Out There

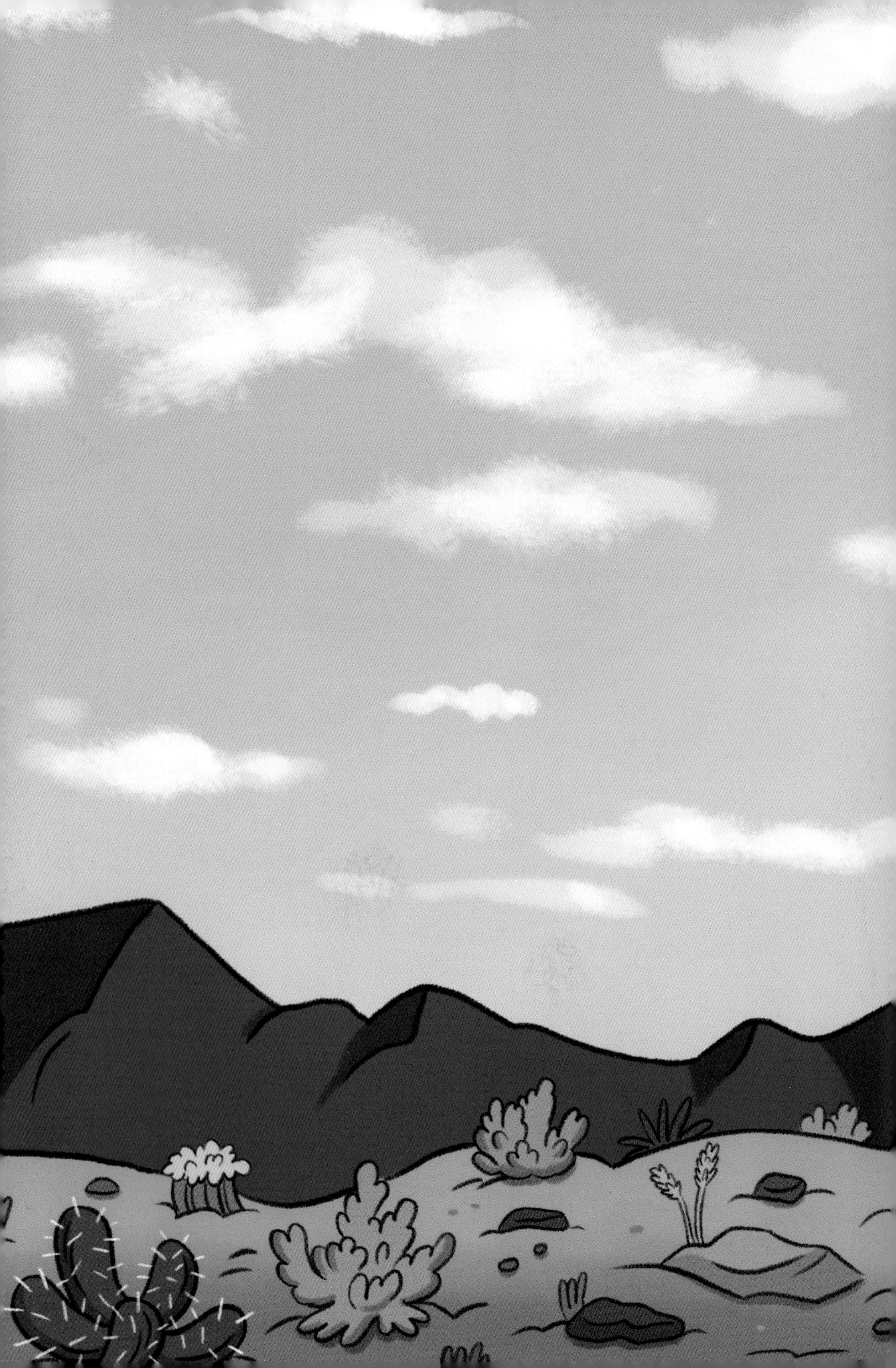

Out There

Seaerra Miller

LB INK

Little, Brown and Company
New York Boston

About This Book

This book was edited by Andrea Colvin and designed by Carolyn Bull.
The production was supervised by Bernadette Flinn, and the production editor was Jake Regier.
The text was set in Seaerra Font 3.

Little, Brown Ink
Hachette Book Group
1290 Avenue of the Americas, New York, NY 10104
Visit us at LBYR.com

First Edition: June 2023

Little, Brown Ink is an imprint of Little, Brown and Company.
The Little, Brown Ink name and logo are trademarks of Hachette Book Group, Inc.

The publisher is not responsible for websites (or their content)
that are not owned by the publisher.

Little, Brown and Company books may be purchased in bulk for business,
educational, or promotional use. For information, please contact your local bookseller
or the Hachette Book Group Special Markets Department at special.markets@hbgusa.com.

Library of Congress Cataloging-in-Publication Data
Names: Miller, Seaerra, author, illustrator.
Title: Out there / Seaerra Miller.
Description: First edition. | New York : Little, Brown and Company, 2023. | Audience: Ages 8–12. | Summary: "Julia goes on
a self-discovery-filled road trip with her UFO-obsessed father to chase a meteor shower." —Provided by publisher.
Identifiers: LCCN 2022031420 | ISBN 9780316591867 (hardcover) | ISBN 9780316591874 (trade paperback) |
ISBN 9780316591850 (ebook)
Subjects: CYAC: Graphic novels. | Fathers and daughters—Fiction. | Friendship—Fiction. | LCGFT: Graphic novels.
Classification: LCC PZ7.7.M5528 Ou 2023 | DDC 741.5/973—dc23/eng/20220726
LC record available at https://lccn.loc.gov/2022031420

ISBNs: 978-0-316-59186-7 (hardcover), 978-0-316-59187-4 (pbk.), 978-0-316-59185-0 (ebook),
978-0-316-34423-4 (ebook), 978-0-316-34433-3 (ebook)

PRINTED IN CHINA

1010

Hardcover: 10 9 8 7 6 5 4 3 2 1

Paperback: 10 9 8 7 6 5 4 3 2 1

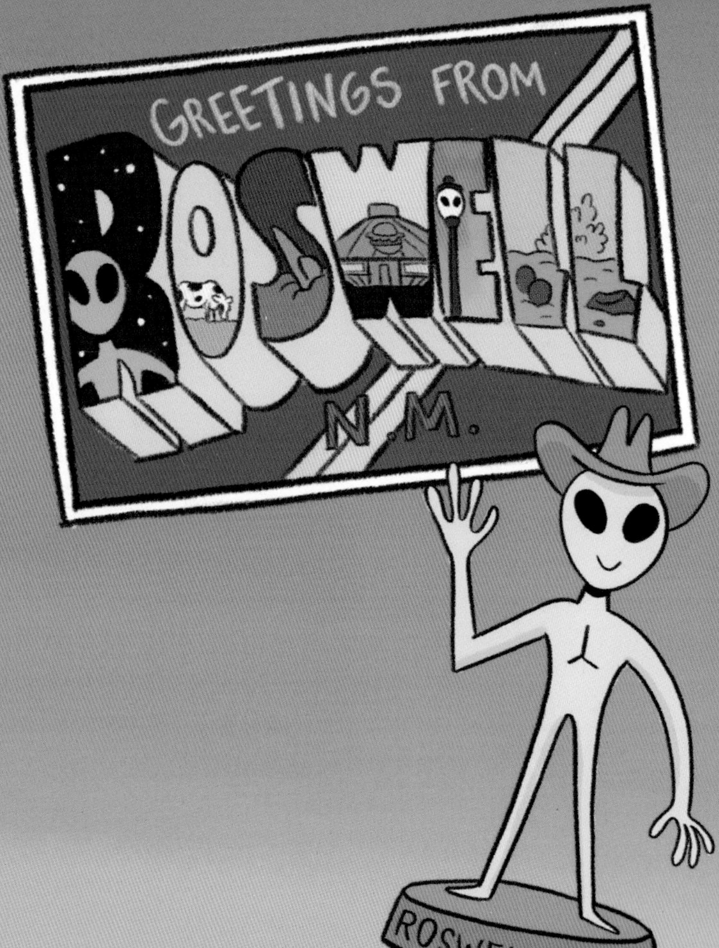
GREETINGS FROM
ROSWELL
N.M.
ROSWELL, NM

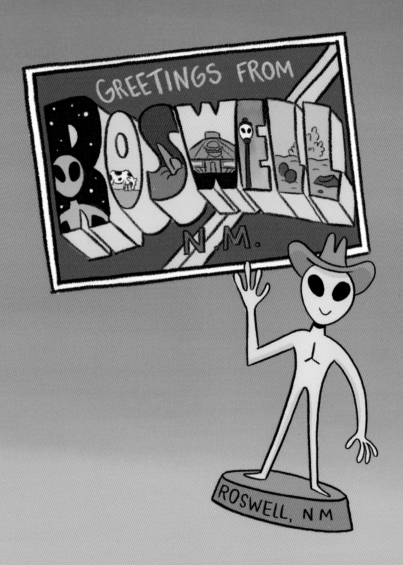

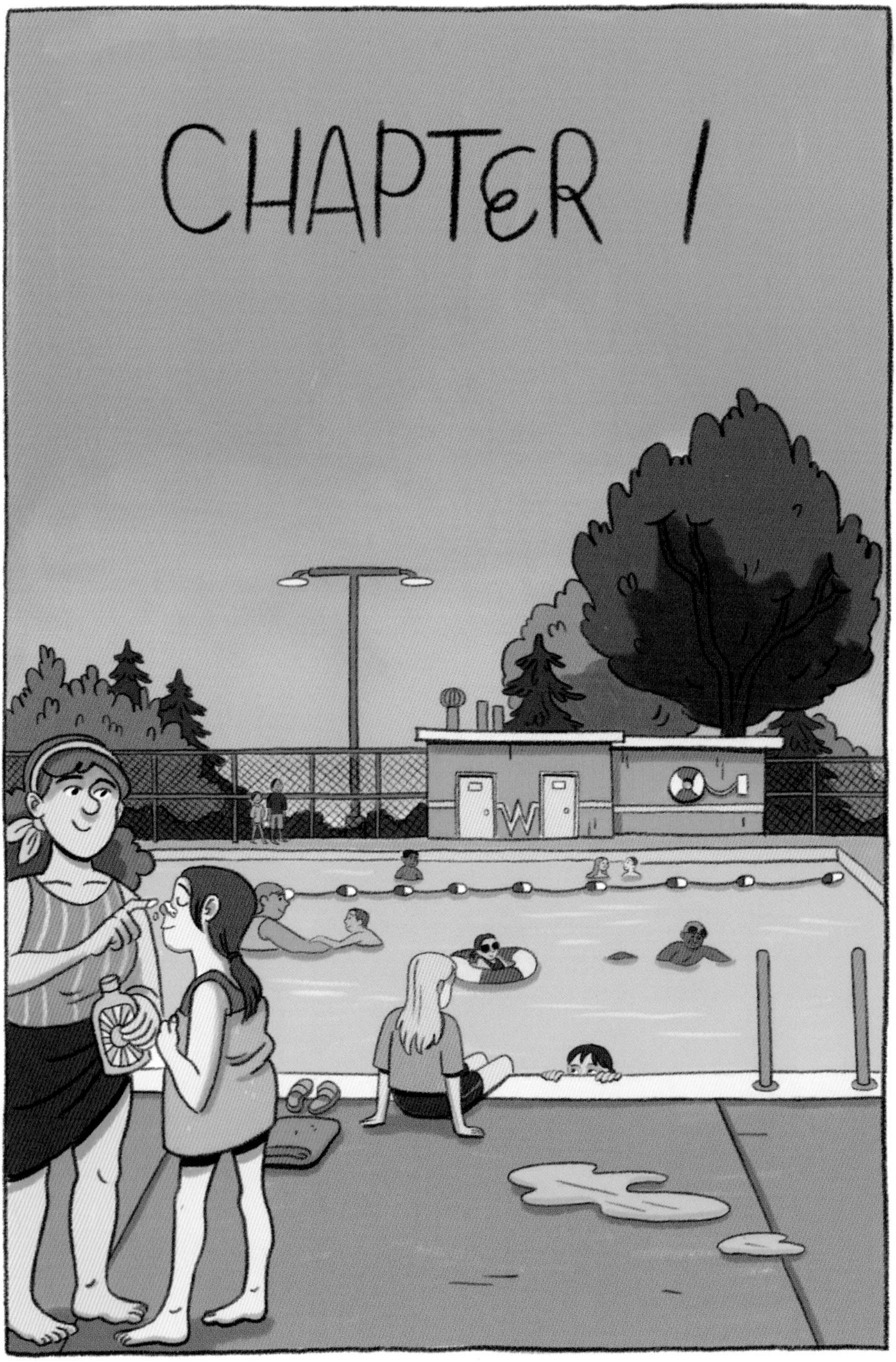
CHAPTER 1
W

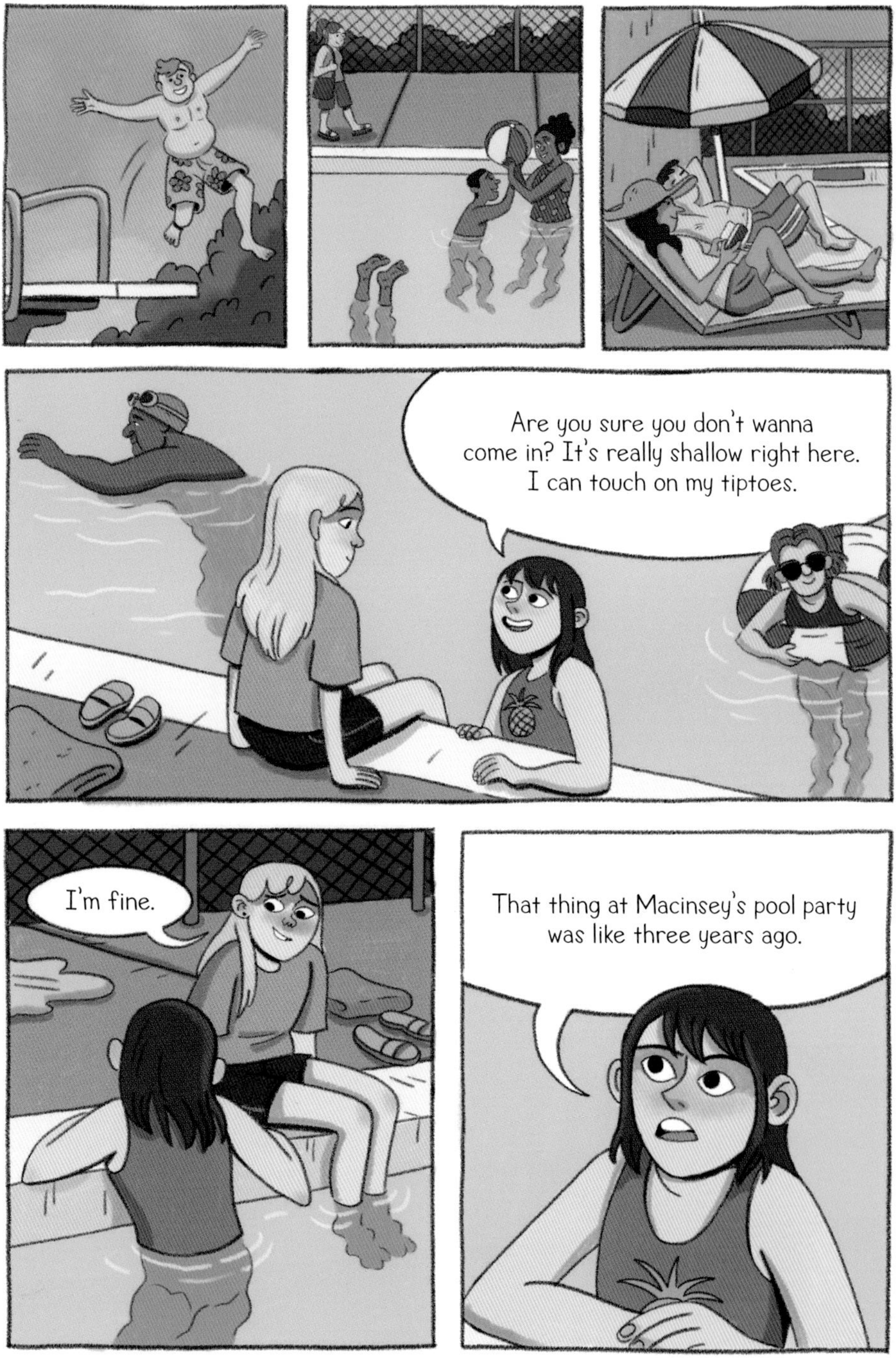
Are you sure you don't wanna come in? It's really shallow right here. I can touch on my tiptoes.
I'm fine.
That thing at Macinsey's pool party was like three years ago.

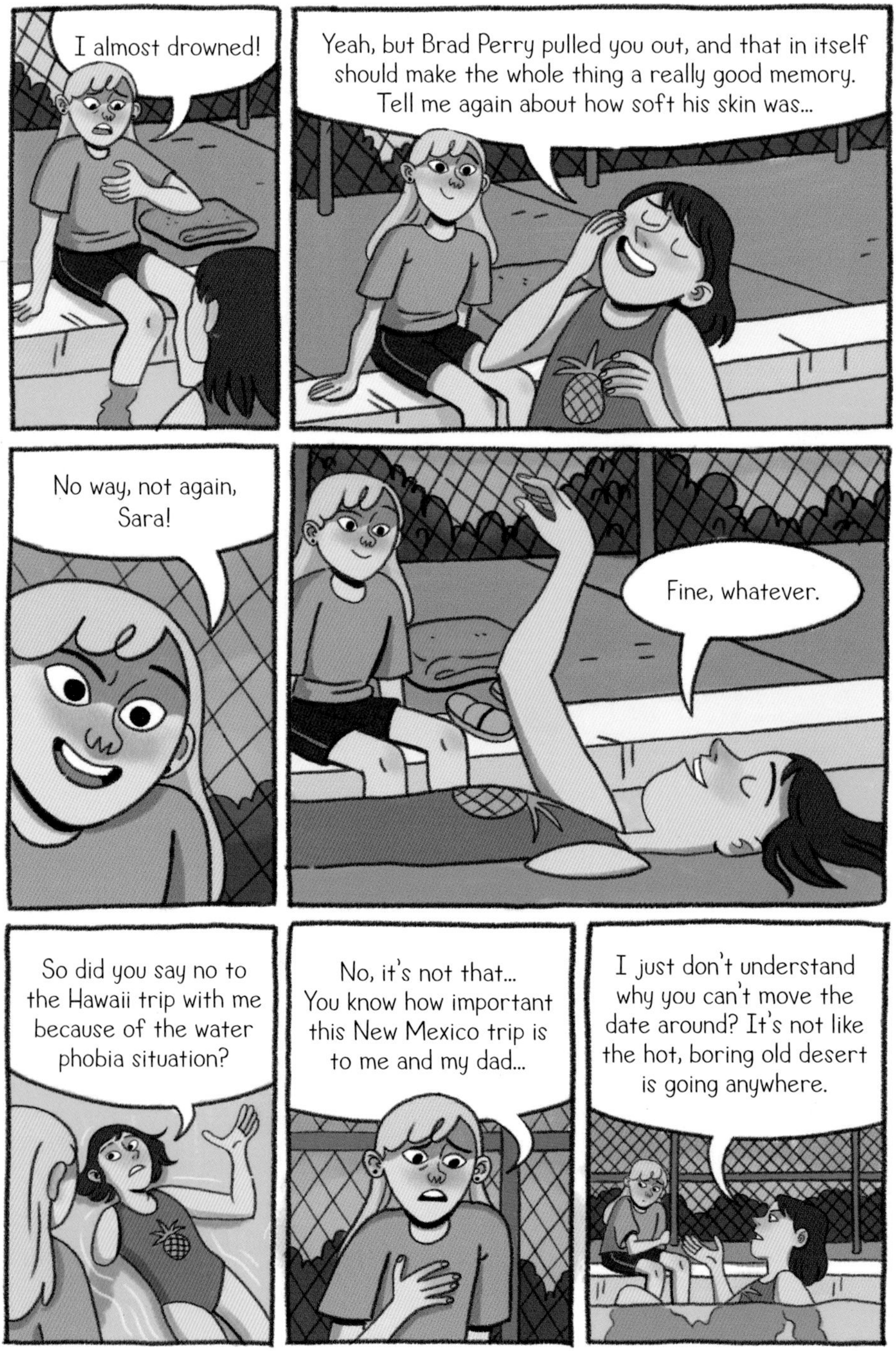
I almost drowned!
Yeah, but Brad Perry pulled you out, and that in itself should make the whole thing a really good memory. Tell me again about how soft his skin was...
No way, not again, Sara!
Fine, whatever.
So did you say no to the Hawaii trip with me because of the water phobia situation?
No, it's not that... You know how important this New Mexico trip is to me and my dad...
I just don't understand why you can't move the date around? It's not like the hot, boring old desert is going anywhere.

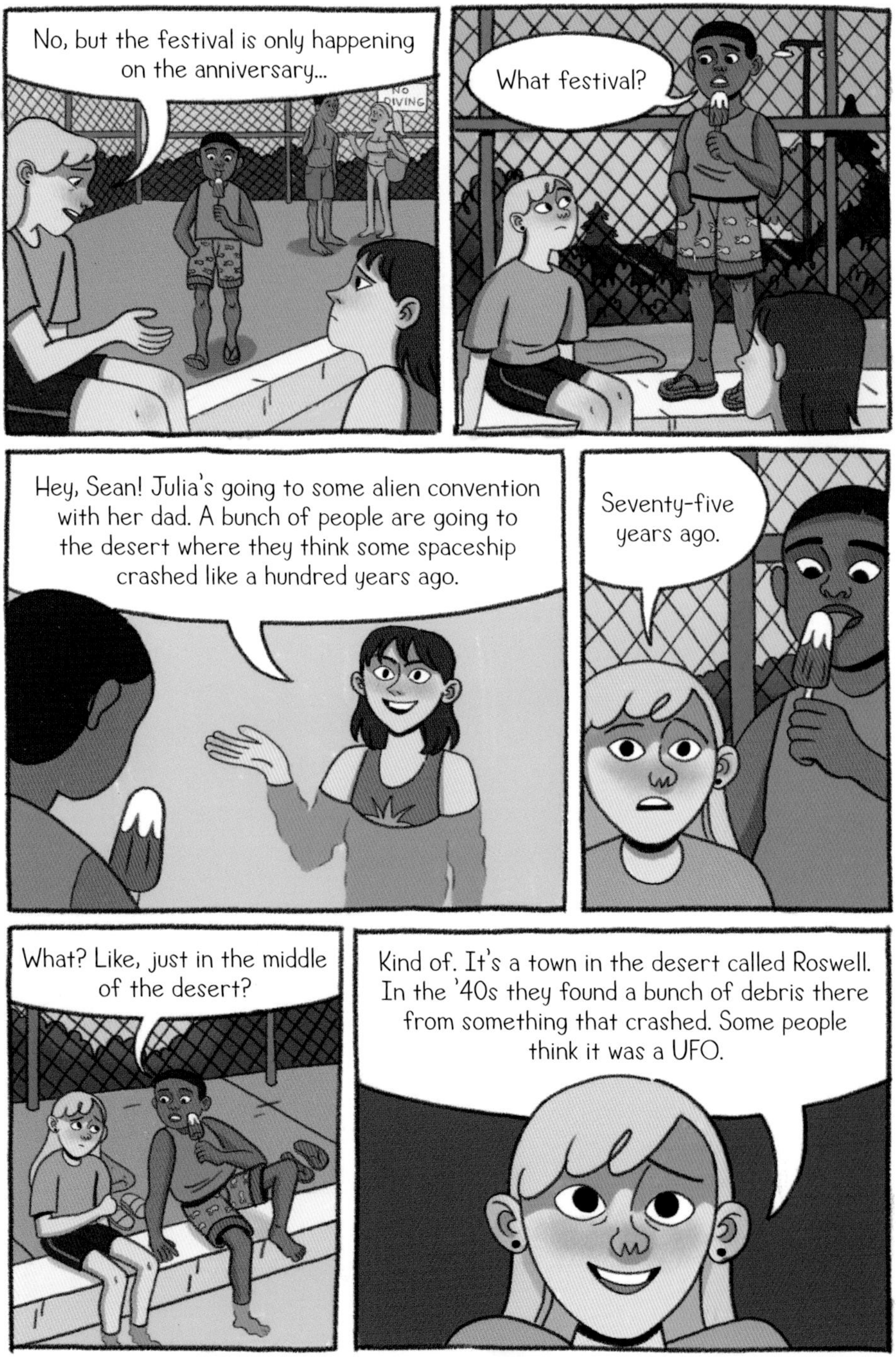
No, but the festival is only happening on the anniversary...
NO DIVING
What festival?
Hey, Sean! Julia's going to some alien convention with her dad. A bunch of people are going to the desert where they think some spaceship crashed like a hundred years ago.
Seventy-five years ago.
What? Like, just in the middle of the desert?
Kind of. It's a town in the desert called Roswell. In the '40s they found a bunch of debris there from something that crashed. Some people think it was a UFO.

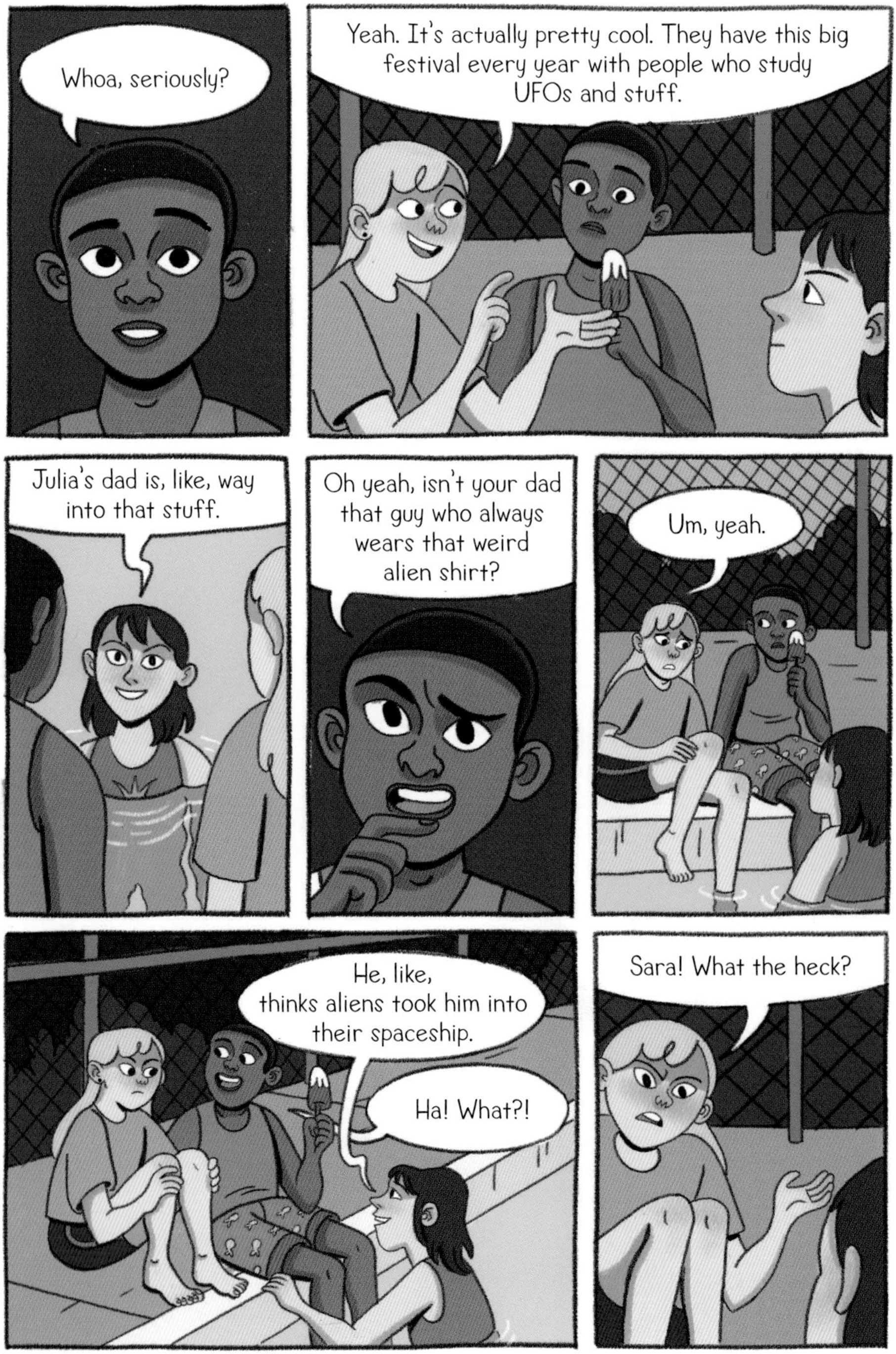
Whoa, seriously?
Yeah. It's actually pretty cool. They have this big festival every year with people who study UFOs and stuff.
Julia's dad is, like, way into that stuff.
Oh yeah, isn't your dad that guy who always wears that weird alien shirt?
Um, yeah.
He, like, thinks aliens took him into their spaceship.
Ha! What?!
Sara! What the heck?

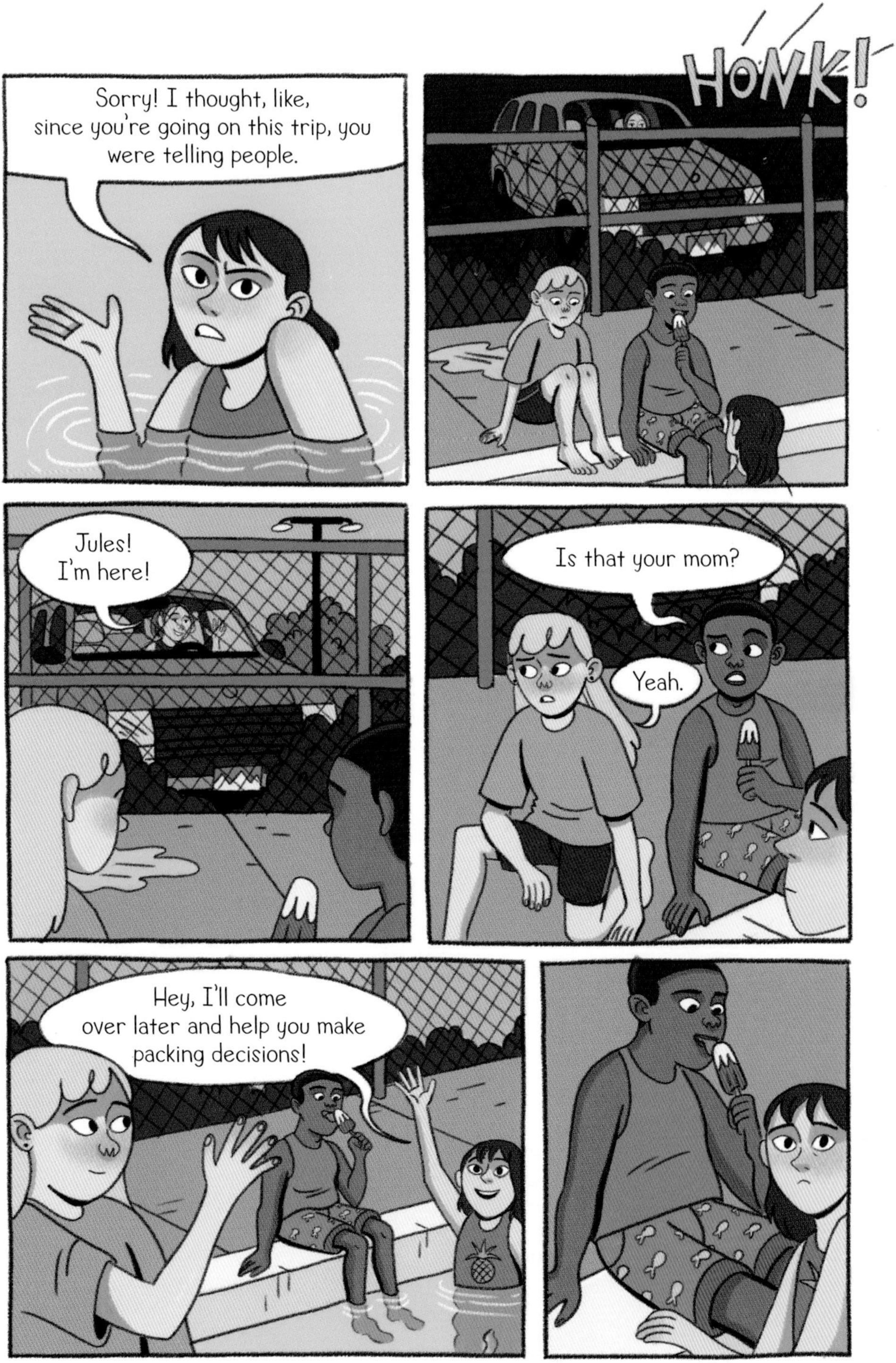
Sorry! I thought, like, since you're going on this trip, you were telling people.
HONK!
Jules! I'm here!
Is that your mom?
Yeah.
Hey, I'll come over later and help you make packing decisions!

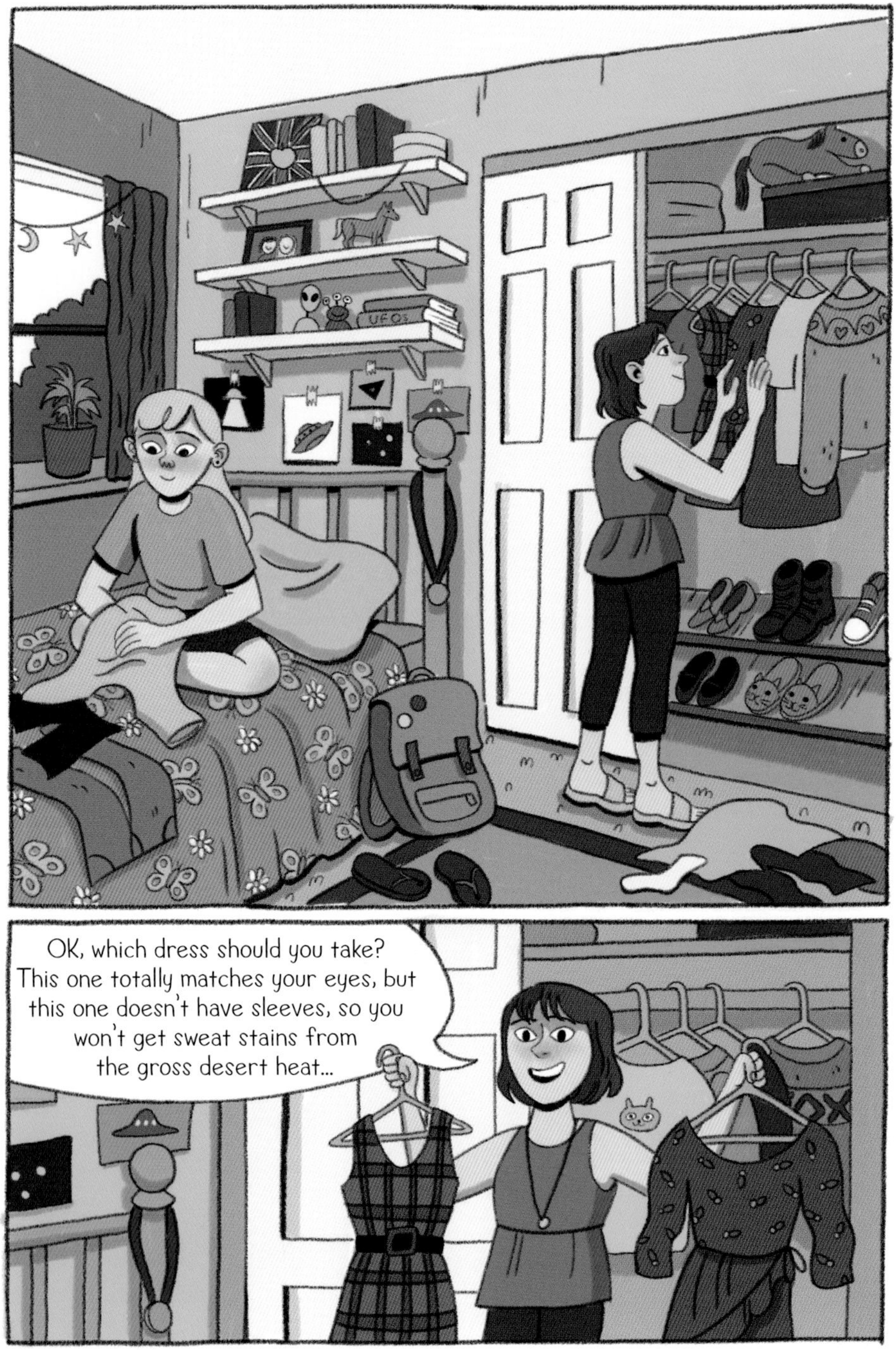
UFOs
OK, which dress should you take? This one totally matches your eyes, but this one doesn't have sleeves, so you won't get sweat stains from the gross desert heat...

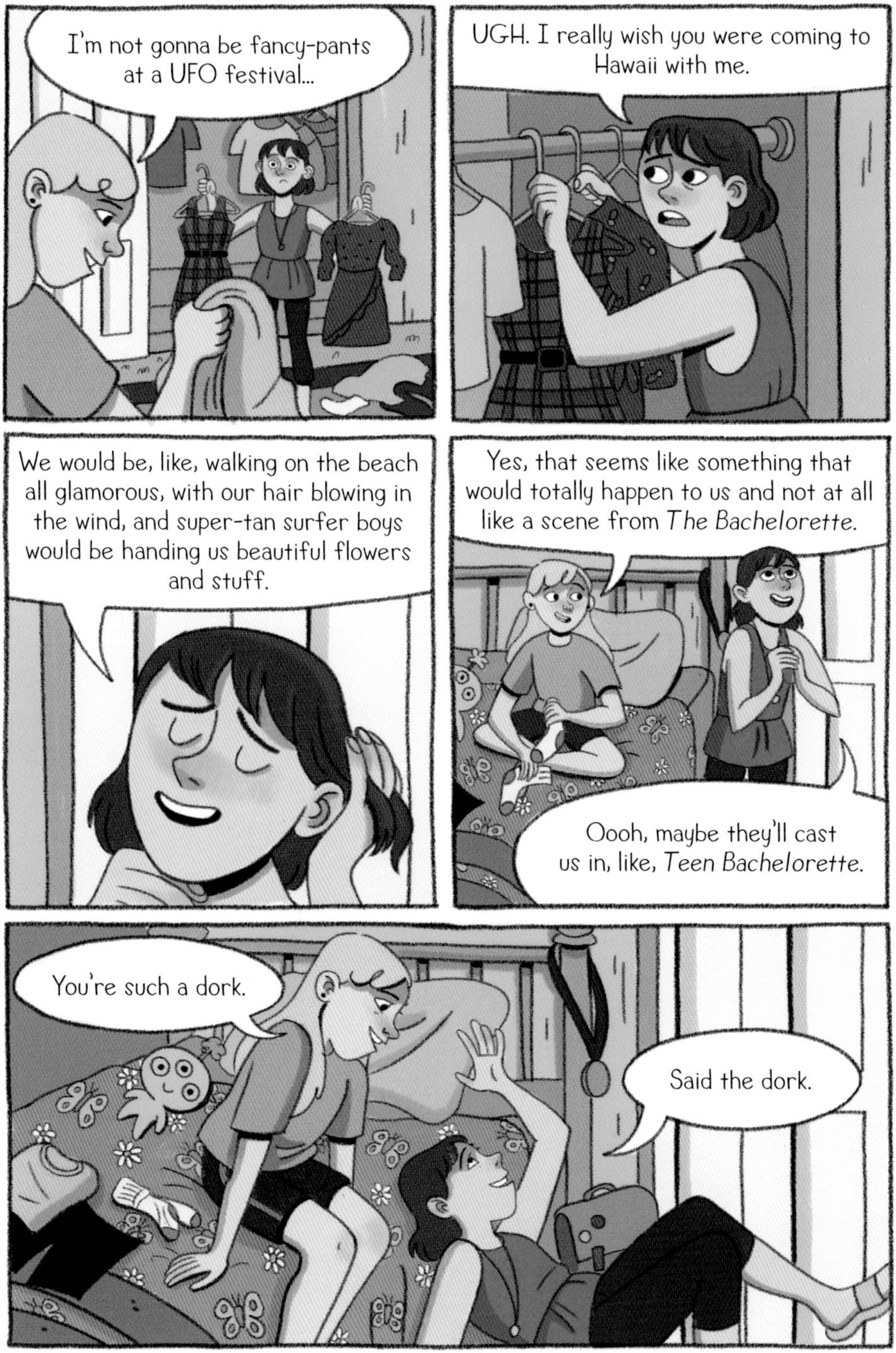
I'm not gonna be fancy-pants at a UFO festival...
UGH. I really wish you were coming to Hawaii with me.
We would be, like, walking on the beach all glamorous, with our hair blowing in the wind, and super-tan surfer boys would be handing us beautiful flowers and stuff.
Yes, that seems like something that would totally happen to us and not at all like a scene from *The Bachelorette*.
Oooh, maybe they'll cast us in, like, *Teen Bachelorette*.
You're such a dork.
Said the dork.

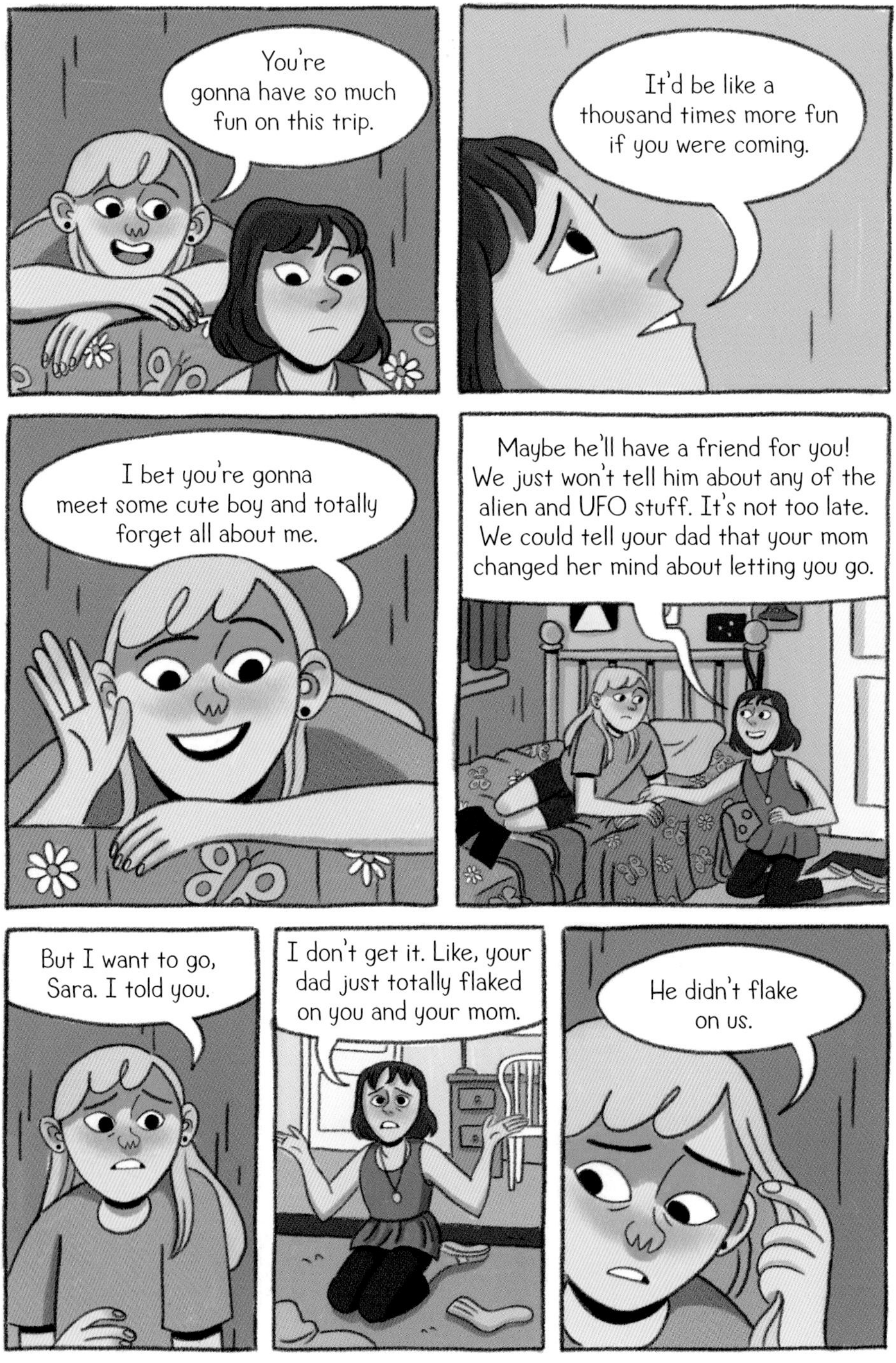
You're gonna have so much fun on this trip.
It'd be like a thousand times more fun if you were coming.
I bet you're gonna meet some cute boy and totally forget all about me.
Maybe he'll have a friend for you! We just won't tell him about any of the alien and UFO stuff. It's not too late. We could tell your dad that your mom changed her mind about letting you go.
But I want to go, Sara. I told you.
I don't get it. Like, your dad just totally flaked on you and your mom.
He didn't flake on us.

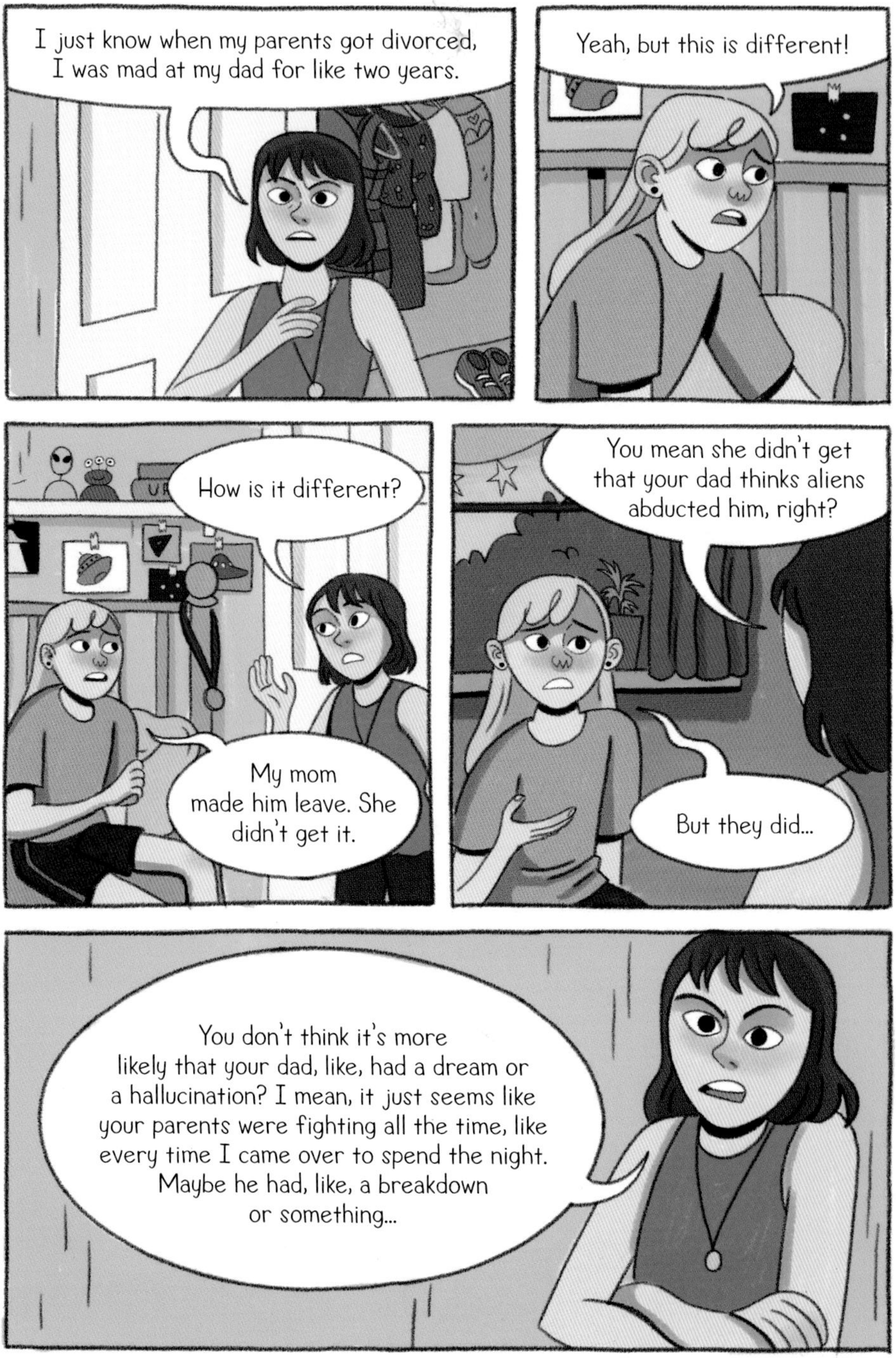
I just know when my parents got divorced, I was mad at my dad for like two years.
Yeah, but this is different!
How is it different?
My mom made him leave. She didn't get it.
You mean she didn't get that your dad thinks aliens abducted him, right?
But they did...
You don't think it's more likely that your dad, like, had a dream or a hallucination? I mean, it just seems like your parents were fighting all the time, like every time I came over to spend the night. Maybe he had, like, a breakdown or something...

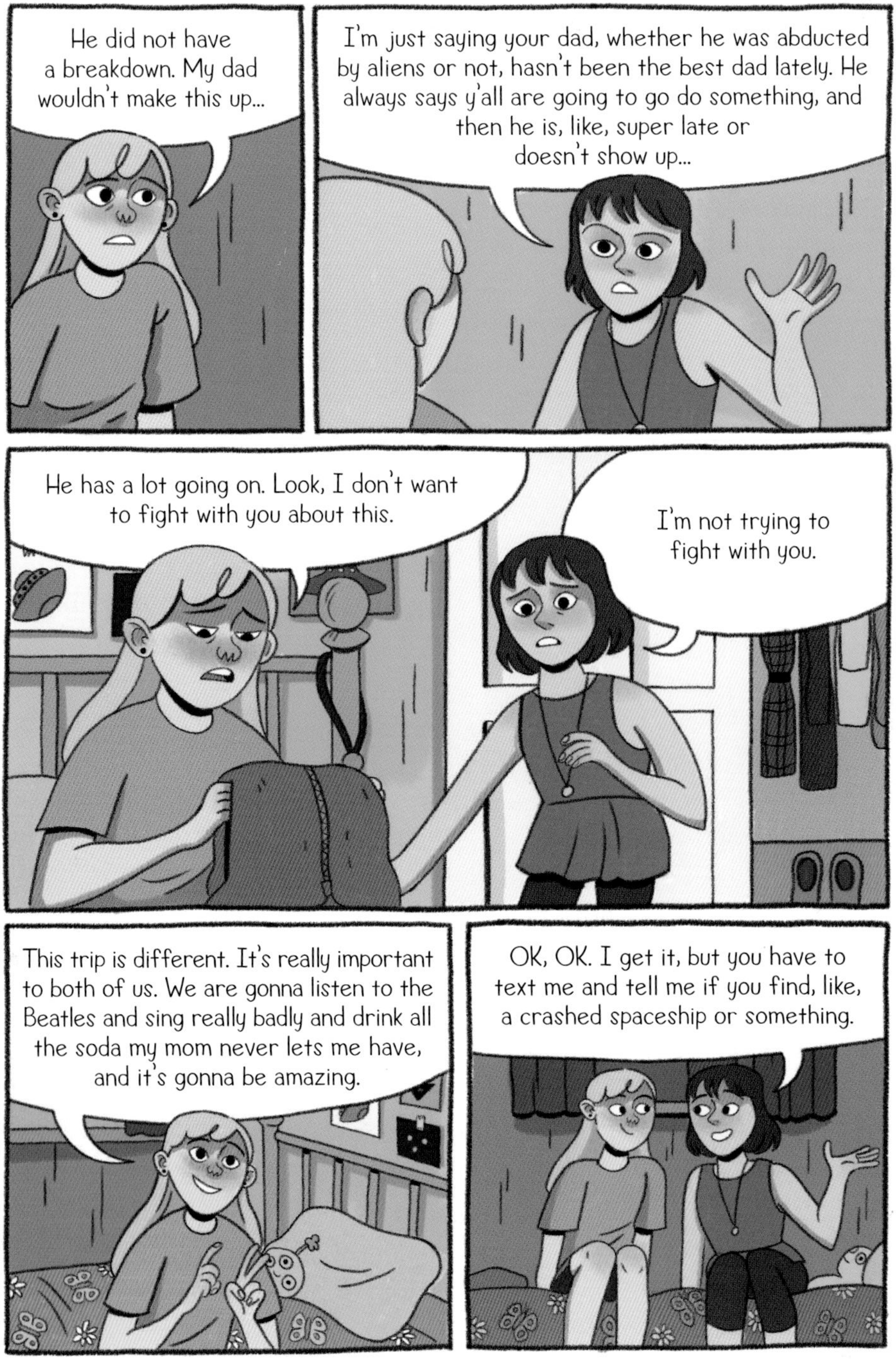
He did not have a breakdown. My dad wouldn't make this up...
I'm just saying your dad, whether he was abducted by aliens or not, hasn't been the best dad lately. He always says y'all are going to go do something, and then he is, like, super late or doesn't show up...
He has a lot going on. Look, I don't want to fight with you about this.
I'm not trying to fight with you.
This trip is different. It's really important to both of us. We are gonna listen to the Beatles and sing really badly and drink all the soda my mom never lets me have, and it's gonna be amazing.
OK, OK. I get it, but you have to text me and tell me if you find, like, a crashed spaceship or something.

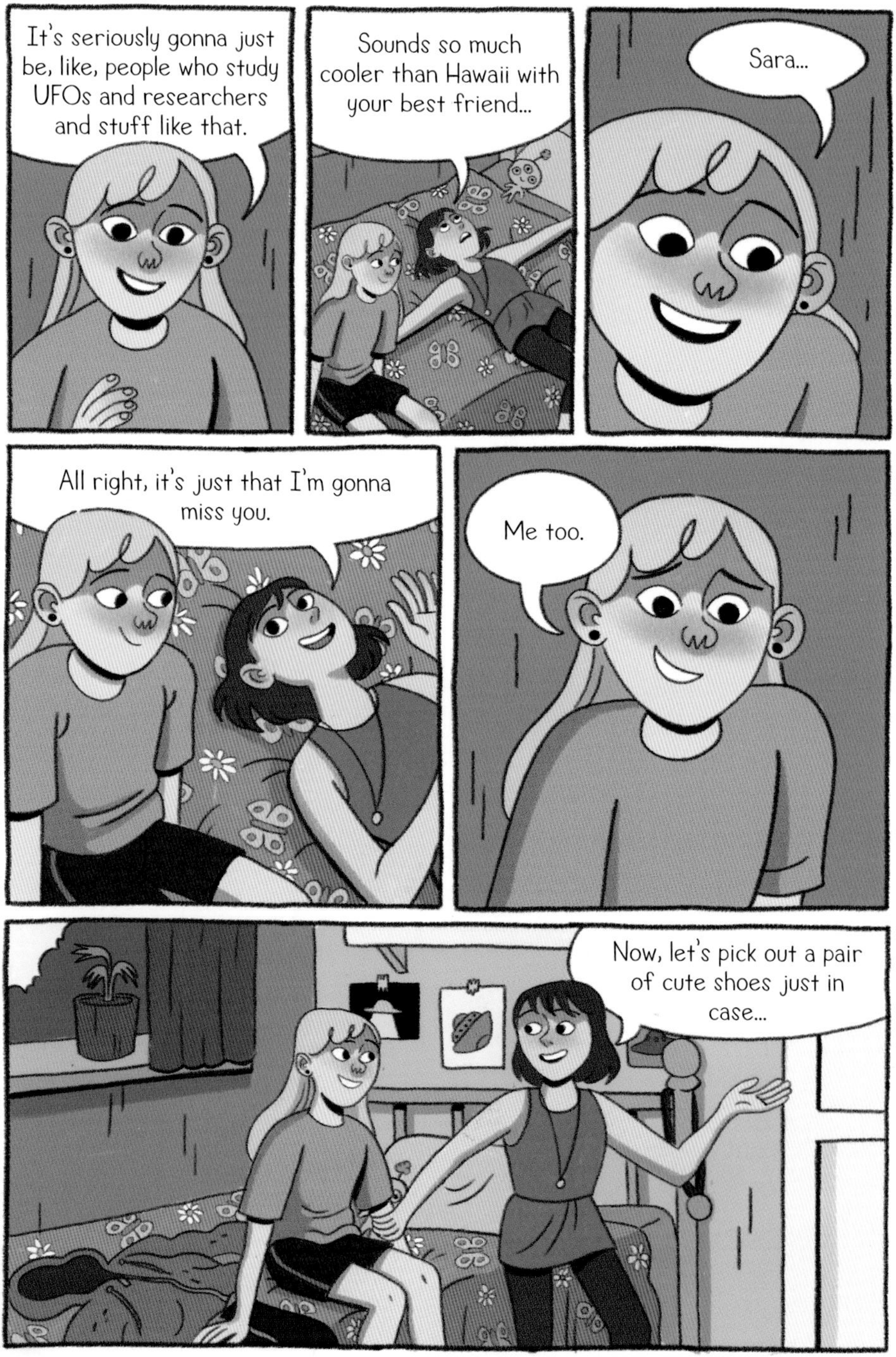
It's seriously gonna just be, like, people who study UFOs and researchers and stuff like that.
Sounds so much cooler than Hawaii with your best friend...
Sara...
All right, it's just that I'm gonna miss you.
Me too.
Now, let's pick out a pair of cute shoes just in case...

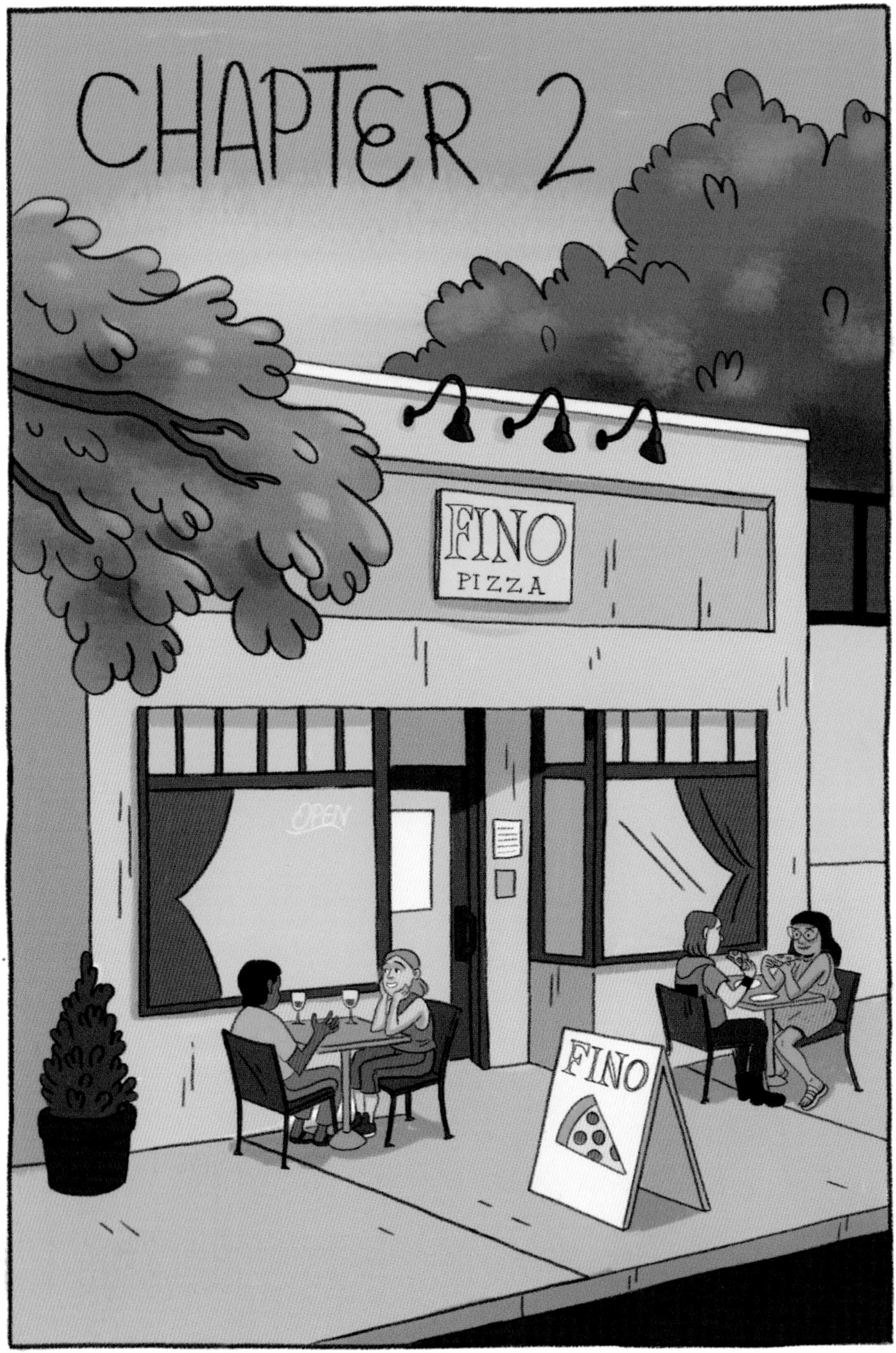
CHAPTER 2
FINO
PIZZA
OPEN
FINO

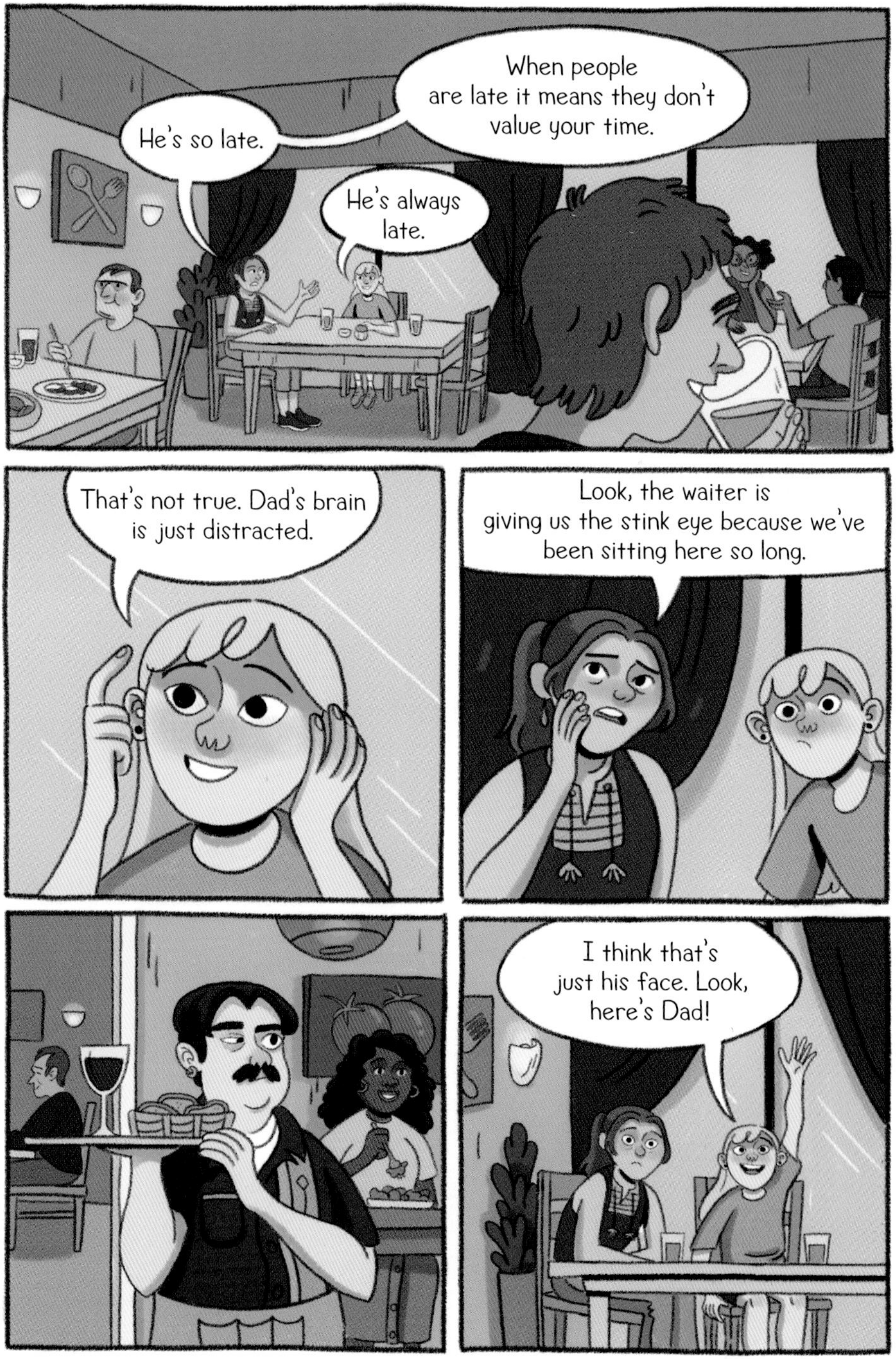
He's so late.
When people are late it means they don't value your time.
He's always late.
That's not true. Dad's brain is just distracted.
Look, the waiter is giving us the stink eye because we've been sitting here so long.
I think that's just his face. Look, here's Dad!

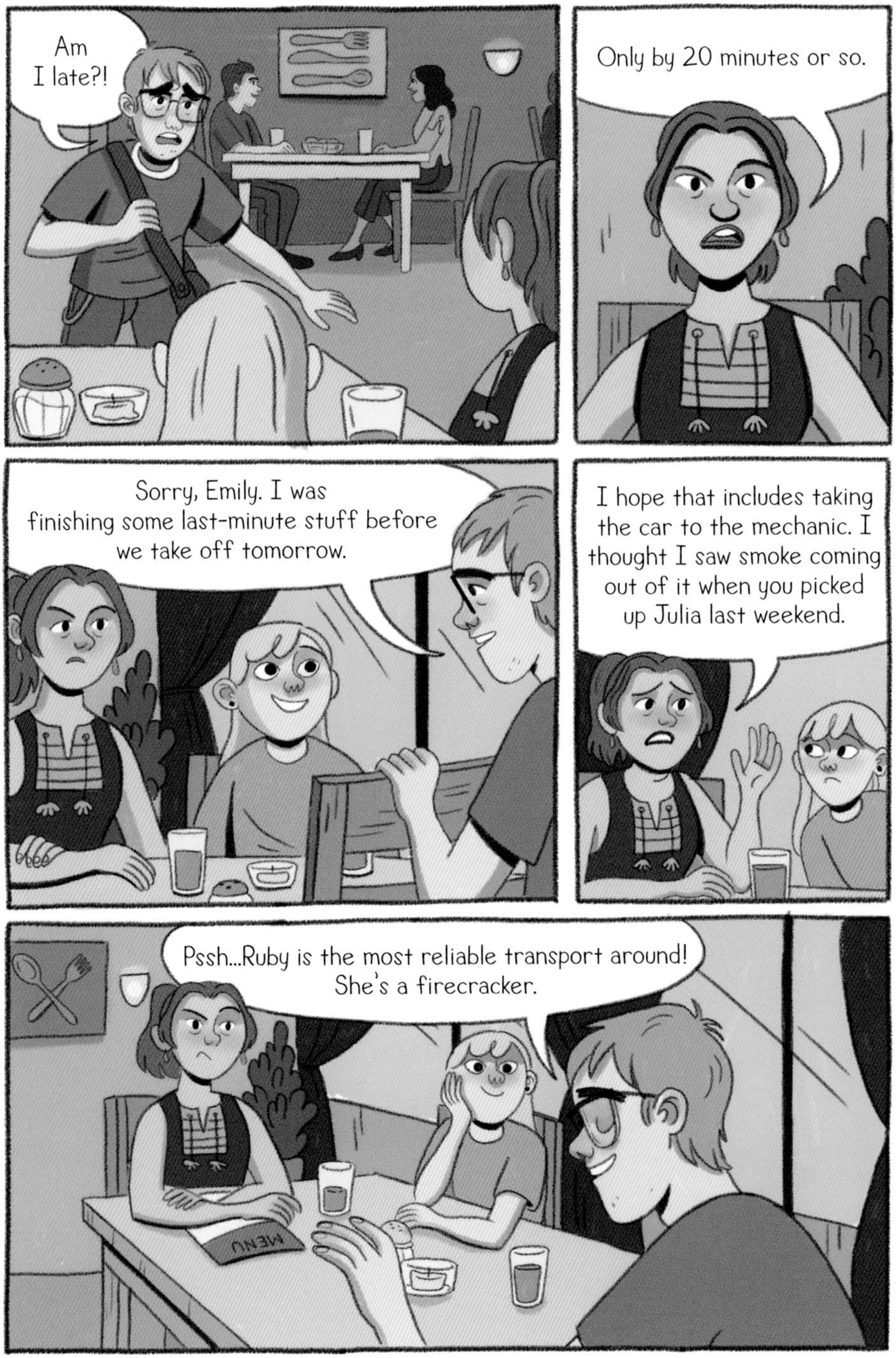
Am I late?!
Only by 20 minutes or so.
Sorry, Emily. I was finishing some last-minute stuff before we take off tomorrow.
I hope that includes taking the car to the mechanic. I thought I saw smoke coming out of it when you picked up Julia last weekend.
Pssh...Ruby is the most reliable transport around! She's a firecracker.
MENU

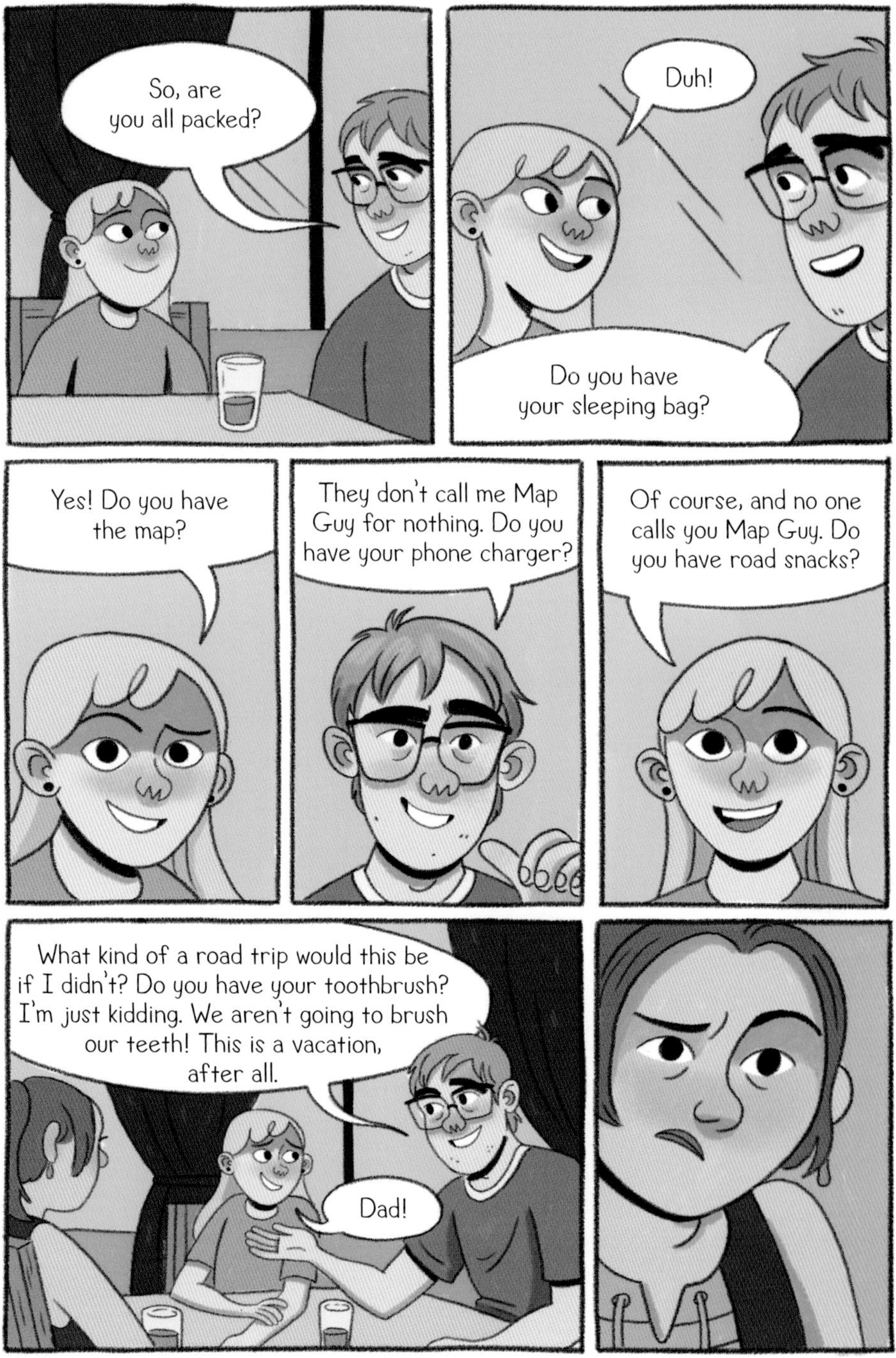
So, are you all packed?
Duh!
Do you have your sleeping bag?
Yes! Do you have the map?
They don't call me Map Guy for nothing. Do you have your phone charger?
Of course, and no one calls you Map Guy. Do you have road snacks?
What kind of a road trip would this be if I didn't? Do you have your toothbrush? I'm just kidding. We aren't going to brush our teeth! This is a vacation, after all.
Dad!

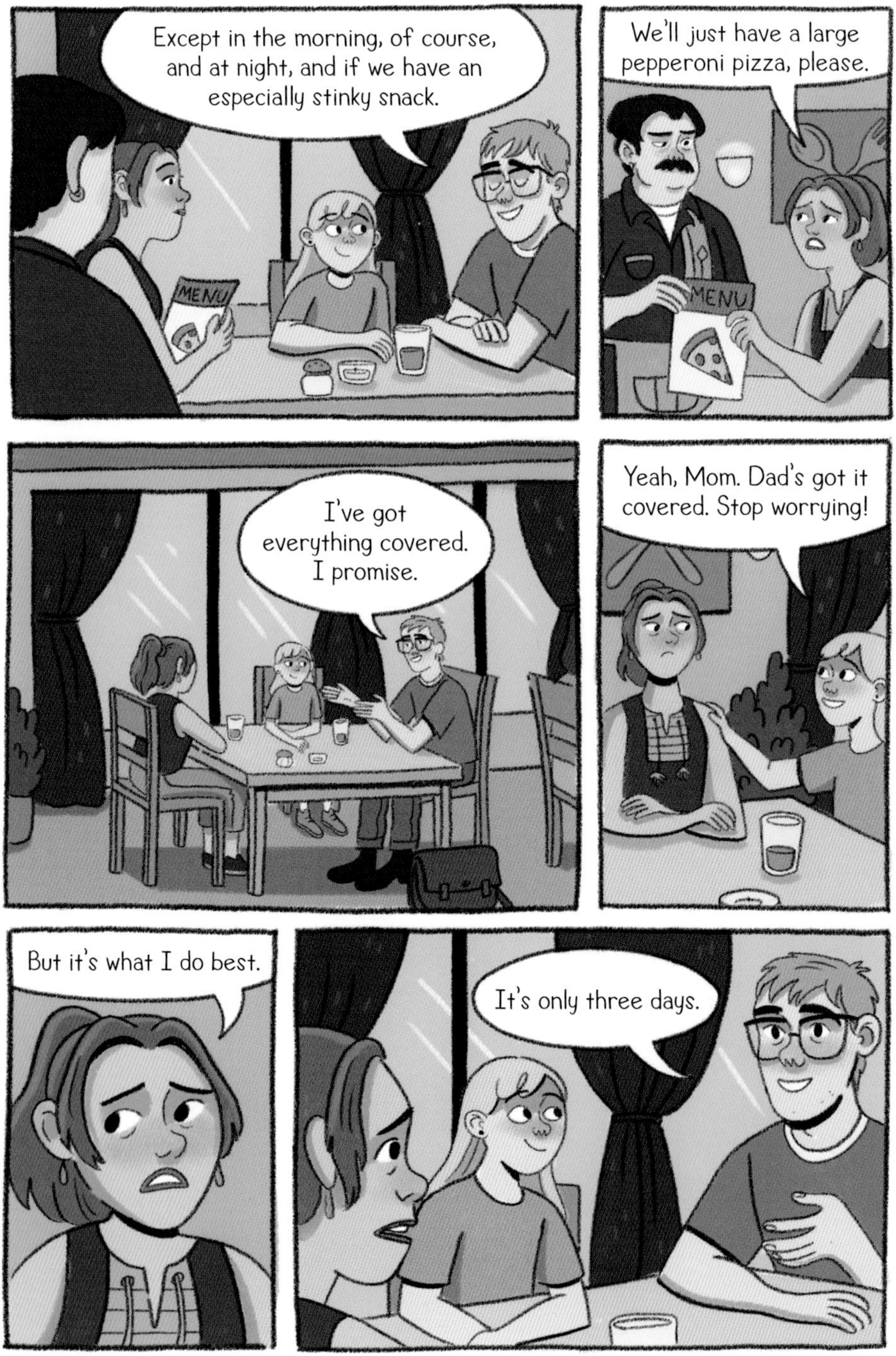
Except in the morning, of course, and at night, and if we have an especially stinky snack.
MENU
We'll just have a large pepperoni pizza, please.
MENU
I've got everything covered. I promise.
Yeah, Mom. Dad's got it covered. Stop worrying!
But it's what I do best.
It's only three days.

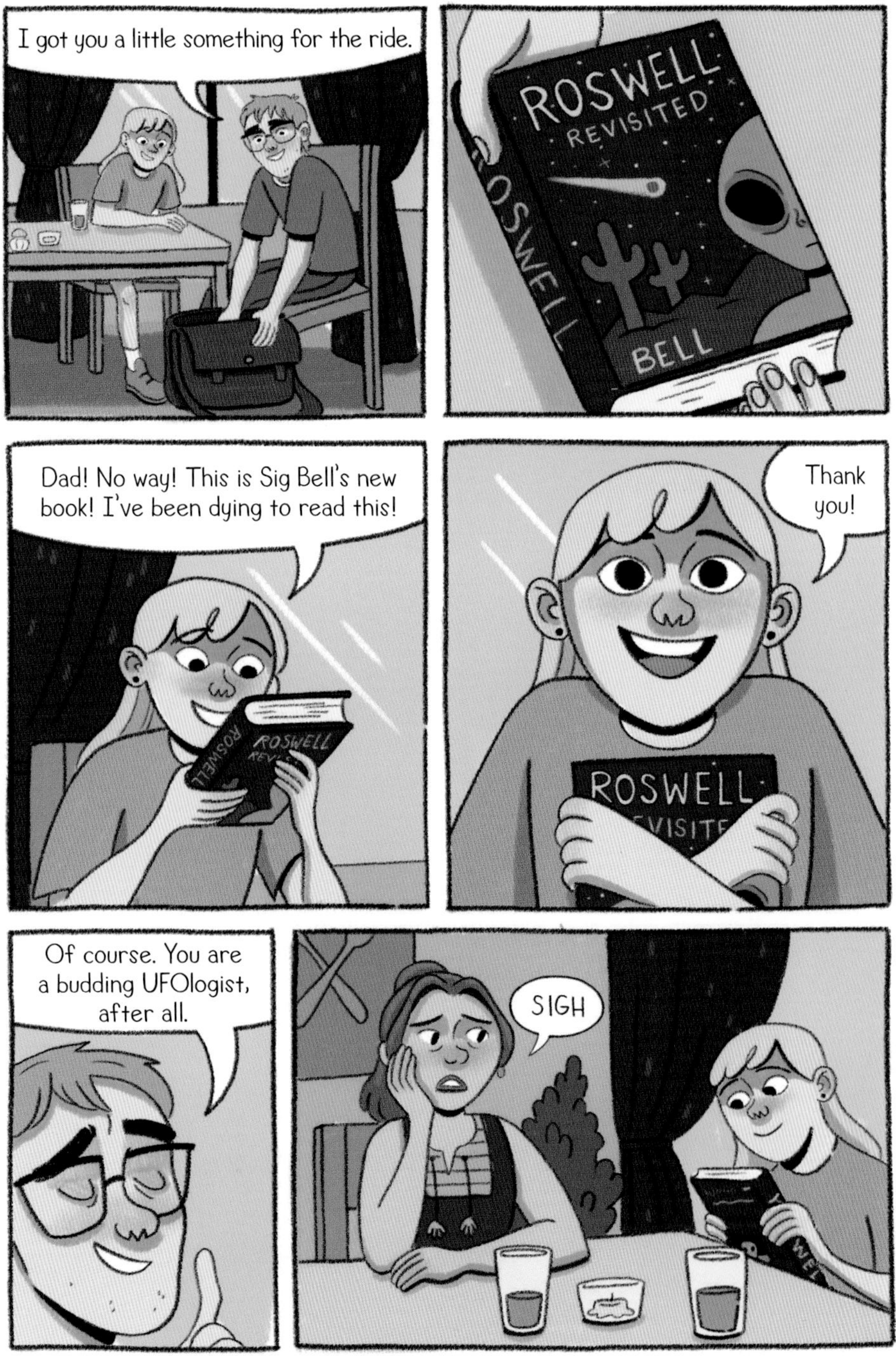
I got you a little something for the ride.
ROSWELL REVISITED
ROSWELL
BELL
Dad! No way! This is Sig Bell's new book! I've been dying to read this!
Thank you!
ROSWELL
Of course. You are a budding UFOlogist, after all.
SIGH

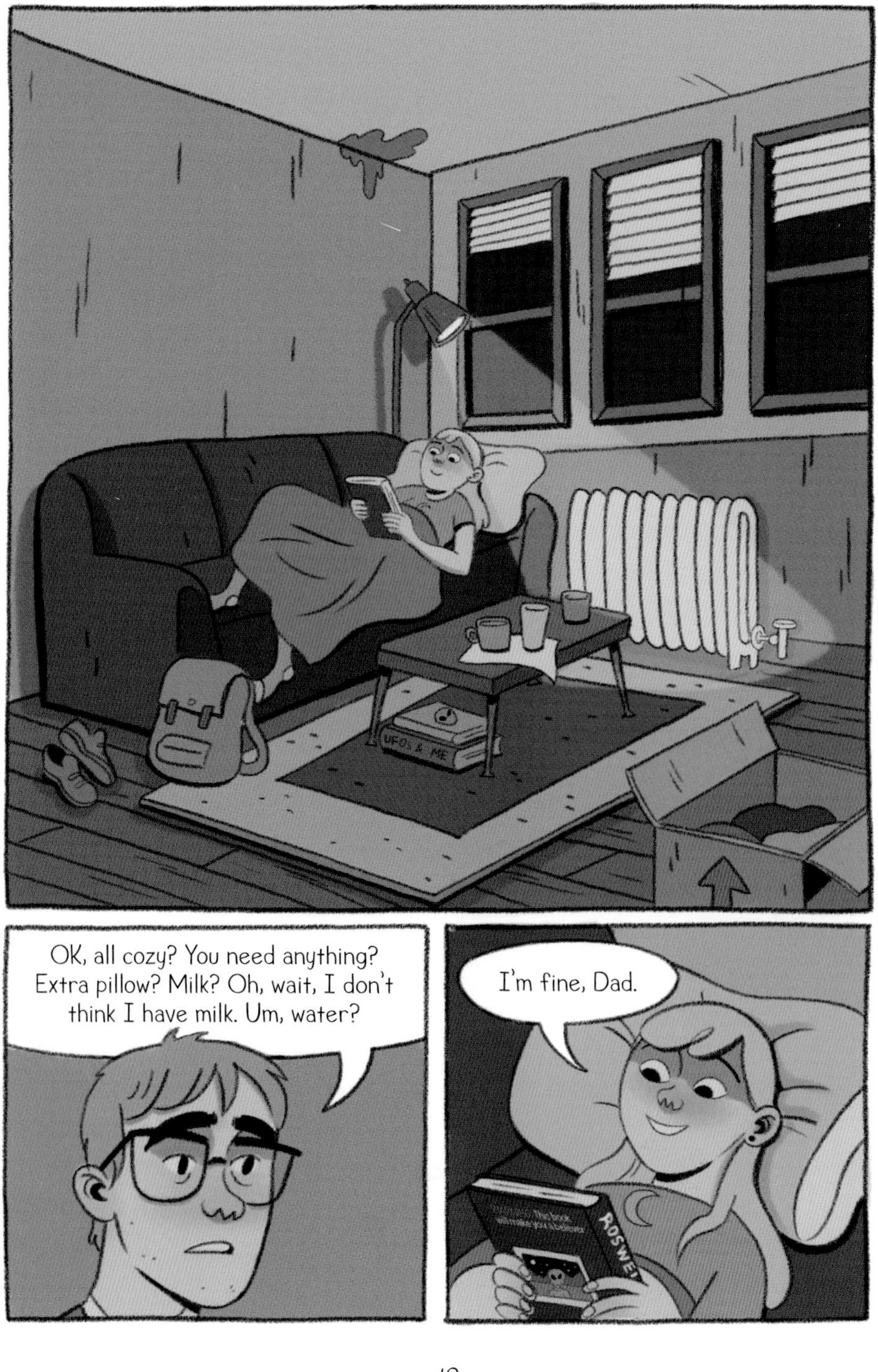
UFOs & ME
OK, all cozy? You need anything? Extra pillow? Milk? Oh, wait, I don't think I have milk. Um, water?
I'm fine, Dad.
ROSWE

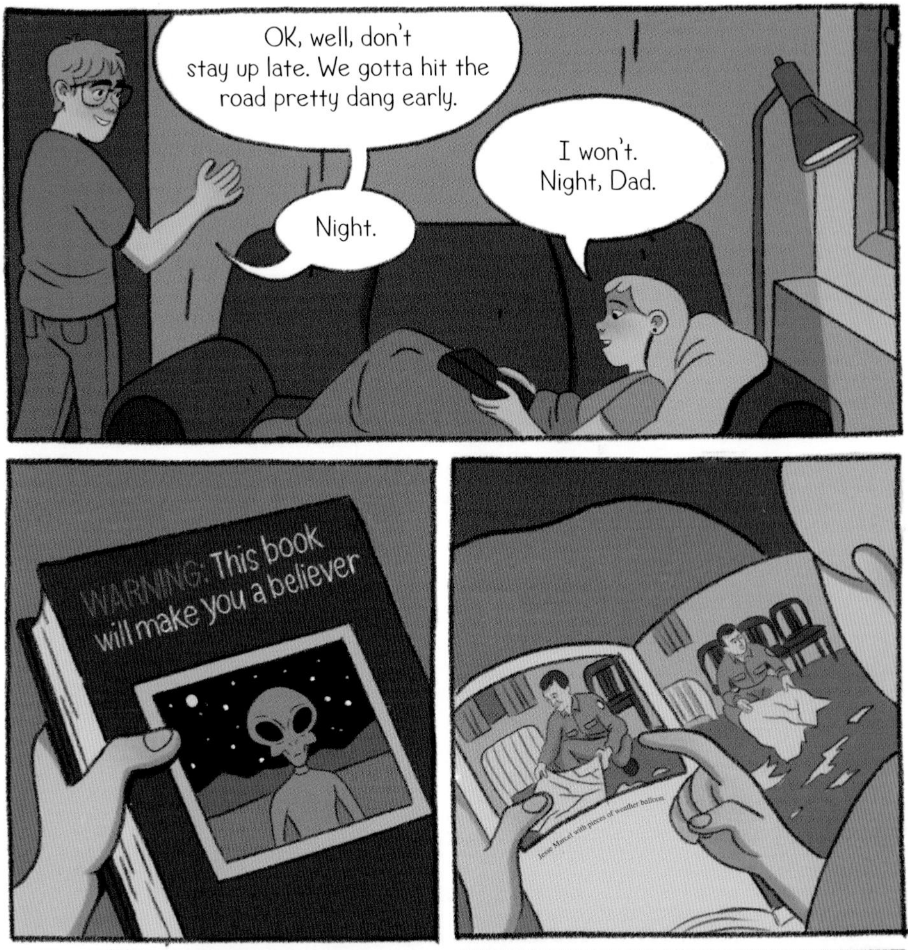
OK, well, don't stay up late. We gotta hit the road pretty dang early.
Night.
I won't. Night, Dad.
WARNING: This book will make you a believer
Jesse Marcel with pieces of weather balloon.
Cool.
ROSWELL REVISITED

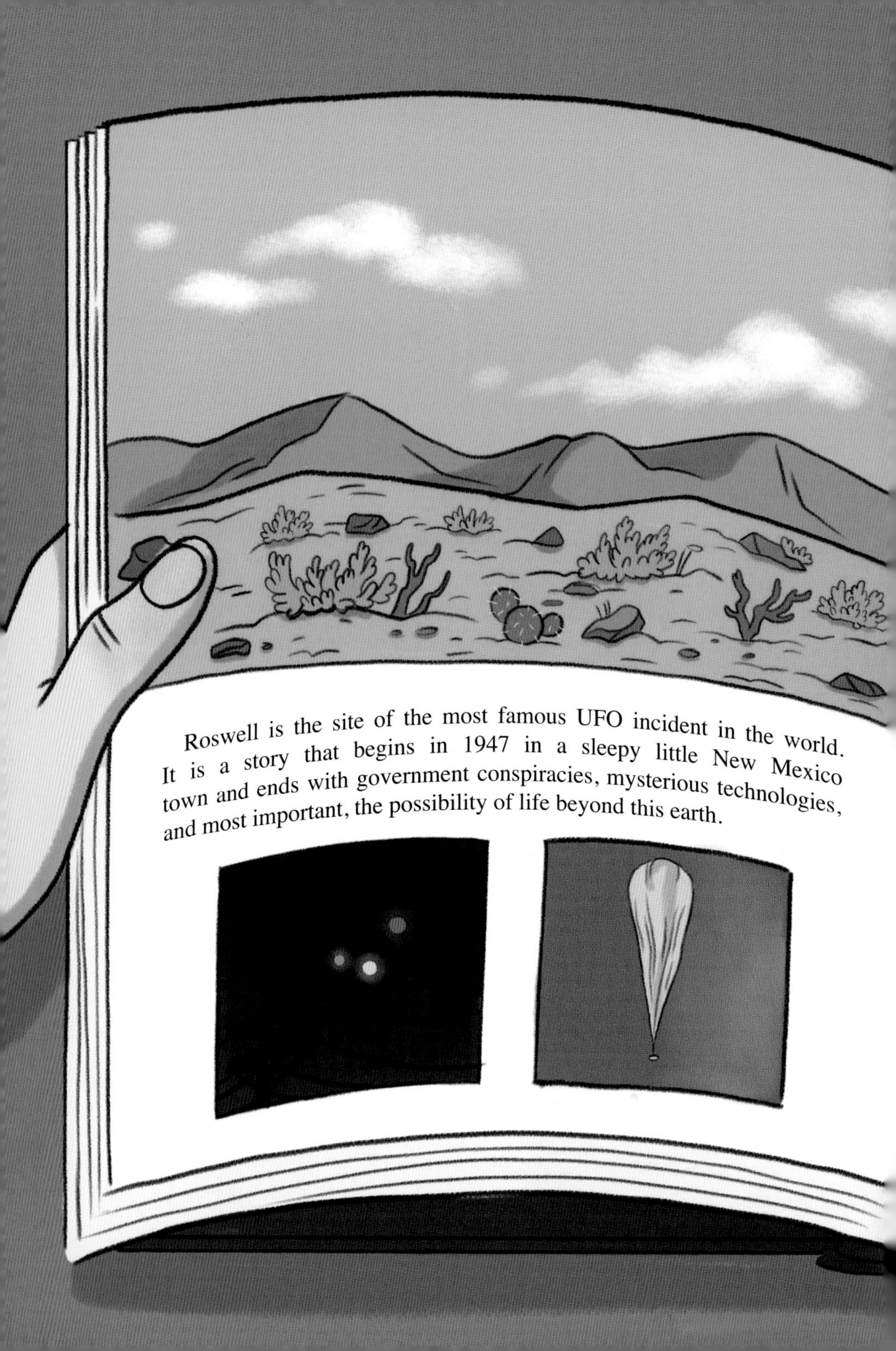
Roswell is the site of the most famous UFO incident in the world. It is a story that begins in 1947 in a sleepy little New Mexico town and ends with government conspiracies, mysterious technologies, and most important, the possibility of life beyond this earth.

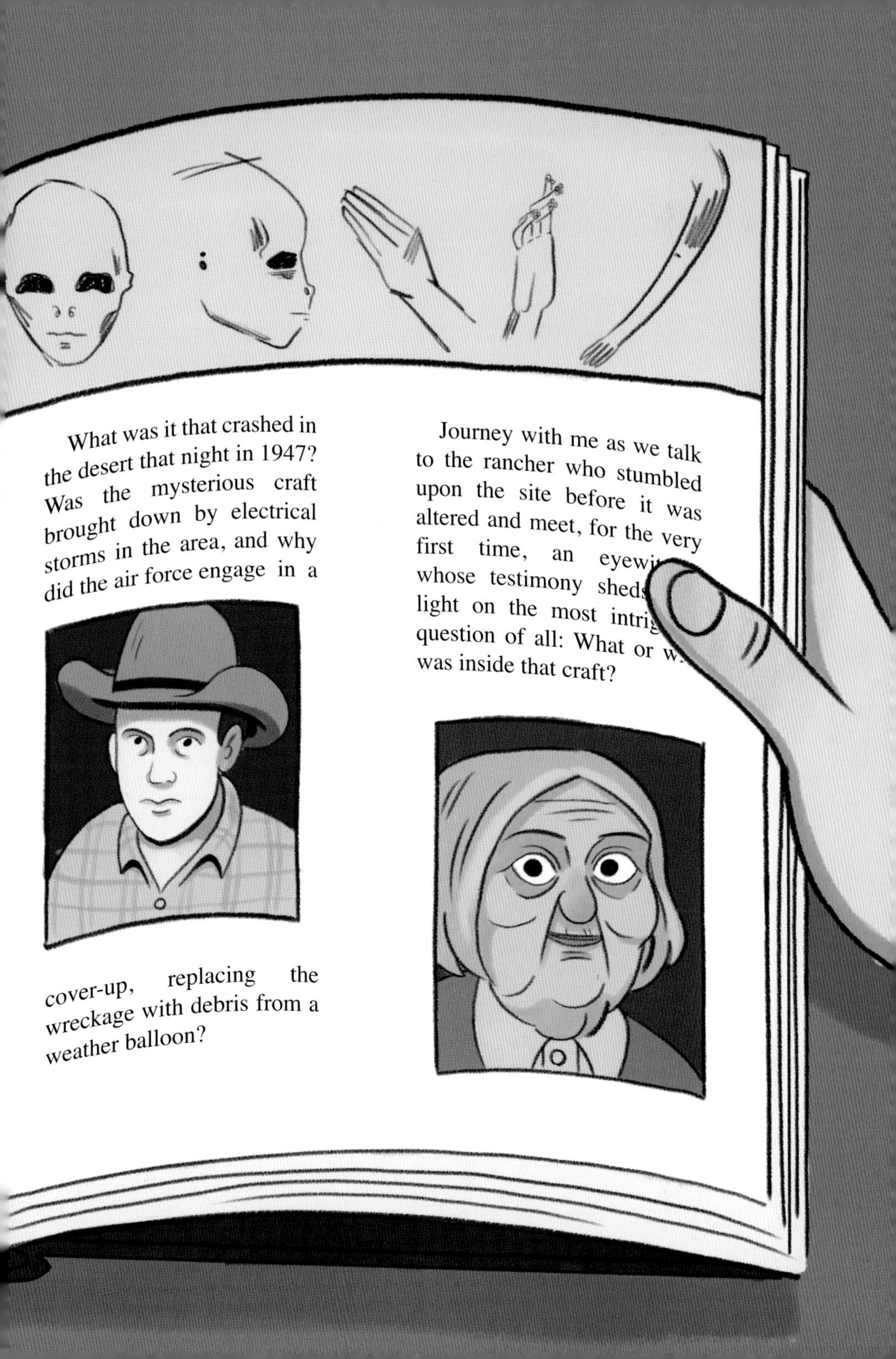
What was it that crashed in the desert that night in 1947? Was the mysterious craft brought down by electrical storms in the area, and why did the air force engage in a cover-up, replacing the wreckage with debris from a weather balloon?
Journey with me as we talk to the rancher who stumbled upon the site before it was altered and meet, for the very first time, an eyewi
whose testimony sheds
light on the most intrig
question of all: What or w
was inside that craft?

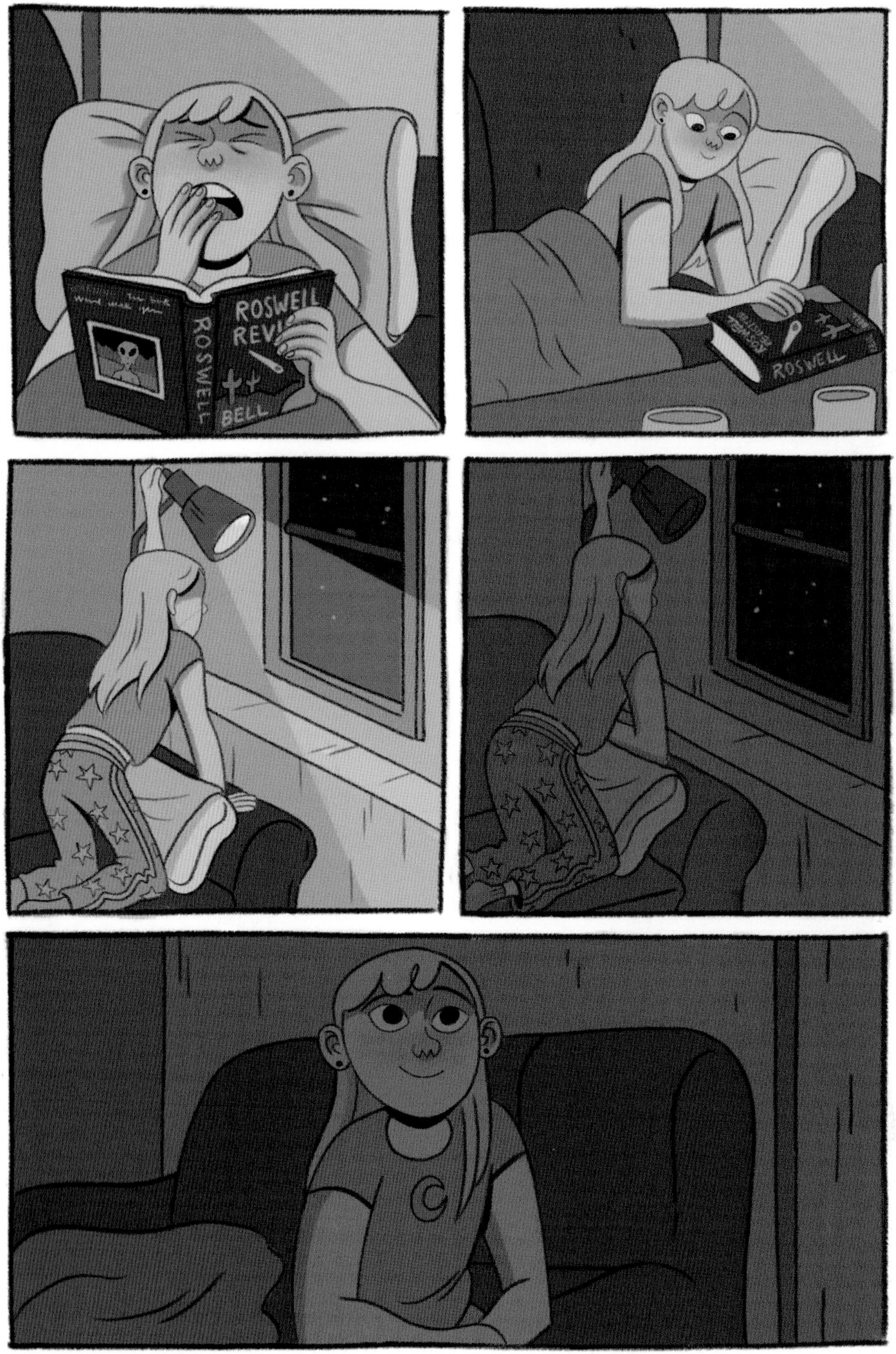
ROSWELL
BELL
ROSWELL

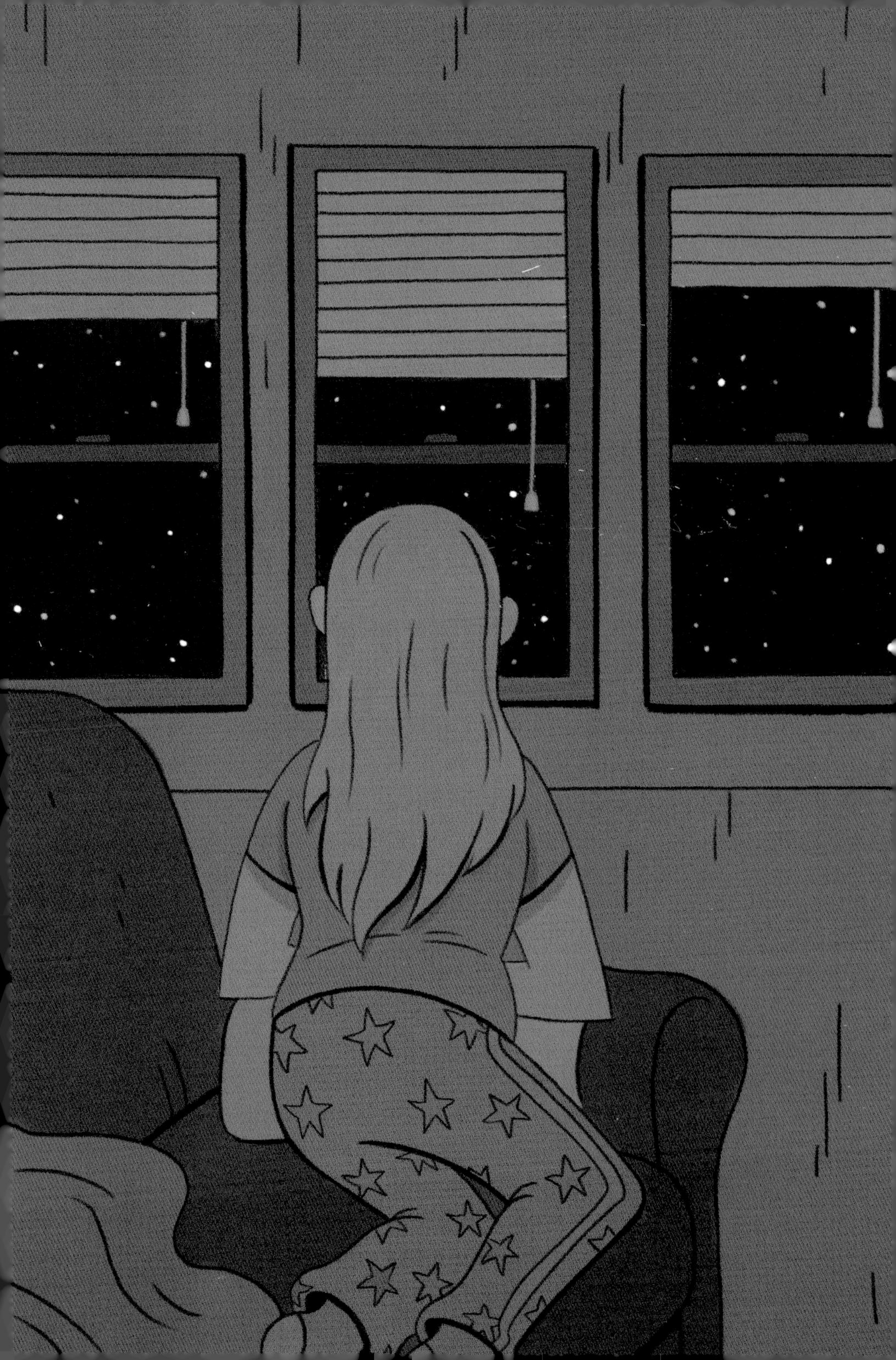

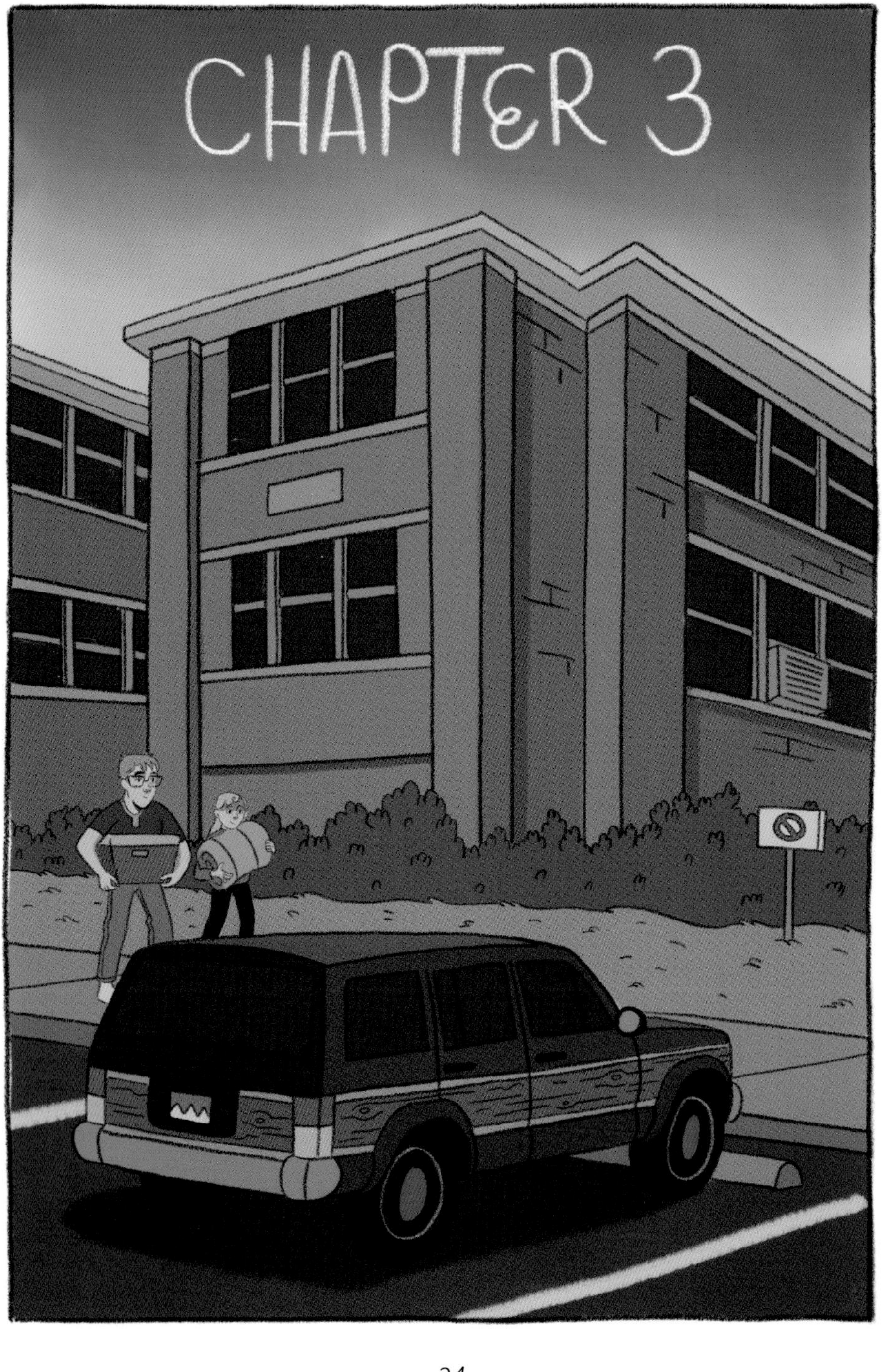
CHAPTER 3

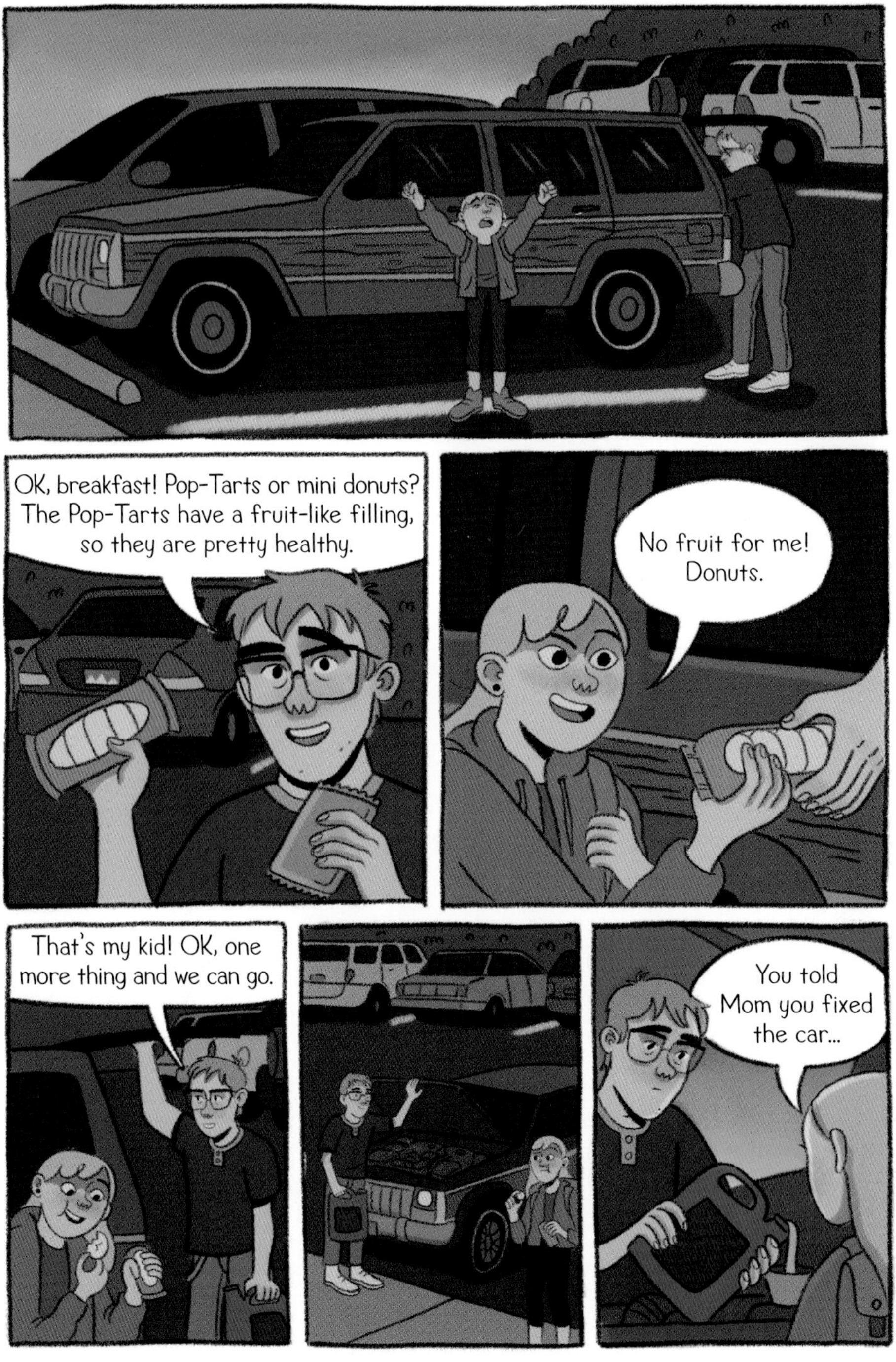
OK, breakfast! Pop-Tarts or mini donuts? The Pop-Tarts have a fruit-like filling, so they are pretty healthy.
No fruit for me! Donuts.
That's my kid! OK, one more thing and we can go.
You told Mom you fixed the car...

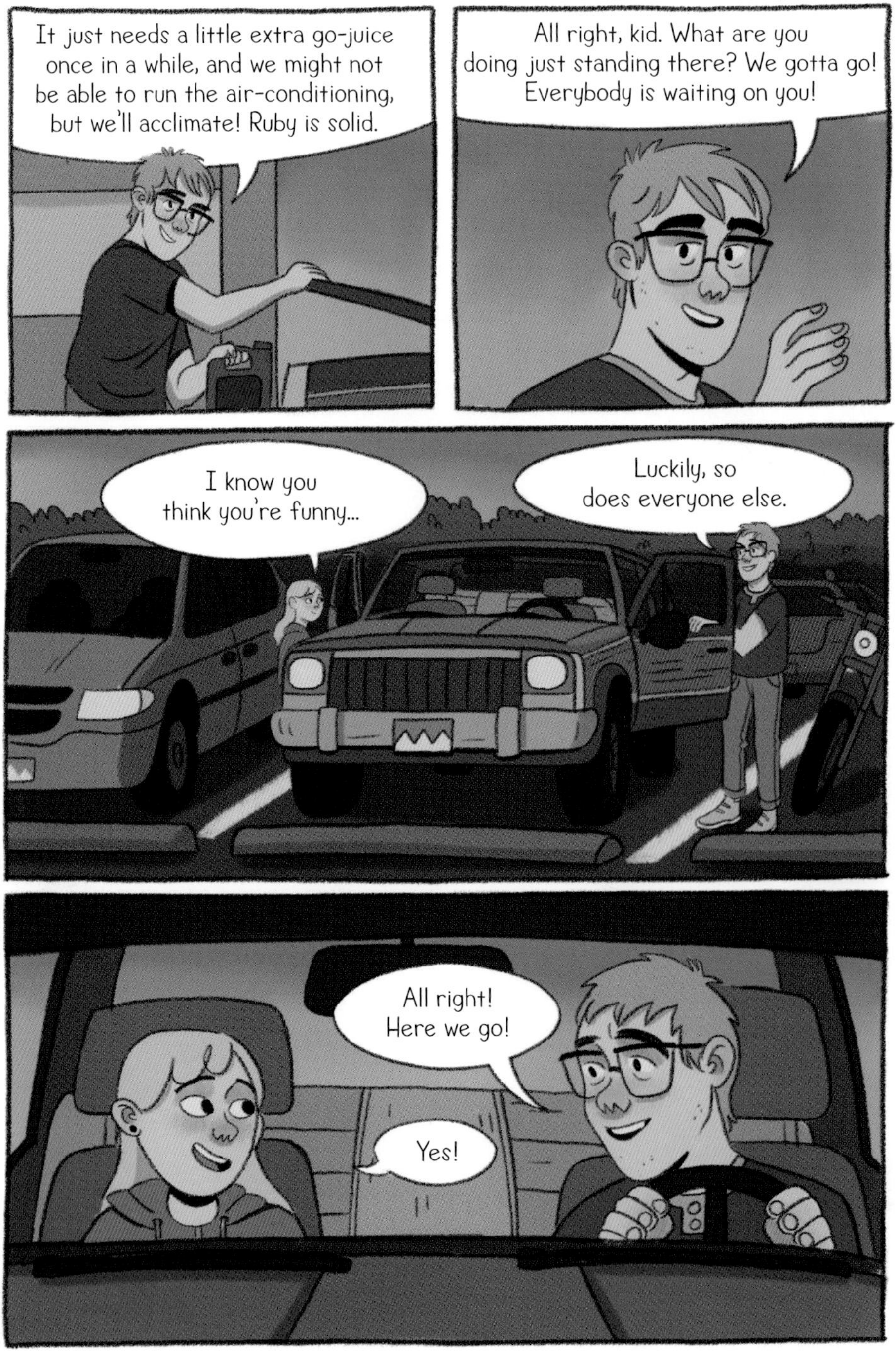
It just needs a little extra go-juice once in a while, and we might not be able to run the air-conditioning, but we'll acclimate! Ruby is solid.
All right, kid. What are you doing just standing there? We gotta go! Everybody is waiting on you!
I know you think you're funny...
Luckily, so does everyone else.
All right! Here we go!
Yes!

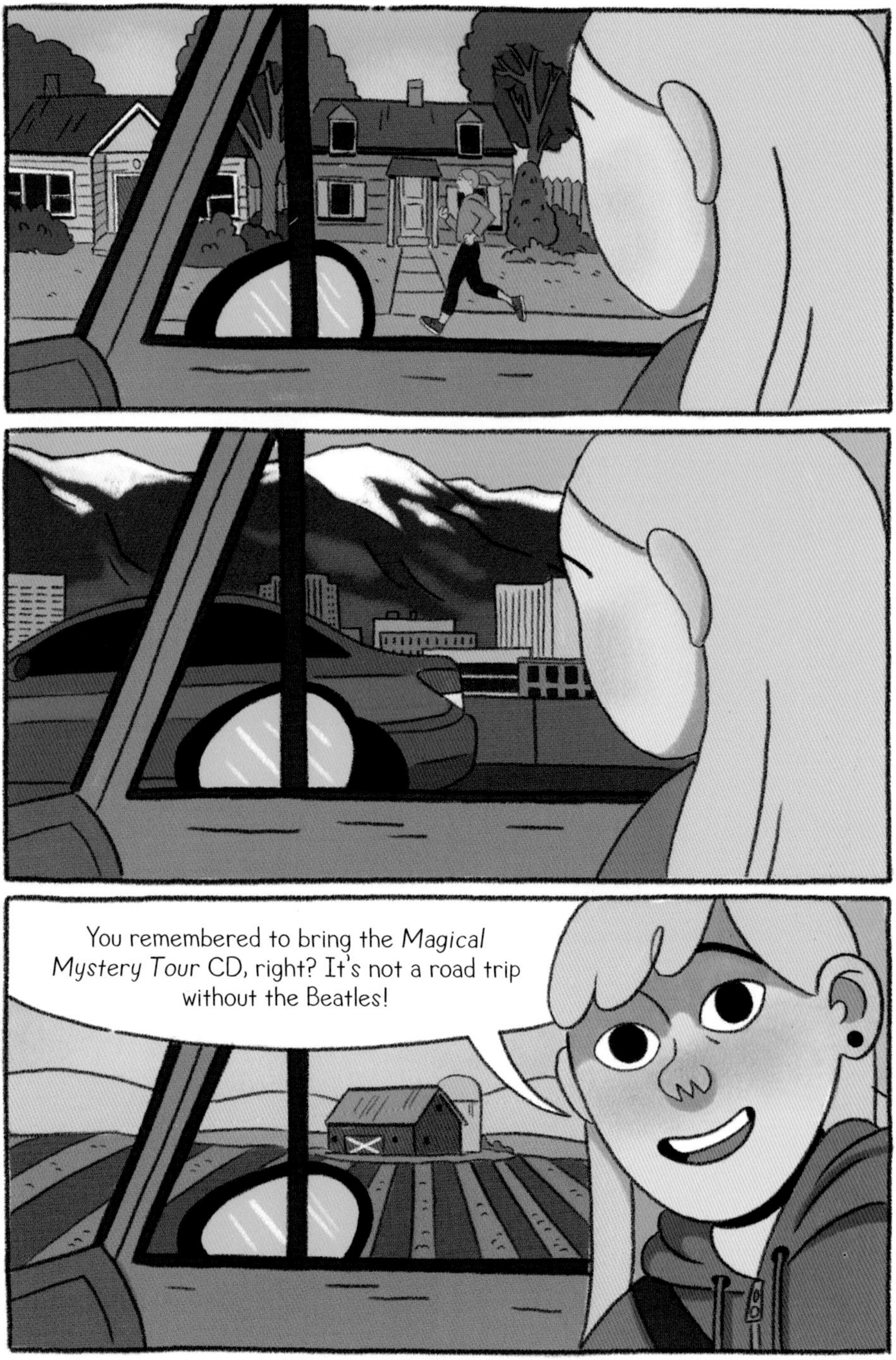
You remembered to bring the *Magical Mystery Tour* CD, right? It's not a road trip without the Beatles!

Oof, sorry.
I totally spaced out.
Oh.
But I have something else! Open the glove compartment!
MAP
NEW MEXICO
SANTA FE
ALBUQUERQUE
CLOVIS
ROSWELL
SACRAMENTO MTS.
70
ROSWELL
You figured it out! The exact place!
MAP

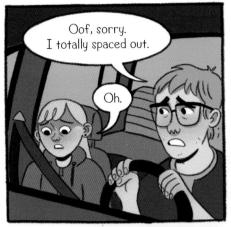

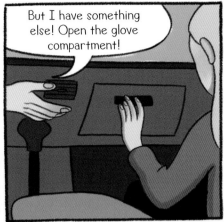

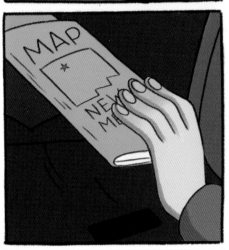

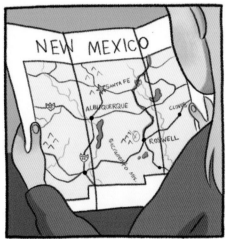

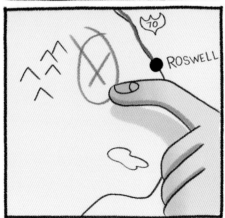

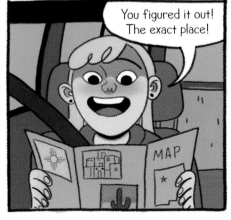

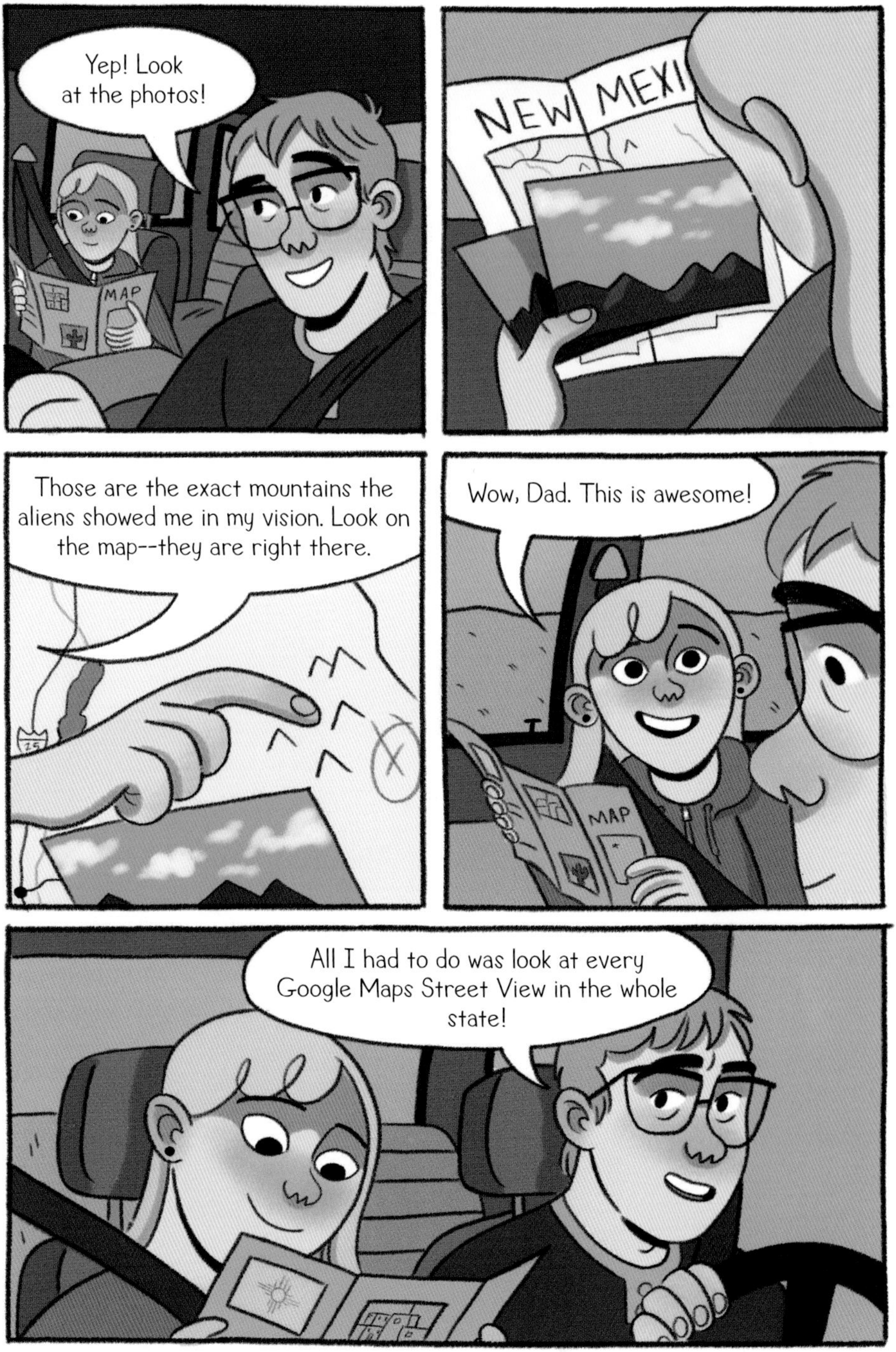
Yep! Look at the photos!
NEW MEXI
MAP
Those are the exact mountains the aliens showed me in my vision. Look on the map--they are right there.
Wow, Dad. This is awesome!
MAP
All I had to do was look at every Google Maps Street View in the whole state!

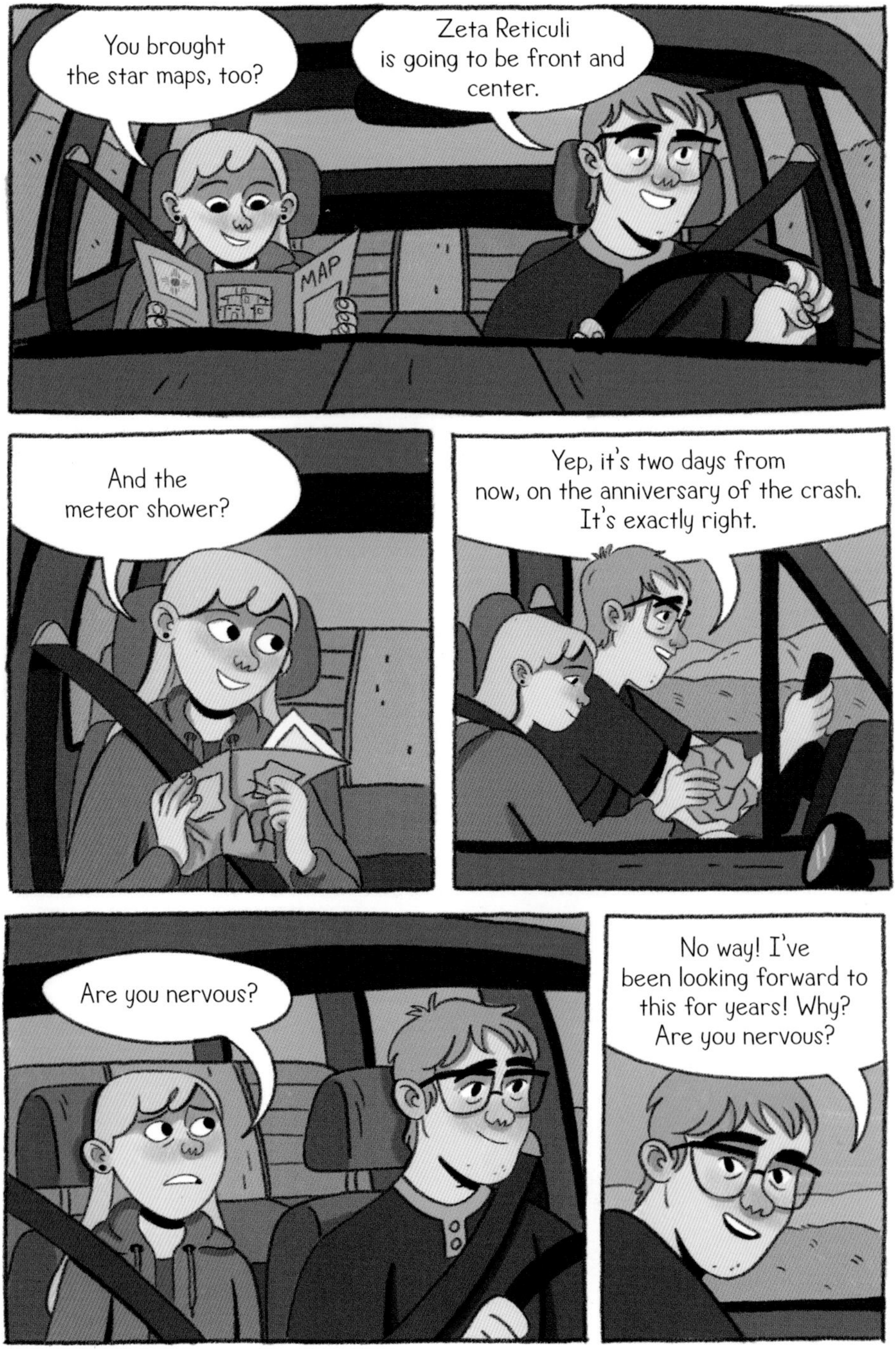
You brought the star maps, too?
Zeta Reticuli is going to be front and center.
MAP
And the meteor shower?
Yep, it's two days from now, on the anniversary of the crash. It's exactly right.
Are you nervous?
No way! I've been looking forward to this for years! Why? Are you nervous?

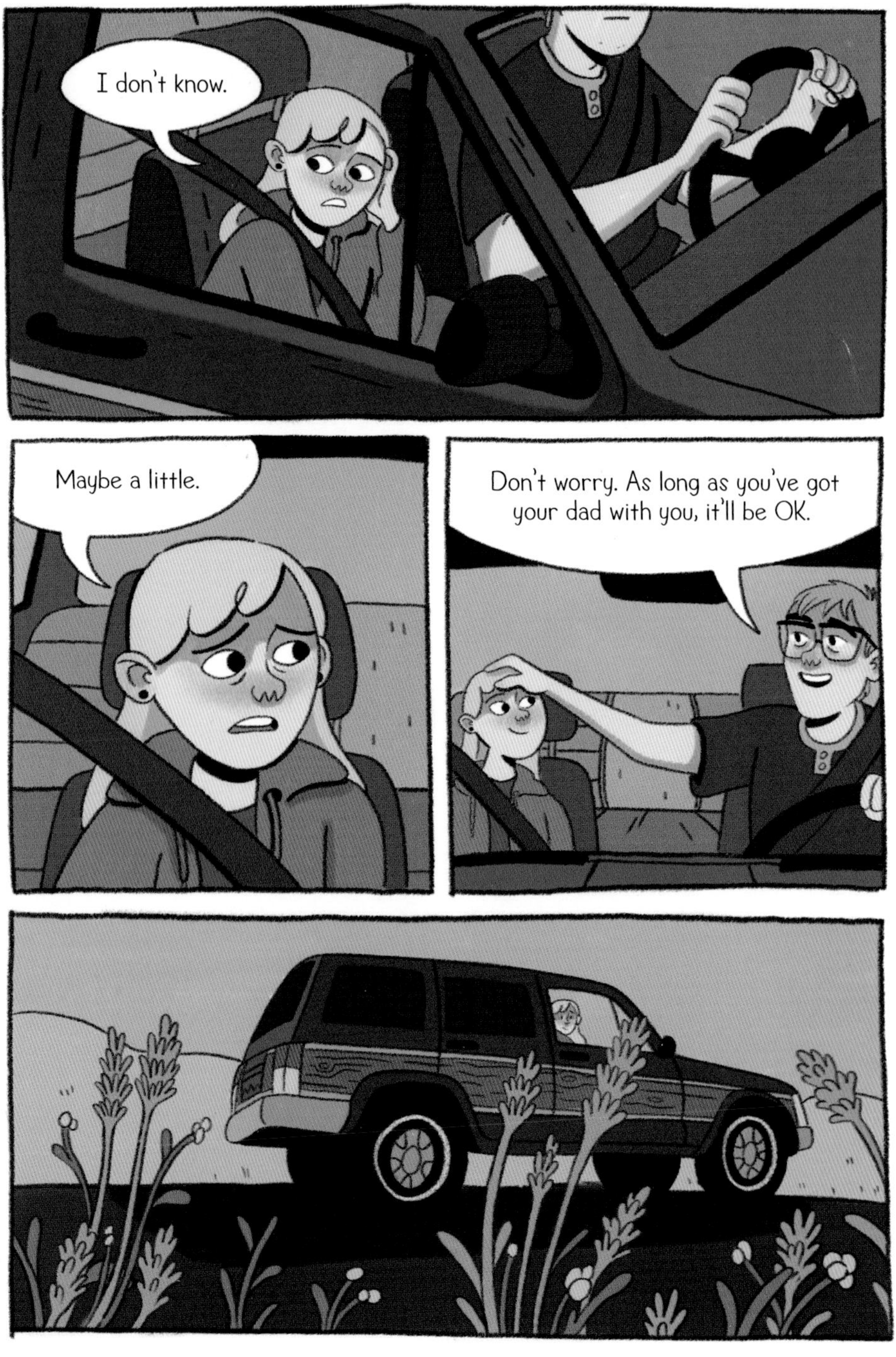
I don't know.
Maybe a little.
Don't worry. As long as you've got your dad with you, it'll be OK.

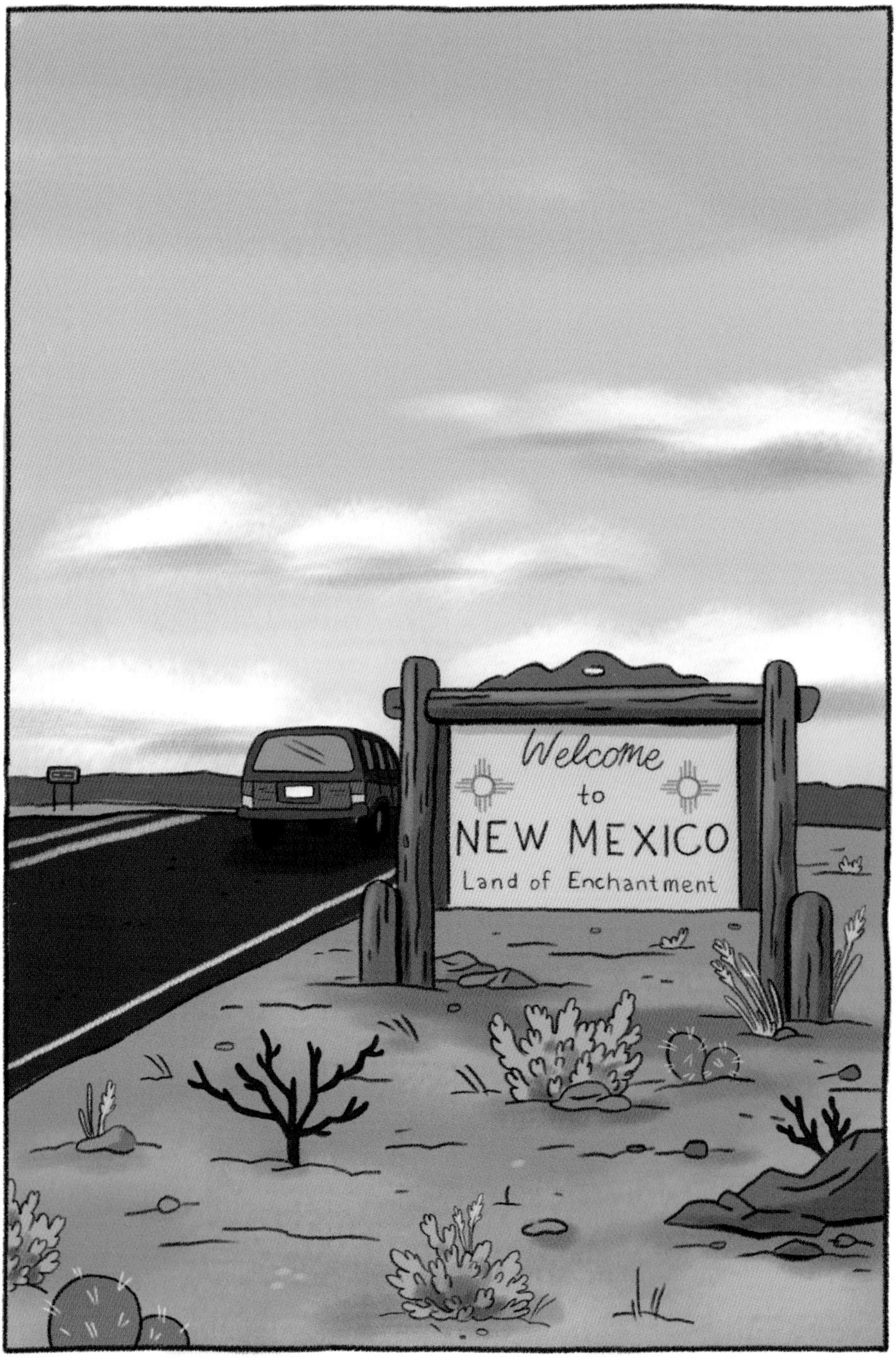
Welcome
to
NEW MEXICO
Land of Enchantment

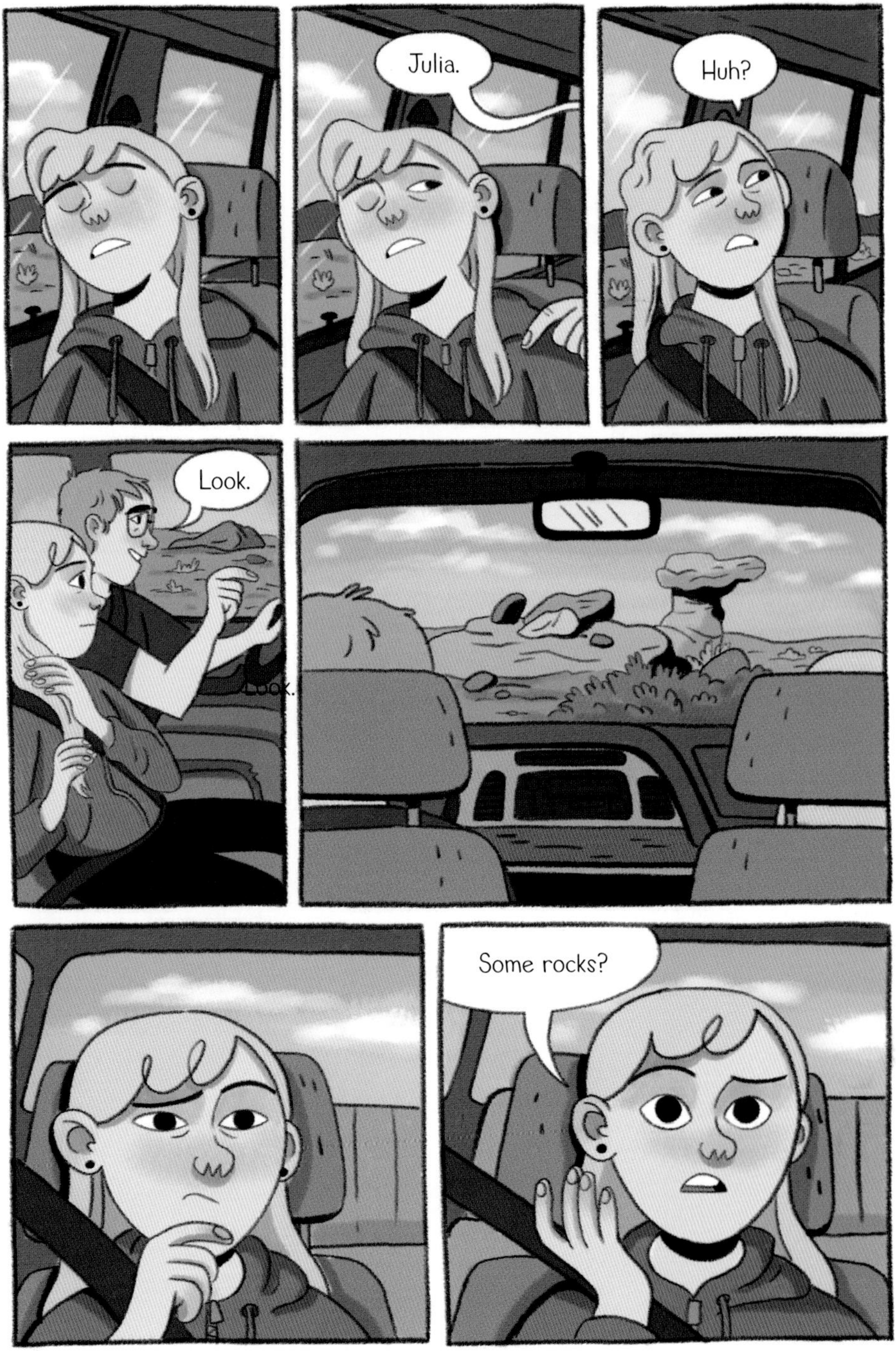
Julia.
Huh?
Look.
Look.
Some rocks?

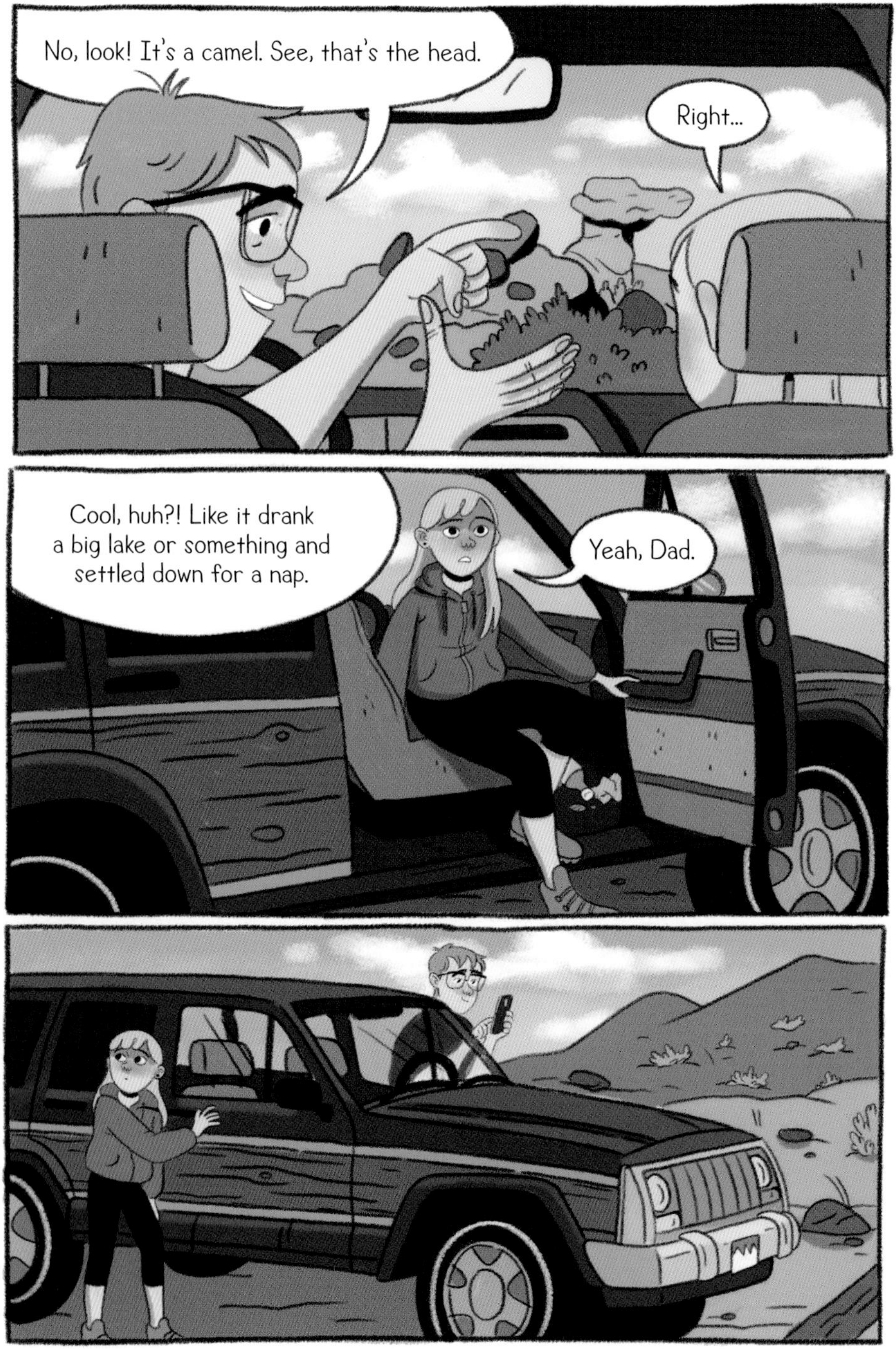
No, look! It's a camel. See, that's the head.
Right...
Cool, huh?! Like it drank a big lake or something and settled down for a nap.
Yeah, Dad.

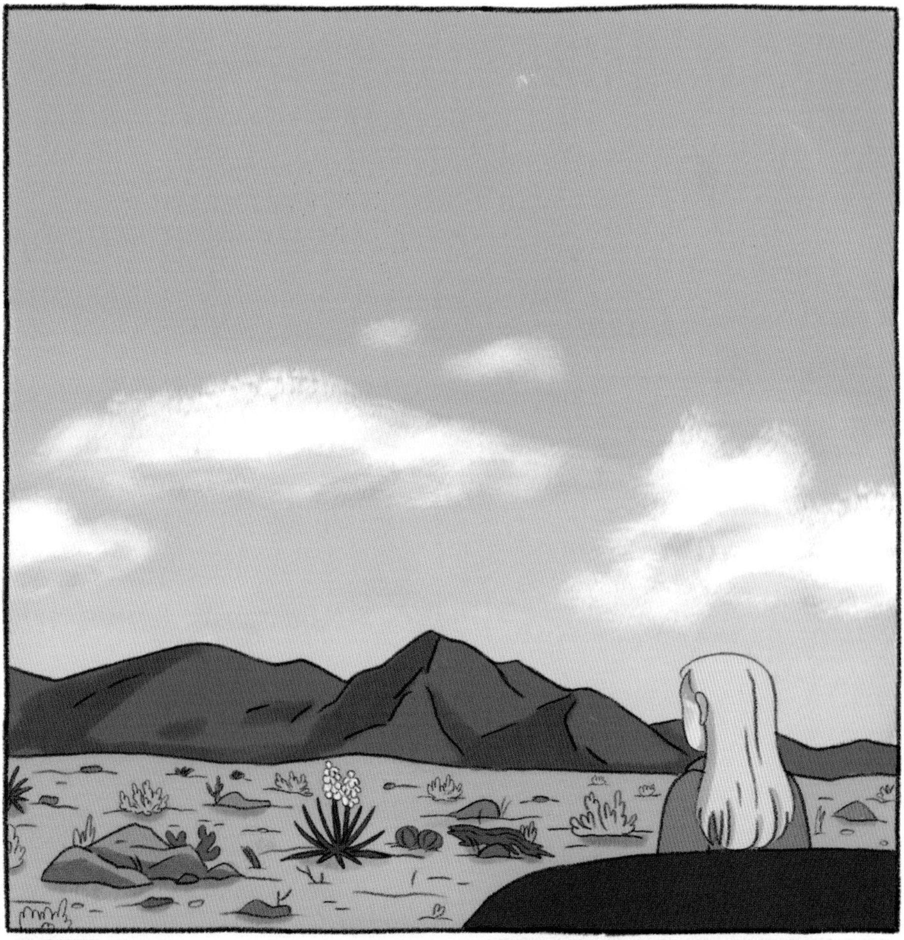

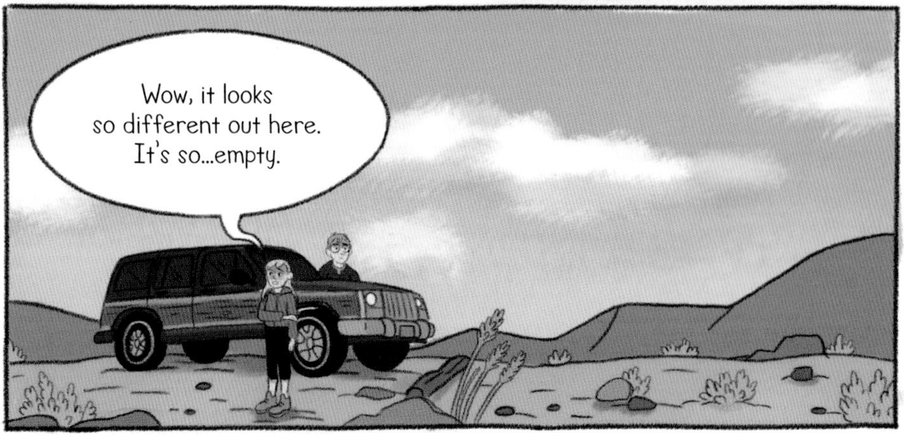
Wow, it looks so different out here. It's so...empty.

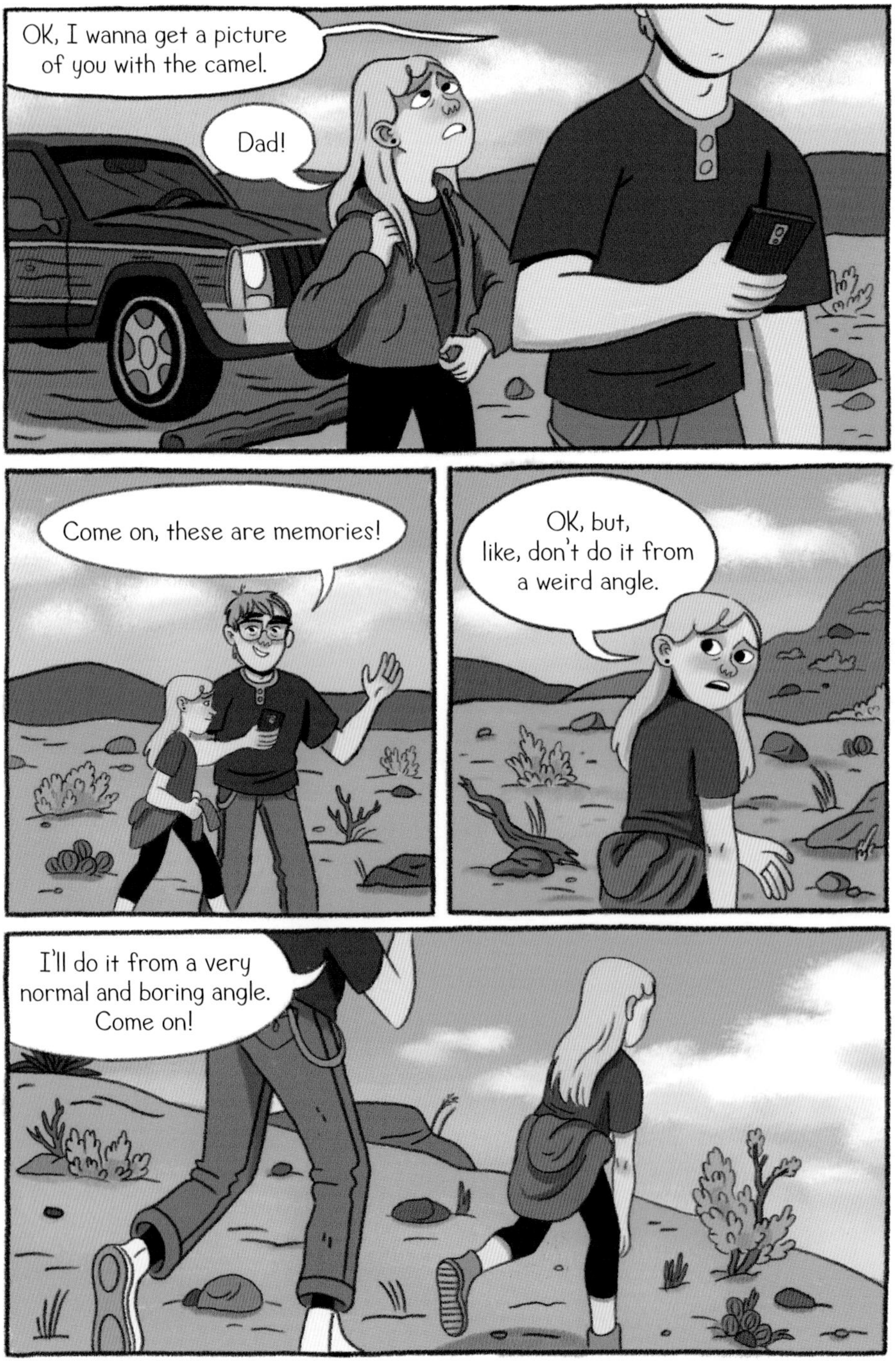
OK, I wanna get a picture of you with the camel.
Dad!
Come on, these are memories!
OK, but, like, don't do it from a weird angle.
I'll do it from a very normal and boring angle. Come on!

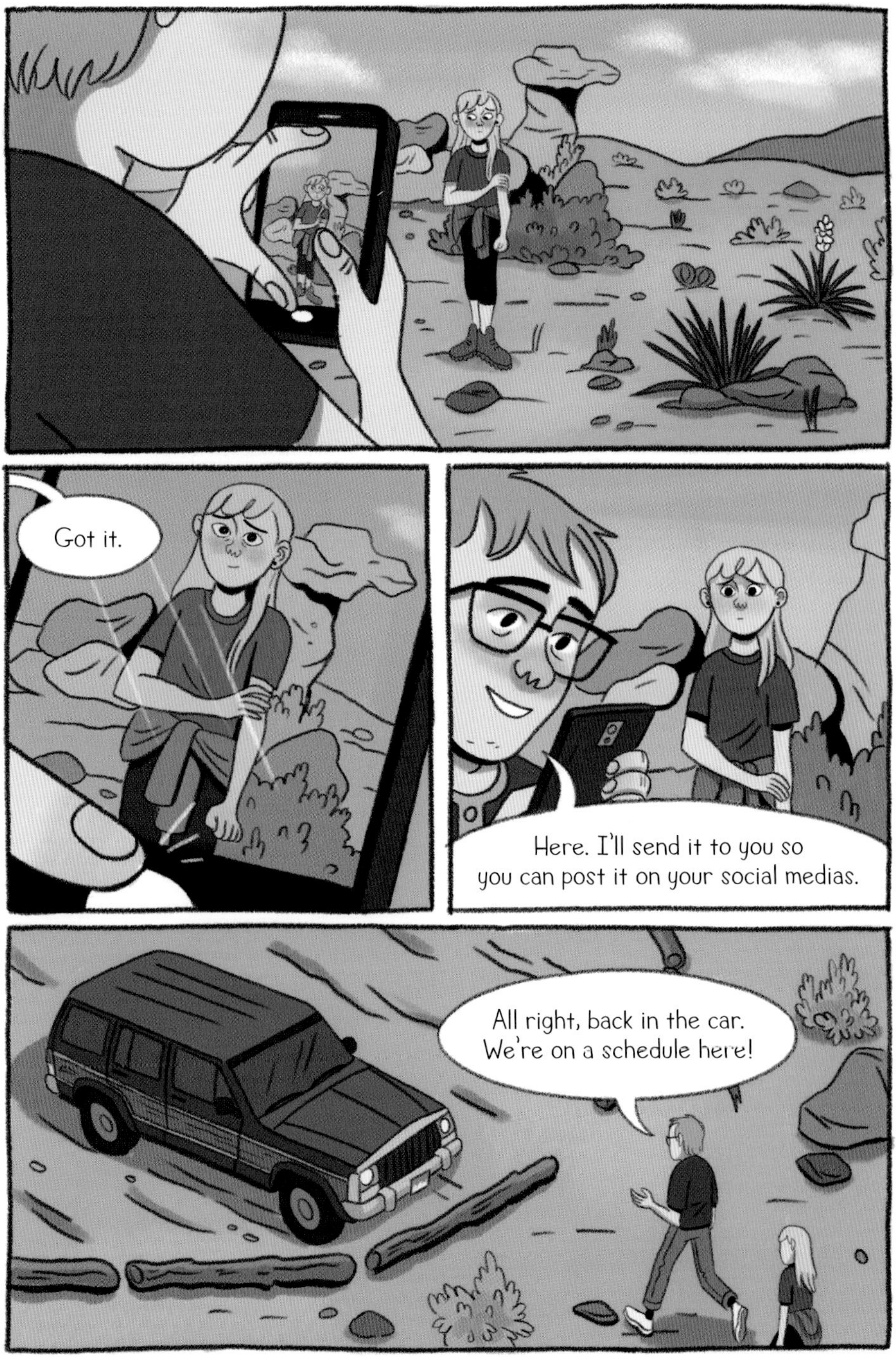
Got it.
Here. I'll send it to you so
you can post it on your social medias.
All right, back in the car.
We're on a schedule here!

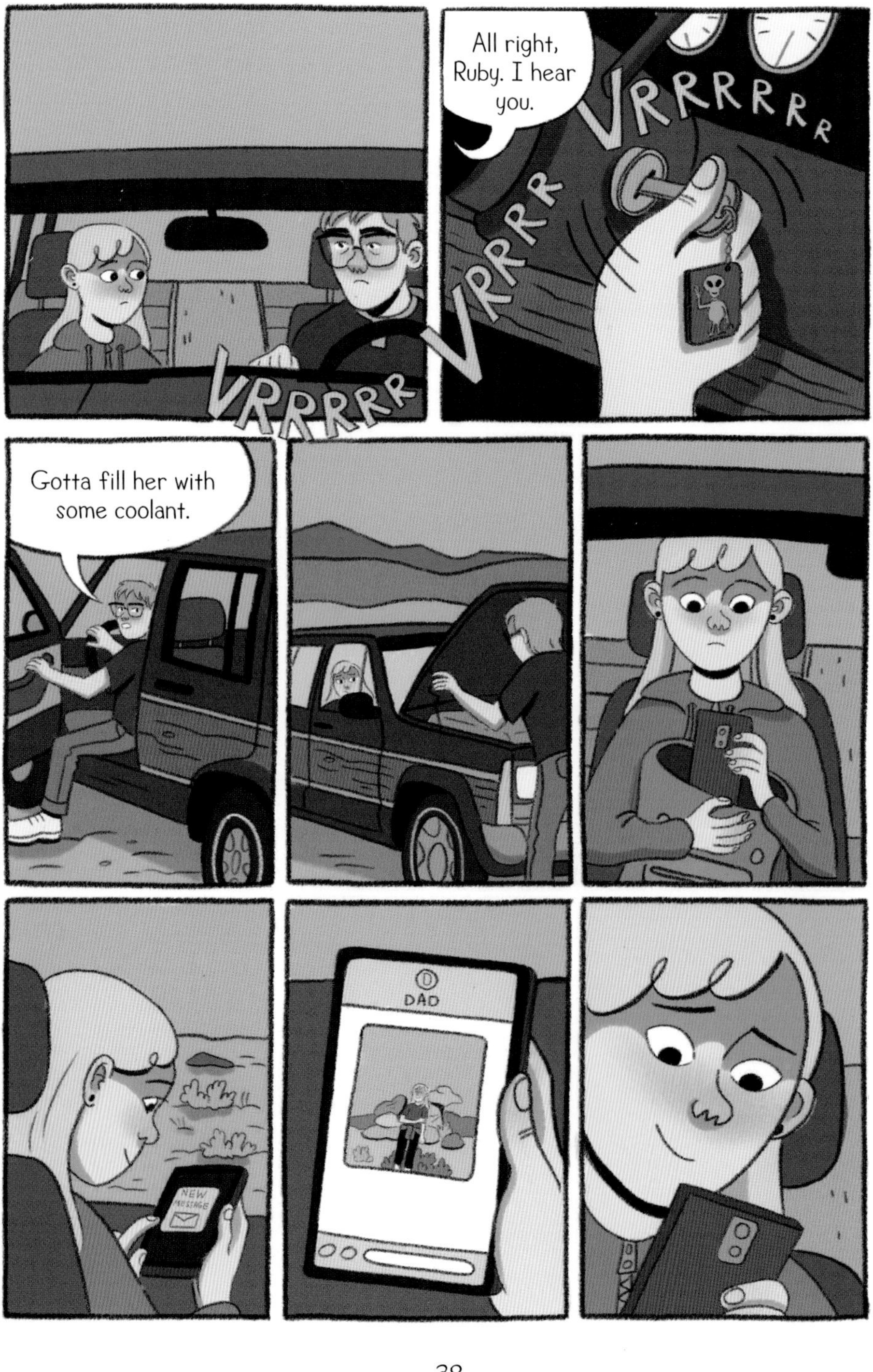
VRRRRRR
VRRRR
All right, Ruby. I hear you.
VRRRRRR
Gotta fill her with some coolant.
DAD
NEW MESSAGE

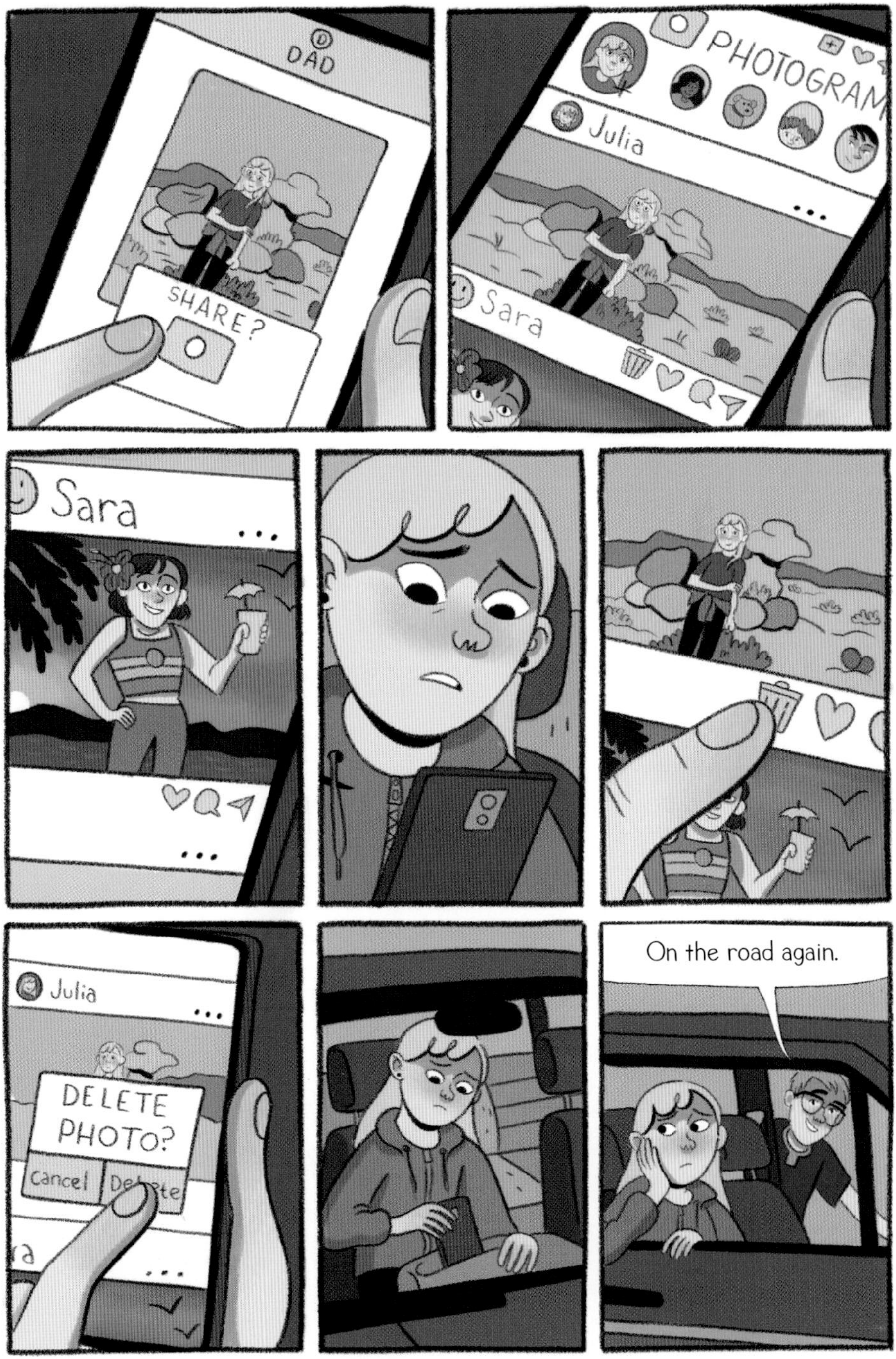
DAD
SHARE?
PHOTOGRAM
Julia
Sara
Sara
Julia
DELETE
PHOTO?
Cancel
Delete
On the road again.

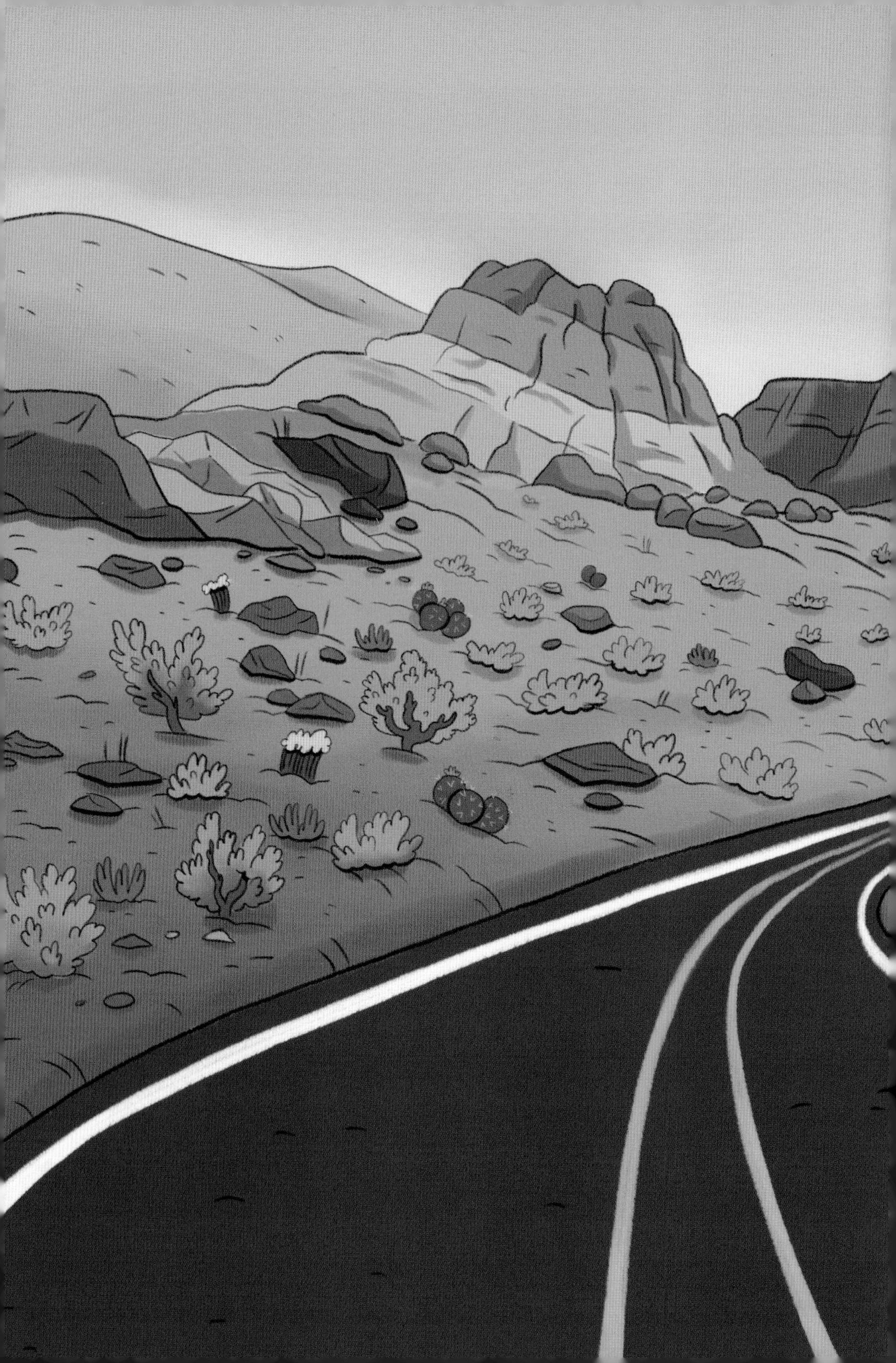

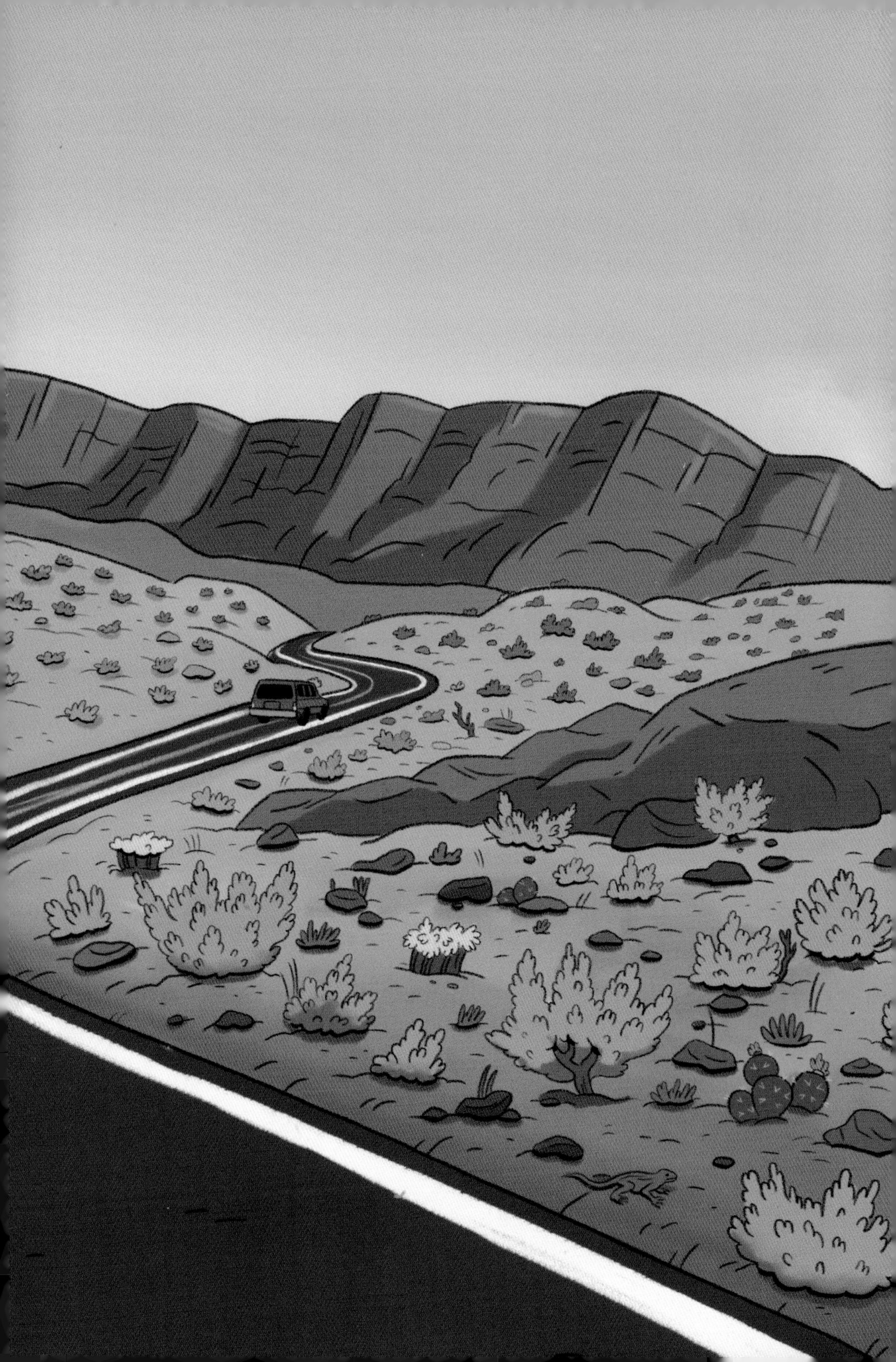

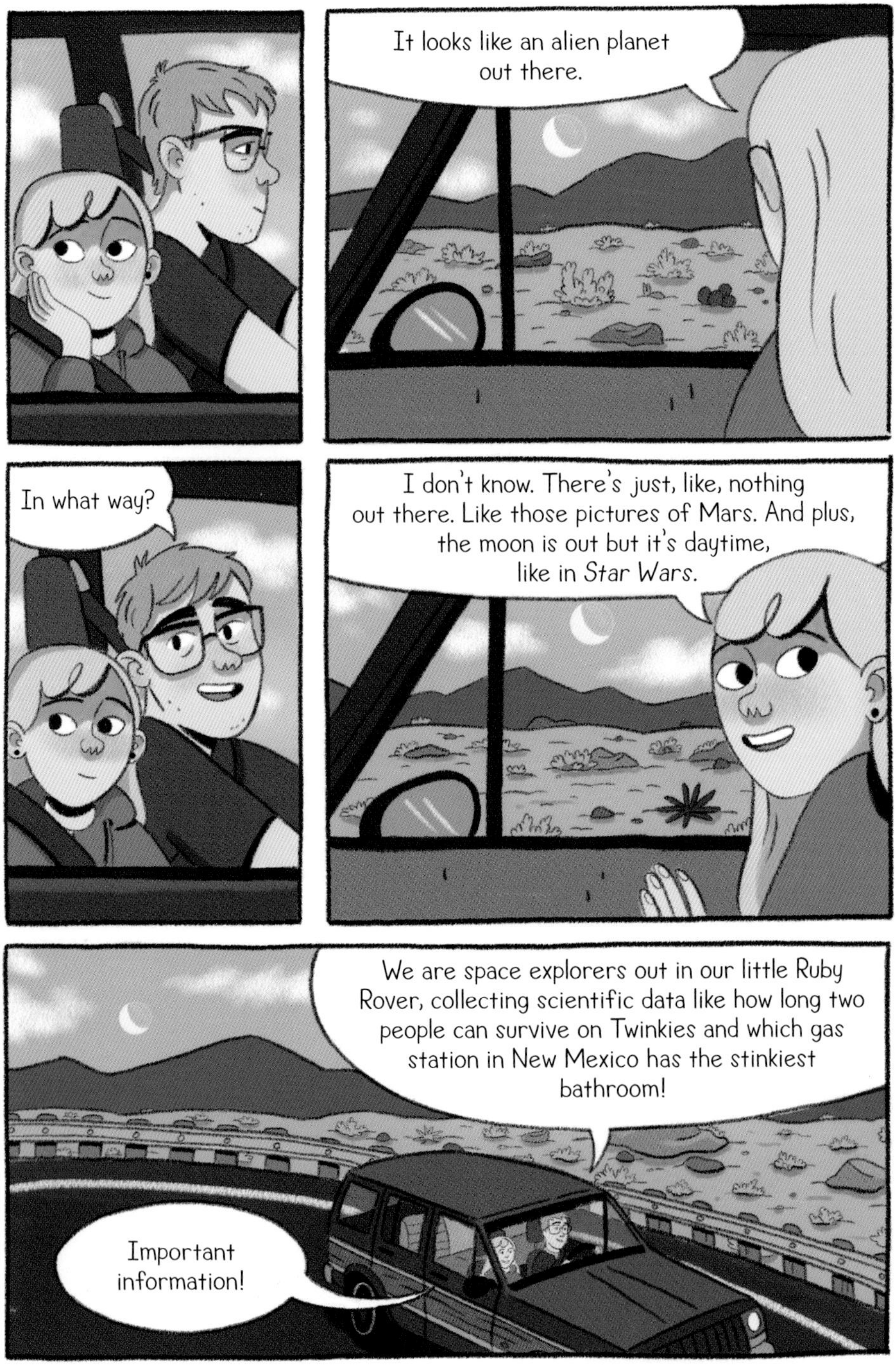
It looks like an alien planet out there.
In what way?
I don't know. There's just, like, nothing out there. Like those pictures of Mars. And plus, the moon is out but it's daytime, like in *Star Wars*.
We are space explorers out in our little Ruby Rover, collecting scientific data like how long two people can survive on Twinkies and which gas station in New Mexico has the stinkiest bathroom!
Important information!

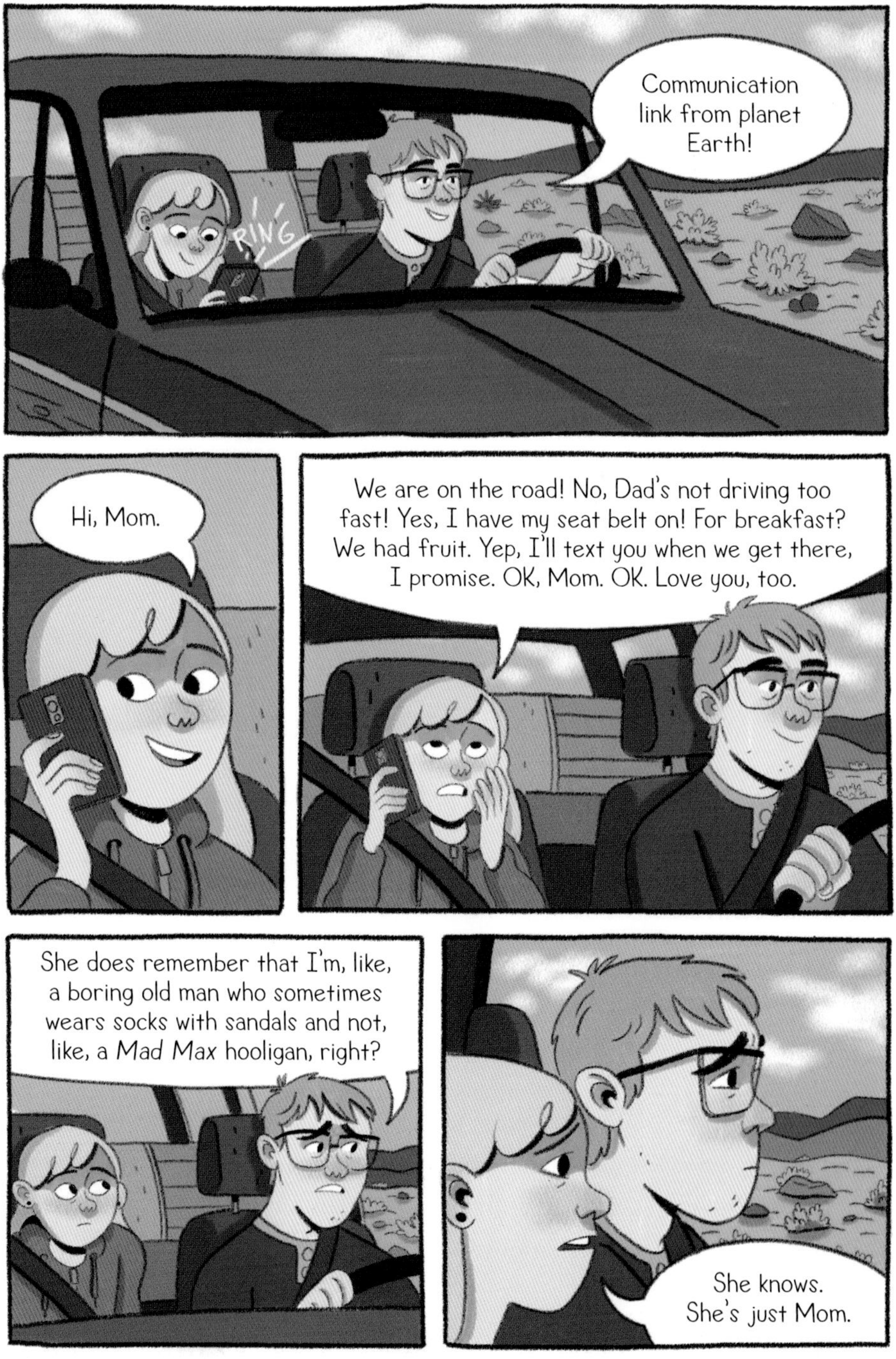
Communication link from planet Earth!
RING
Hi, Mom.
We are on the road! No, Dad's not driving too fast! Yes, I have my seat belt on! For breakfast? We had fruit. Yep, I'll text you when we get there, I promise. OK, Mom. OK. Love you, too.
She does remember that I'm, like, a boring old man who sometimes wears socks with sandals and not, like, a *Mad Max* hooligan, right?
She knows. She's just Mom.

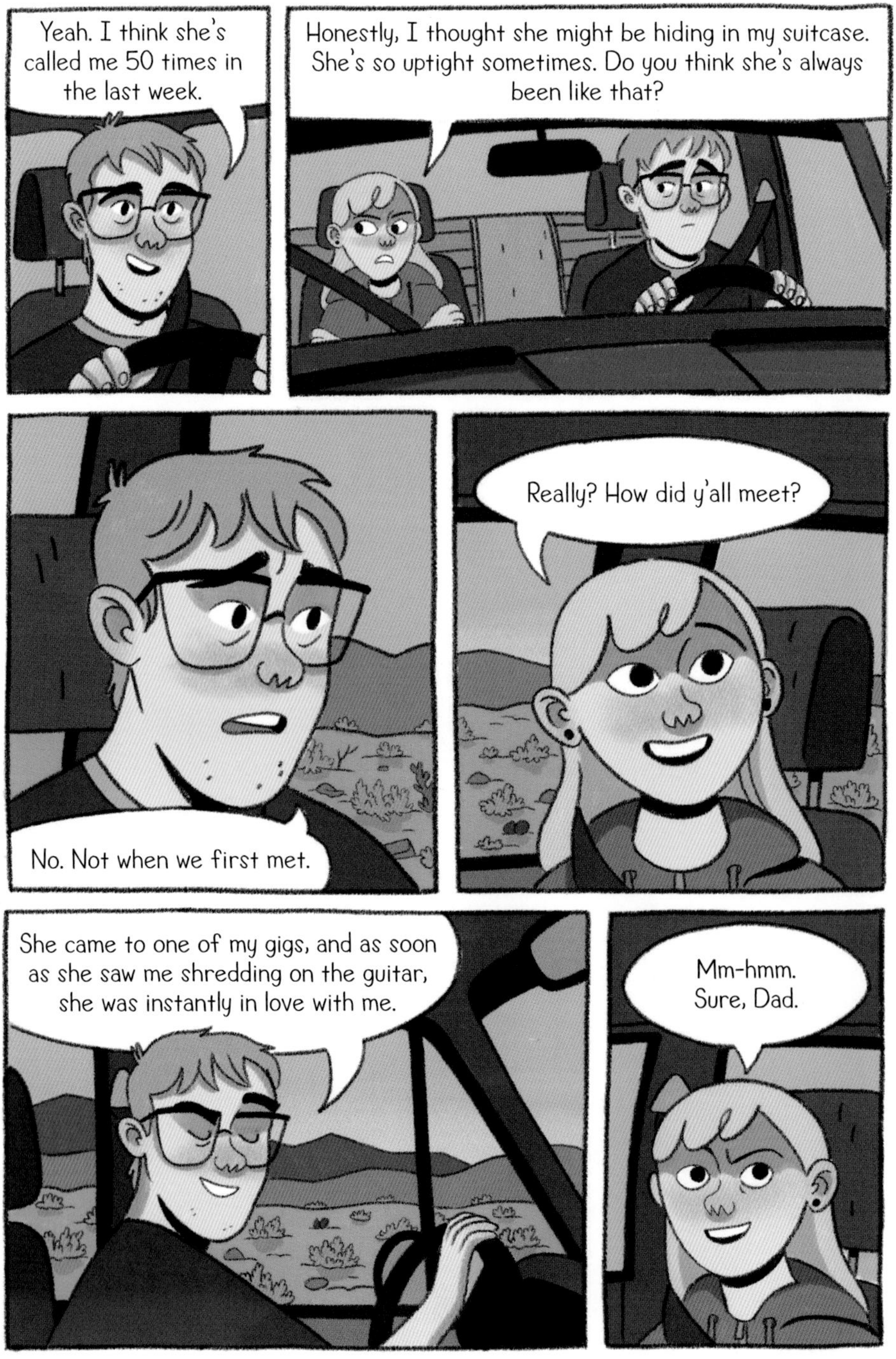
Yeah. I think she's called me 50 times in the last week.
Honestly, I thought she might be hiding in my suitcase. She's so uptight sometimes. Do you think she's always been like that?
No. Not when we first met.
Really? How did y'all meet?
She came to one of my gigs, and as soon as she saw me shredding on the guitar, she was instantly in love with me.
Mm-hmm. Sure, Dad.

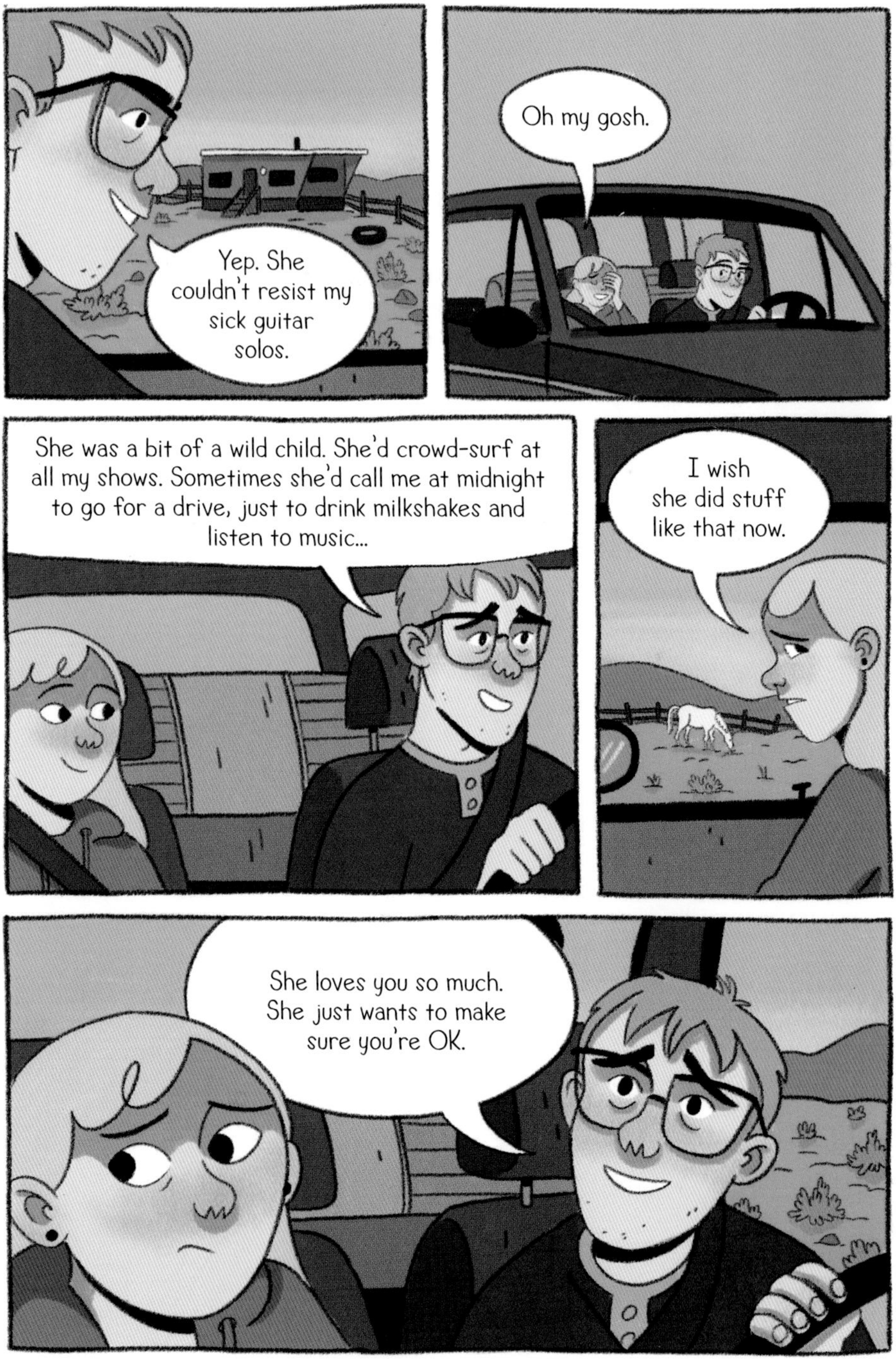
Yep. She couldn't resist my sick guitar solos.
Oh my gosh.
She was a bit of a wild child. She'd crowd-surf at all my shows. Sometimes she'd call me at midnight to go for a drive, just to drink milkshakes and listen to music...
I wish she did stuff like that now.
She loves you so much. She just wants to make sure you're OK.

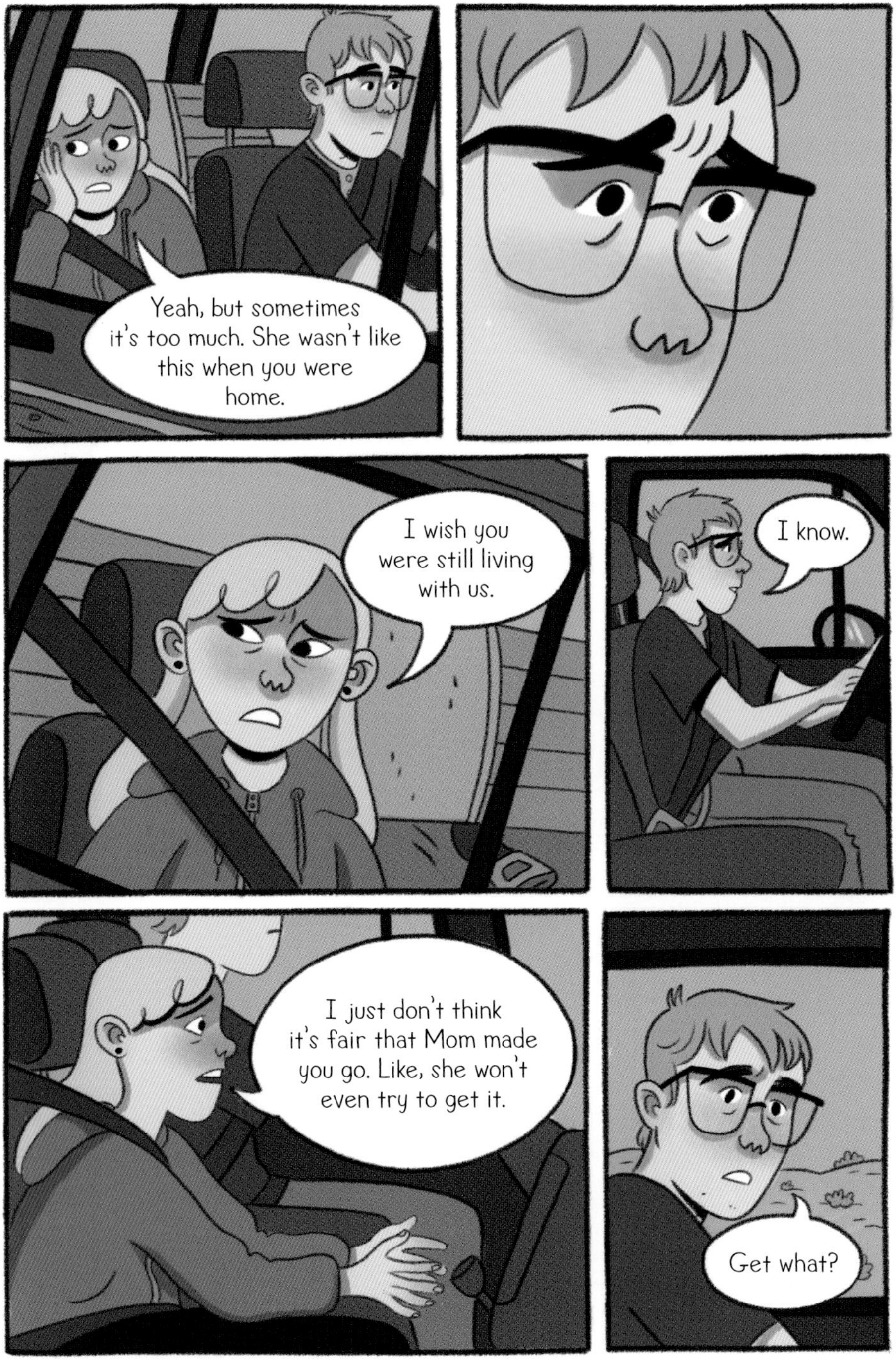
Yeah, but sometimes it's too much. She wasn't like this when you were home.
I wish you were still living with us.
I know.
I just don't think it's fair that Mom made you go. Like, she won't even try to get it.
Get what?

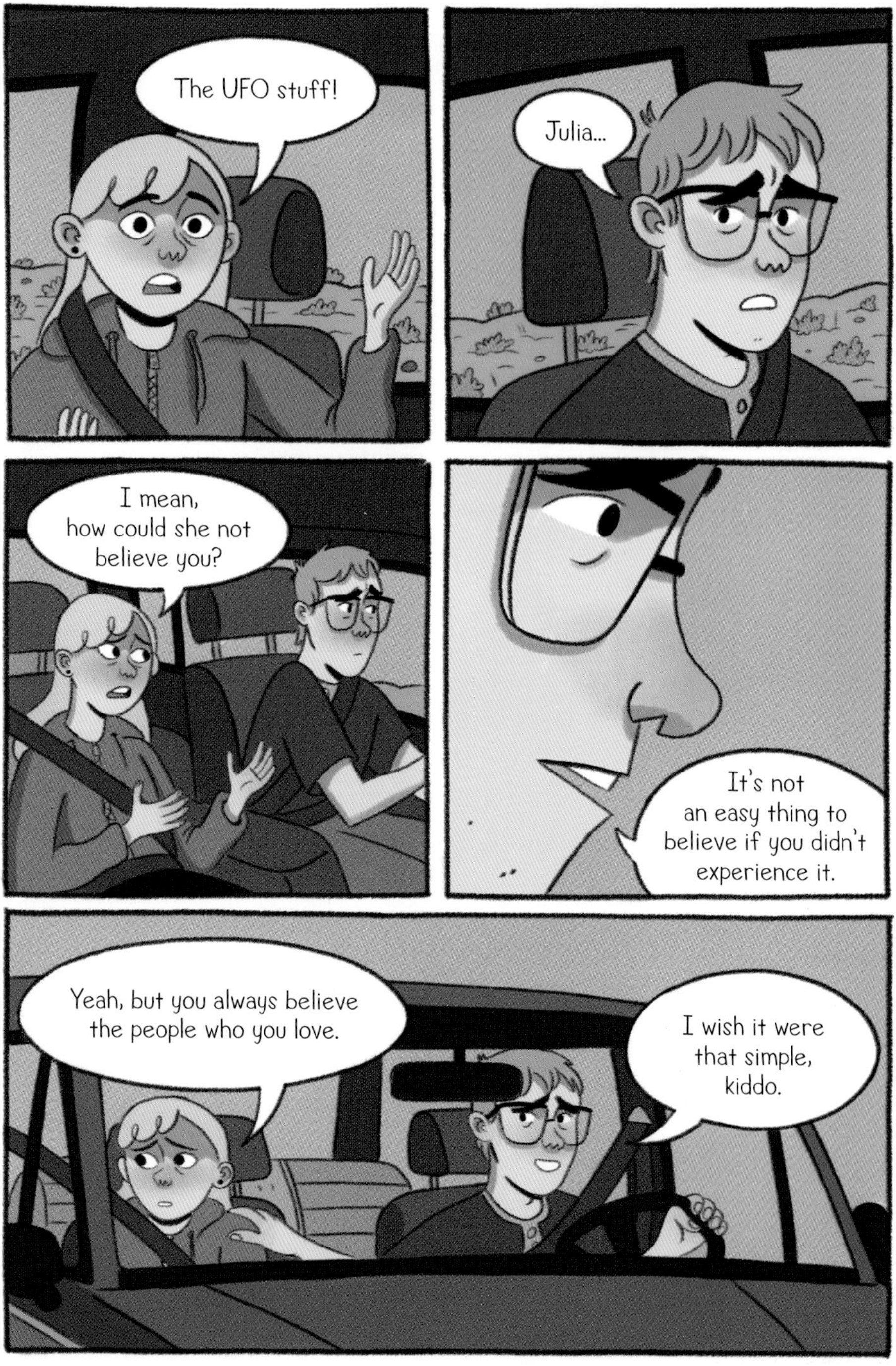
The UFO stuff!
Julia...
I mean, how could she not believe you?
It's not an easy thing to believe if you didn't experience it.
Yeah, but you always believe the people who you love.
I wish it were that simple, kiddo.

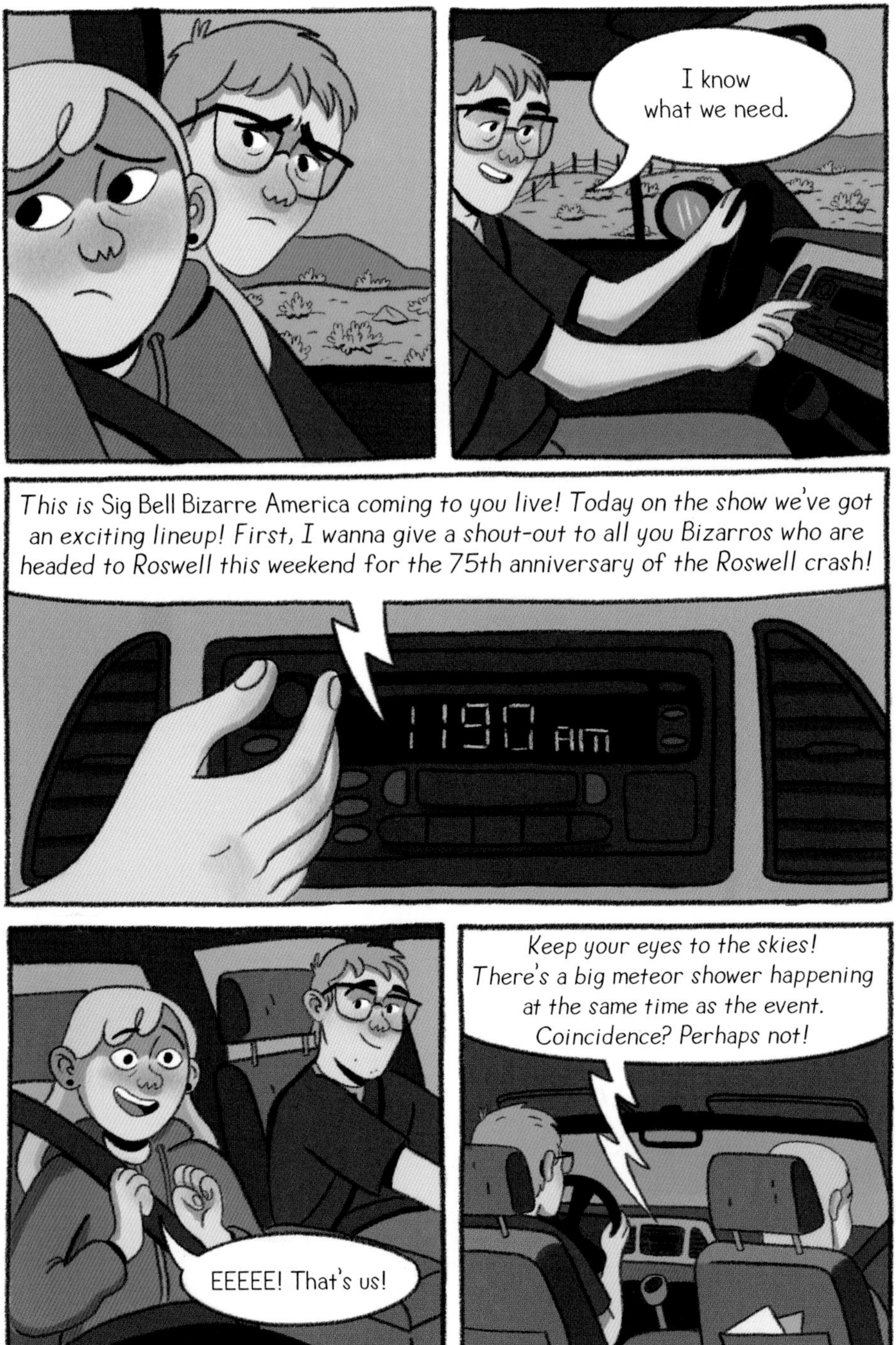
I know what we need.
This is Sig Bell Bizarre America coming to you live! Today on the show we've got an exciting lineup! First, I wanna give a shout-out to all you Bizarros who are headed to Roswell this weekend for the 75th anniversary of the Roswell crash!
1190 AM
EEEEE! That's us!
Keep your eyes to the skies! There's a big meteor shower happening at the same time as the event. Coincidence? Perhaps not!

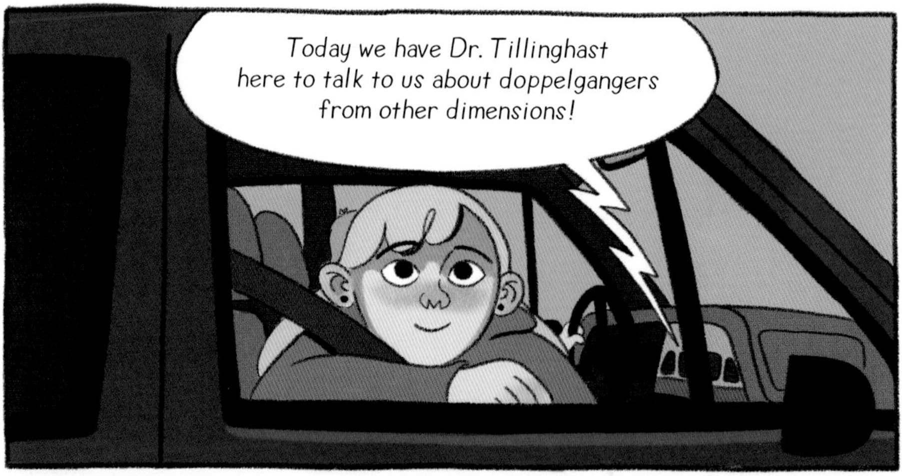
Today we have Dr. Tillinghast here to talk to us about doppelgangers from other dimensions!

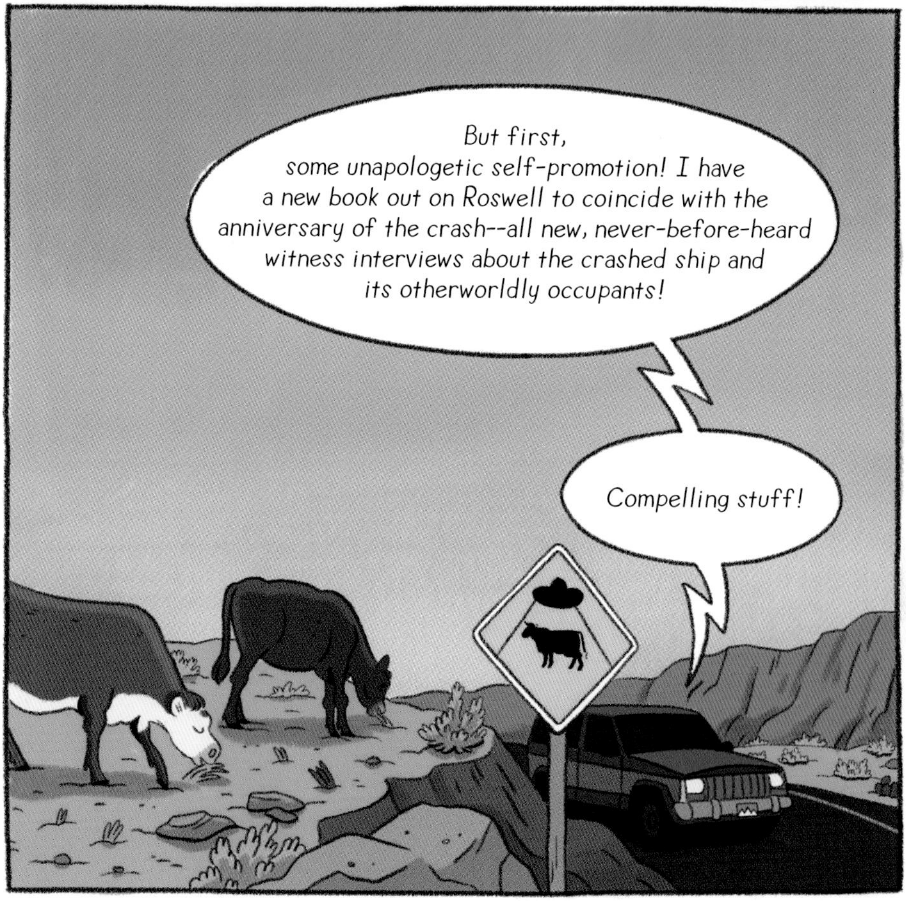
But first, some unapologetic self-promotion! I have a new book out on Roswell to coincide with the anniversary of the crash--all new, never-before-heard witness interviews about the crashed ship and its otherworldly occupants!
Compelling stuff!

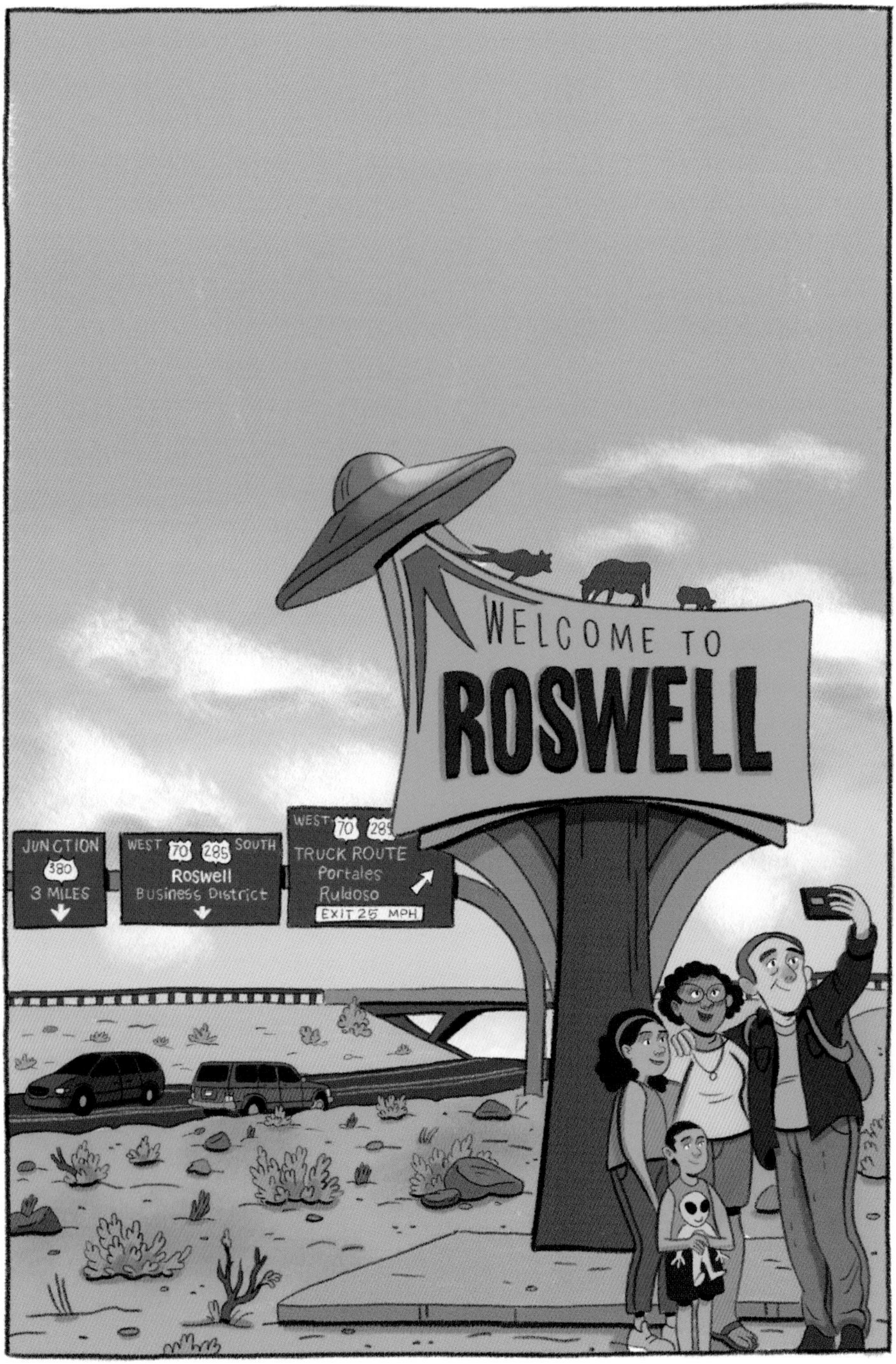
WELCOME TO
ROSWELL
JUNCTION
380
3 MILES
WEST 70 285 SOUTH
Roswell
Business District
TRUCK ROUTE
Portales
Ruidoso
EXIT 25 MPH

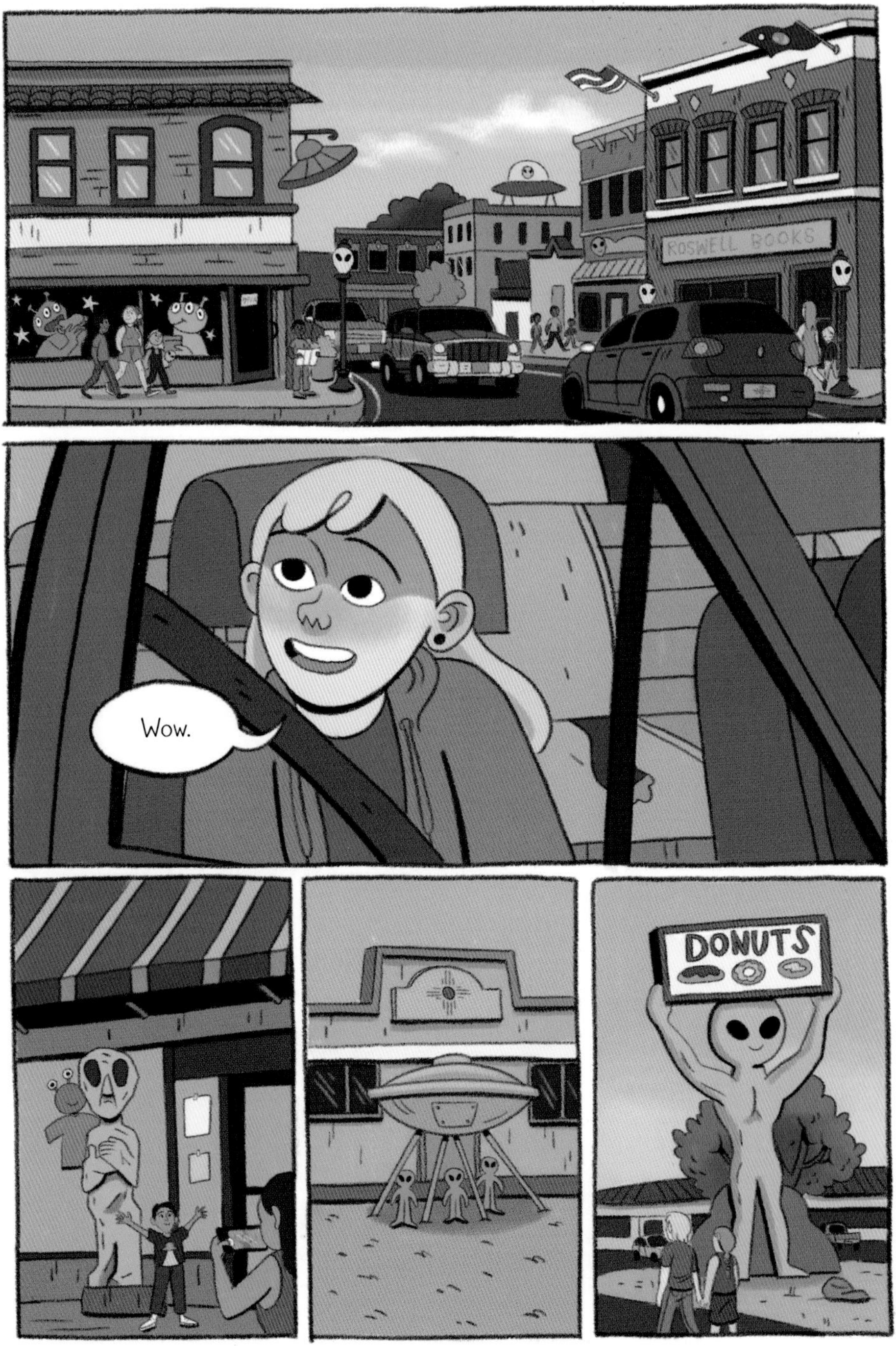
ROSWELL BOOKS
Wow.
DONUTS

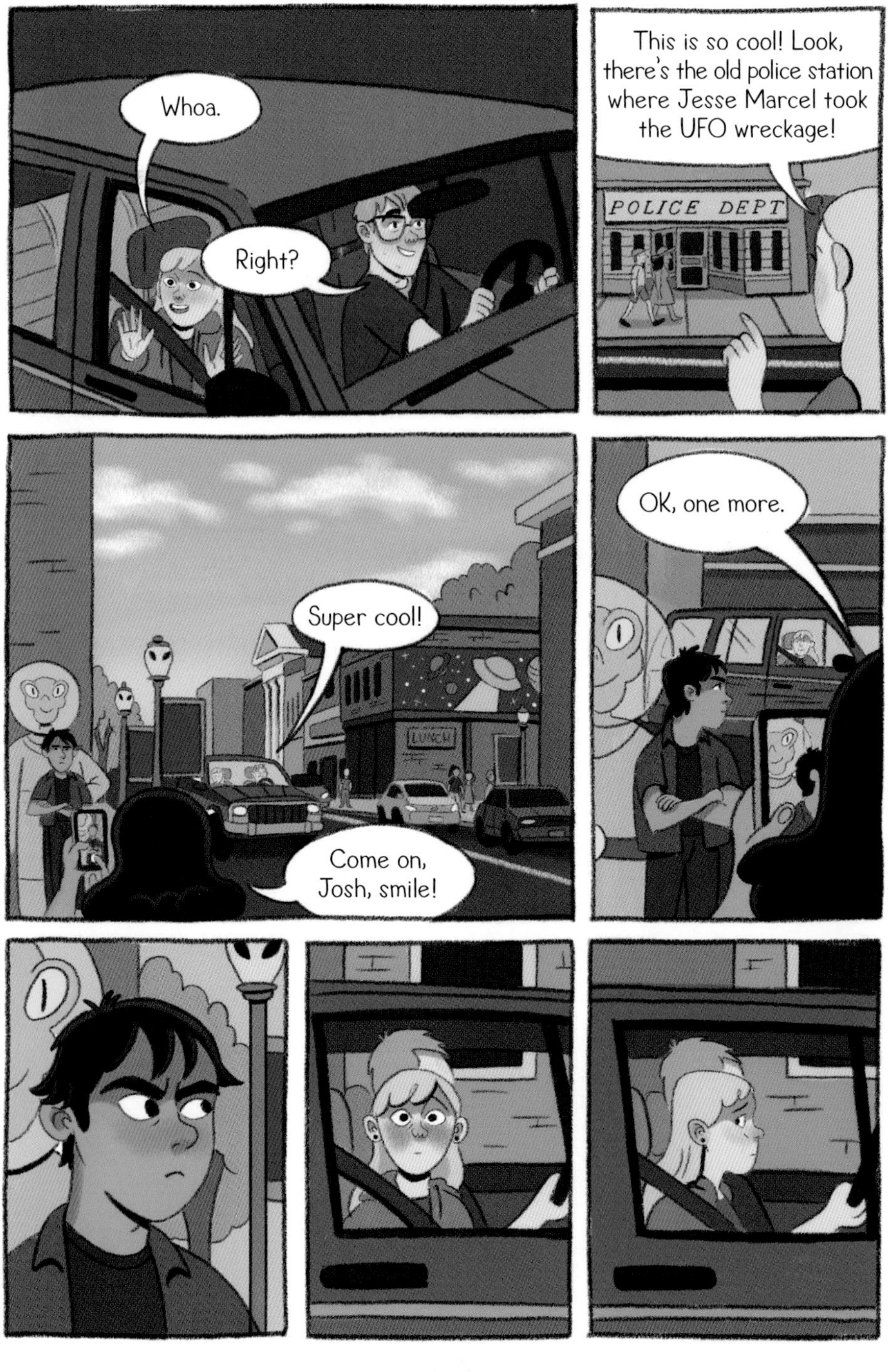
Whoa.
Right?
This is so cool! Look, there's the old police station where Jesse Marcel took the UFO wreckage!
POLICE DEPT
Super cool!
LUNCH
Come on, Josh, smile!
OK, one more.

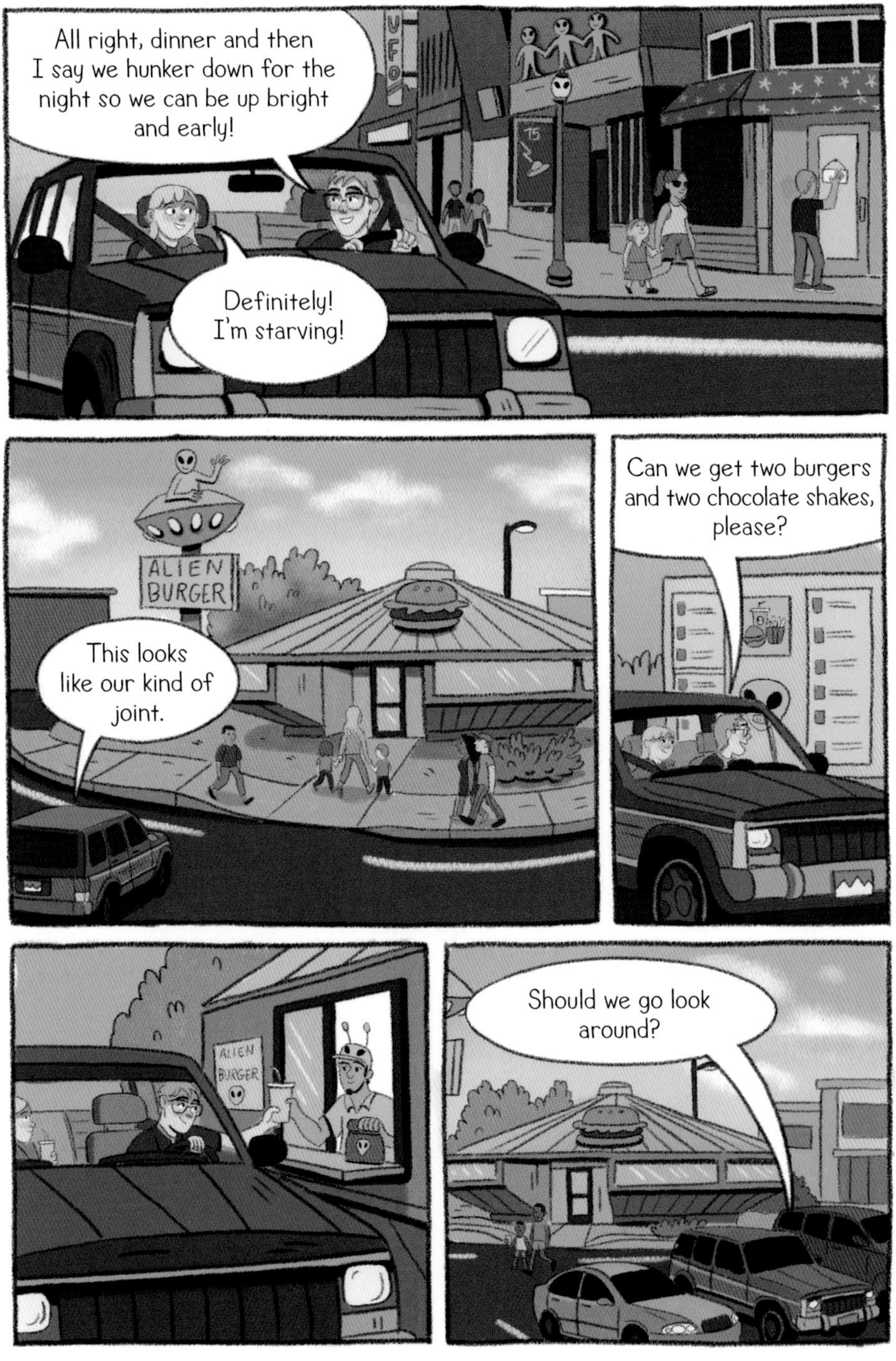

UFO
All right, dinner and then I say we hunker down for the night so we can be up bright and early!
Definitely! I'm starving!
ALIEN BURGER
This looks like our kind of joint.
Can we get two burgers and two chocolate shakes, please?
ALIEN BURGER
Should we go look around?

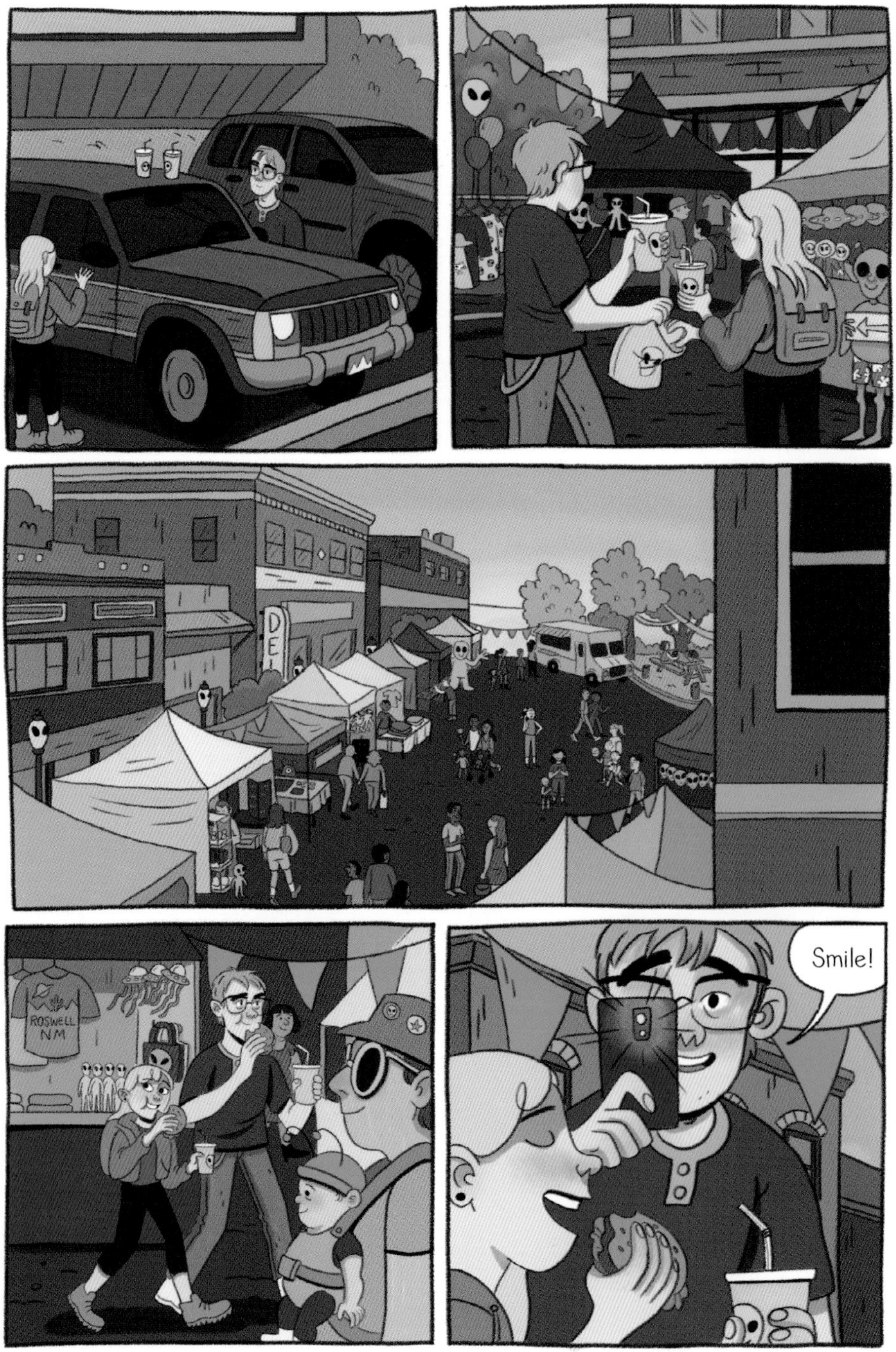
ROSWELL
NM
Smile!

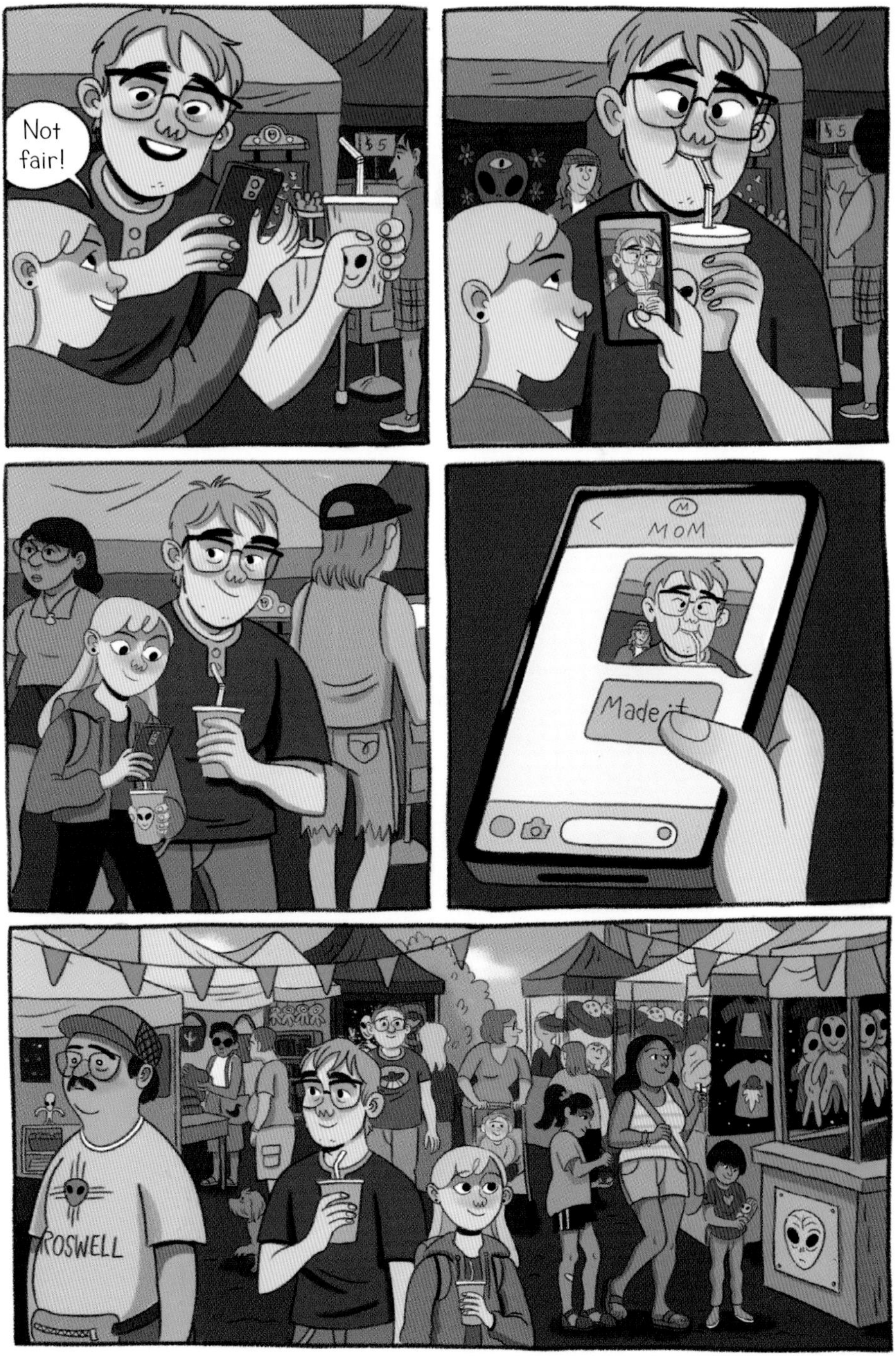
Not fair!
$5
$5
MOM
Made it
ROSWELL

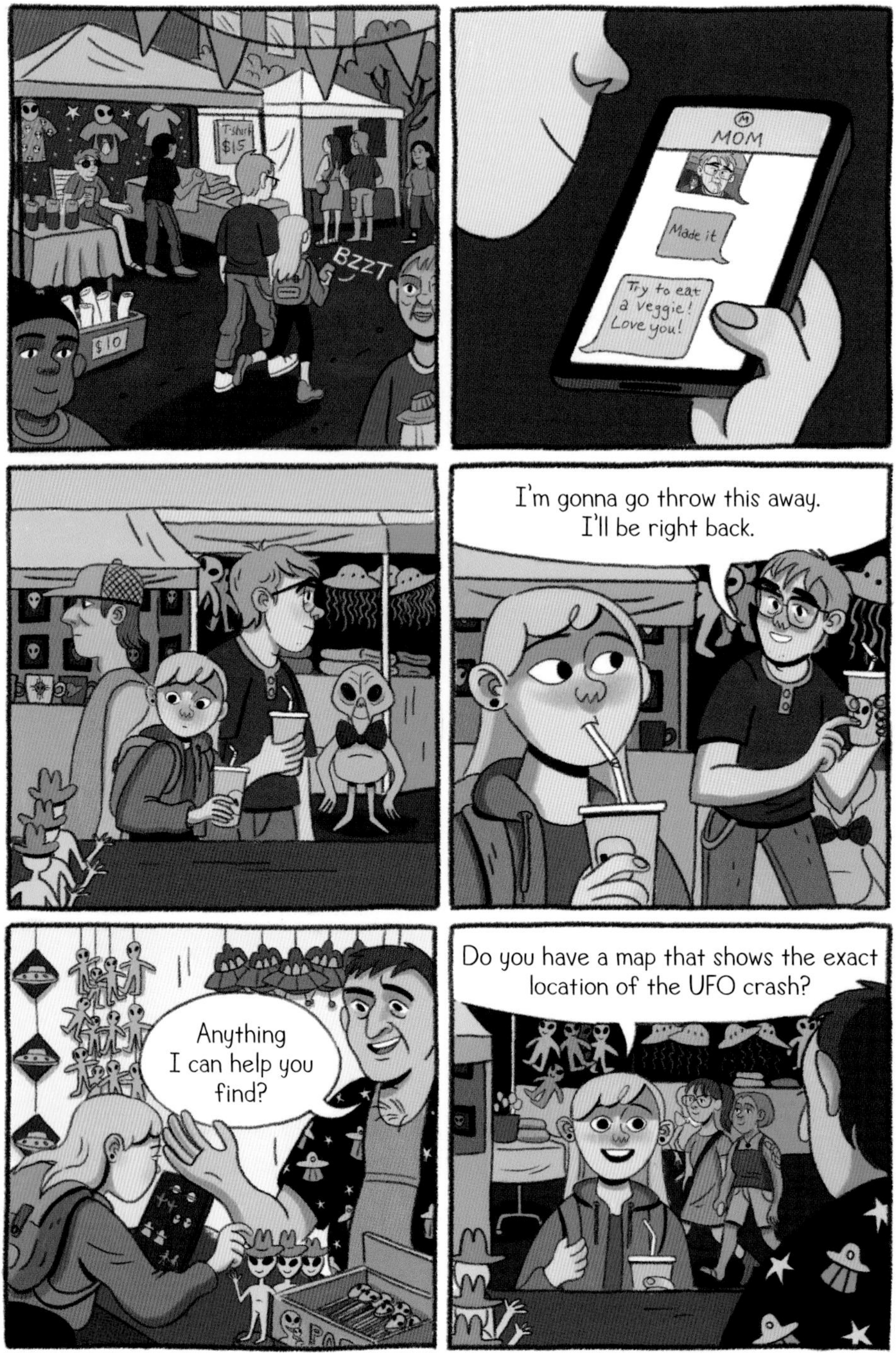
T-shirt $15
$10
BZZT
MOM
Made it
Try to eat a veggie! Love you!
I'm gonna go throw this away. I'll be right back.
Anything I can help you find?
Do you have a map that shows the exact location of the UFO crash?

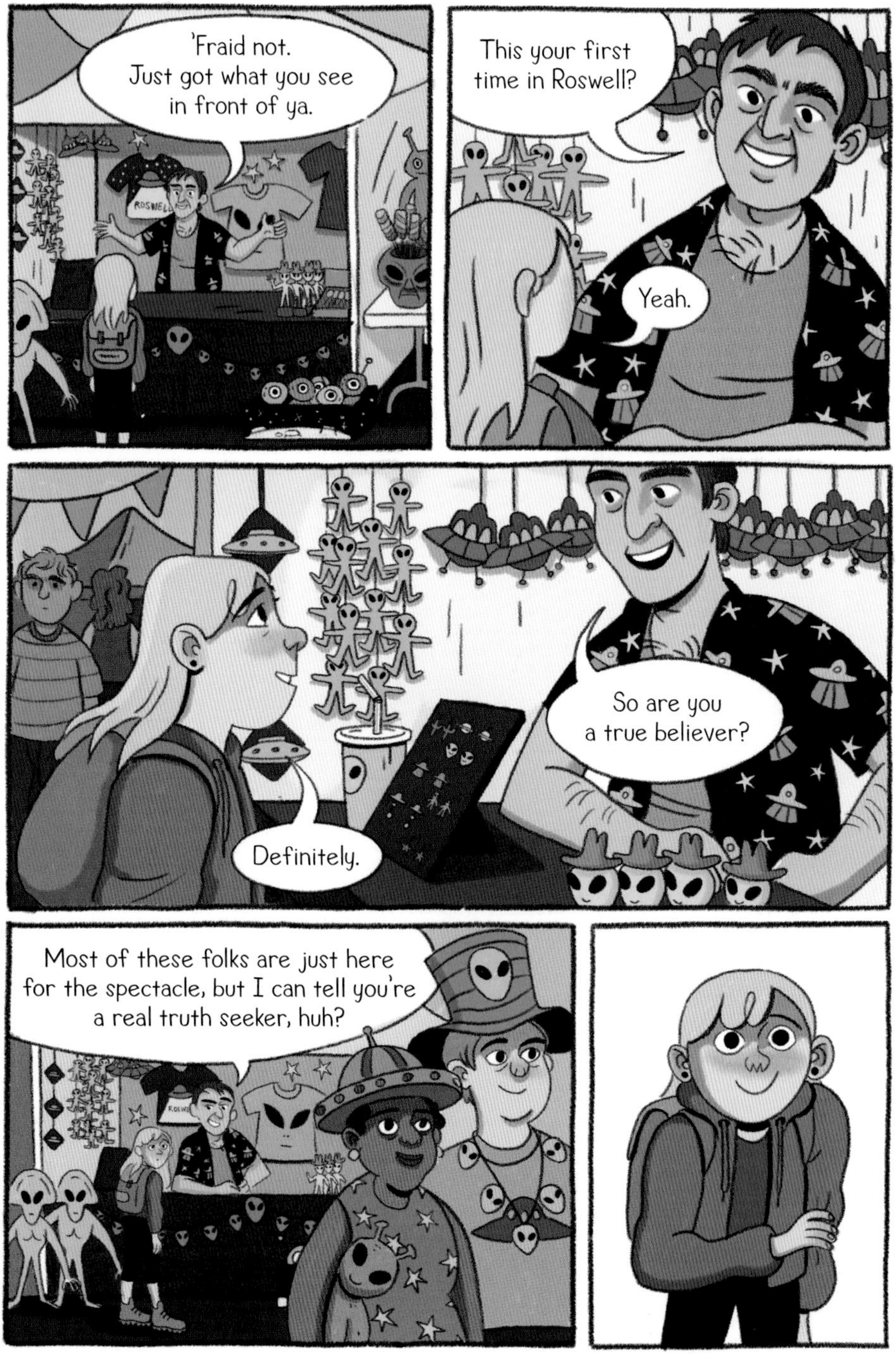
'Fraid not.
Just got what you see
in front of ya.
ROSWELL
This your first
time in Roswell?
Yeah.
So are you
a true believer?
Definitely.
Most of these folks are just here
for the spectacle, but I can tell you're
a real truth seeker, huh?
ROSWELL

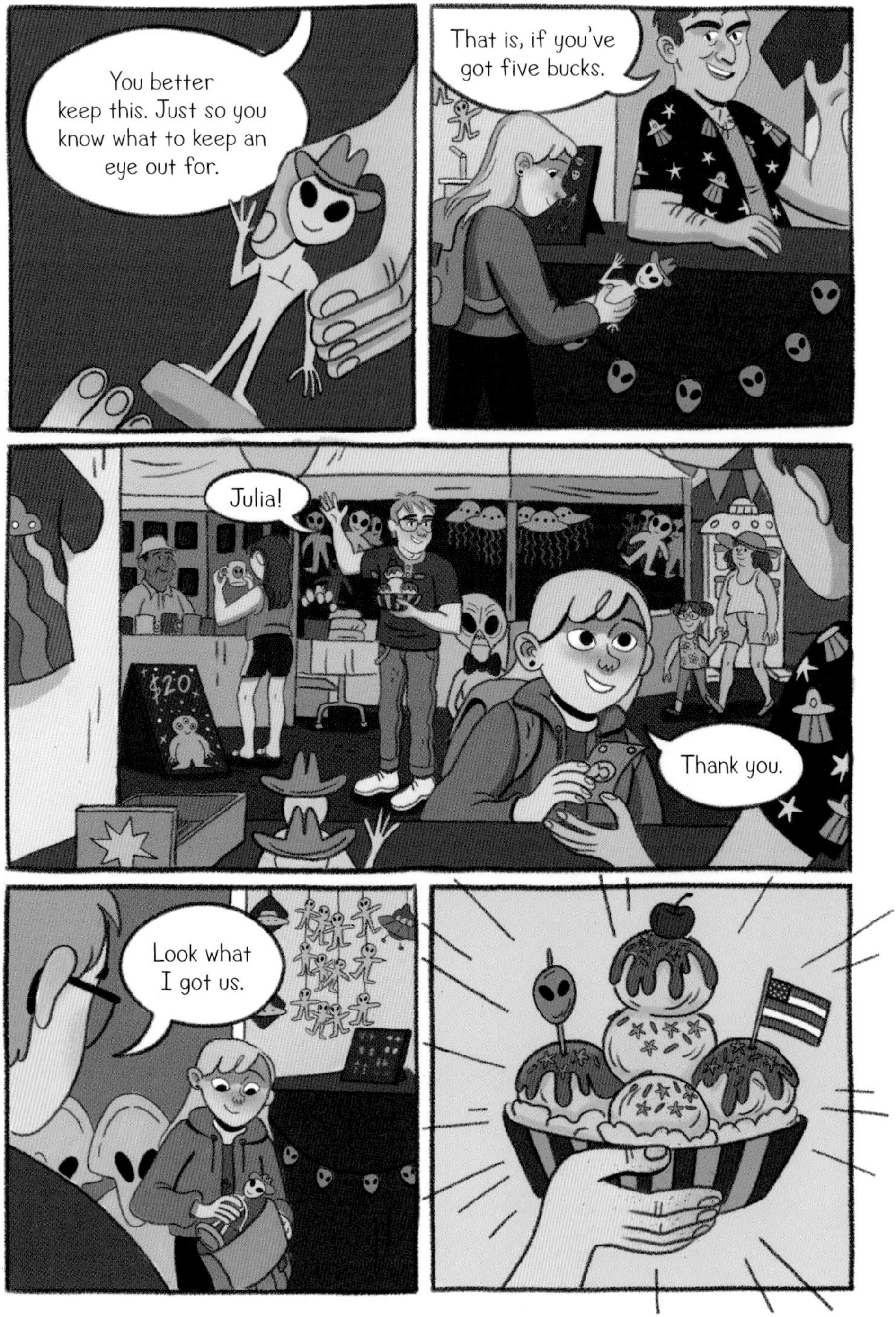
You better keep this. Just so you know what to keep an eye out for.
That is, if you've got five bucks.
Julia!
$20
Thank you.
Look what I got us.

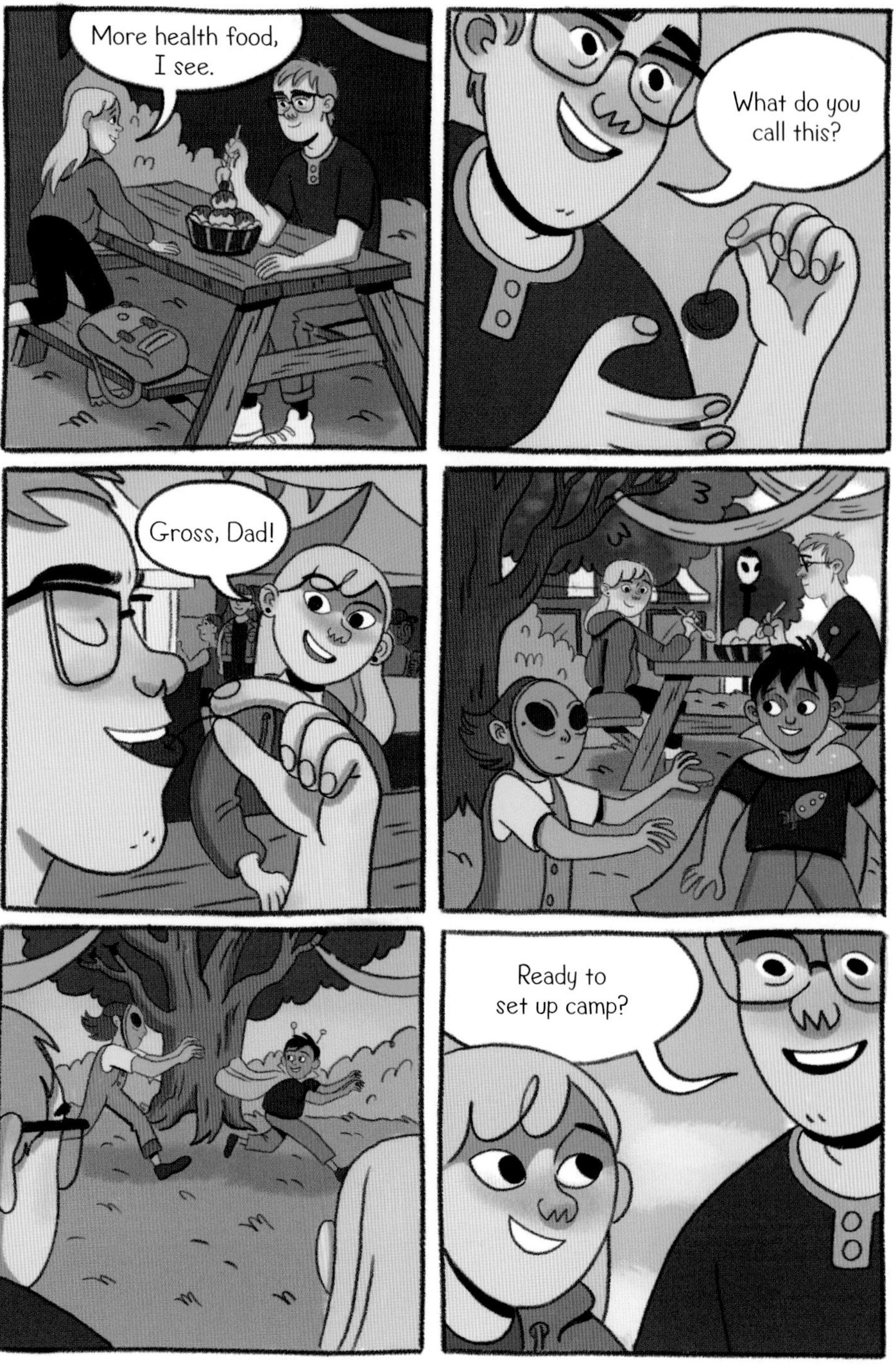
More health food, I see.
What do you call this?
Gross, Dad!
Ready to set up camp?

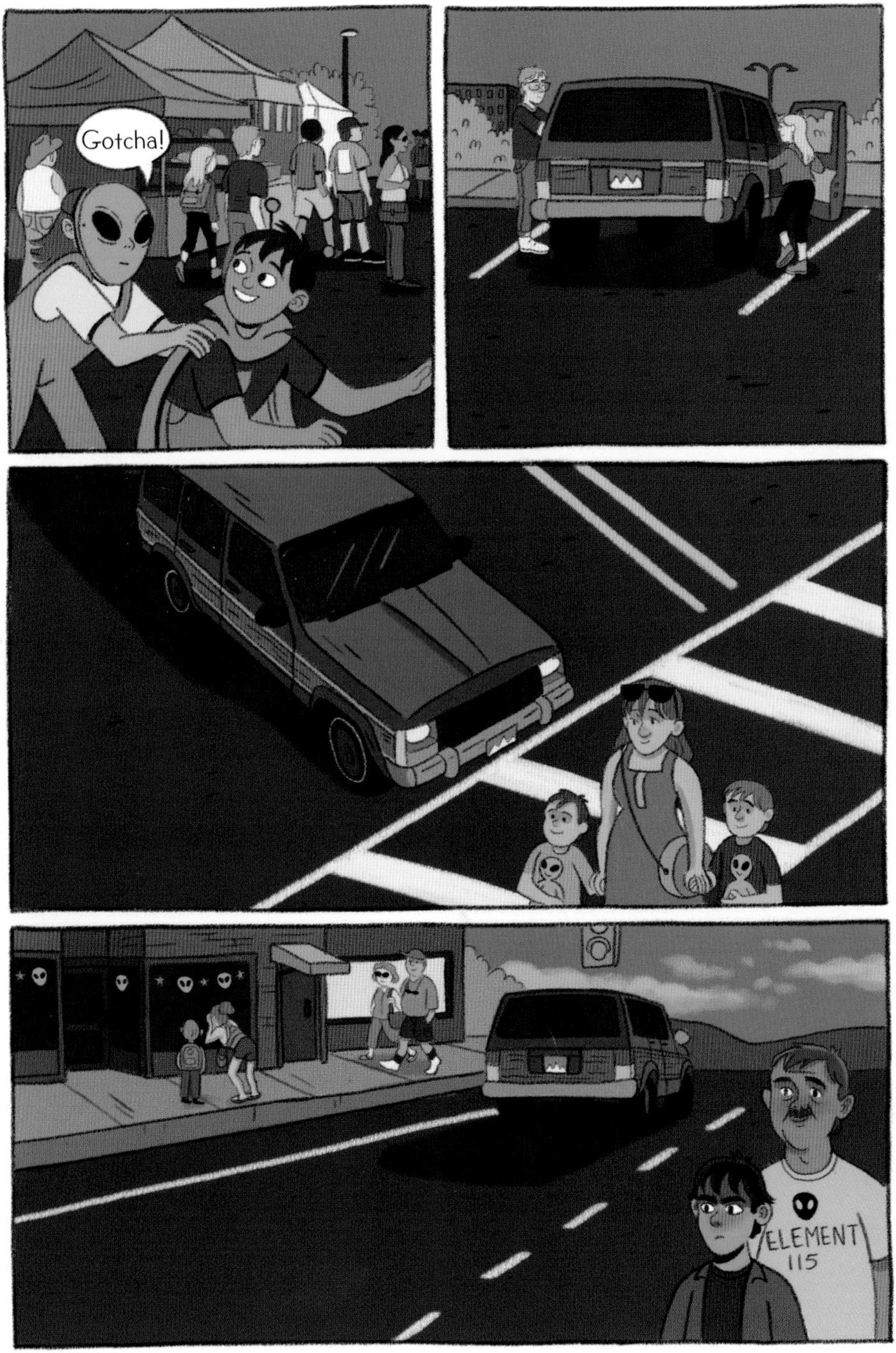
Gotcha!
ELEMENT
115

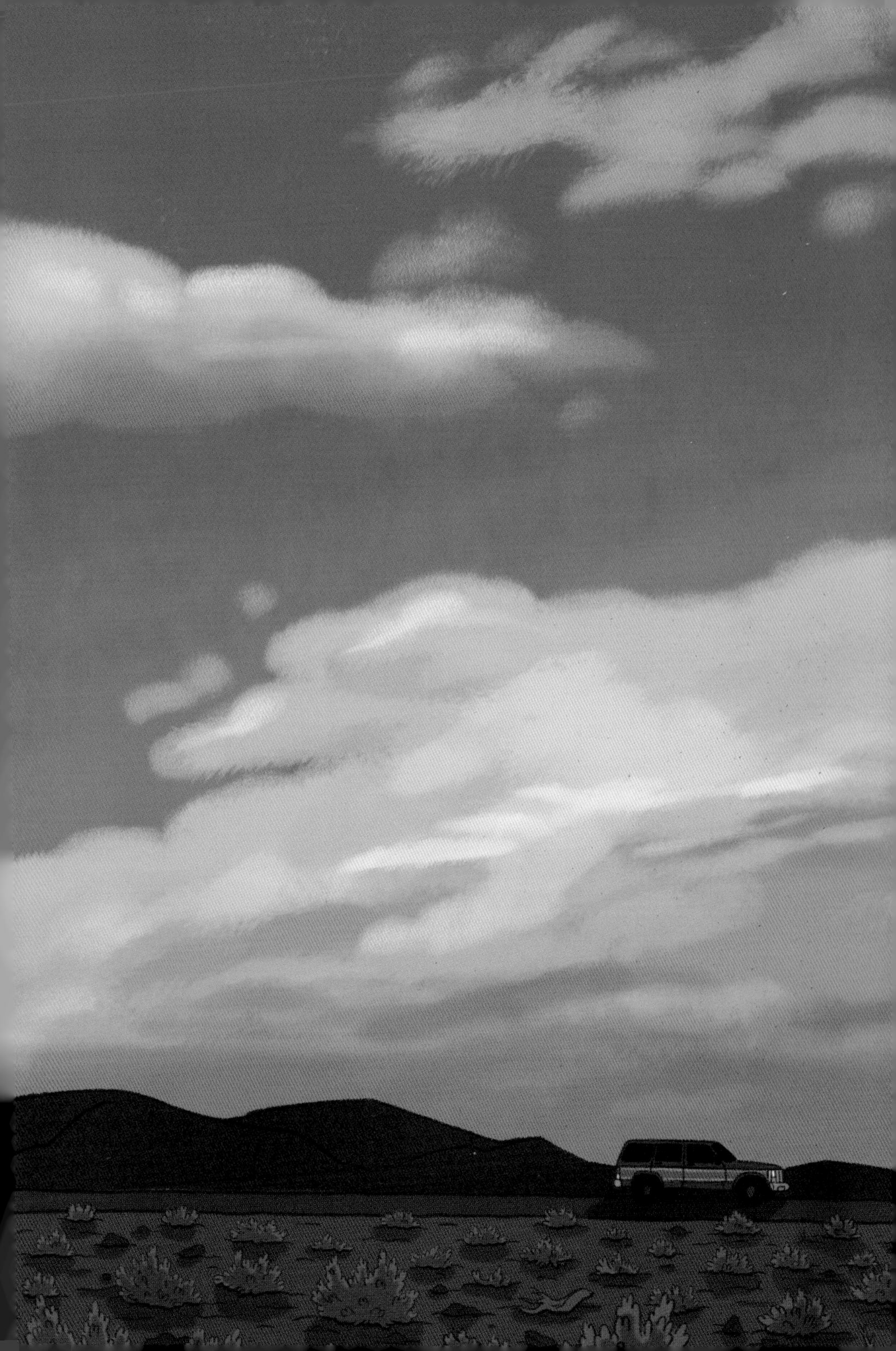

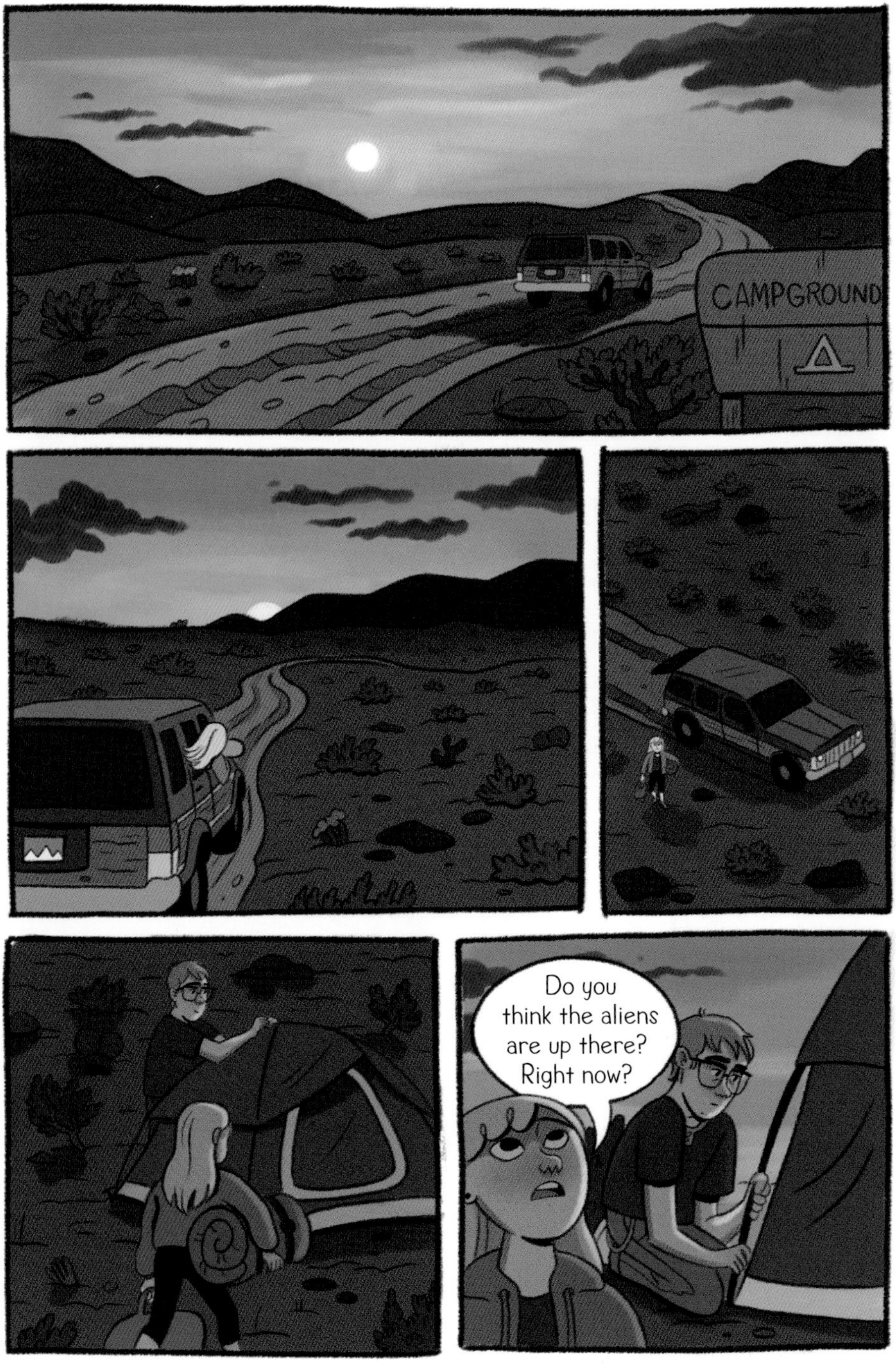
CAMPGROUND
Do you think the aliens are up there? Right now?

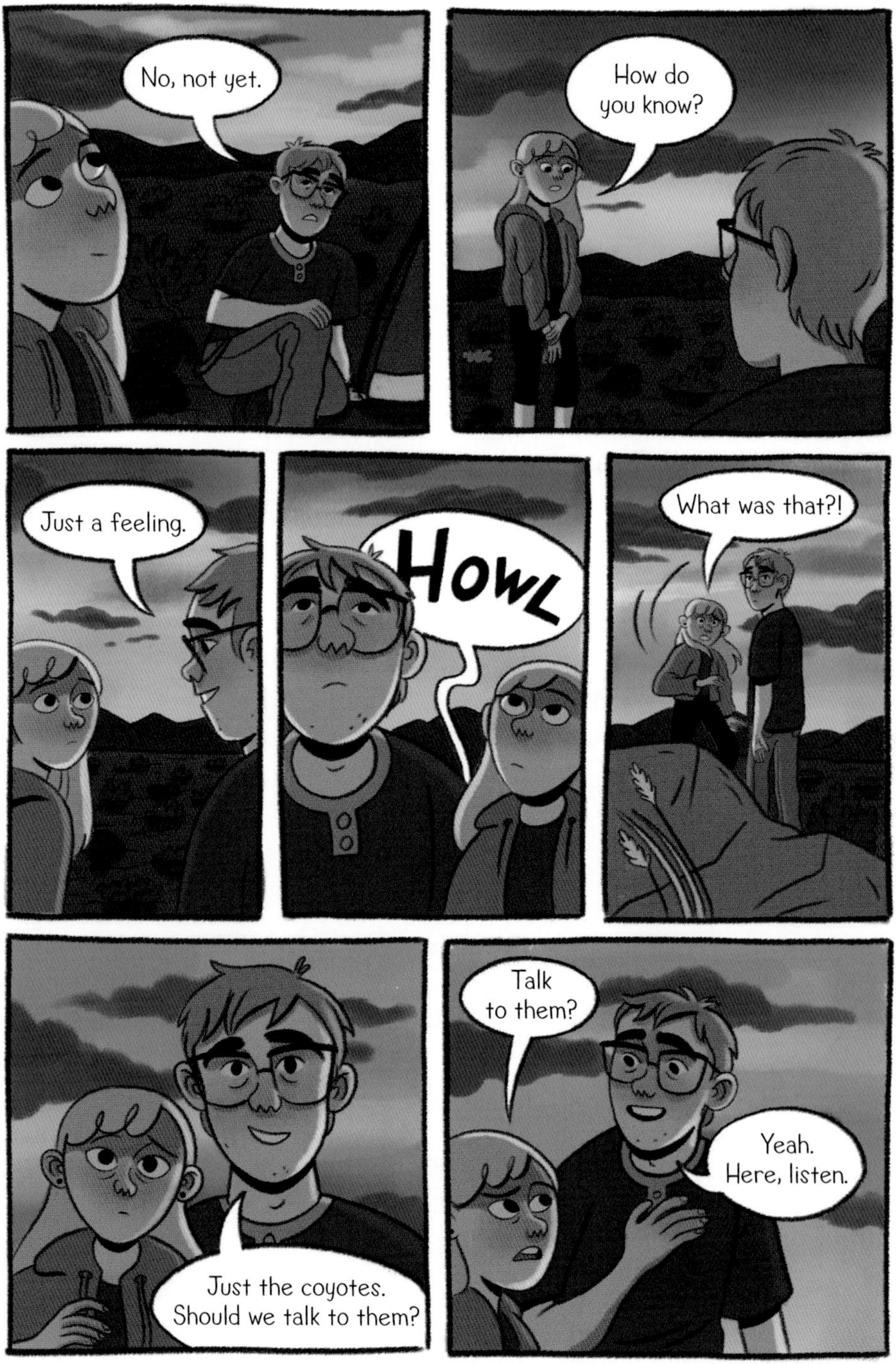
No, not yet.
How do you know?
Just a feeling.
HOWL
What was that?!
Just the coyotes. Should we talk to them?
Talk to them?
Yeah. Here, listen.

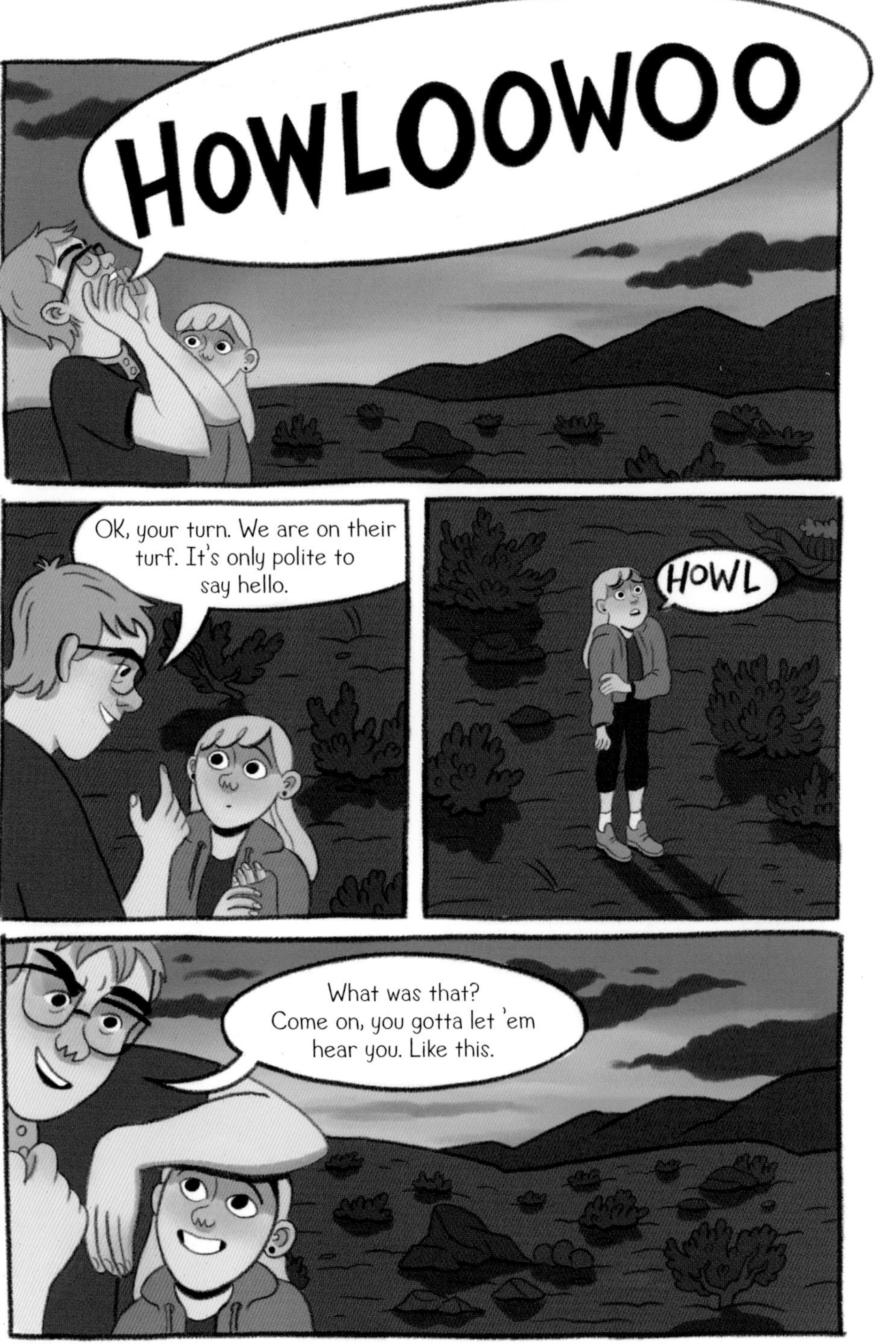
HOWLOOWOO
OK, your turn. We are on their turf. It's only polite to say hello.
HOWL
What was that? Come on, you gotta let 'em hear you. Like this.

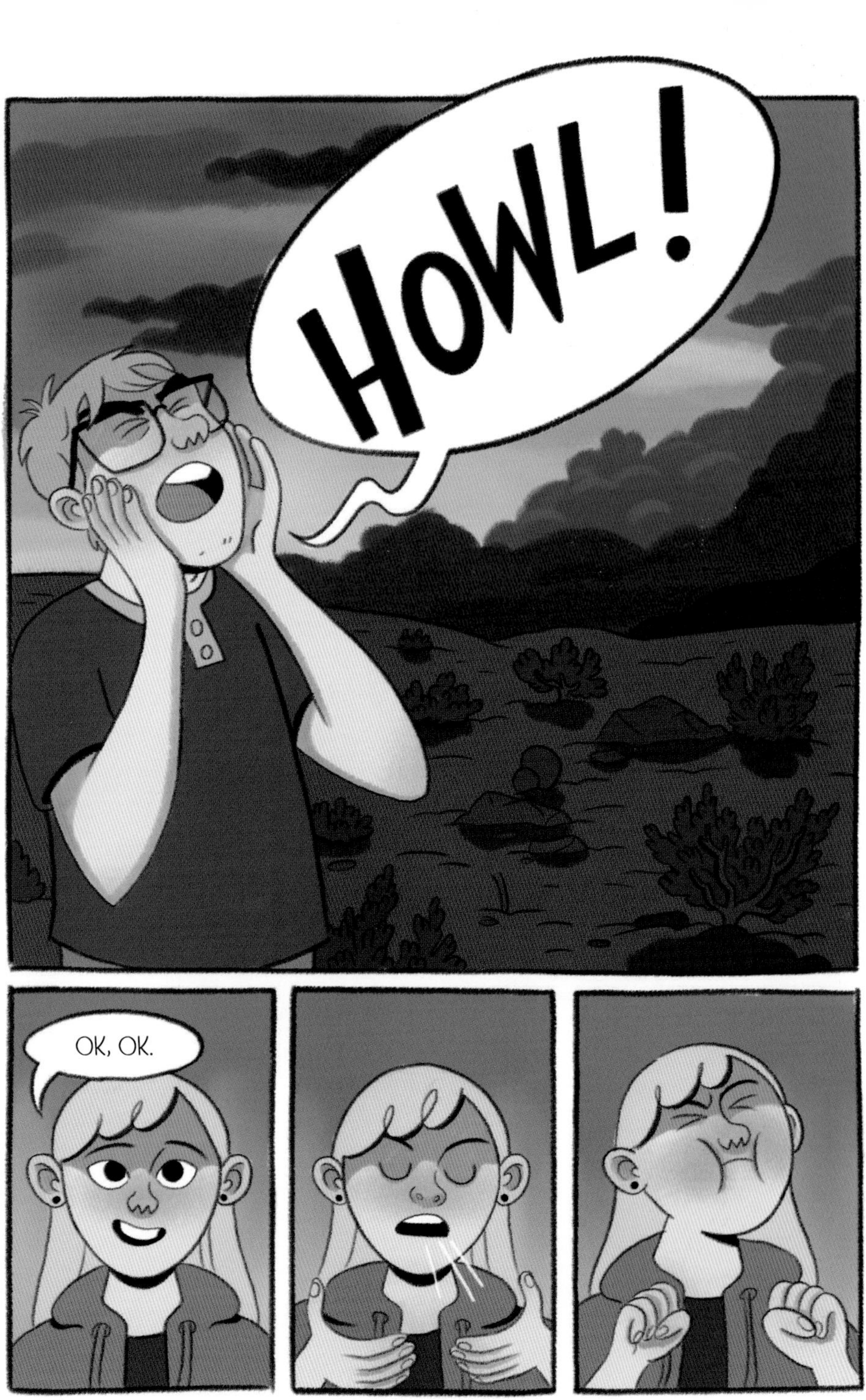
HOWL!
OK, OK.

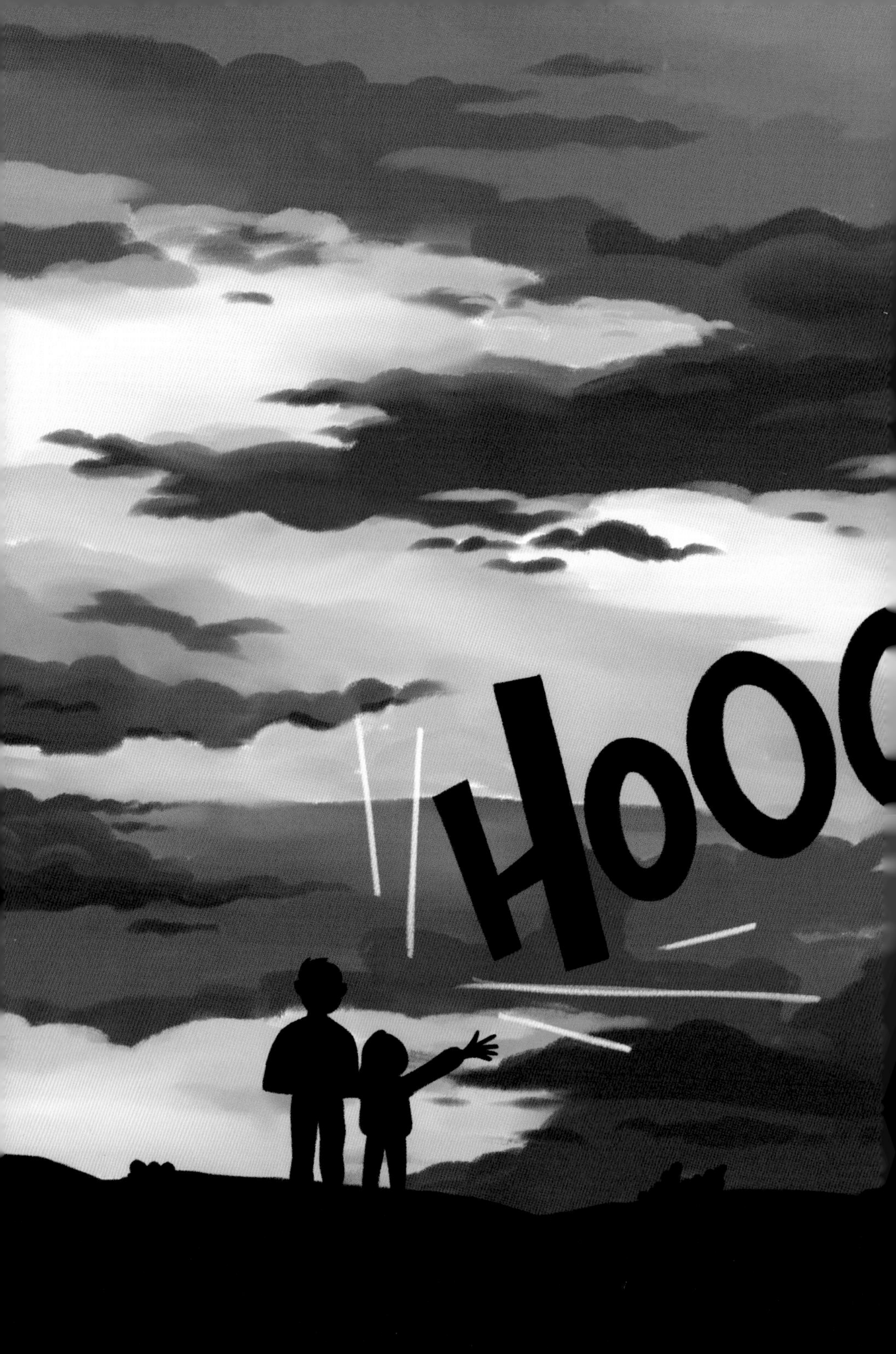
HOOO

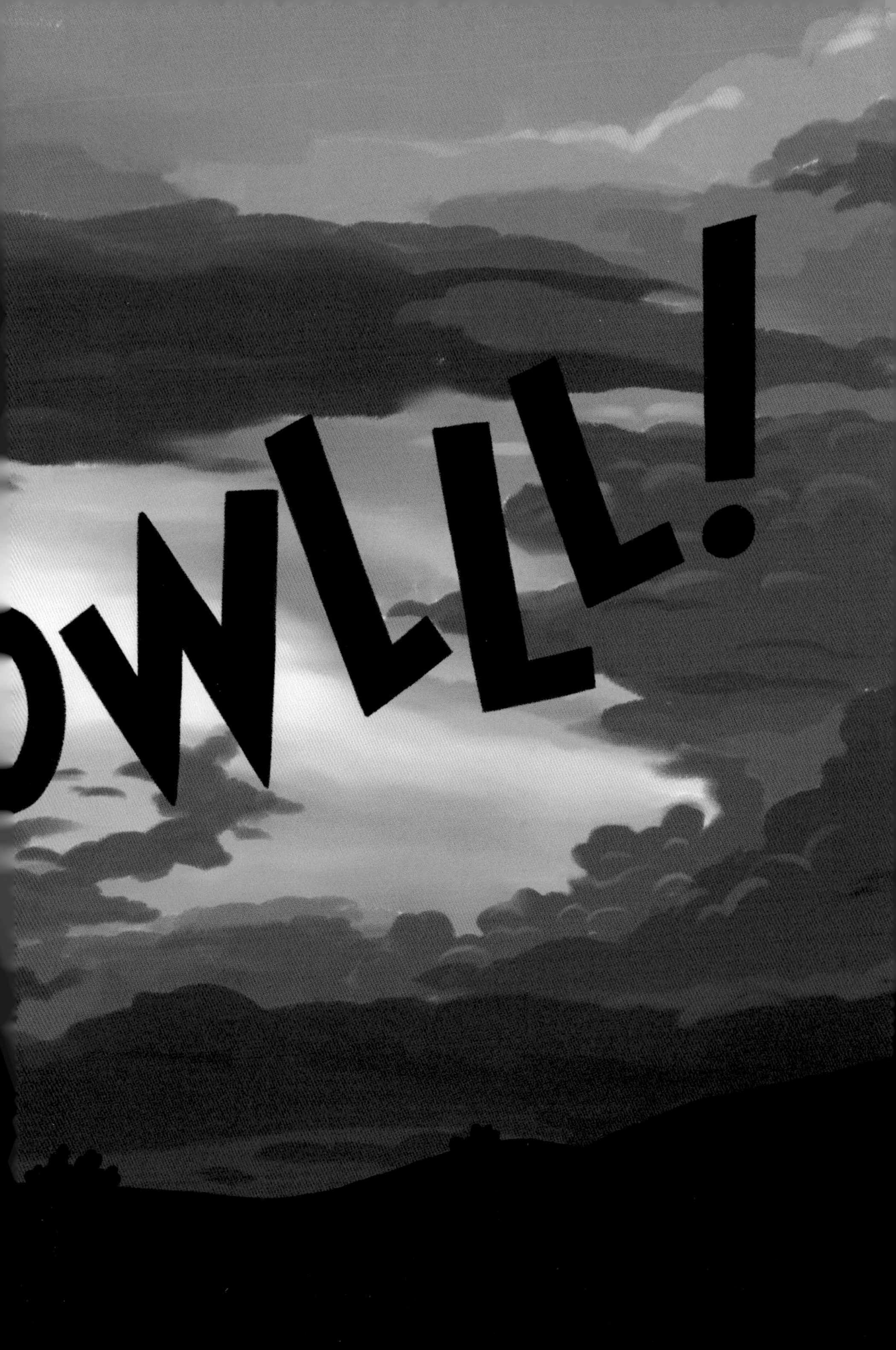
OWLLL!

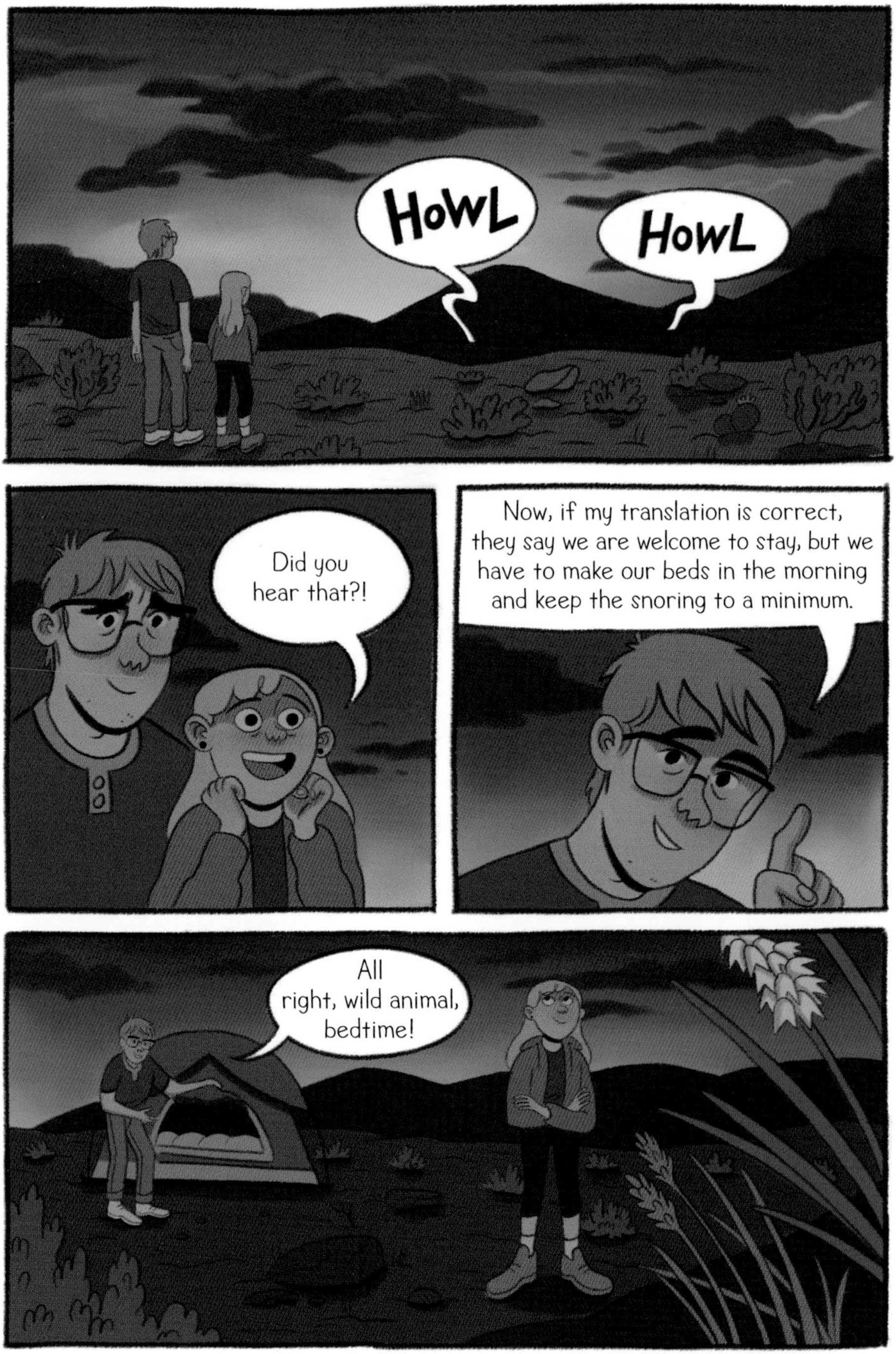
HOWL
HOWL
Did you hear that?!
Now, if my translation is correct, they say we are welcome to stay, but we have to make our beds in the morning and keep the snoring to a minimum.
All right, wild animal, bedtime!

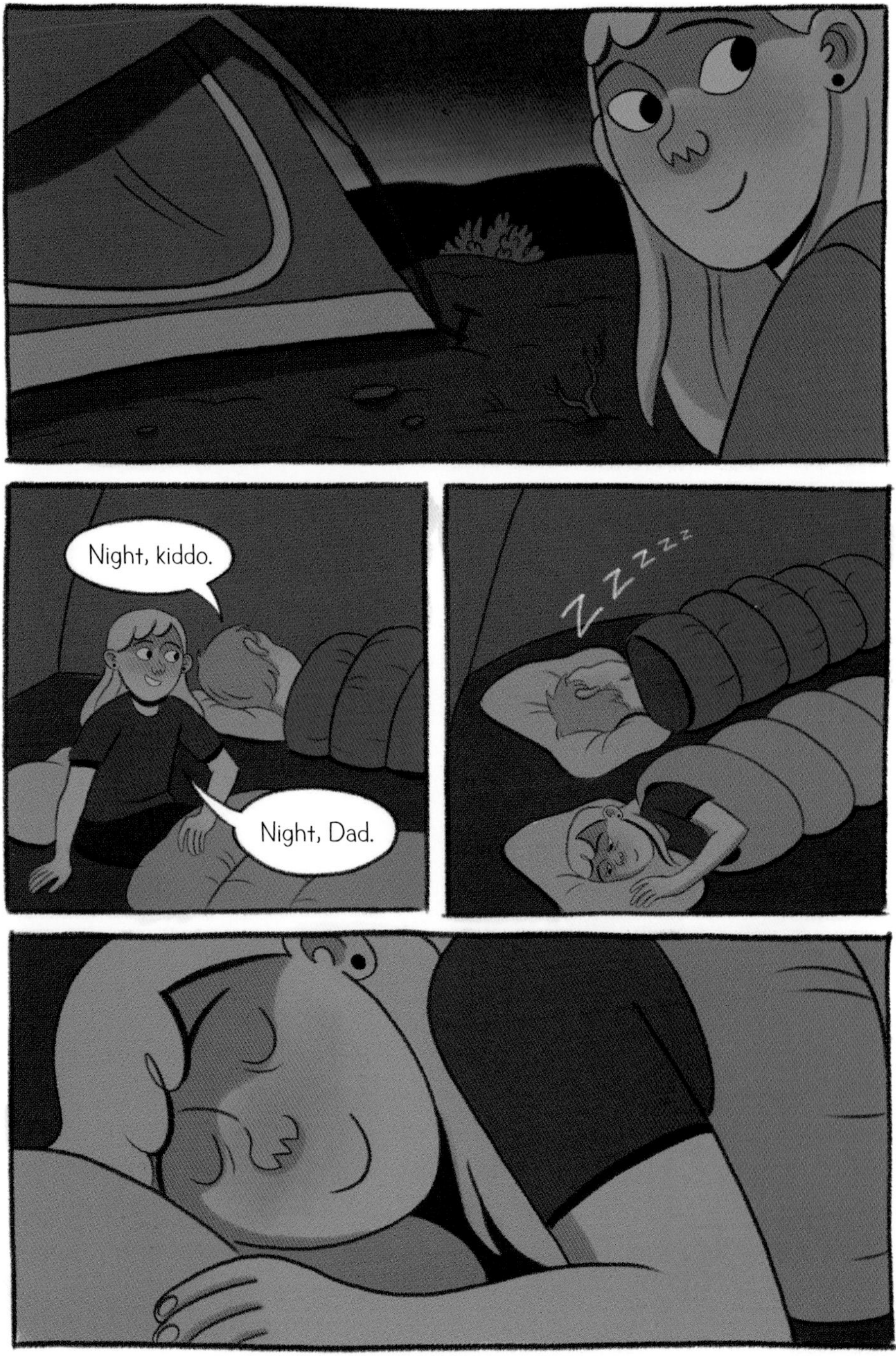
Night, kiddo.
Night, Dad.
ZZZzzz

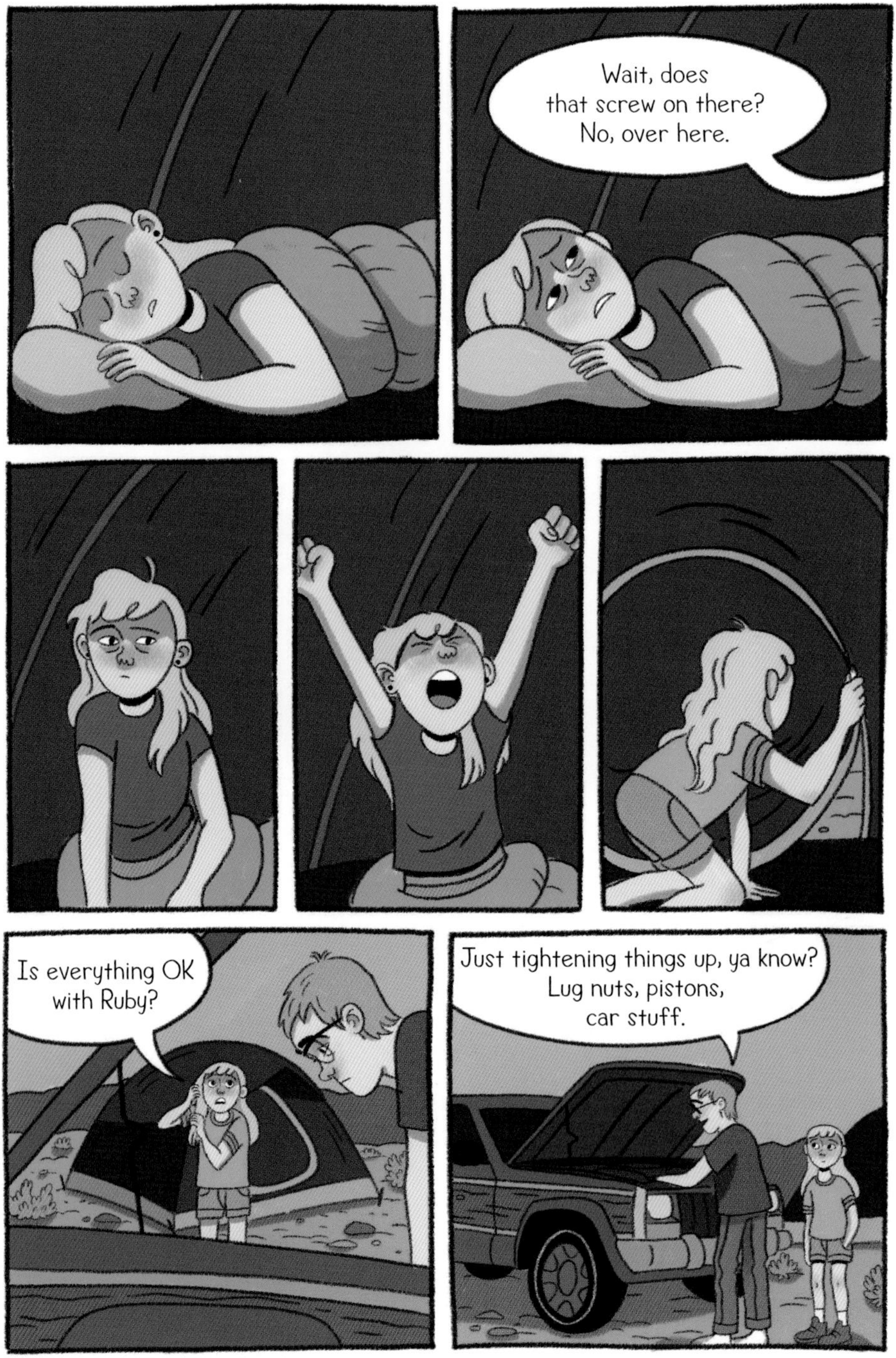
Wait, does
that screw on there?
No, over here.
Is everything OK
with Ruby?
Just tightening things up, ya know?
Lug nuts, pistons,
car stuff.

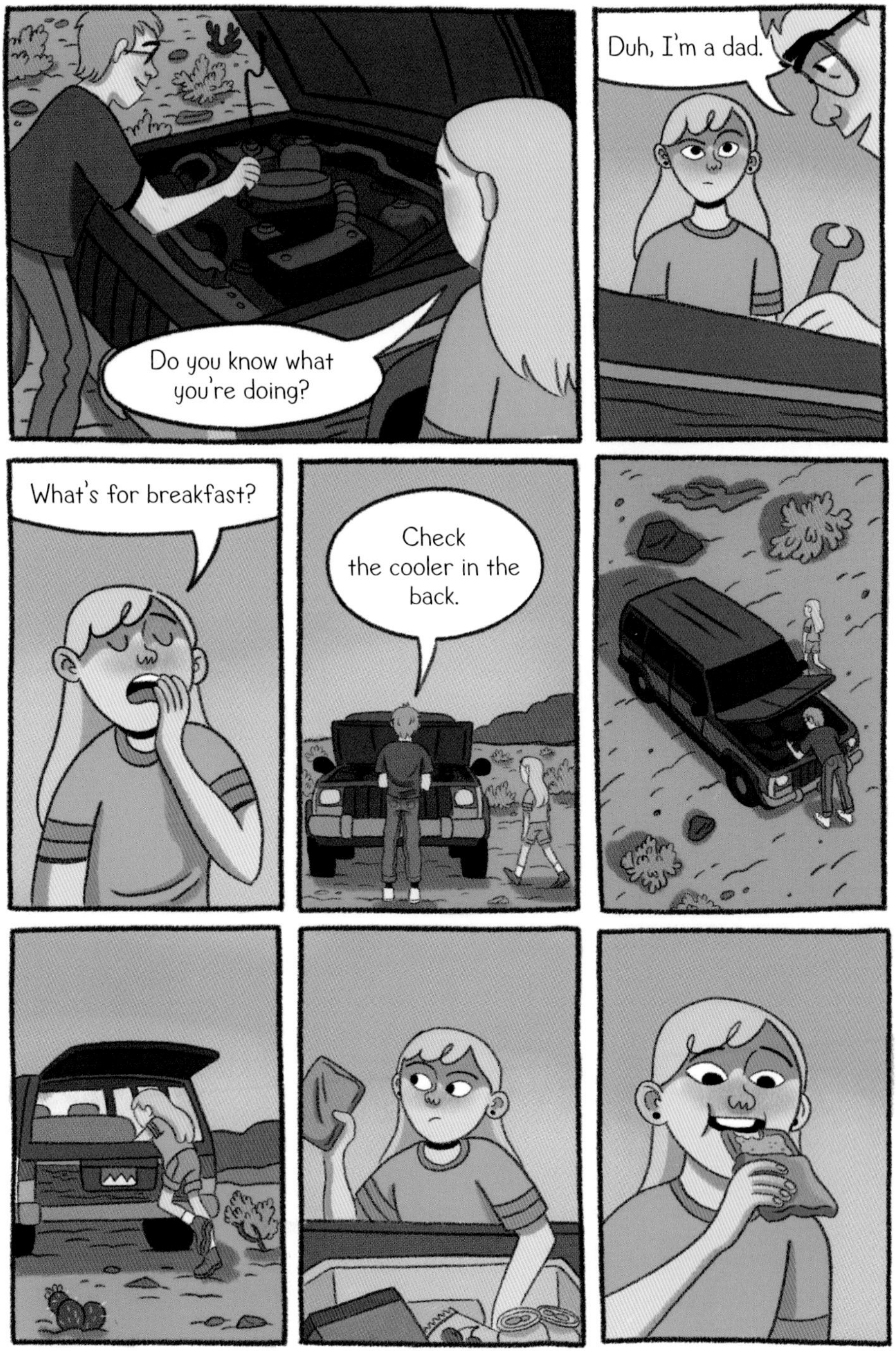
Do you know what you're doing?
Duh, I'm a dad.
What's for breakfast?
Check the cooler in the back.

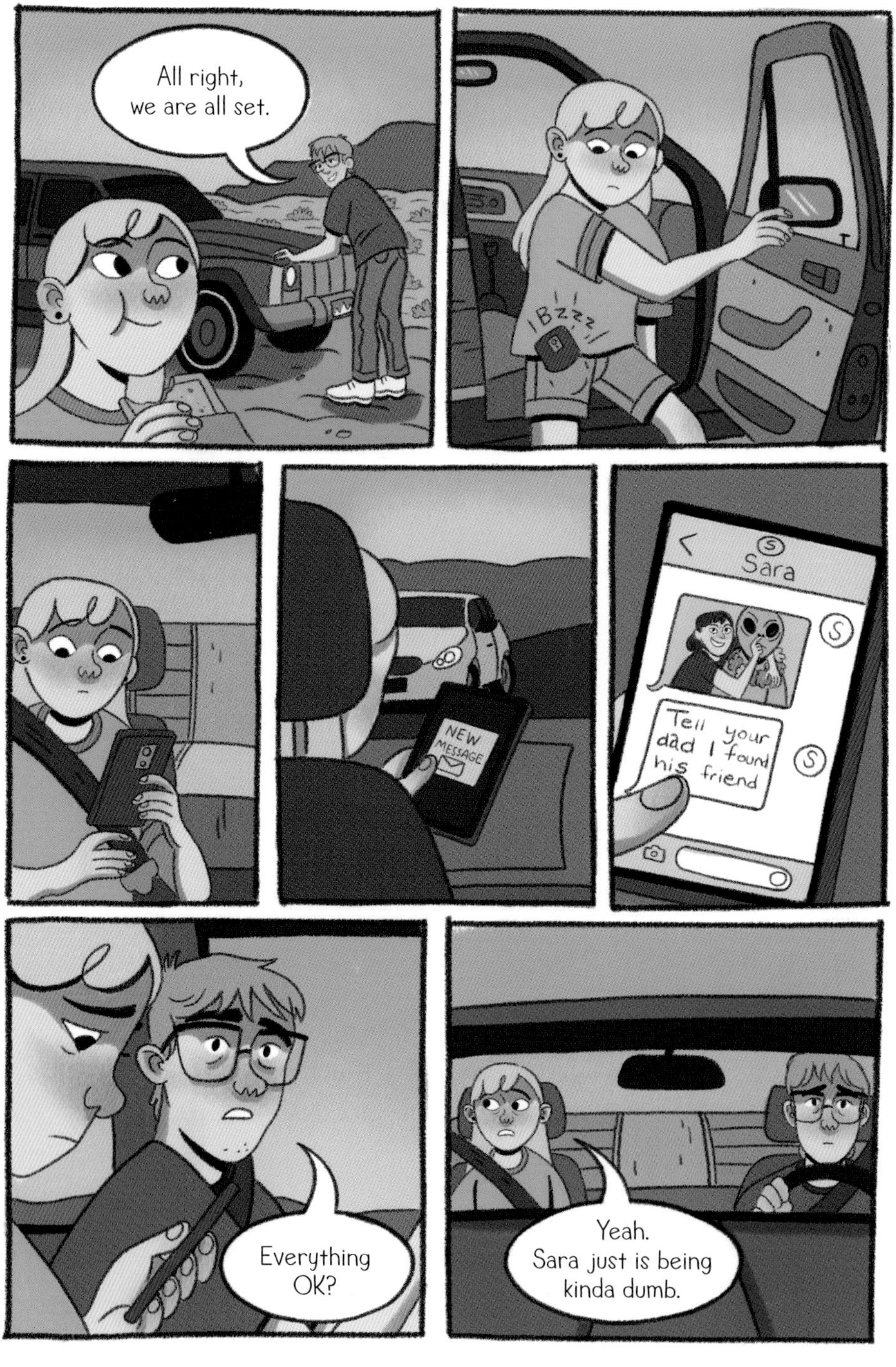
All right, we are all set.
Bzzz
NEW MESSAGE
Sara
Tell your dad I found his friend
Everything OK?
Yeah. Sara just is being kinda dumb.

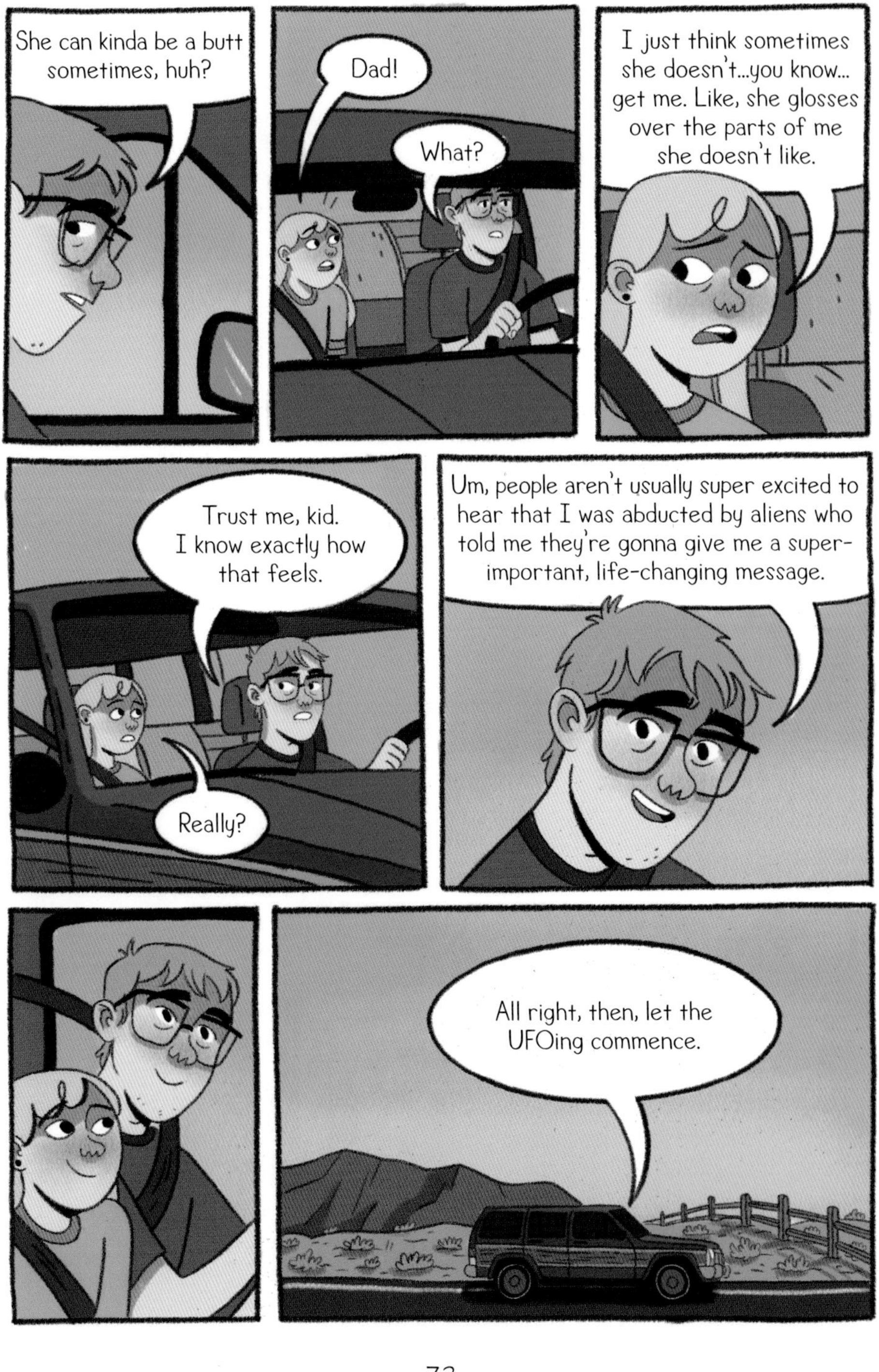
She can kinda be a butt sometimes, huh?
Dad!
What?
I just think sometimes she doesn't...you know... get me. Like, she glosses over the parts of me she doesn't like.
Trust me, kid. I know exactly how that feels.
Really?
Um, people aren't usually super excited to hear that I was abducted by aliens who told me they're gonna give me a super-important, life-changing message.
All right, then, let the UFOing commence.

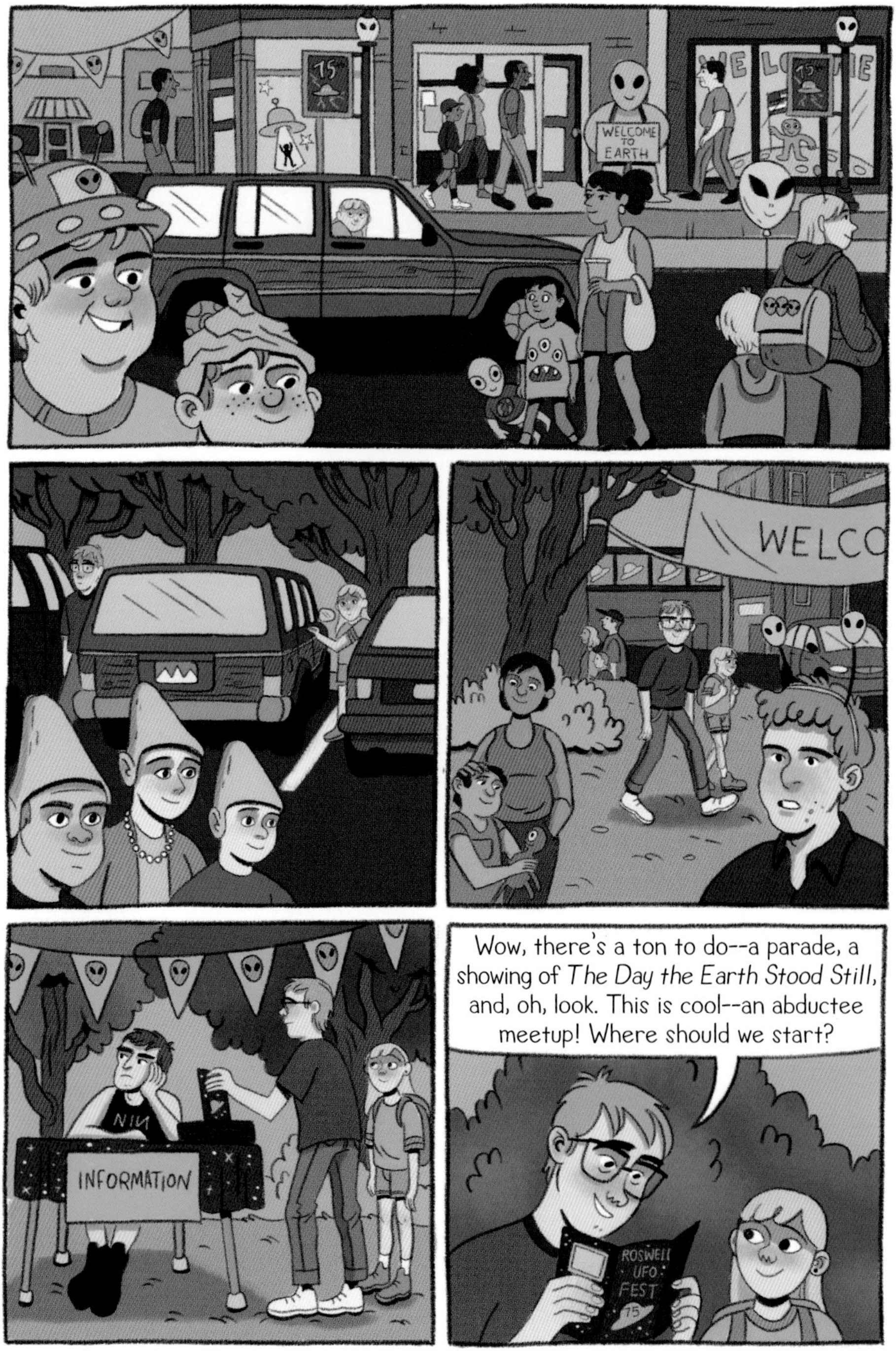
WELCOME TO EARTH
WELCO
INFORMATION
NIN
Wow, there's a ton to do--a parade, a showing of *The Day the Earth Stood Still*, and, oh, look. This is cool--an abductee meetup! Where should we start?
ROSWELL UFO FEST
75

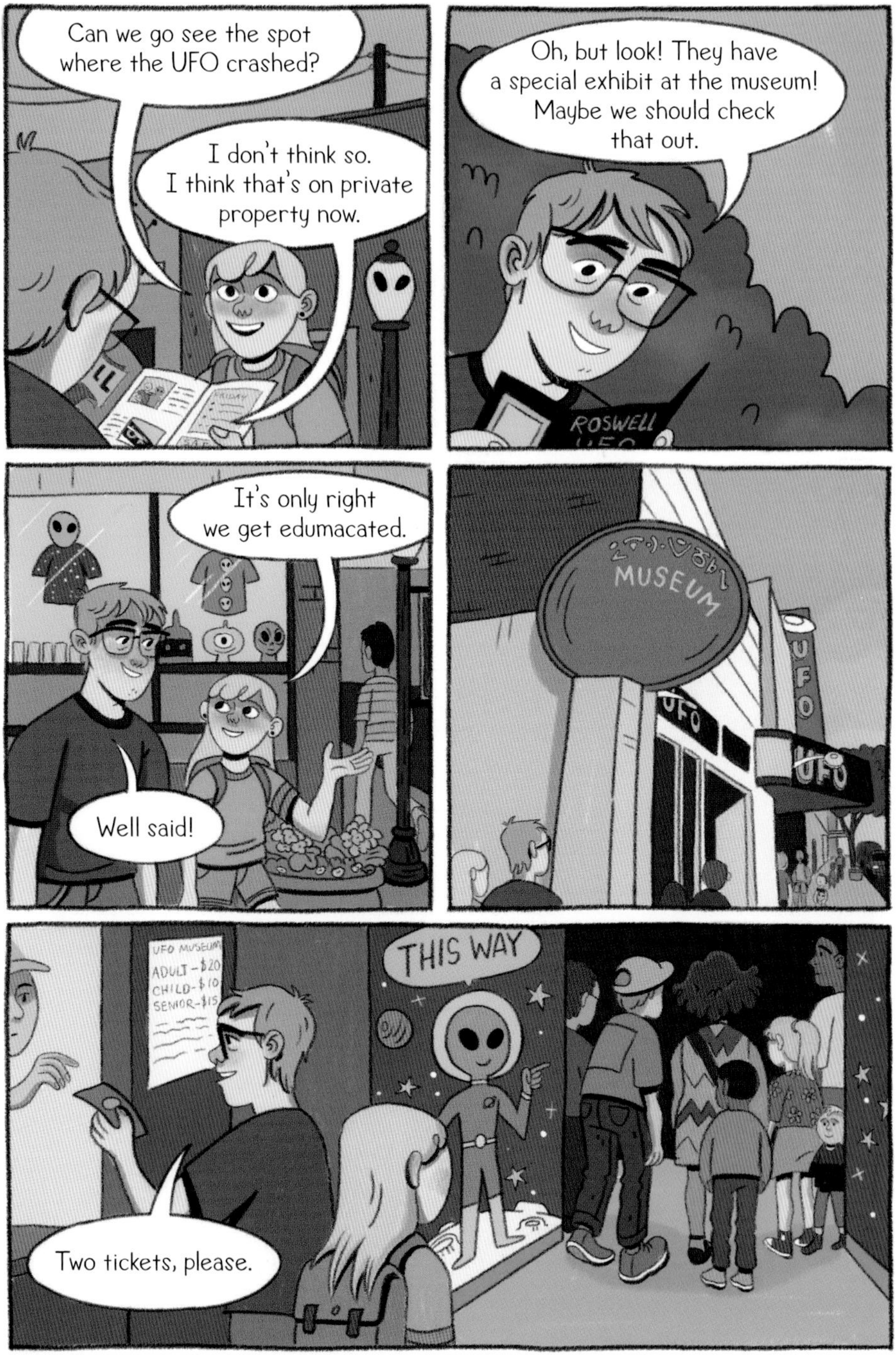
Can we go see the spot where the UFO crashed?
I don't think so. I think that's on private property now.
Oh, but look! They have a special exhibit at the museum! Maybe we should check that out.
ROSWELL
It's only right we get edumacated.
Well said!
MUSEUM
UFO
UFO
UFO
UFO MUSEUM
ADULT - $20
CHILD - $10
SENIOR - $15
THIS WAY
Two tickets, please.

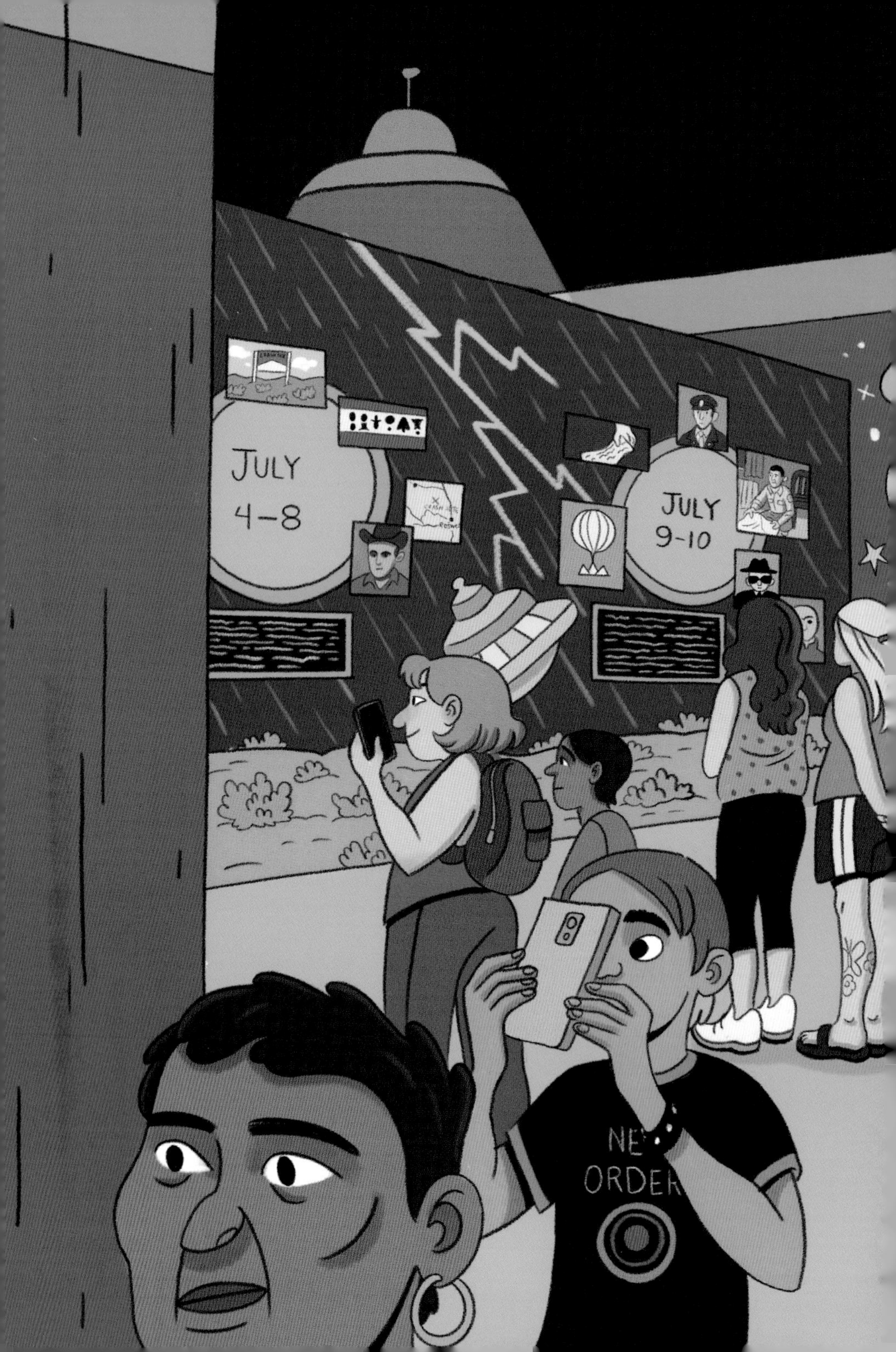
JULY
4–8
JULY
9-10
NEW
ORDER

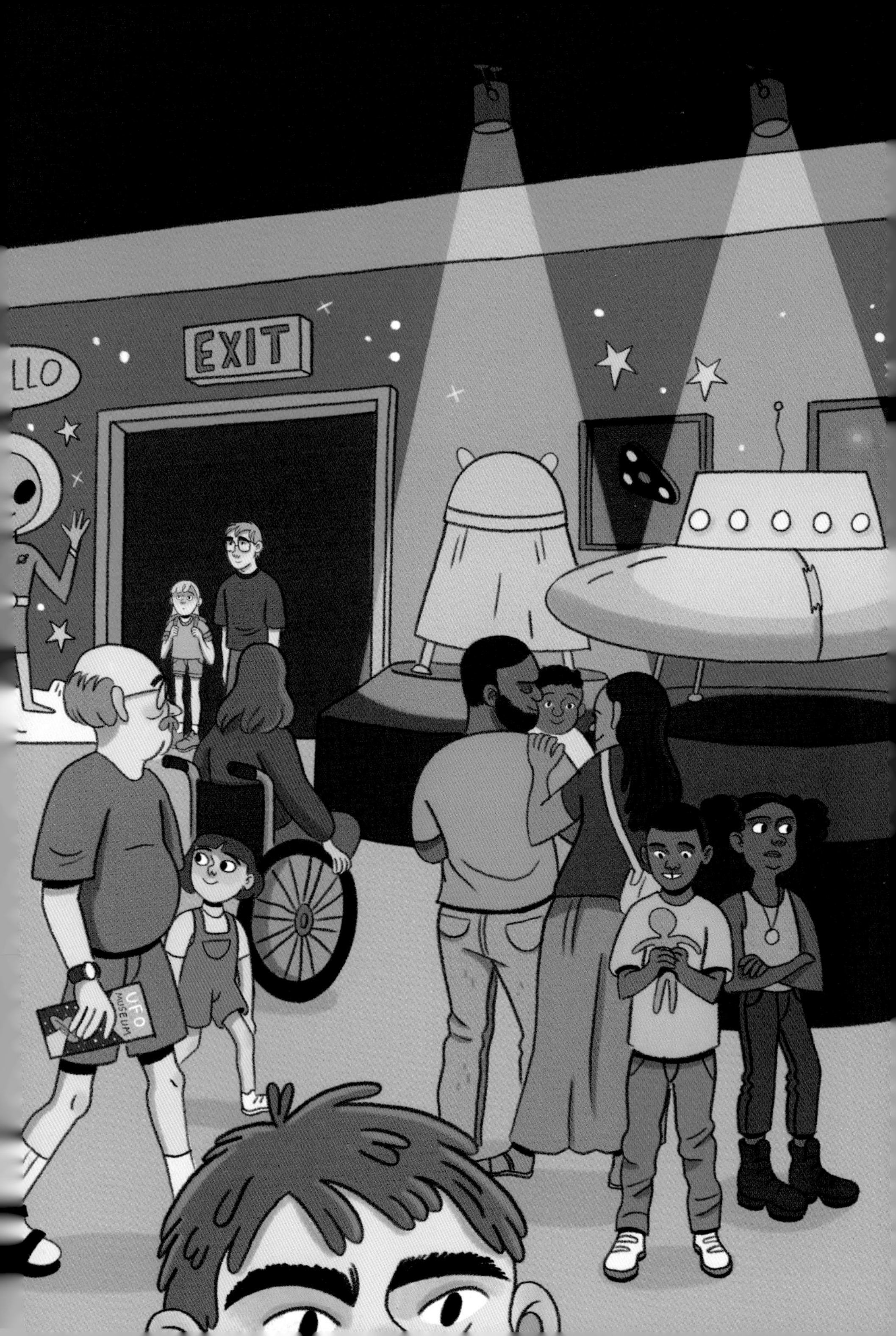
LLO
EXIT
UFO MUSEUM

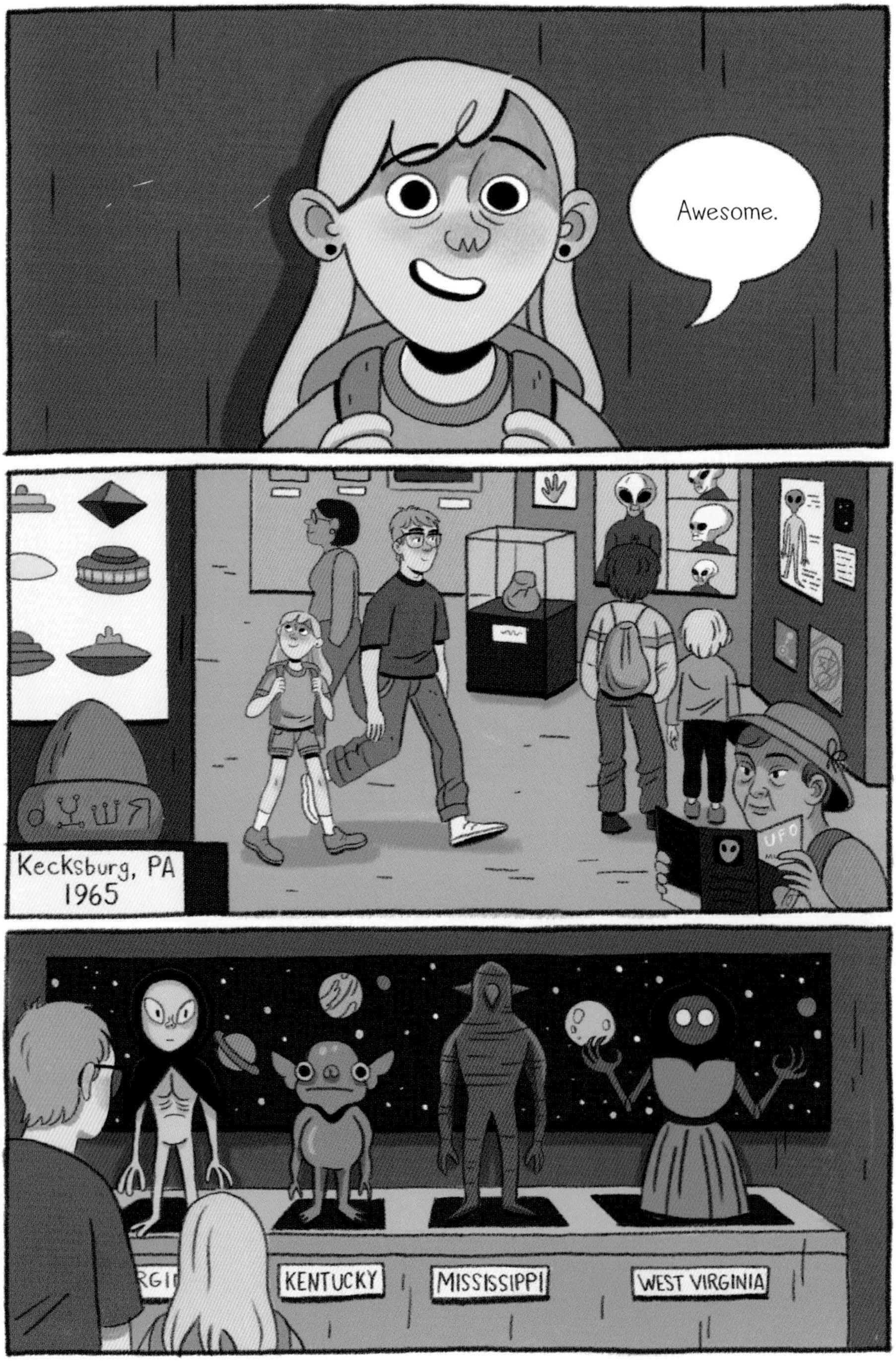
Awesome.
Kecksburg, PA
1965
UFO
KENTUCKY
MISSISSIPPI
WEST VIRGINIA

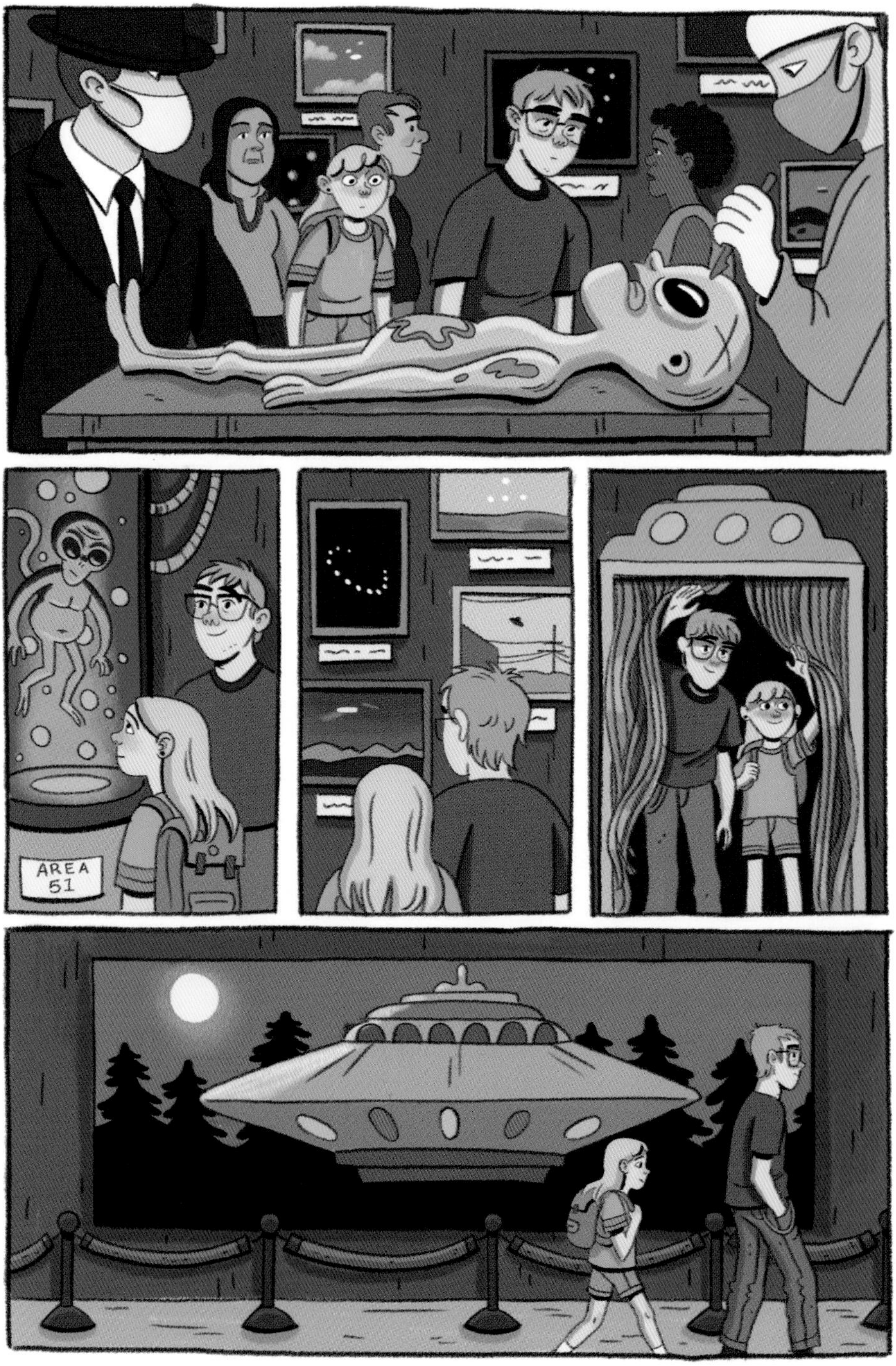
AREA 51

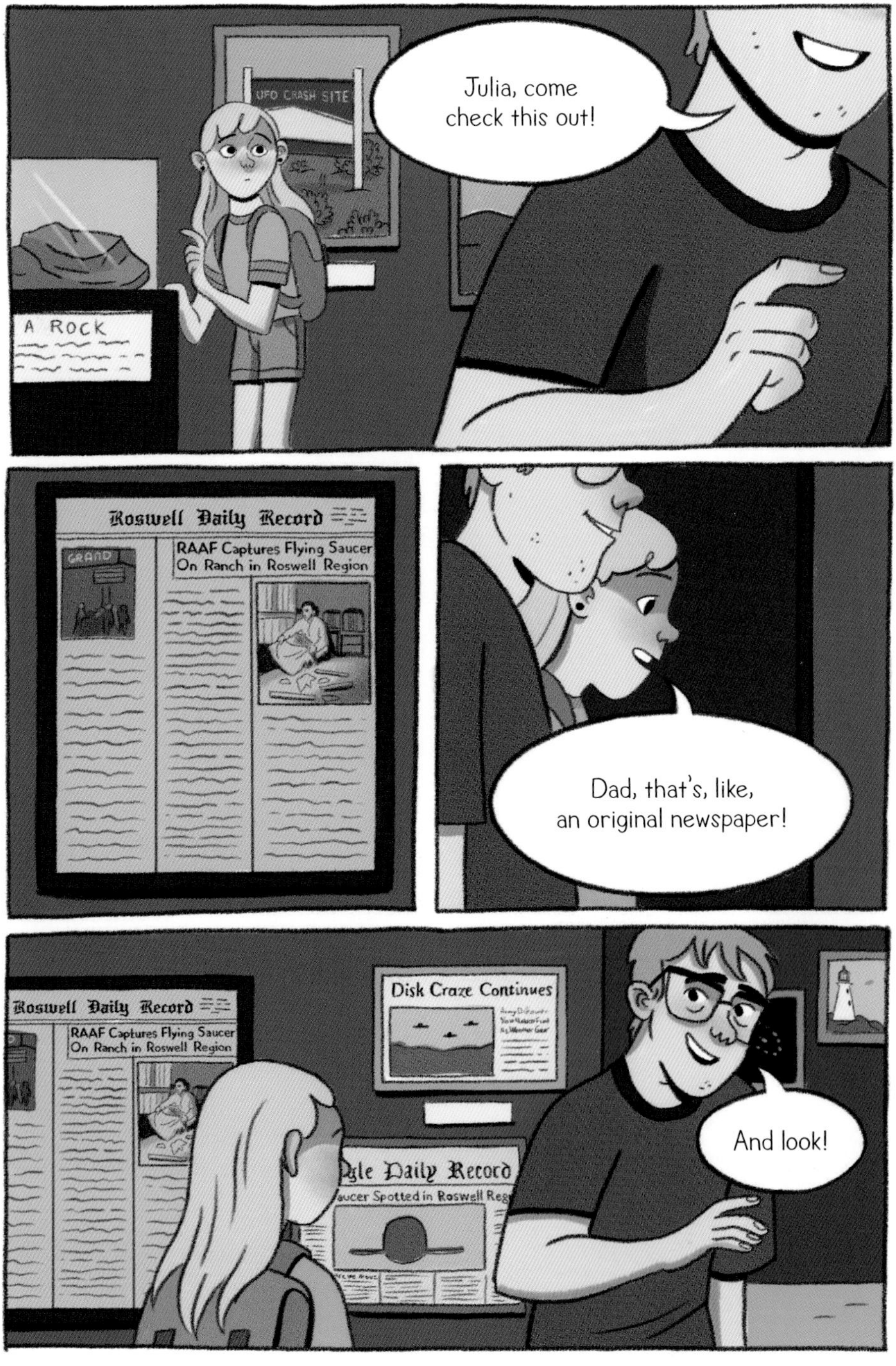
UFO CRASH SITE
A ROCK
Julia, come check this out!
Roswell Daily Record
RAAF Captures Flying Saucer On Ranch in Roswell Region
GRAND
Dad, that's, like, an original newspaper!
Roswell Daily Record
RAAF Captures Flying Saucer On Ranch in Roswell Region
Disk Craze Continues
And look!

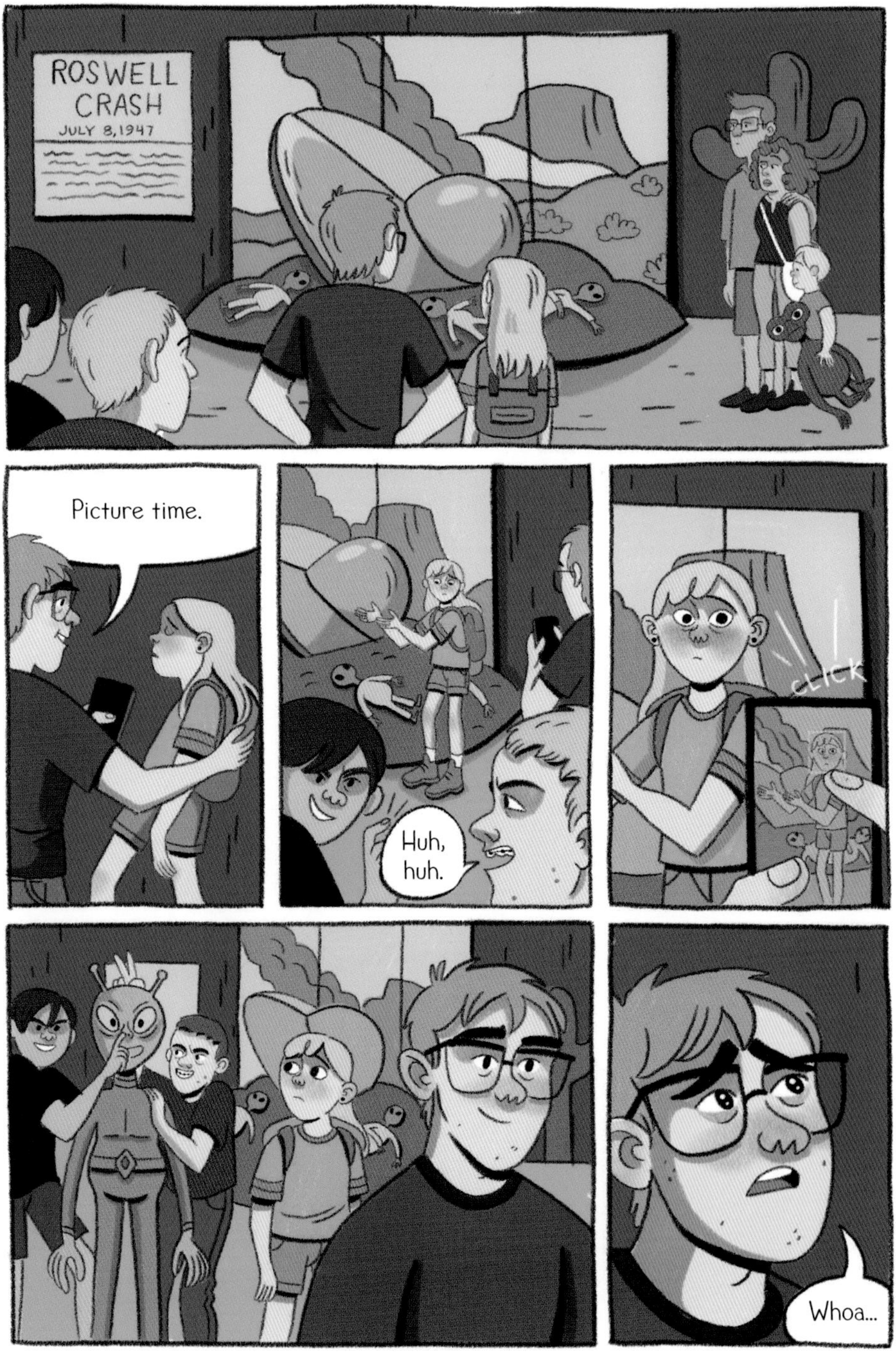
ROSWELL CRASH
JULY 8, 1947
Picture time.
Huh, huh.
CLICK
Whoa...

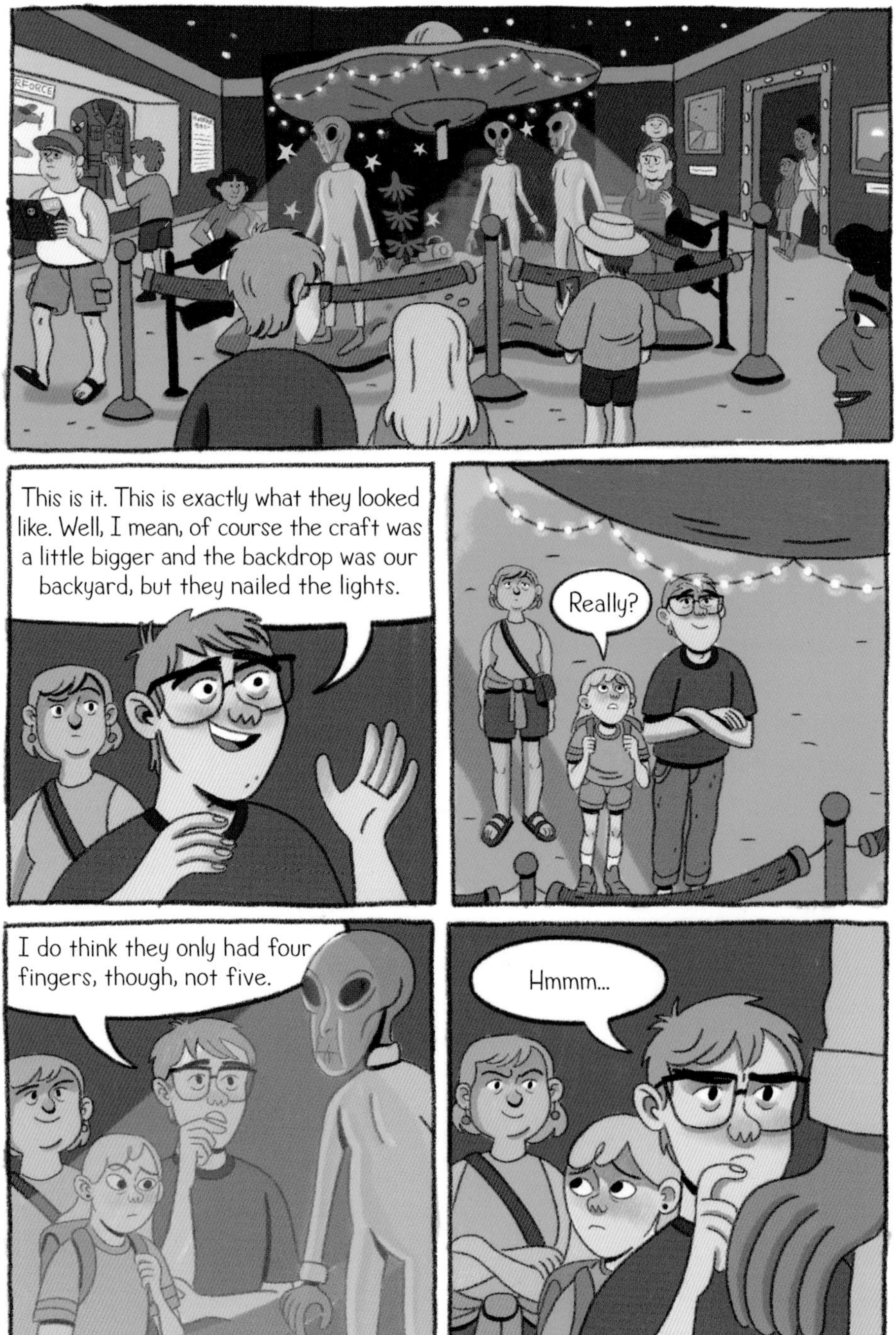
RFORCE
This is it. This is exactly what they looked like. Well, I mean, of course the craft was a little bigger and the backdrop was our backyard, but they nailed the lights.
Really?
I do think they only had four fingers, though, not five.
Hmmm...

Maybe we should check out the big exhibit.

Lead the way!

OST DEBRIS FOUND

Hidden from the public for over 50 years, new remnants of the Roswell UFO have been recovered.

Dad! This is amazing! Oh my gosh!

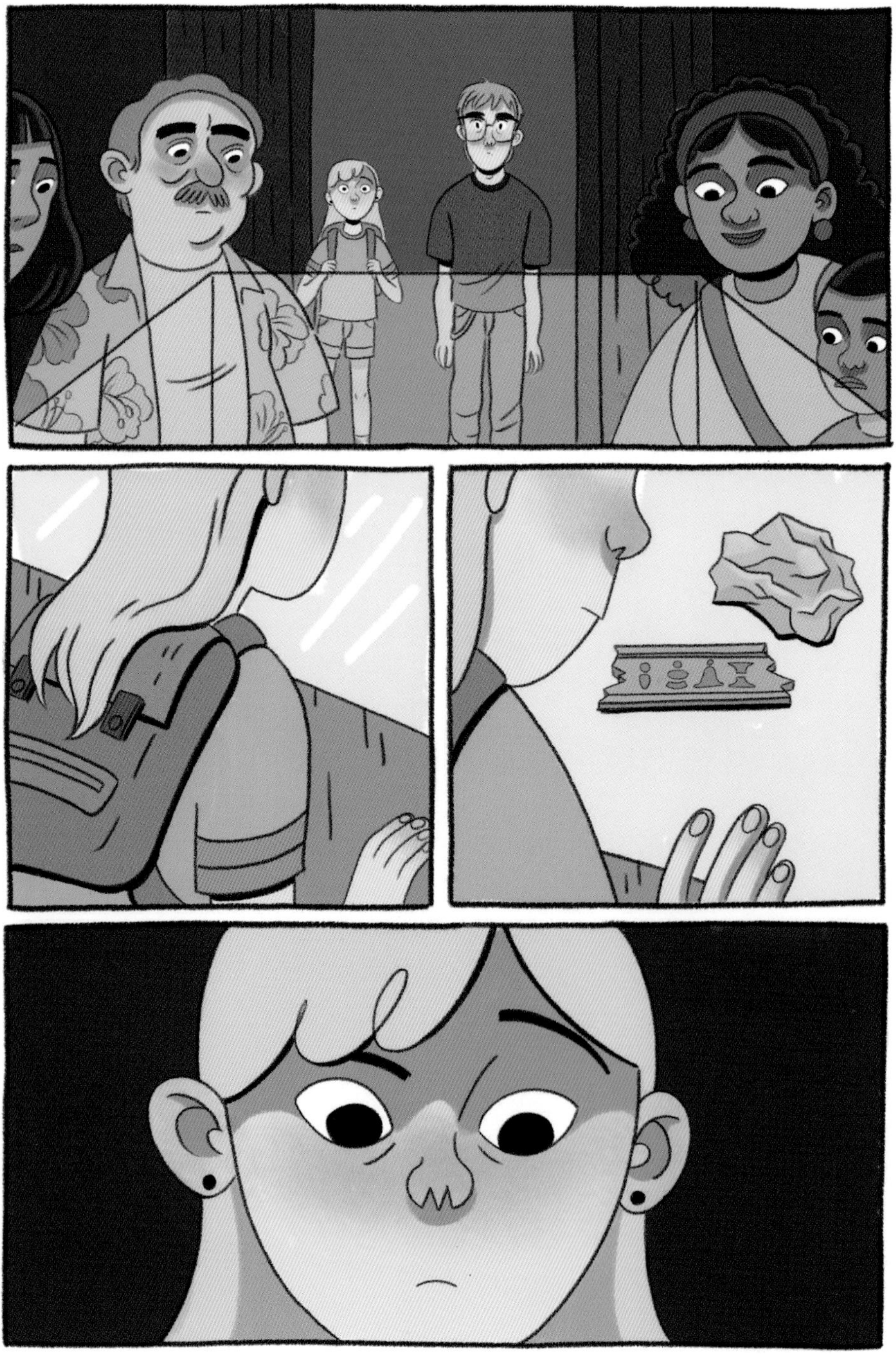

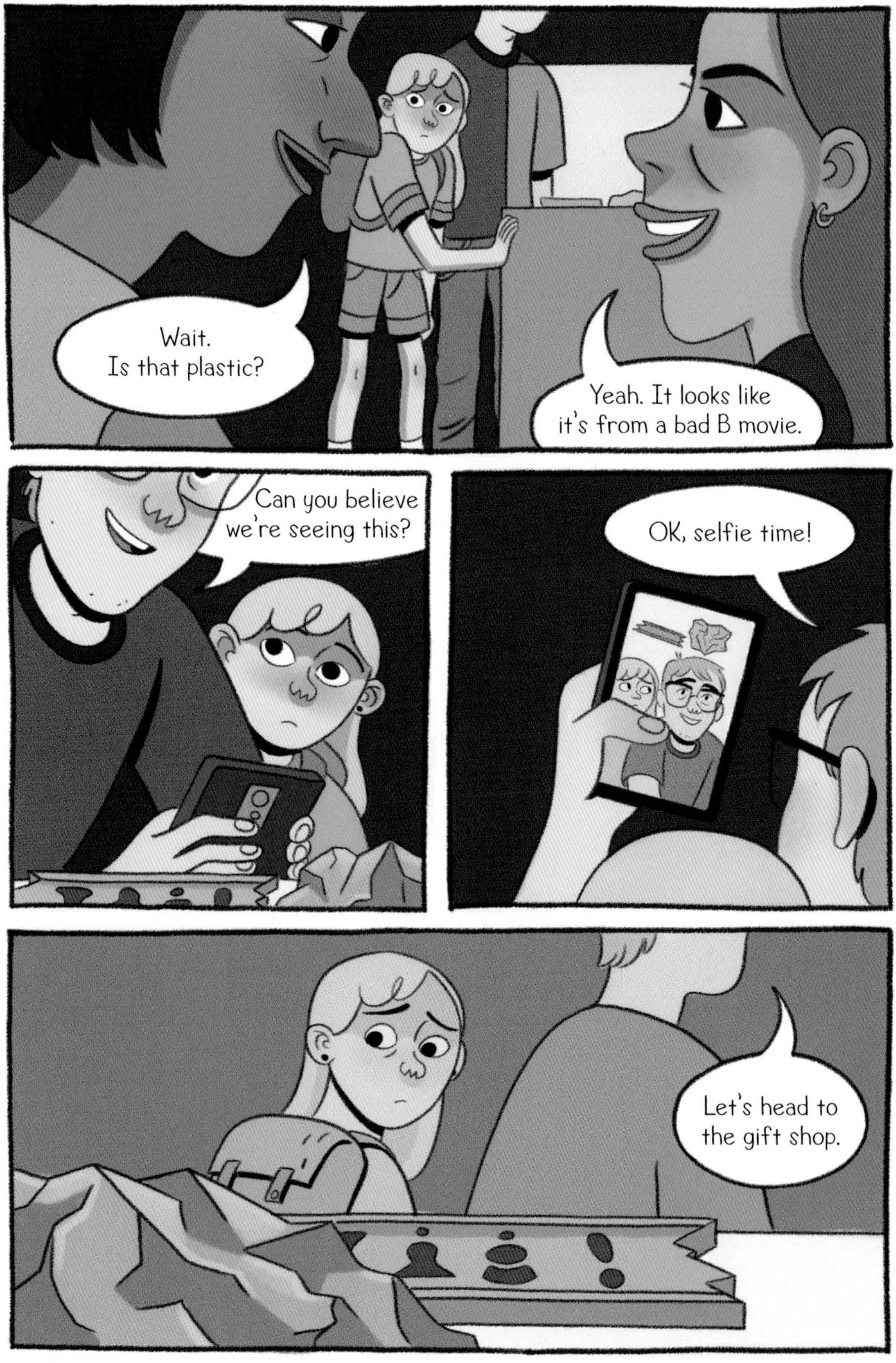
Wait.
Is that plastic?
Yeah. It looks like
it's from a bad B movie.
Can you believe
we're seeing this?
OK, selfie time!
Let's head to
the gift shop.

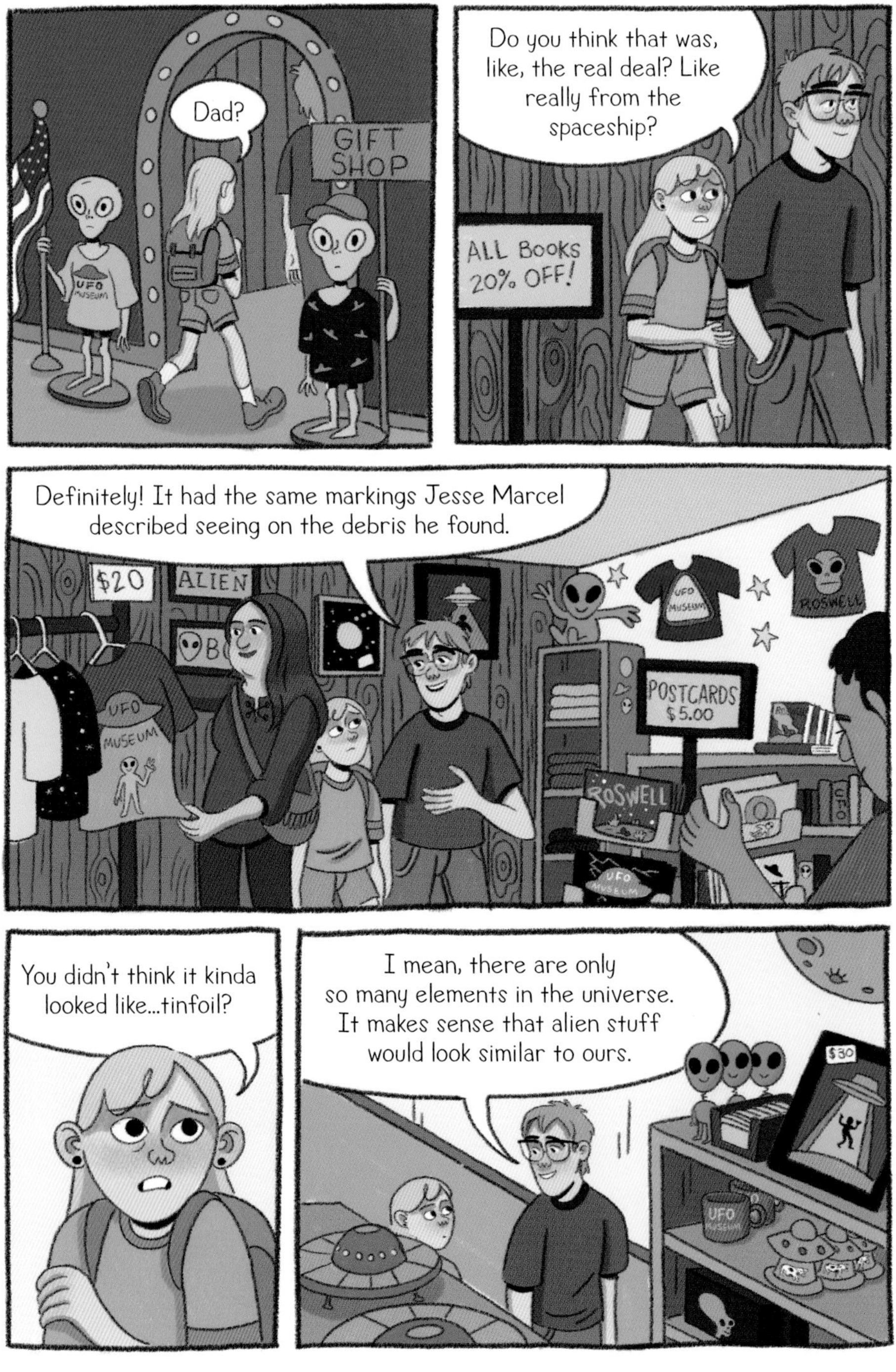
Dad?
GIFT SHOP
UFO MUSEUM
Do you think that was, like, the real deal? Like really from the spaceship?
ALL BOOKS 20% OFF!
Definitely! It had the same markings Jesse Marcel described seeing on the debris he found.
$20
ALIEN
UFO MUSEUM
POSTCARDS $5.00
ROSWELL
You didn't think it kinda looked like...tinfoil?
I mean, there are only so many elements in the universe. It makes sense that alien stuff would look similar to ours.
$30
UFO MUSEUM

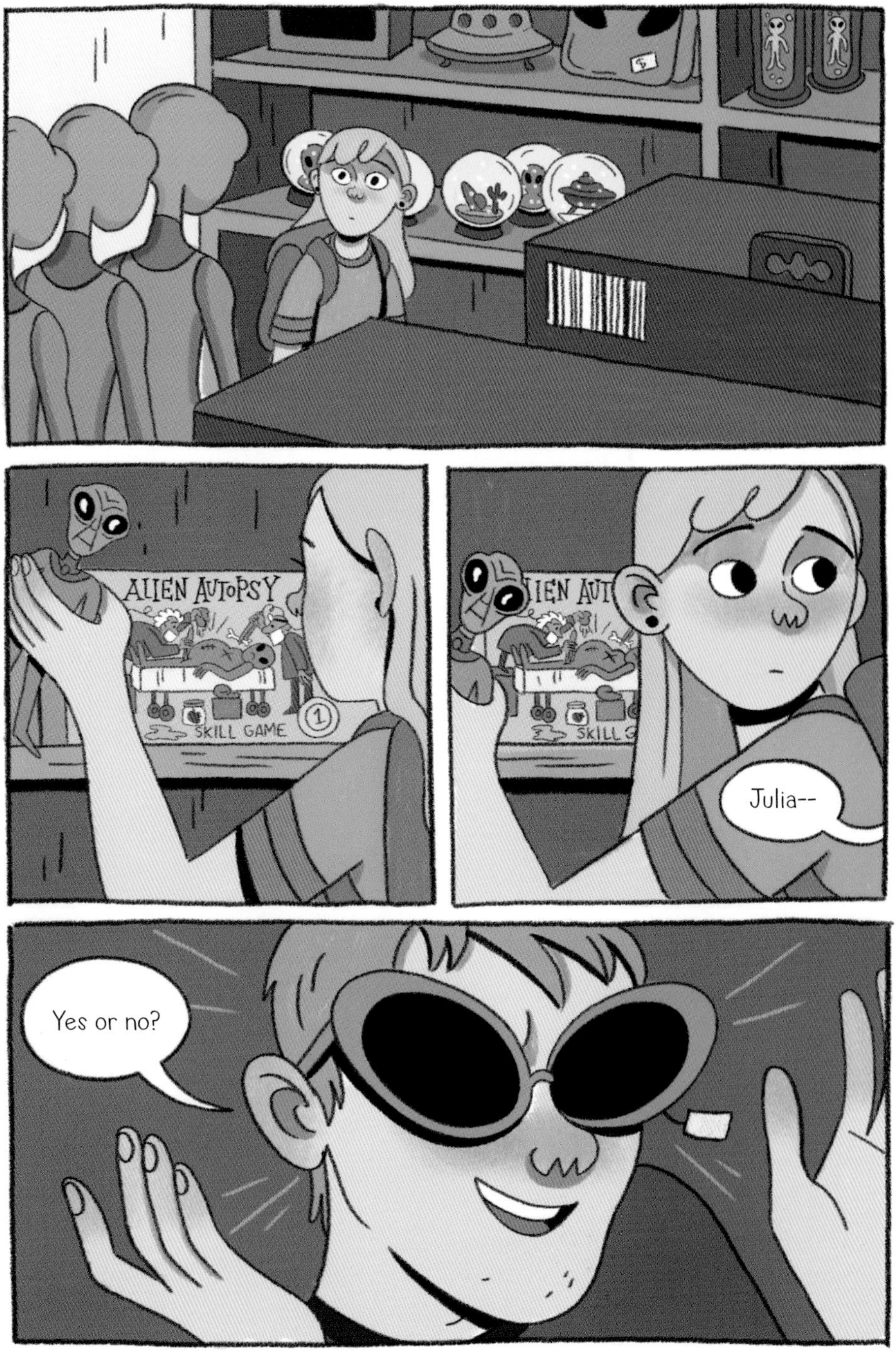
ALIEN AUTOPSY
SKILL GAME
1
Julia--
Yes or no?

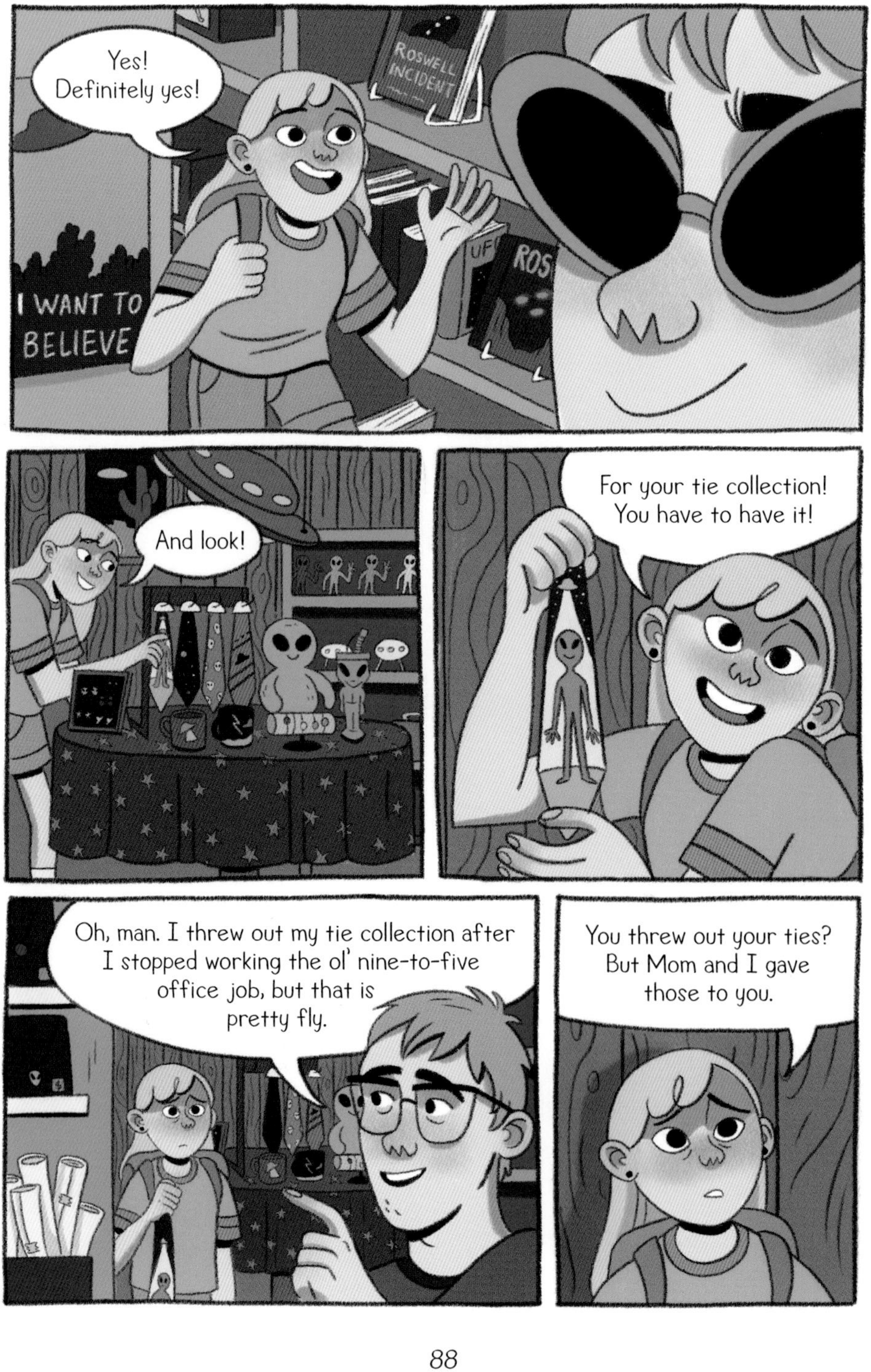
Yes! Definitely yes!
ROSWELL INCIDENT
I WANT TO BELIEVE
ROS
UFO
And look!
For your tie collection! You have to have it!
Oh, man. I threw out my tie collection after I stopped working the ol' nine-to-five office job, but that is pretty fly.
You threw out your ties? But Mom and I gave those to you.

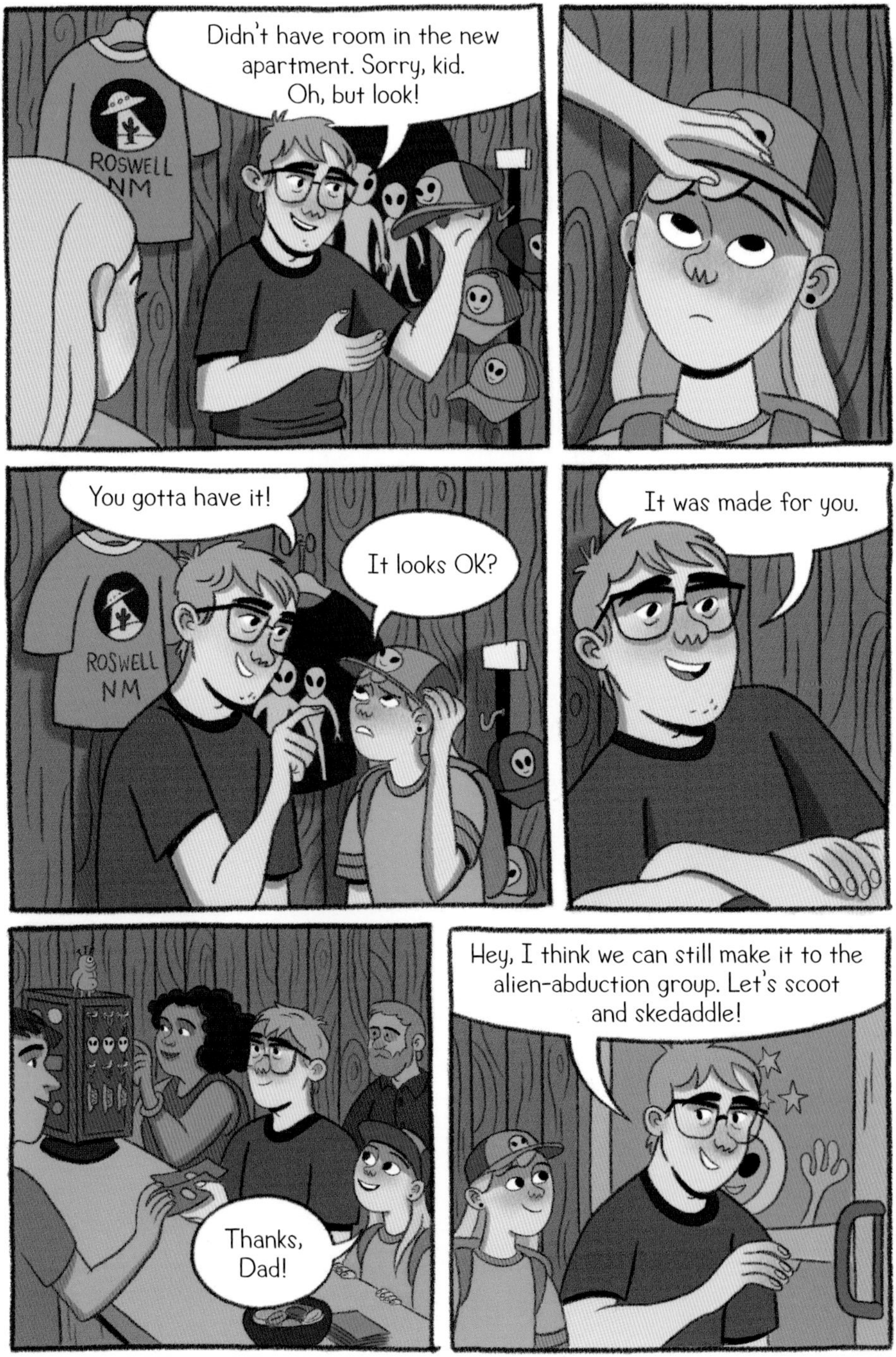
Didn't have room in the new apartment. Sorry, kid. Oh, but look!
ROSWELL NM
You gotta have it!
It looks OK?
ROSWELL NM
It was made for you.
Thanks, Dad!
Hey, I think we can still make it to the alien-abduction group. Let's scoot and skedaddle!

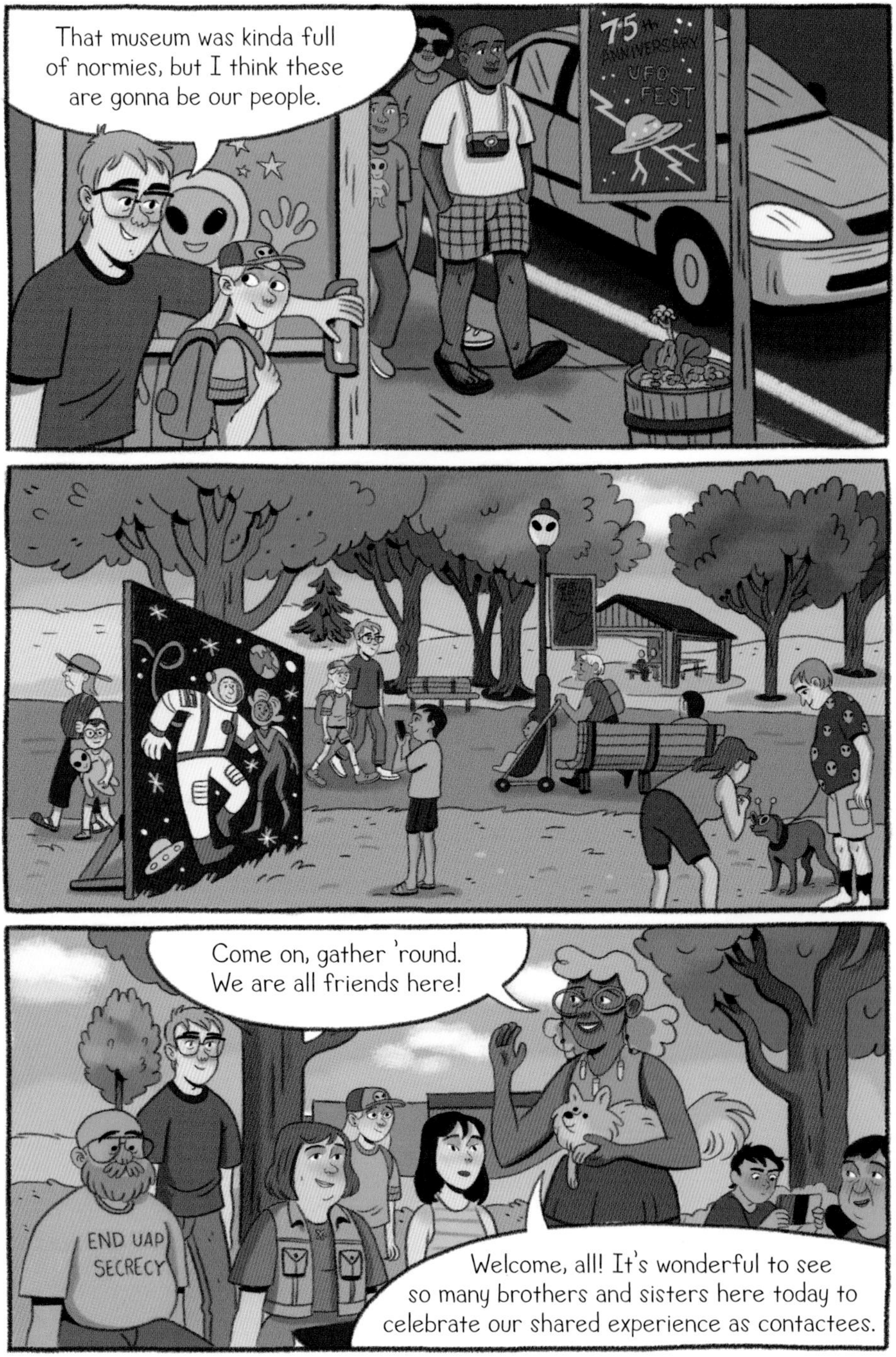

That museum was kinda full of normies, but I think these are gonna be our people.
75th ANNIVERSARY UFO FEST
Come on, gather 'round. We are all friends here!
END UAP SECRECY
Welcome, all! It's wonderful to see so many brothers and sisters here today to celebrate our shared experience as contactees.

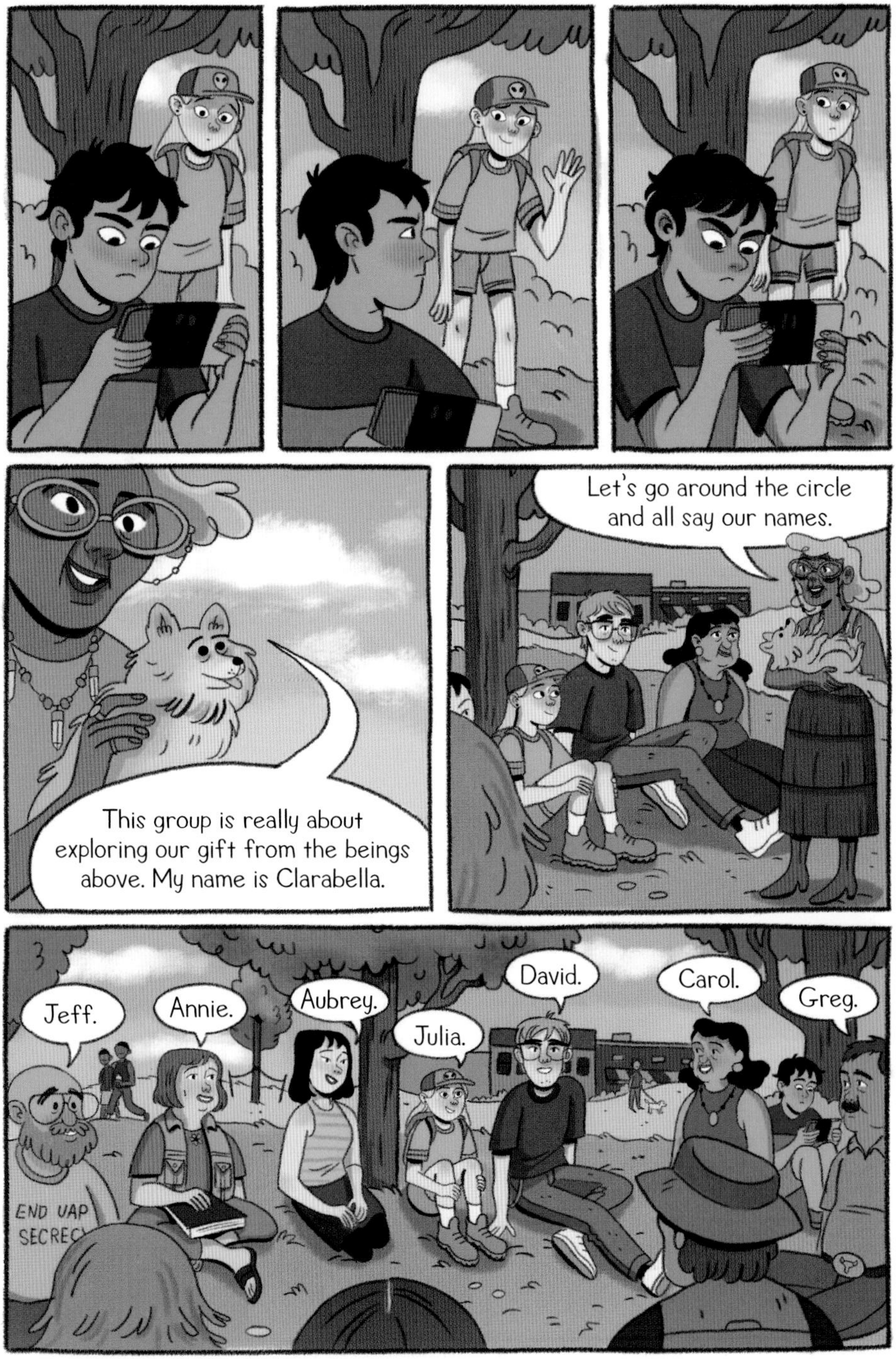
This group is really about exploring our gift from the beings above. My name is Clarabella.
Let's go around the circle and all say our names.
Jeff.
Annie.
Aubrey.
Julia.
David.
Carol.
Greg.
END UAP SECREC

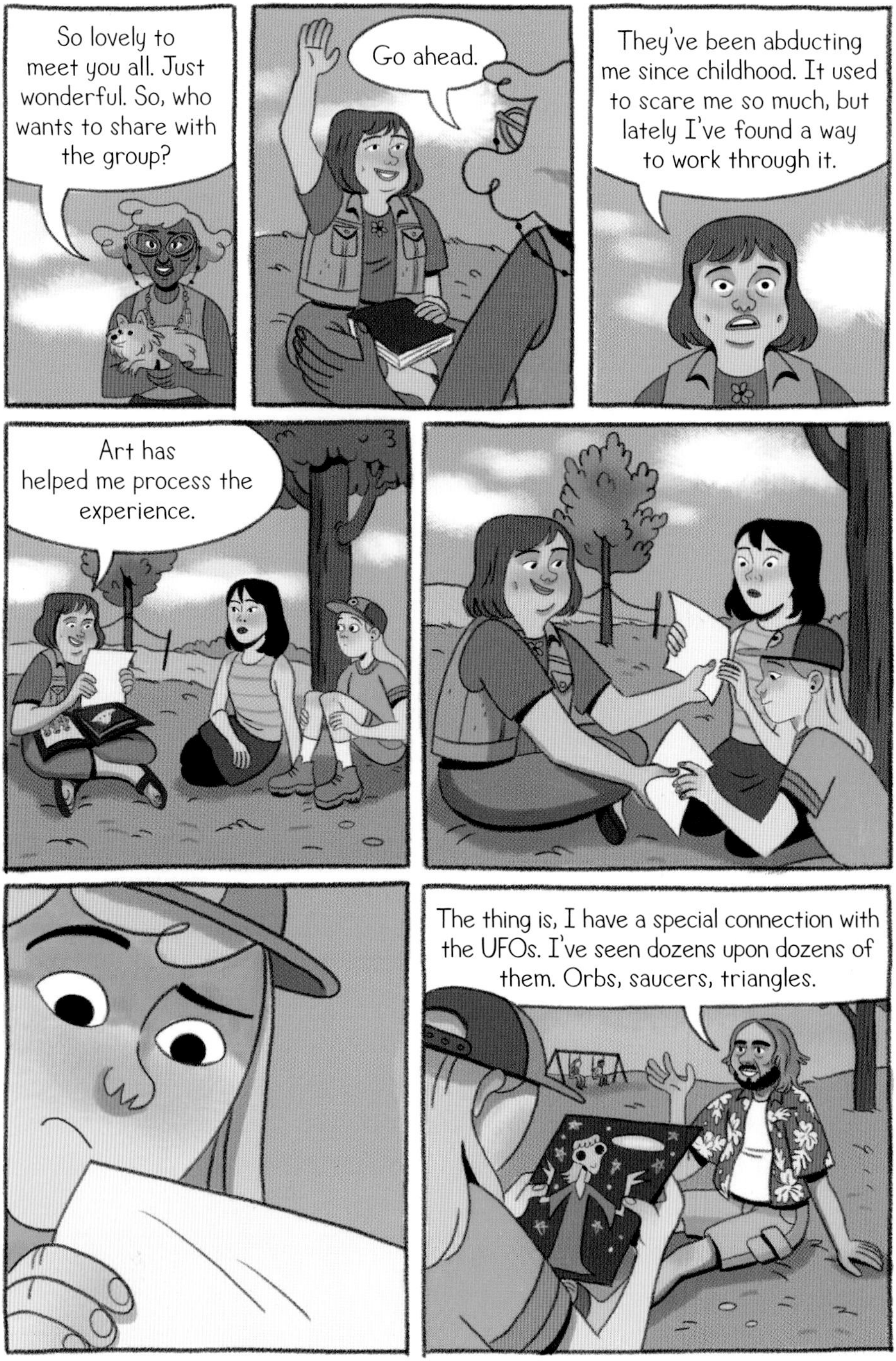

So lovely to meet you all. Just wonderful. So, who wants to share with the group?
Go ahead.
They've been abducting me since childhood. It used to scare me so much, but lately I've found a way to work through it.
Art has helped me process the experience.
The thing is, I have a special connection with the UFOs. I've seen dozens upon dozens of them. Orbs, saucers, triangles.

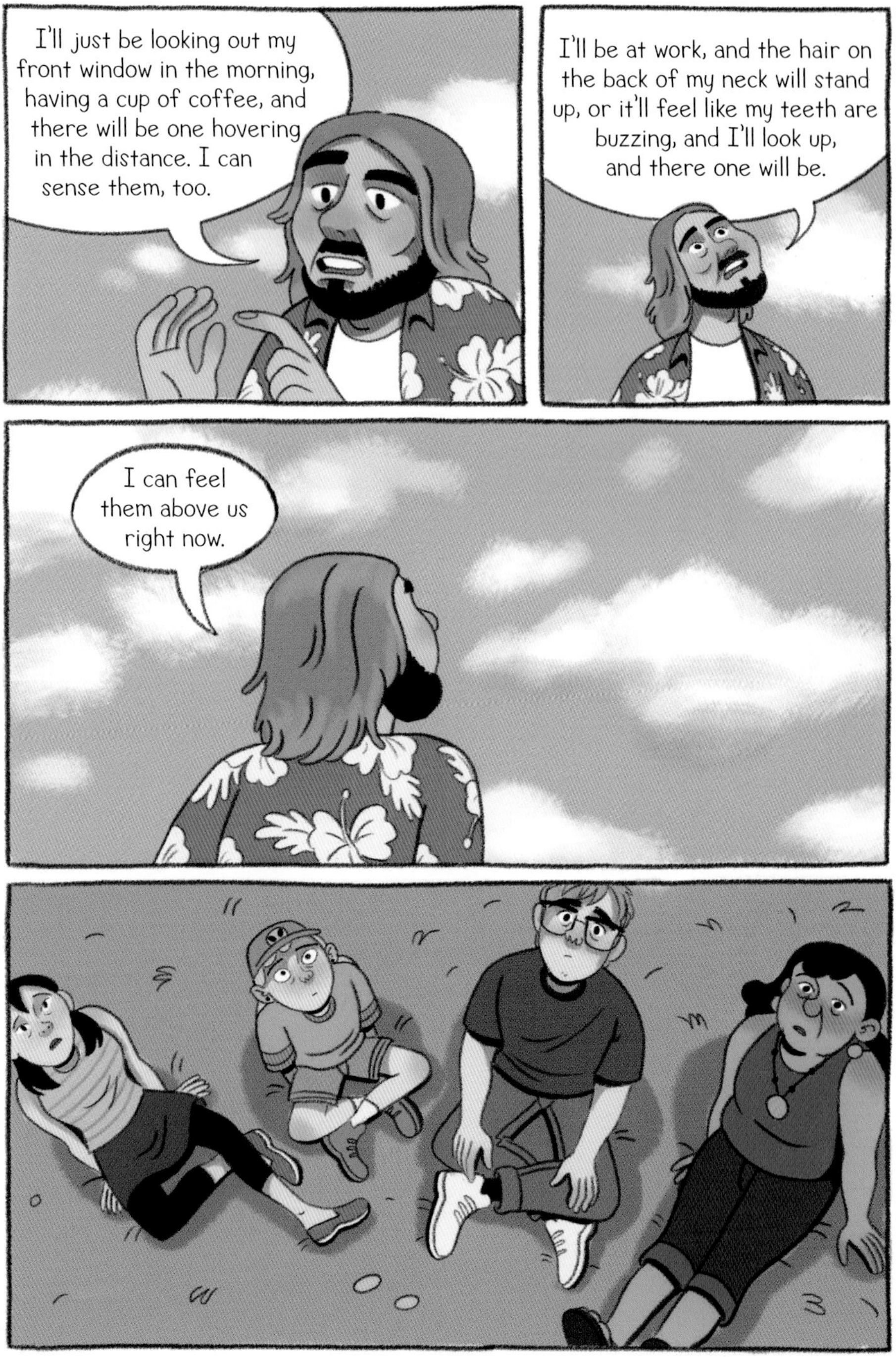
I'll just be looking out my front window in the morning, having a cup of coffee, and there will be one hovering in the distance. I can sense them, too.
I'll be at work, and the hair on the back of my neck will stand up, or it'll feel like my teeth are buzzing, and I'll look up, and there one will be.
I can feel them above us right now.

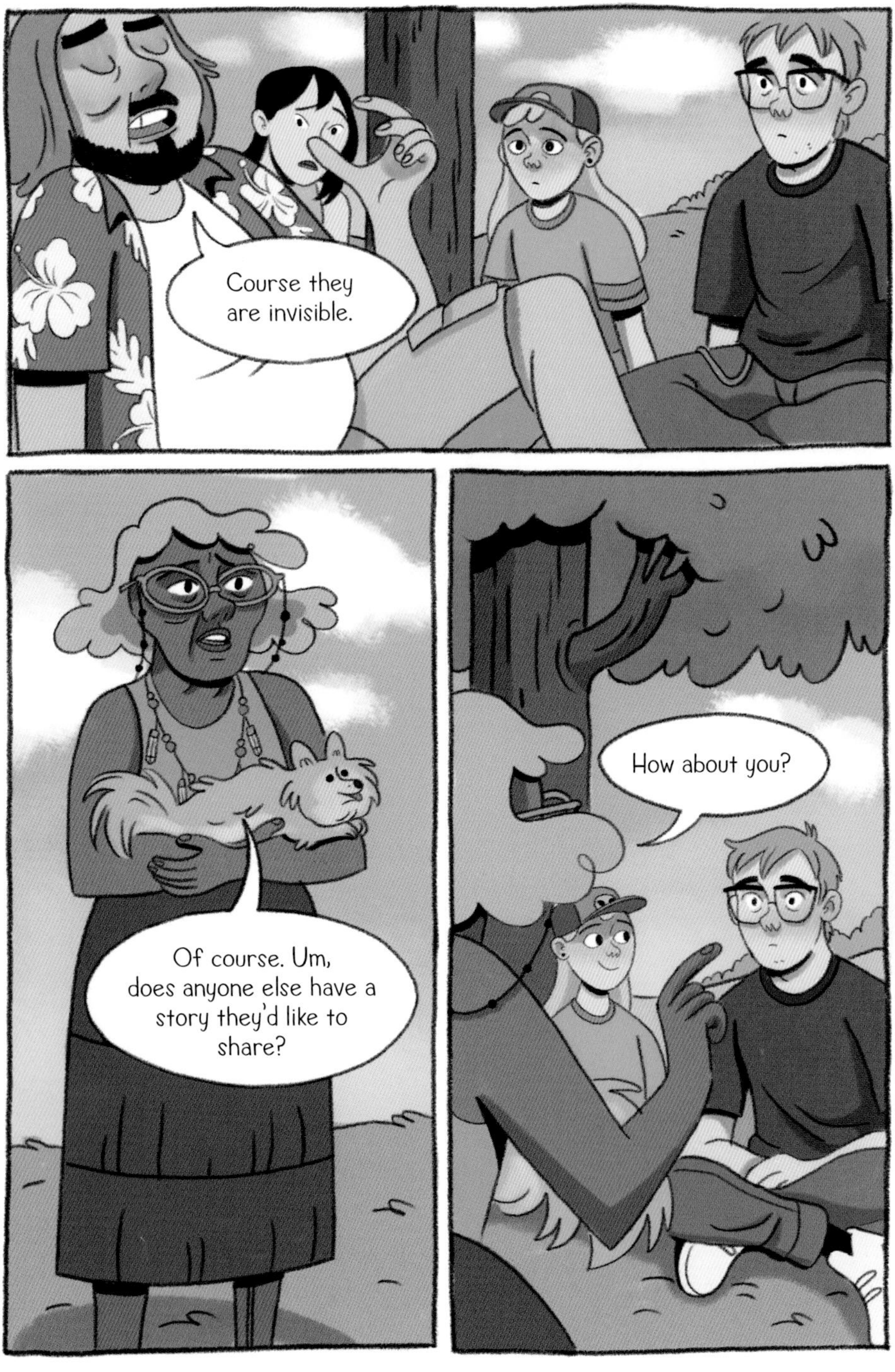
Course they are invisible.
Of course. Um, does anyone else have a story they'd like to share?
How about you?

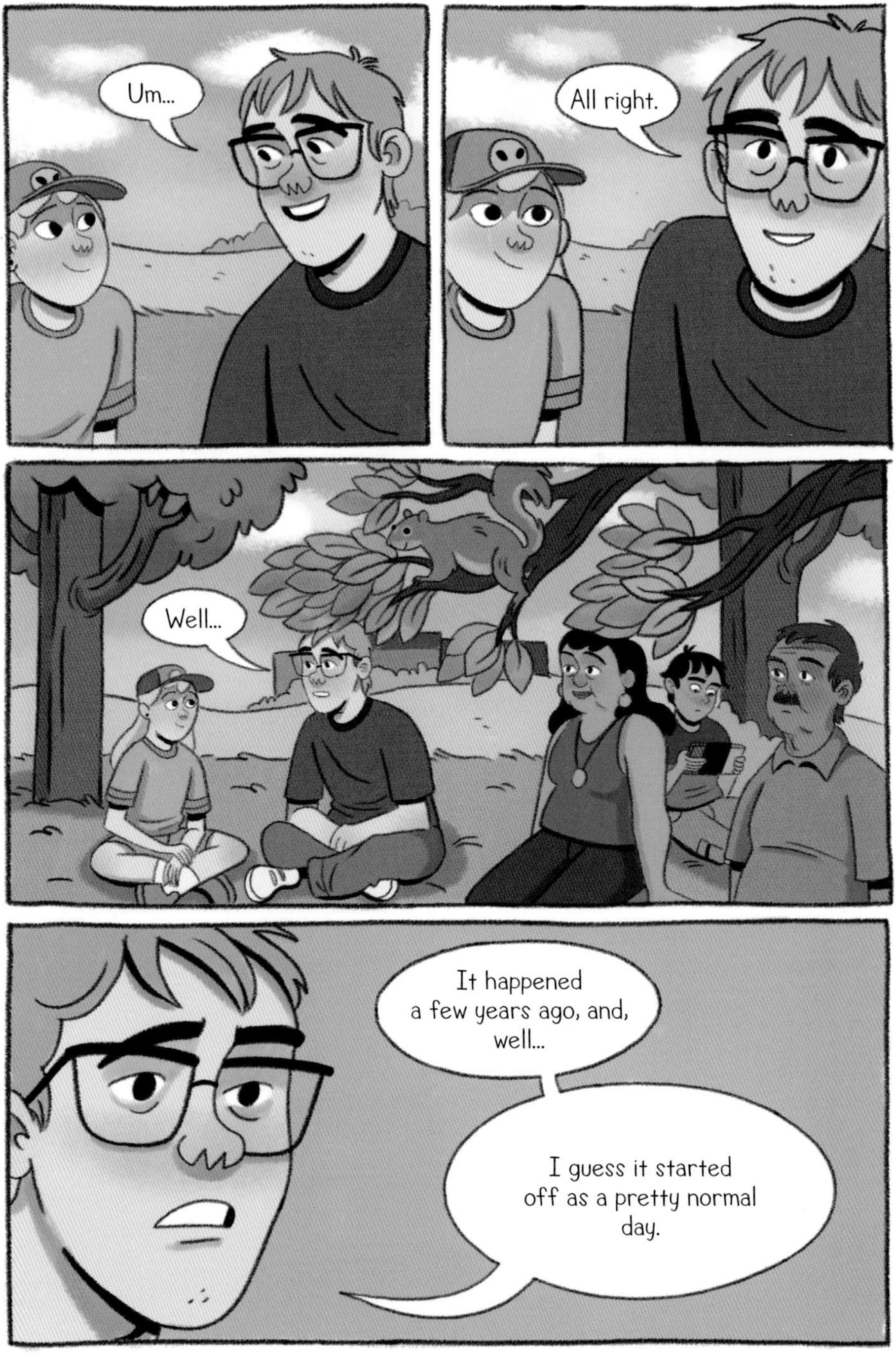
Um...
All right.
Well...
It happened a few years ago, and, well...
I guess it started off as a pretty normal day.

"It was a Saturday, so I was home. It'd been a terrible week at work, and I was exhausted. But as the day progressed, I felt something more than that.

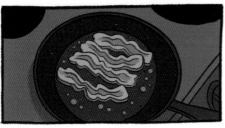

"Something was off. Everything was too still. All day there was no wind, not even a breeze. I didn't hear birds chirping or insects buzzing.

"I was fixated on the feeling, but when I mentioned it to my wife, she thought I was losing it. I was so distracted that I absentmindedly poured bacon grease down the drain and clogged it. My wife and I got into this huge fight. We were fighting a lot back then.

"She was so mad, and we ended up going to bed without speaking. I couldn't fall asleep, and not just because of the fight. It was too quiet.

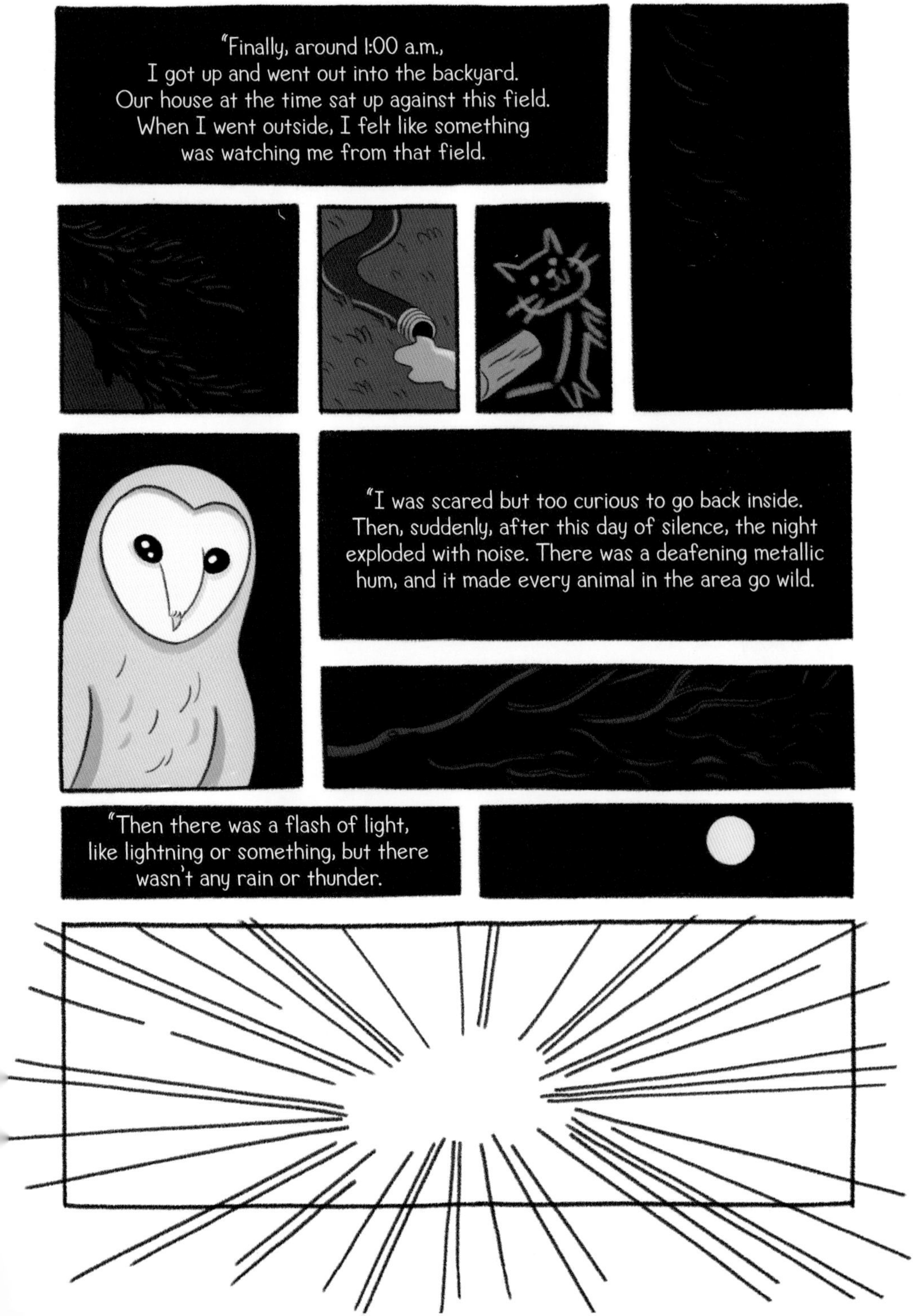
"Finally, around 1:00 a.m., I got up and went out into the backyard. Our house at the time sat up against this field. When I went outside, I felt like something was watching me from that field.
"I was scared but too curious to go back inside. Then, suddenly, after this day of silence, the night exploded with noise. There was a deafening metallic hum, and it made every animal in the area go wild.
"Then there was a flash of light, like lightning or something, but there wasn't any rain or thunder.

"The next thing I knew, I was...somewhere else. There were stars everywhere. I had never seen so many stars, and I couldn't move.

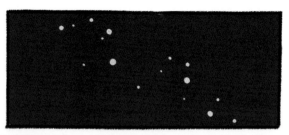

"I could only look straight ahead, and I was lying flat on my back against something cold and hard. I could see shadowy figures all around me. I wanted to call out to them, but I couldn't speak. Then it was like I just knew that I could talk to them in my head.

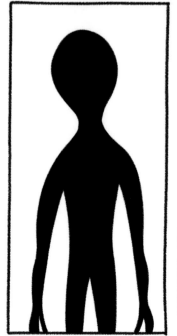

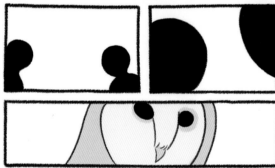

"When I did, one of them stepped into view. Its eyes were huge and black, but I wasn't scared. I knew it wasn't going to hurt me. More of them came forward.

98

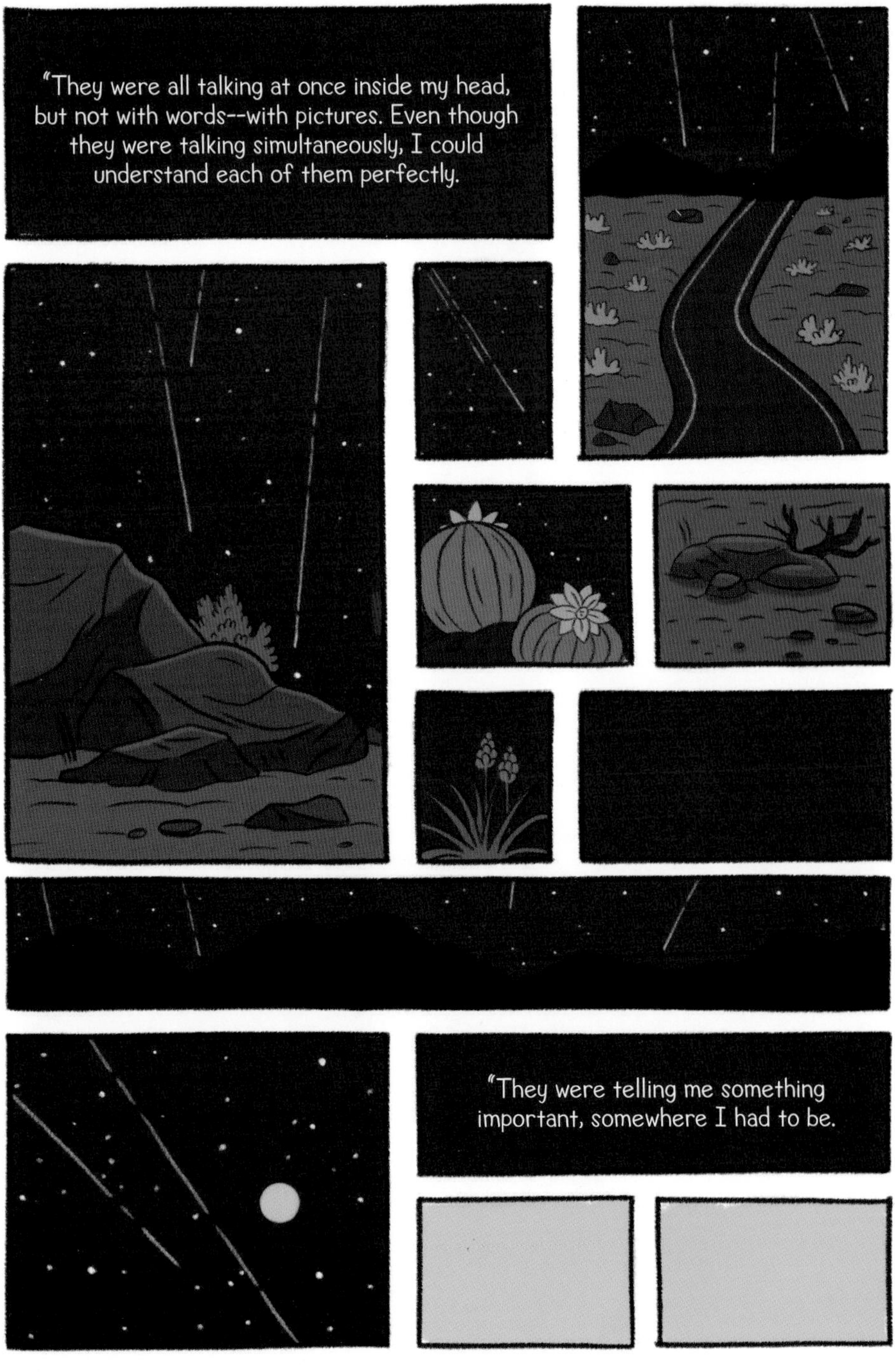
"They were all talking at once inside my head, but not with words--with pictures. Even though they were talking simultaneously, I could understand each of them perfectly.
"They were telling me something important, somewhere I had to be.

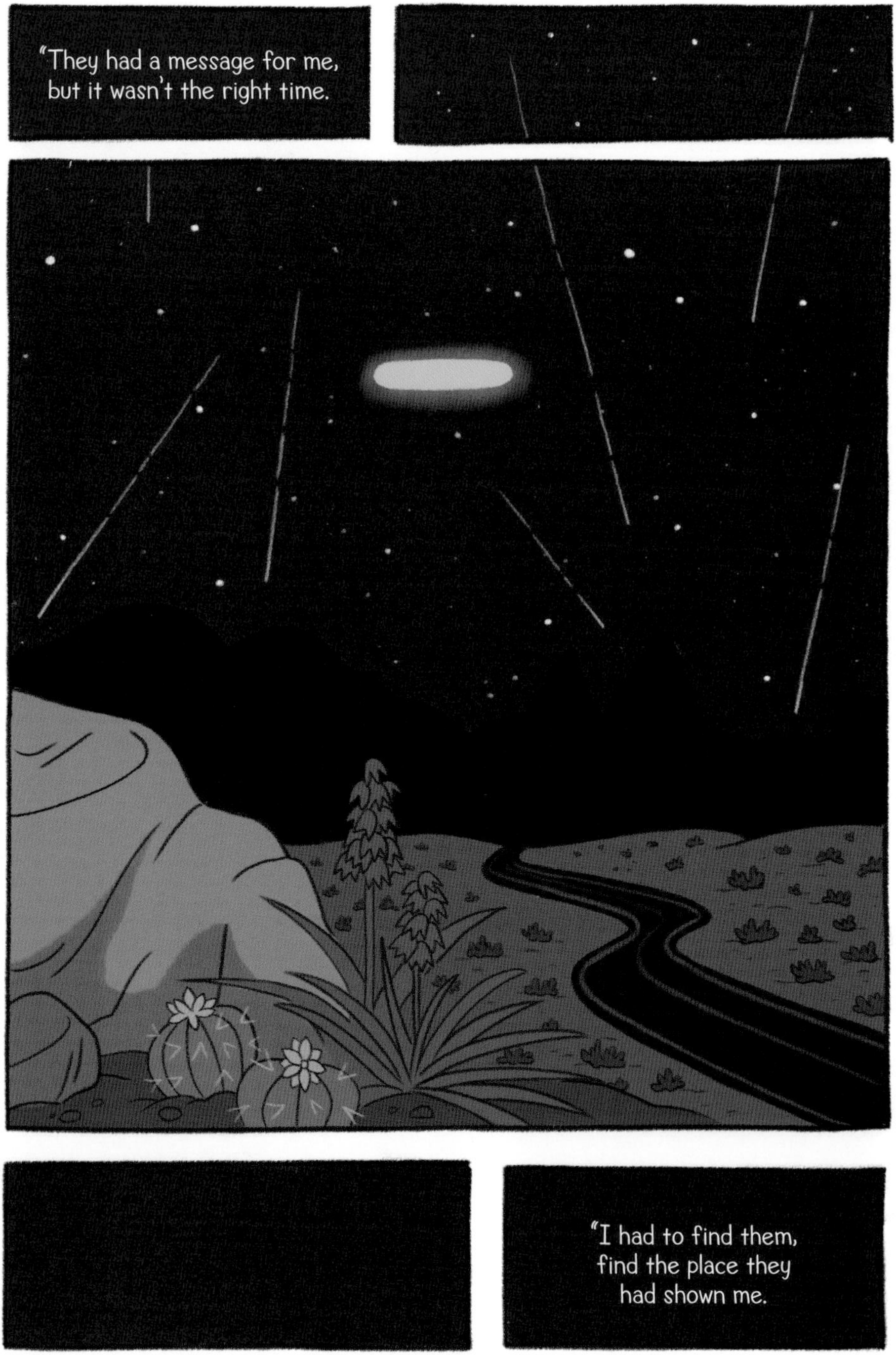
"They had a message for me,
but it wasn't the right time.
"I had to find them,
find the place they
had shown me.

"I don't remember much else before waking up on a lawn chair in the backyard.

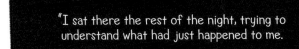

"I sat there the rest of the night, trying to understand what had just happened to me.

"When the sun rose, I went back to bed. My wife was still fast asleep, totally unaware of what had just happened to me, but I knew I was completely changed."

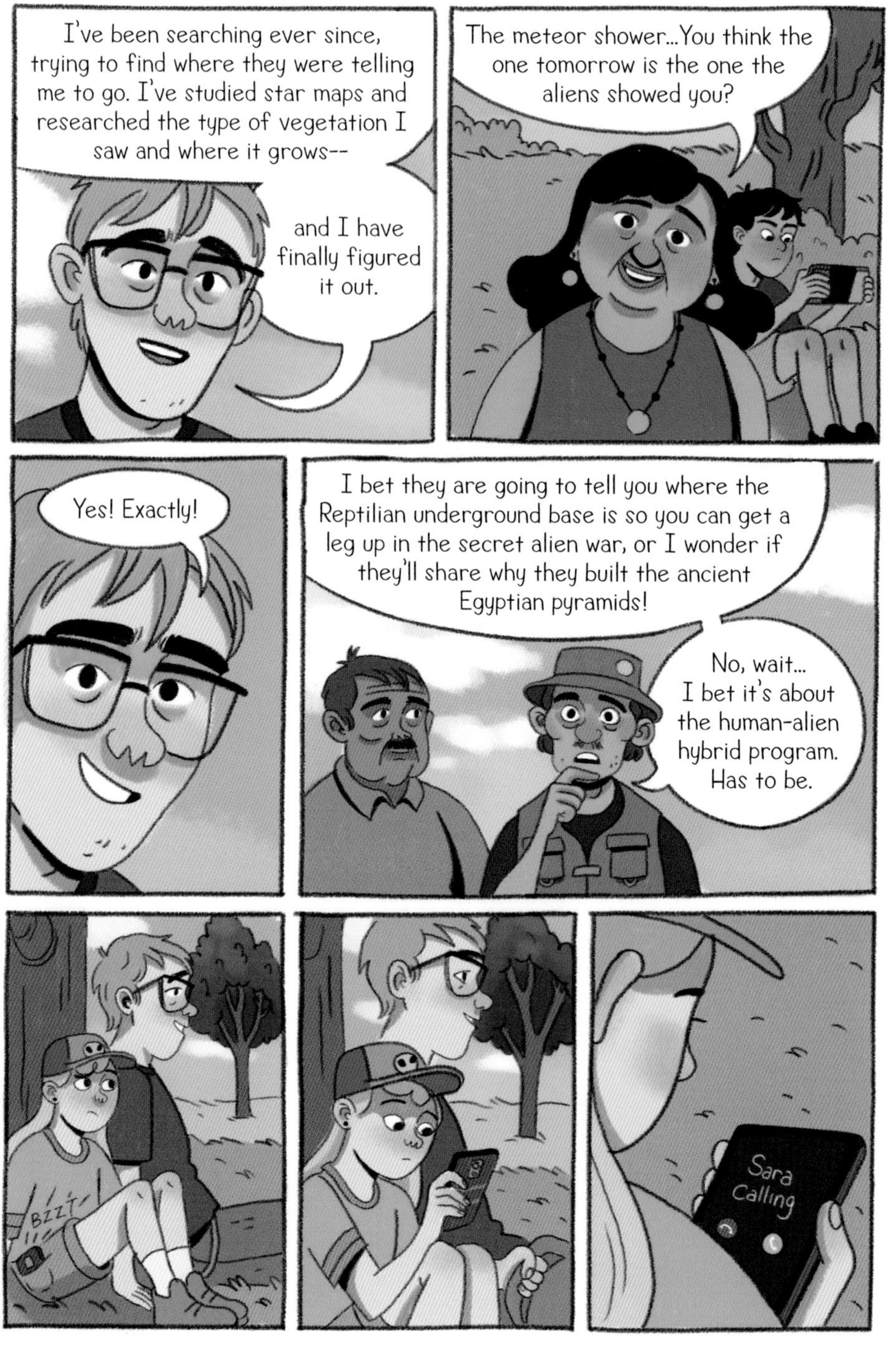
I've been searching ever since, trying to find where they were telling me to go. I've studied star maps and researched the type of vegetation I saw and where it grows--
and I have finally figured it out.
The meteor shower...You think the one tomorrow is the one the aliens showed you?
Yes! Exactly!
I bet they are going to tell you where the Reptilian underground base is so you can get a leg up in the secret alien war, or I wonder if they'll share why they built the ancient Egyptian pyramids!
No, wait... I bet it's about the human-alien hybrid program. Has to be.
BZZT
Sara Calling

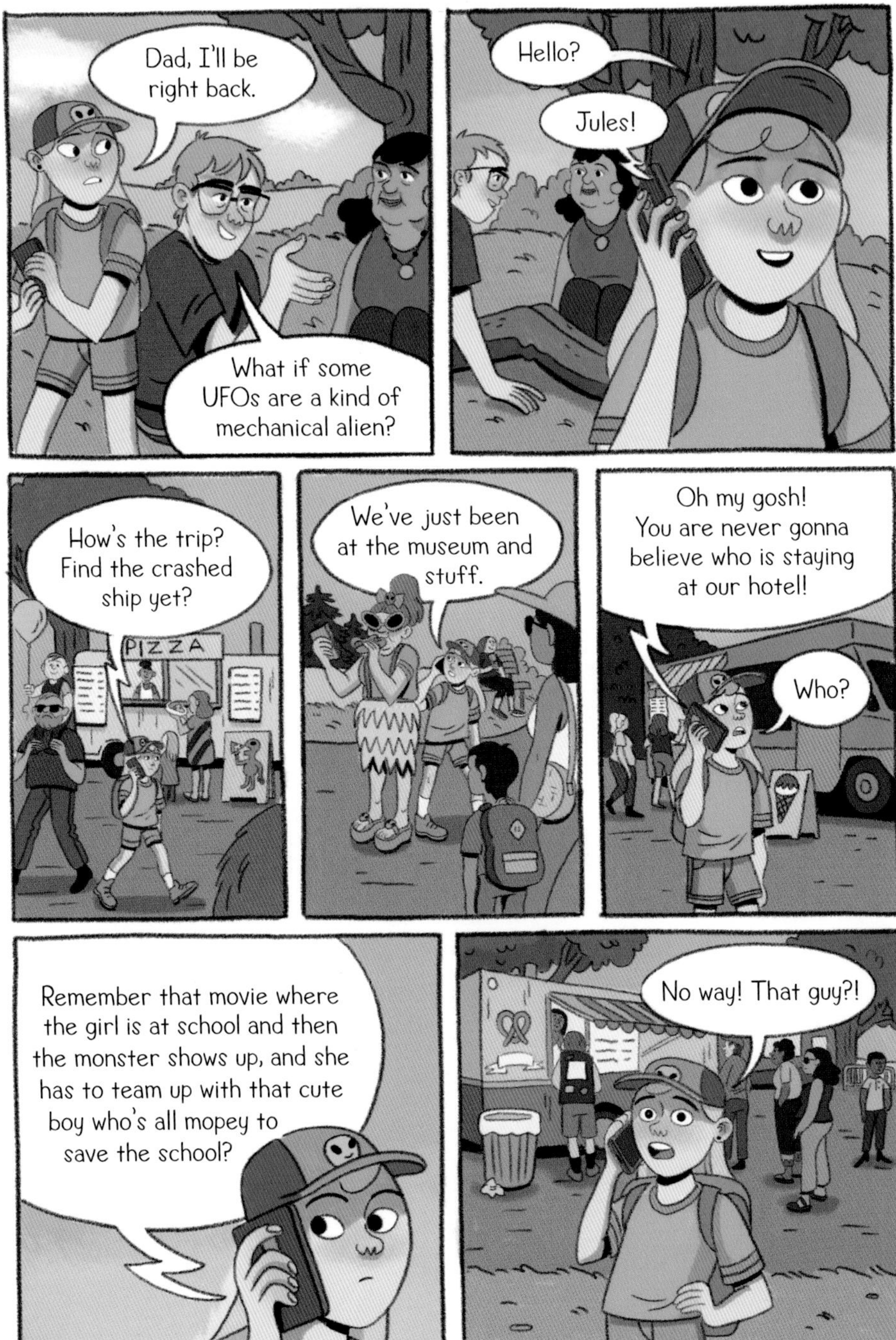
Dad, I'll be right back.
What if some UFOs are a kind of mechanical alien?
Hello?
Jules!
How's the trip? Find the crashed ship yet?
PIZZA
We've just been at the museum and stuff.
Oh my gosh! You are never gonna believe who is staying at our hotel!
Who?
Remember that movie where the girl is at school and then the monster shows up, and she has to team up with that cute boy who's all mopey to save the school?
No way! That guy?!

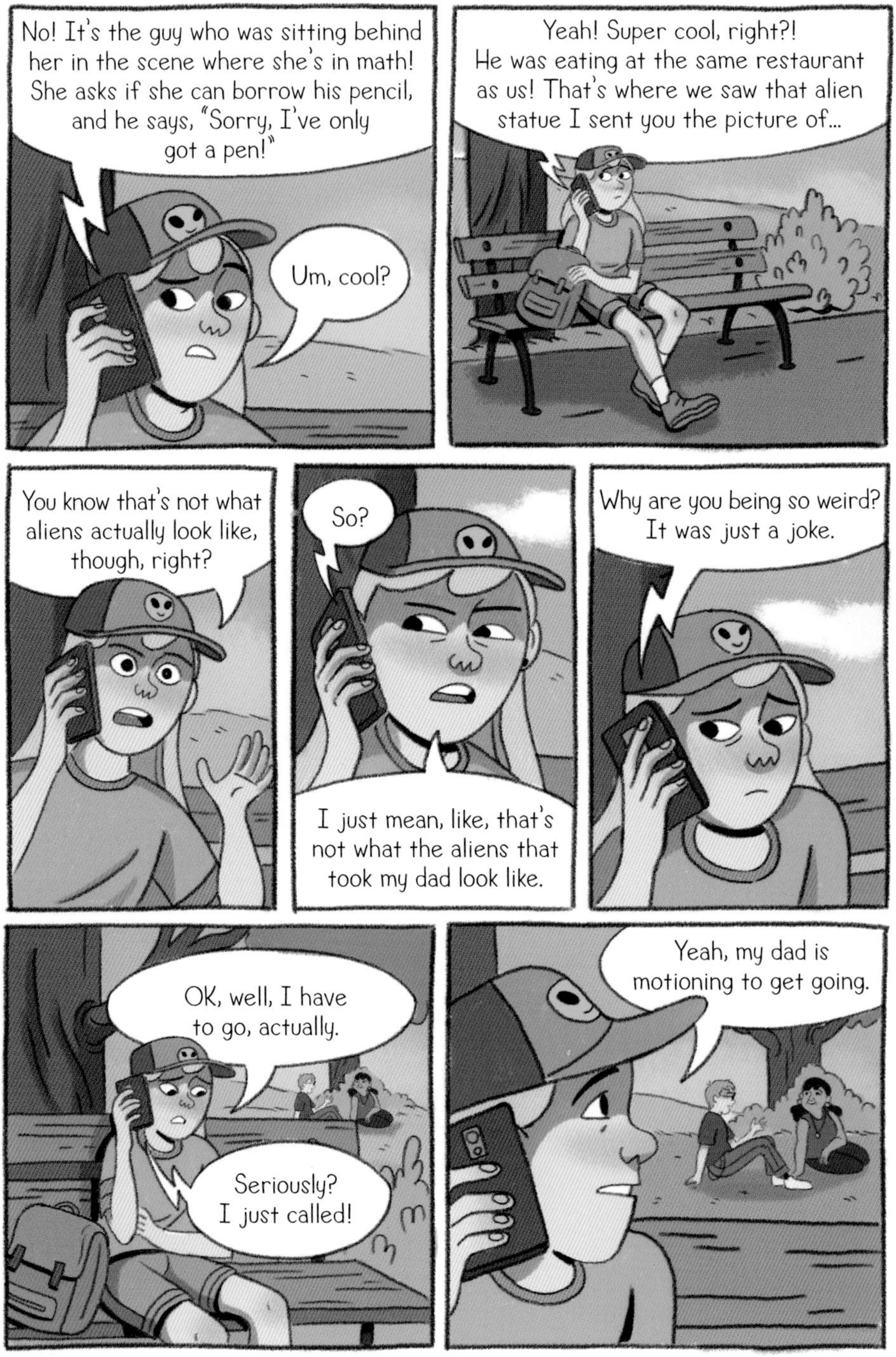
No! It's the guy who was sitting behind her in the scene where she's in math! She asks if she can borrow his pencil, and he says, "Sorry, I've only got a pen!"
Um, cool?
Yeah! Super cool, right?! He was eating at the same restaurant as us! That's where we saw that alien statue I sent you the picture of...
You know that's not what aliens actually look like, though, right?
So?
I just mean, like, that's not what the aliens that took my dad look like.
Why are you being so weird? It was just a joke.
OK, well, I have to go, actually.
Seriously? I just called!
Yeah, my dad is motioning to get going.

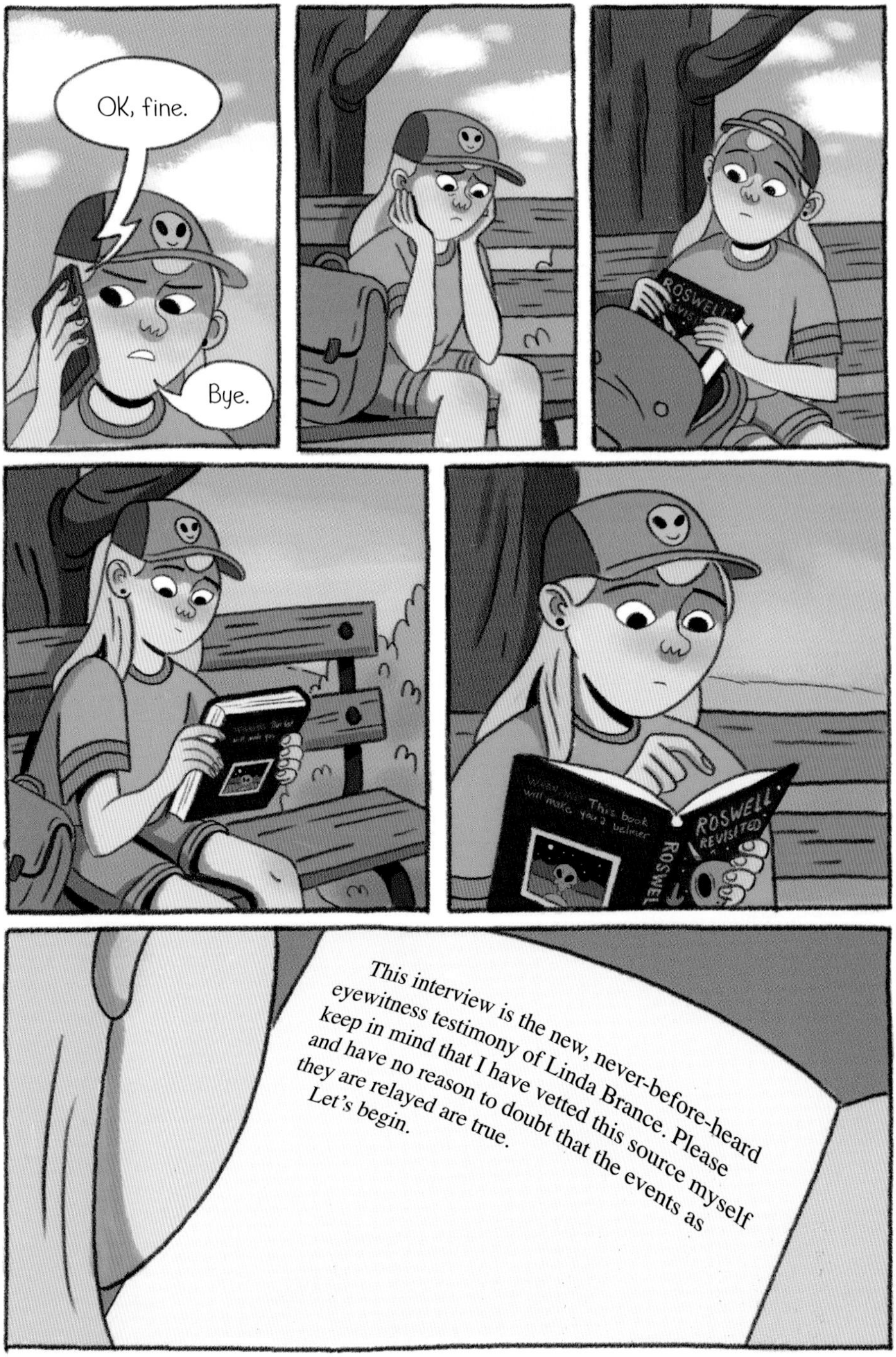
OK, fine.
Bye.
ROSWELL REVISITED
ROSWELL
This interview is the new, never-before-heard eyewitness testimony of Linda Brance. Please keep in mind that I have vetted this source myself and have no reason to doubt that the events as they are relayed are true.
Let's begin.

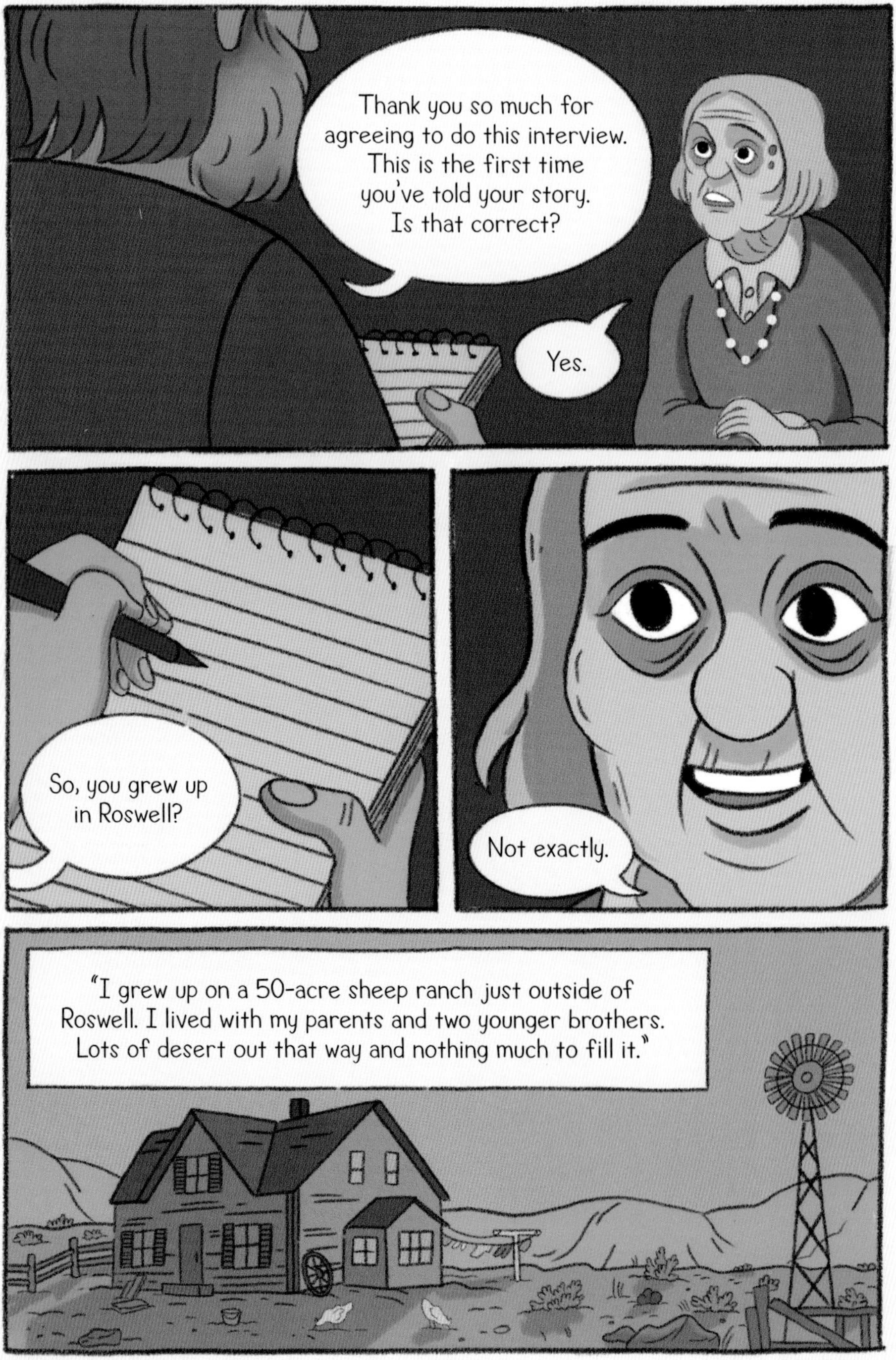

Thank you so much for agreeing to do this interview. This is the first time you've told your story. Is that correct?
Yes.
So, you grew up in Roswell?
Not exactly.
"I grew up on a 50-acre sheep ranch just outside of Roswell. I lived with my parents and two younger brothers. Lots of desert out that way and nothing much to fill it."

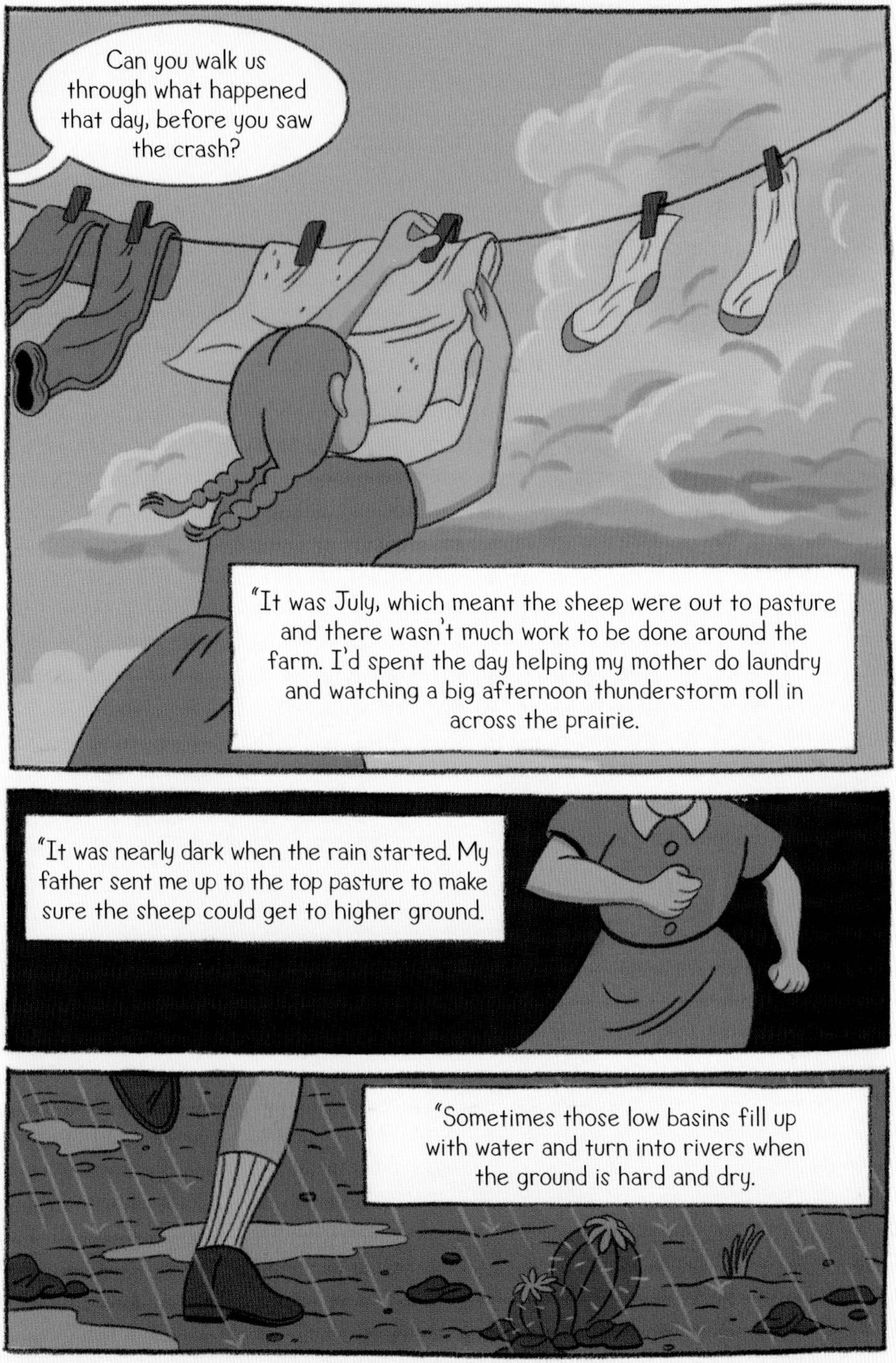

Can you walk us through what happened that day, before you saw the crash?
"It was July, which meant the sheep were out to pasture and there wasn't much work to be done around the farm. I'd spent the day helping my mother do laundry and watching a big afternoon thunderstorm roll in across the prairie.
"It was nearly dark when the rain started. My father sent me up to the top pasture to make sure the sheep could get to higher ground.
"Sometimes those low basins fill up with water and turn into rivers when the ground is hard and dry.

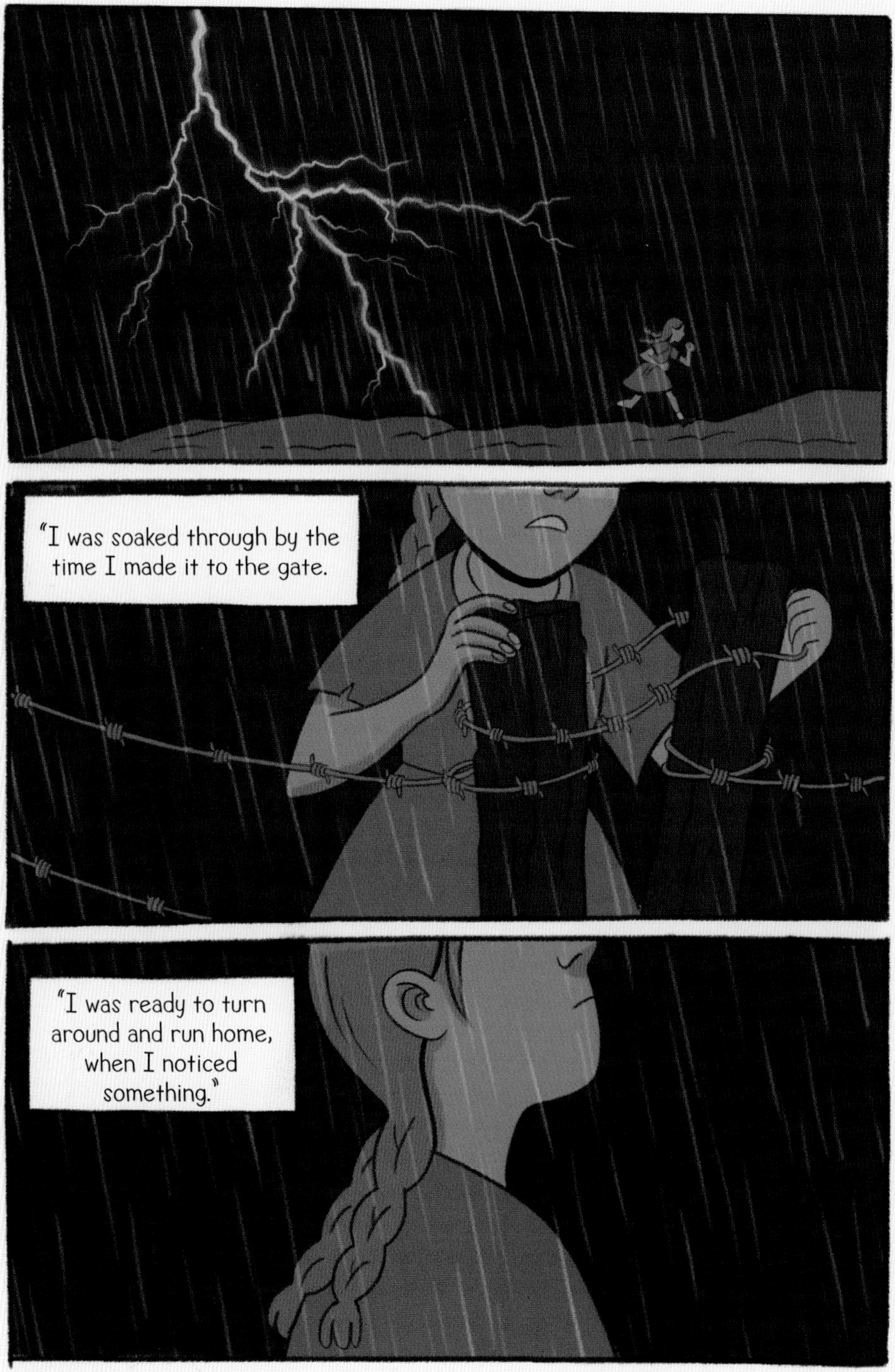
"I was soaked through by the time I made it to the gate.
"I was ready to turn around and run home, when I noticed something."

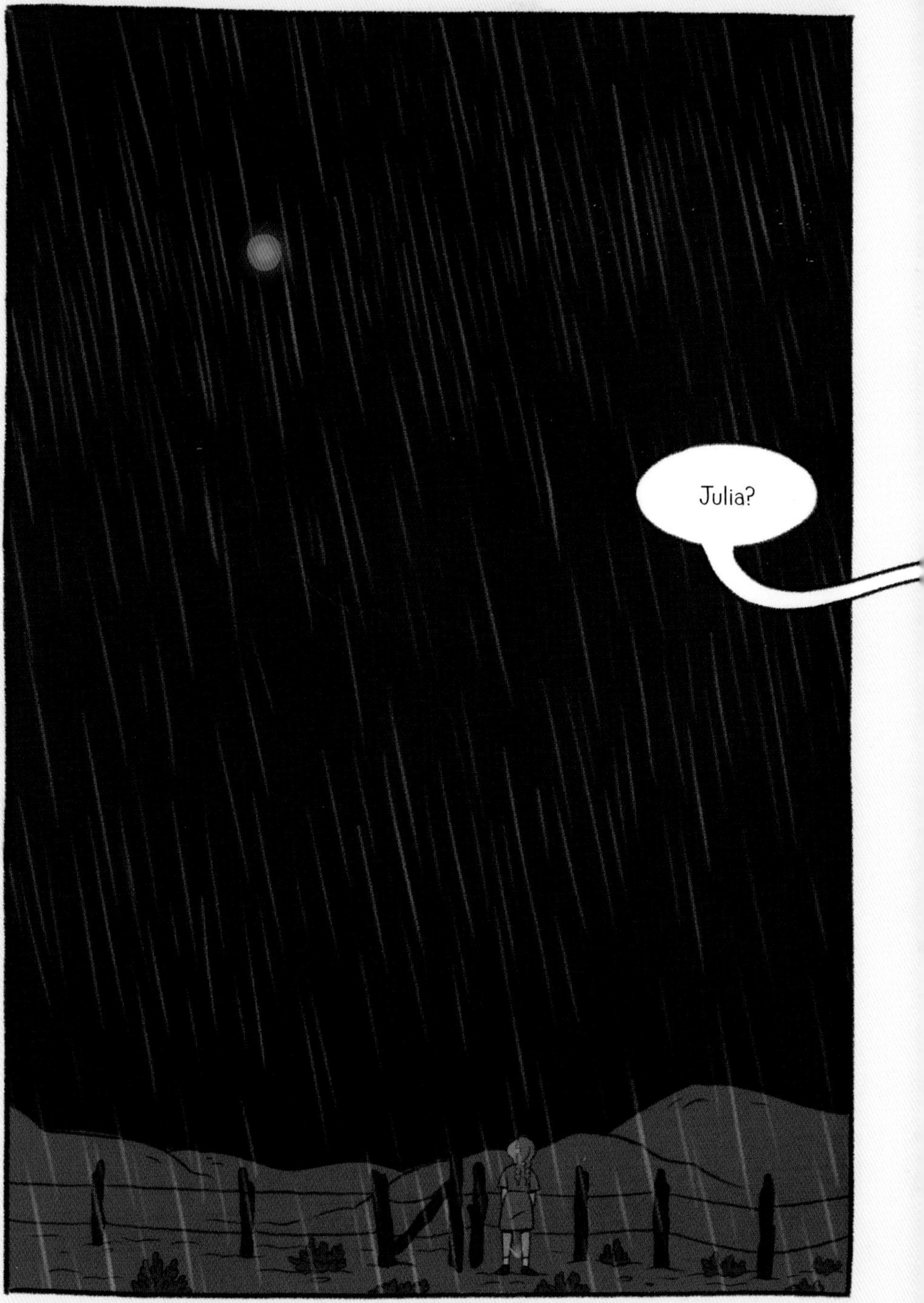
Julia?

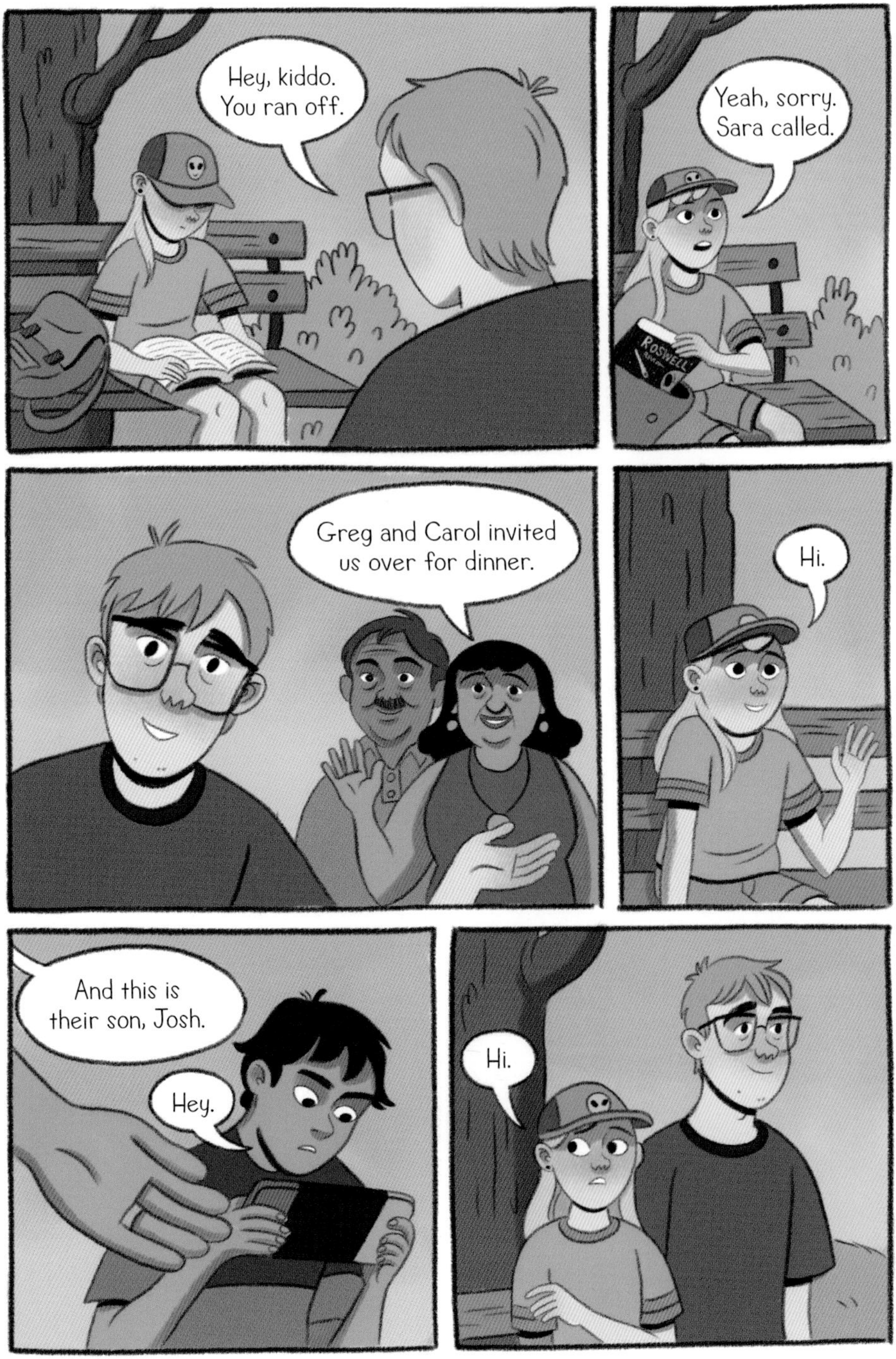
Hey, kiddo. You ran off.
Yeah, sorry. Sara called.
ROSWELL
Greg and Carol invited us over for dinner.
Hi.
And this is their son, Josh.
Hey.
Hi.

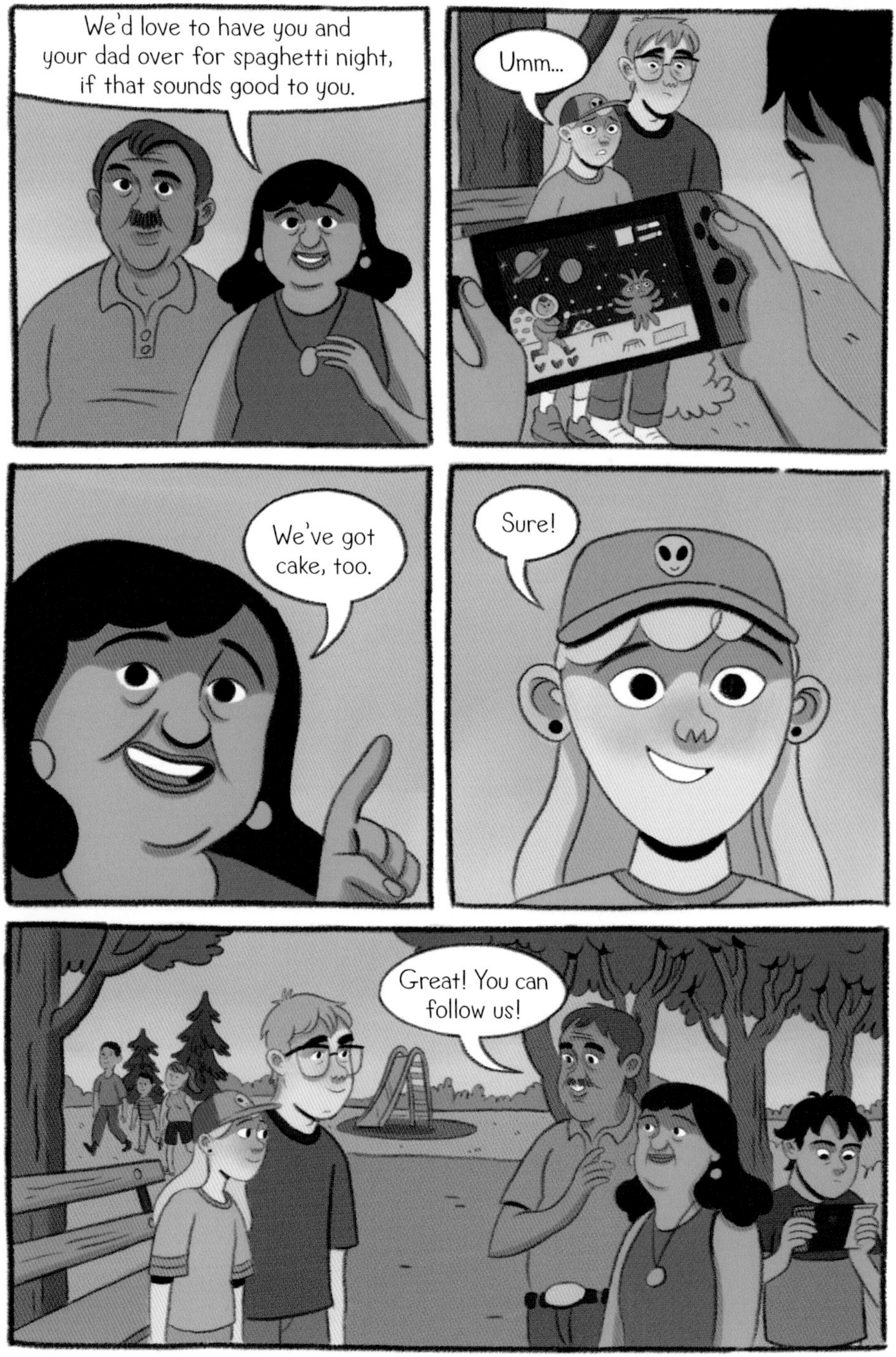
We'd love to have you and your dad over for spaghetti night, if that sounds good to you.
Umm...
We've got cake, too.
Sure!
Great! You can follow us!

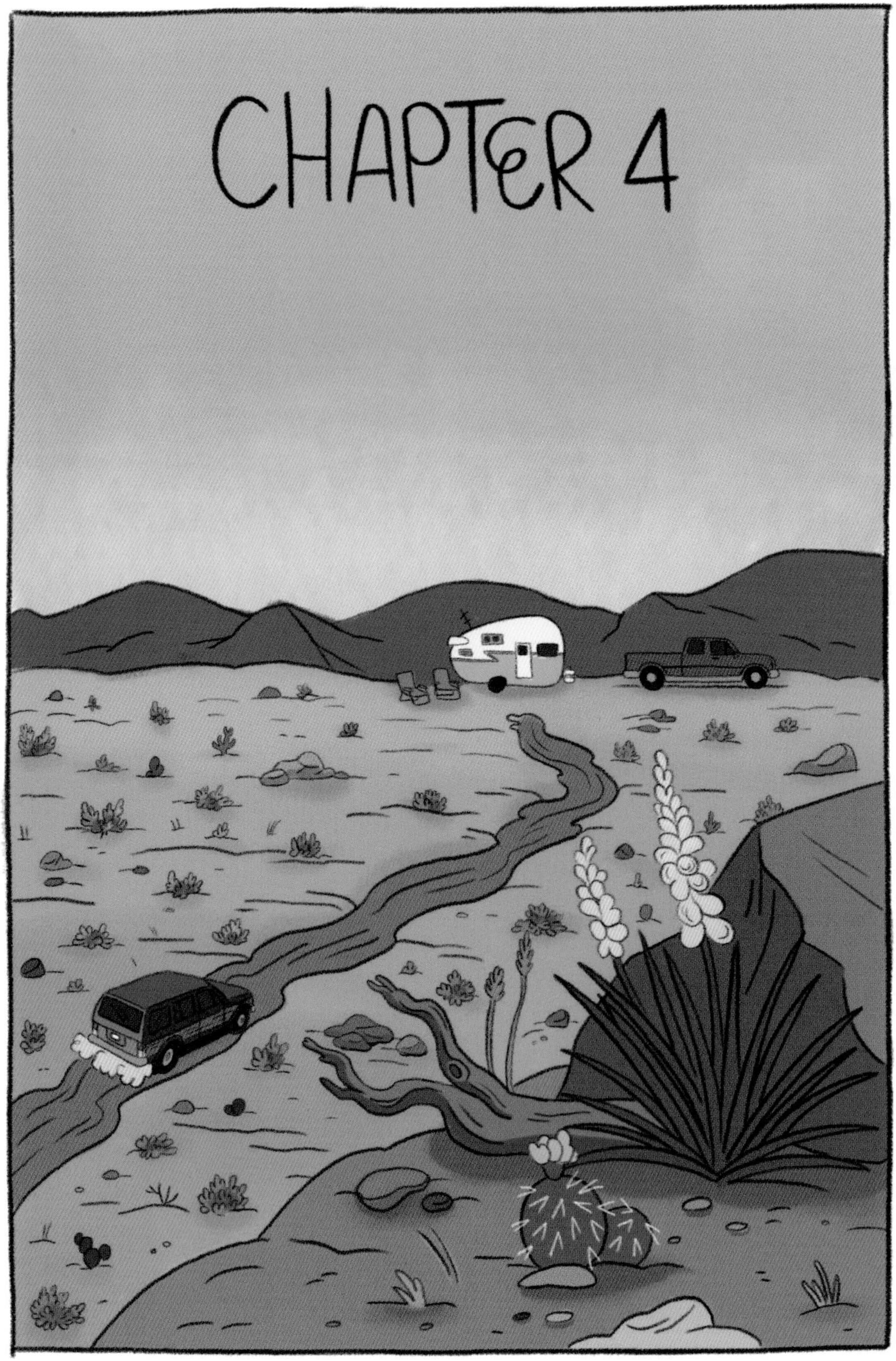
CHAPTER 4

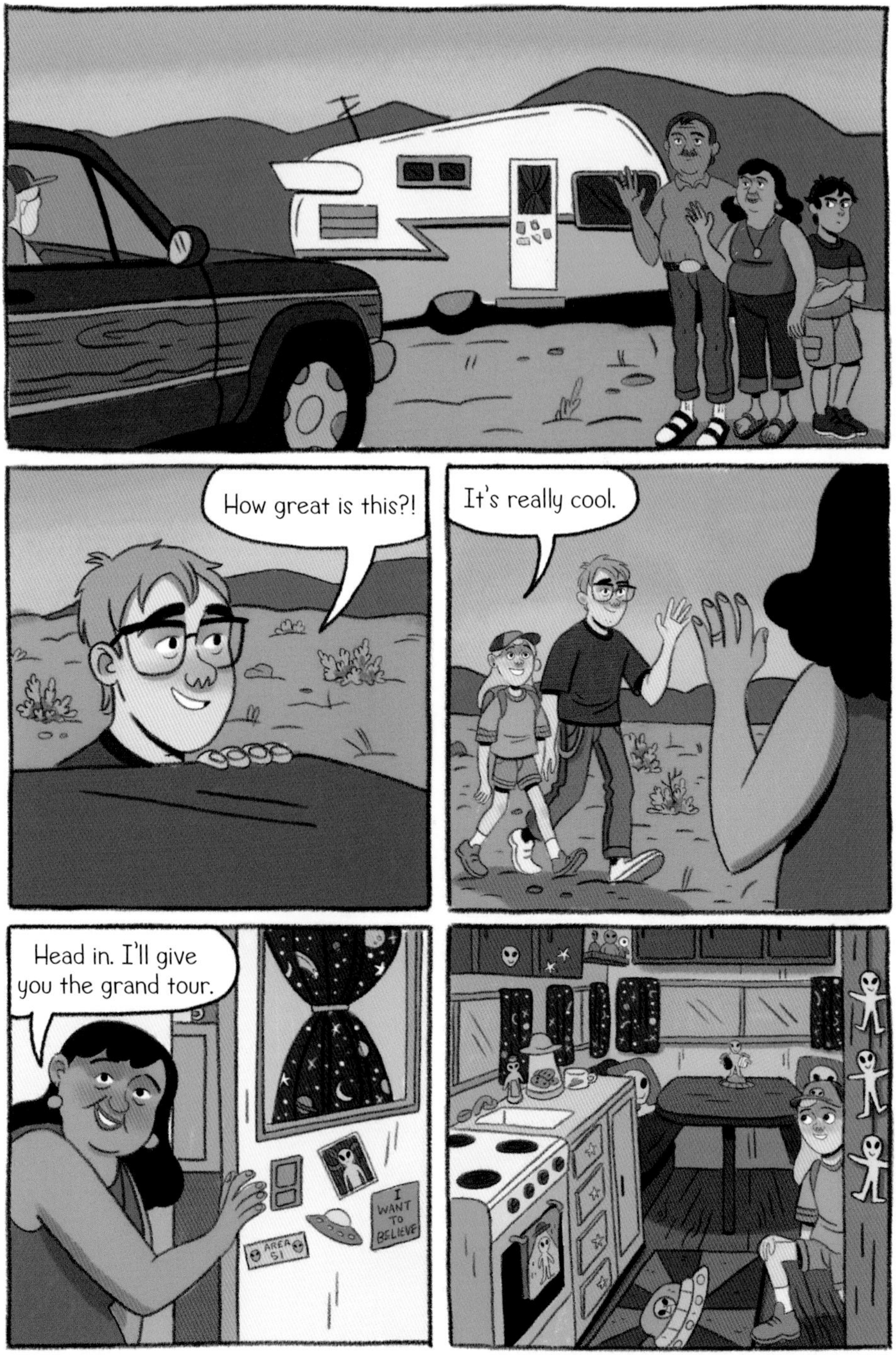
How great is this?!
It's really cool.
Head in. I'll give you the grand tour.
I WANT TO BELIEVE
AREA 51

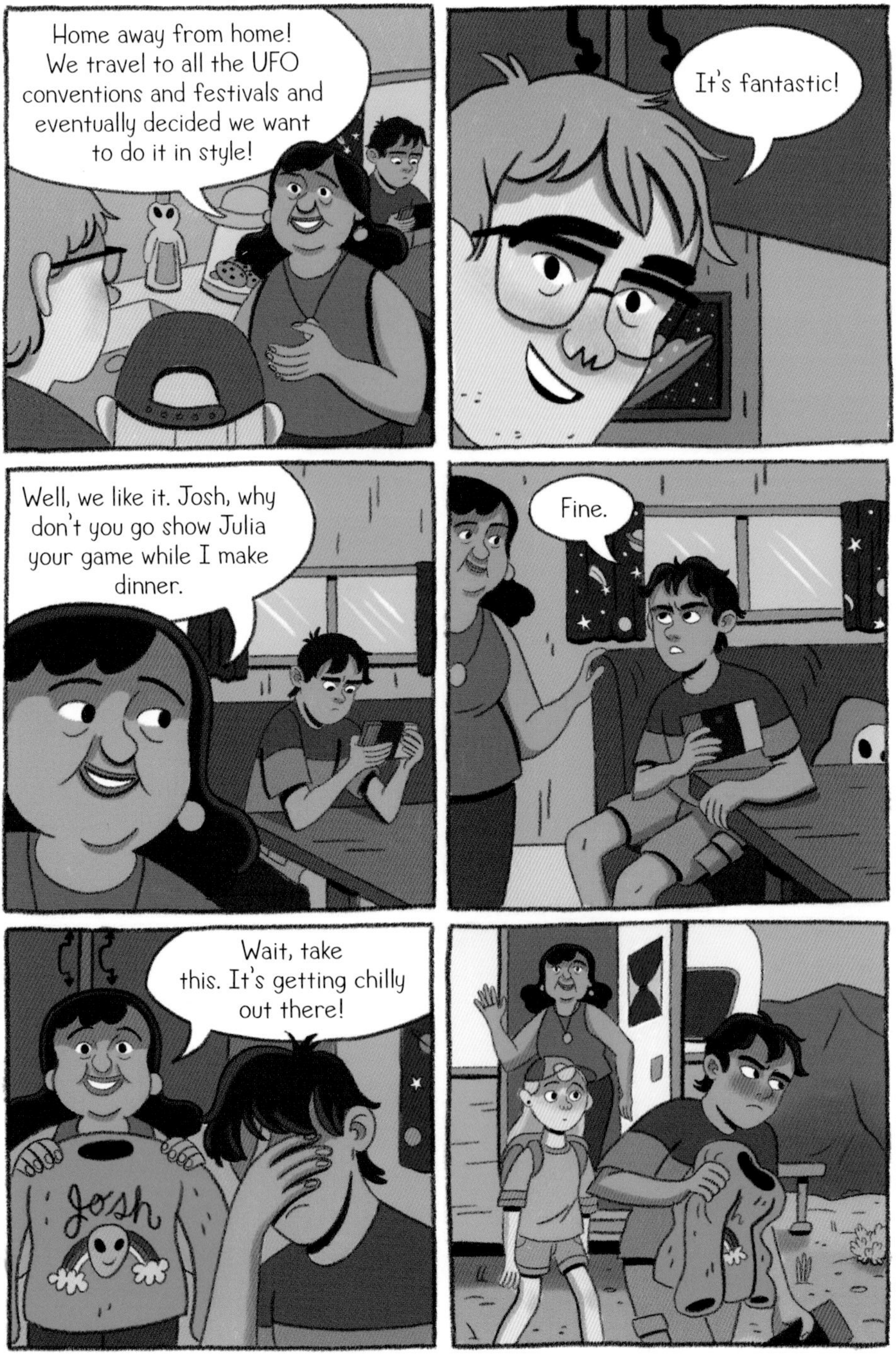
Home away from home! We travel to all the UFO conventions and festivals and eventually decided we want to do it in style!
It's fantastic!
Well, we like it. Josh, why don't you go show Julia your game while I make dinner.
Fine.
Wait, take this. It's getting chilly out there!
Josh

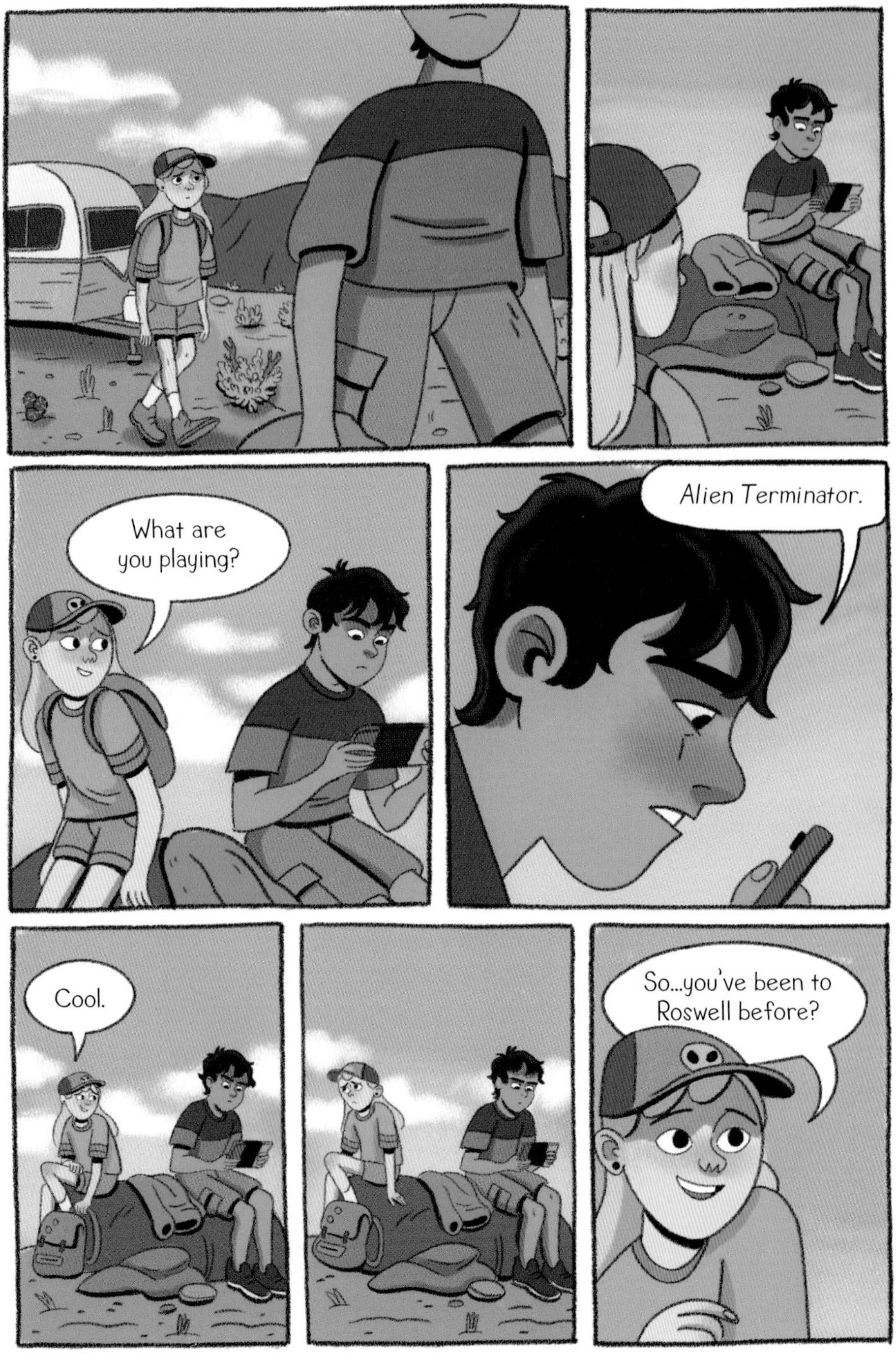
What are you playing?
Alien Terminator.
Cool.
So...you've been to Roswell before?

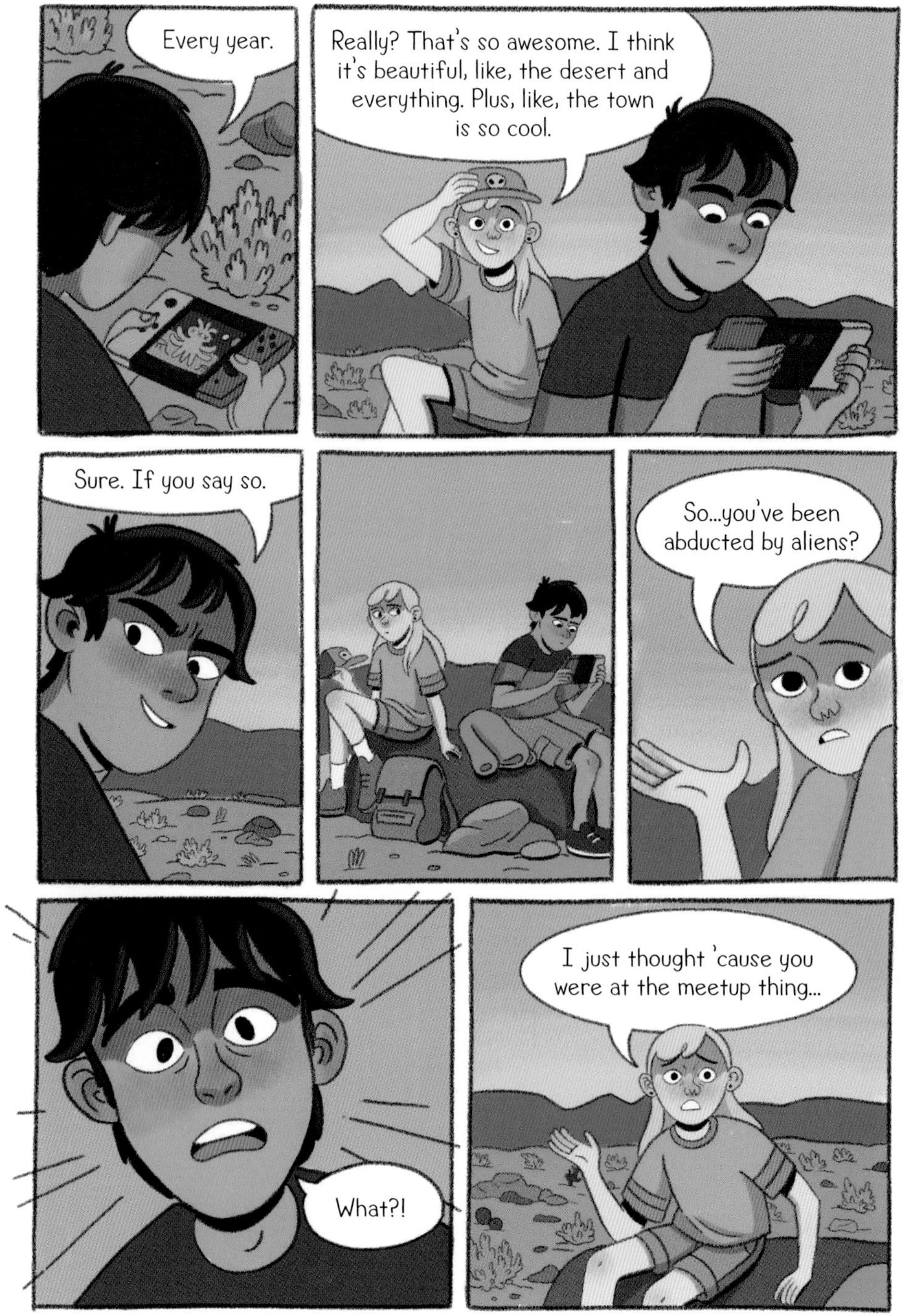

Every year.
Really? That's so awesome. I think it's beautiful, like, the desert and everything. Plus, like, the town is so cool.
Sure. If you say so.
So...you've been abducted by aliens?
What?!
I just thought 'cause you were at the meetup thing...

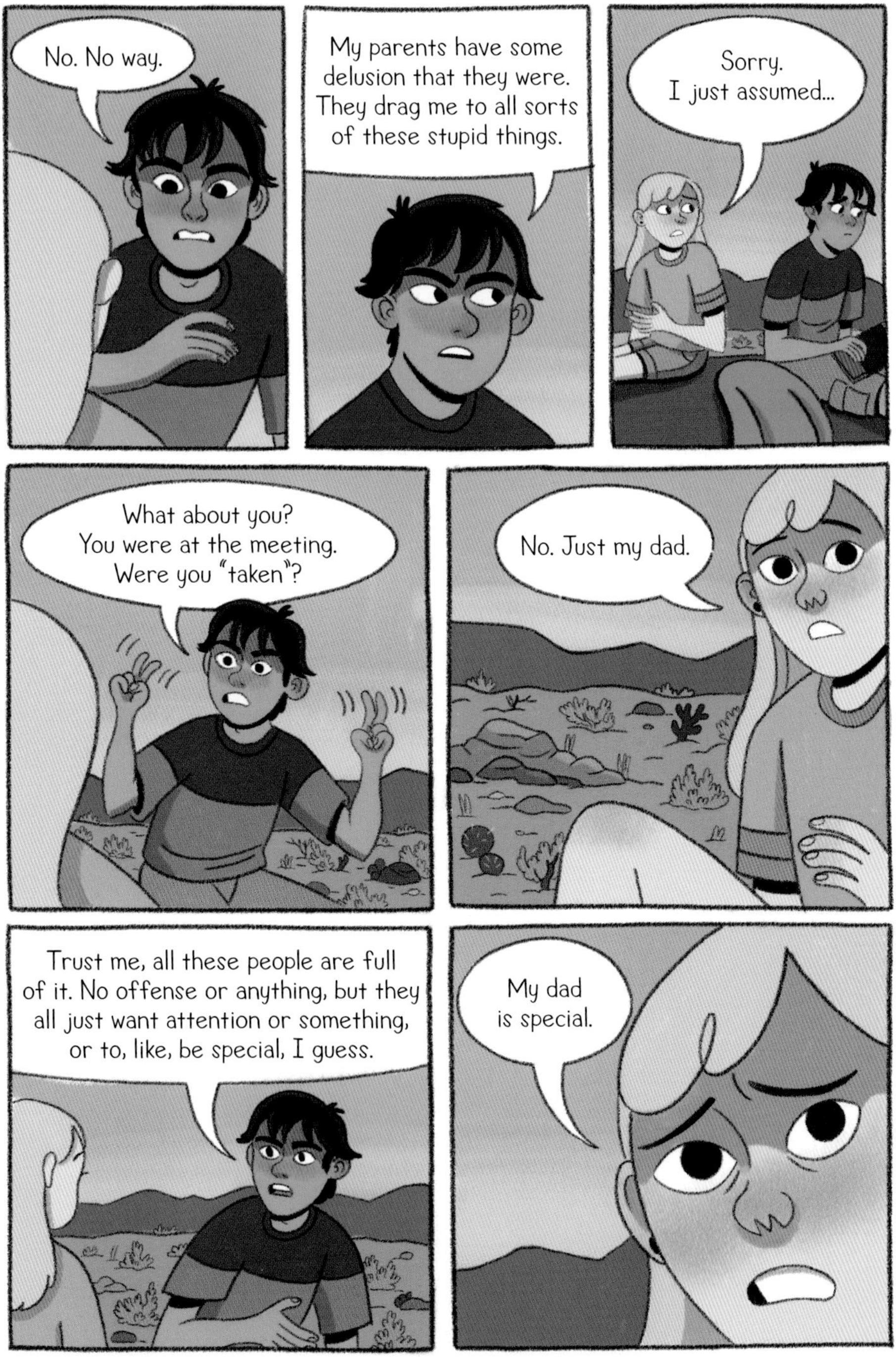
No. No way.
My parents have some delusion that they were. They drag me to all sorts of these stupid things.
Sorry. I just assumed...
What about you? You were at the meeting. Were you "taken"?
No. Just my dad.
Trust me, all these people are full of it. No offense or anything, but they all just want attention or something, or to, like, be special, I guess.
My dad is special.

You really think aliens came from like a billion trillion miles away, looked all over Earth just to find your dad standing in the backyard in his underwear, and thought they'd, like, take him to space, just for kicks?

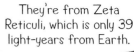

They're from Zeta Reticuli, which is only 39 light-years from Earth.

Seriously? Do you hear yourself? Your dad is just as full of it as the rest of them.

You don't even know him.

Whatever.

You travel all over to all these UFO conventions, and, like, you really don't believe any of it's real?! What about Rendlesham Forest or the Phoenix Lights?

I'm not saying that people don't see lights in the sky or some weird stuff. I'm saying my parents do this not because aliens kidnapped them, but because it makes them feel important.

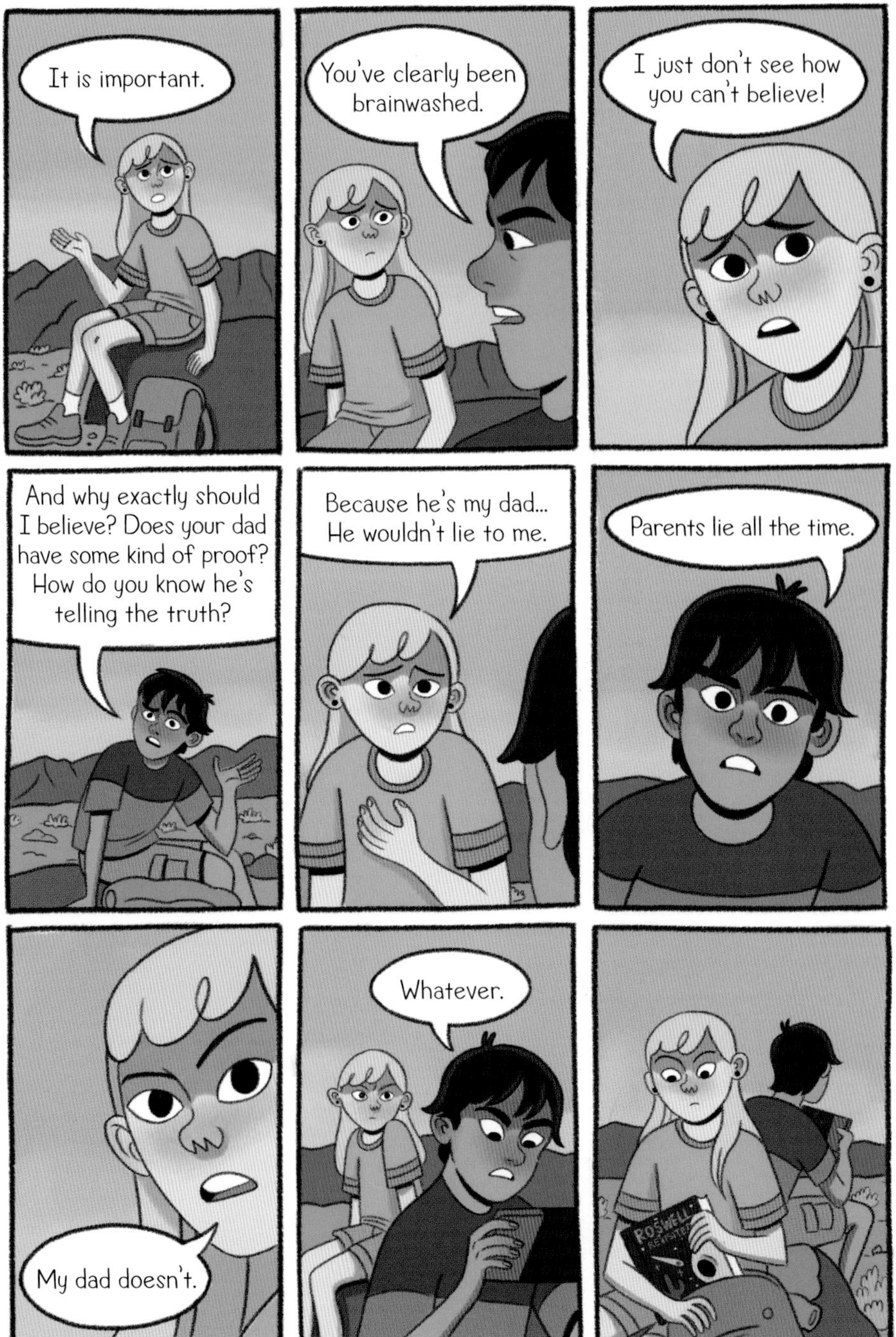
It is important.
You've clearly been brainwashed.
I just don't see how you can't believe!
And why exactly should I believe? Does your dad have some kind of proof? How do you know he's telling the truth?
Because he's my dad... He wouldn't lie to me.
Parents lie all the time.
My dad doesn't.
Whatever.
ROSWELL REVISITED

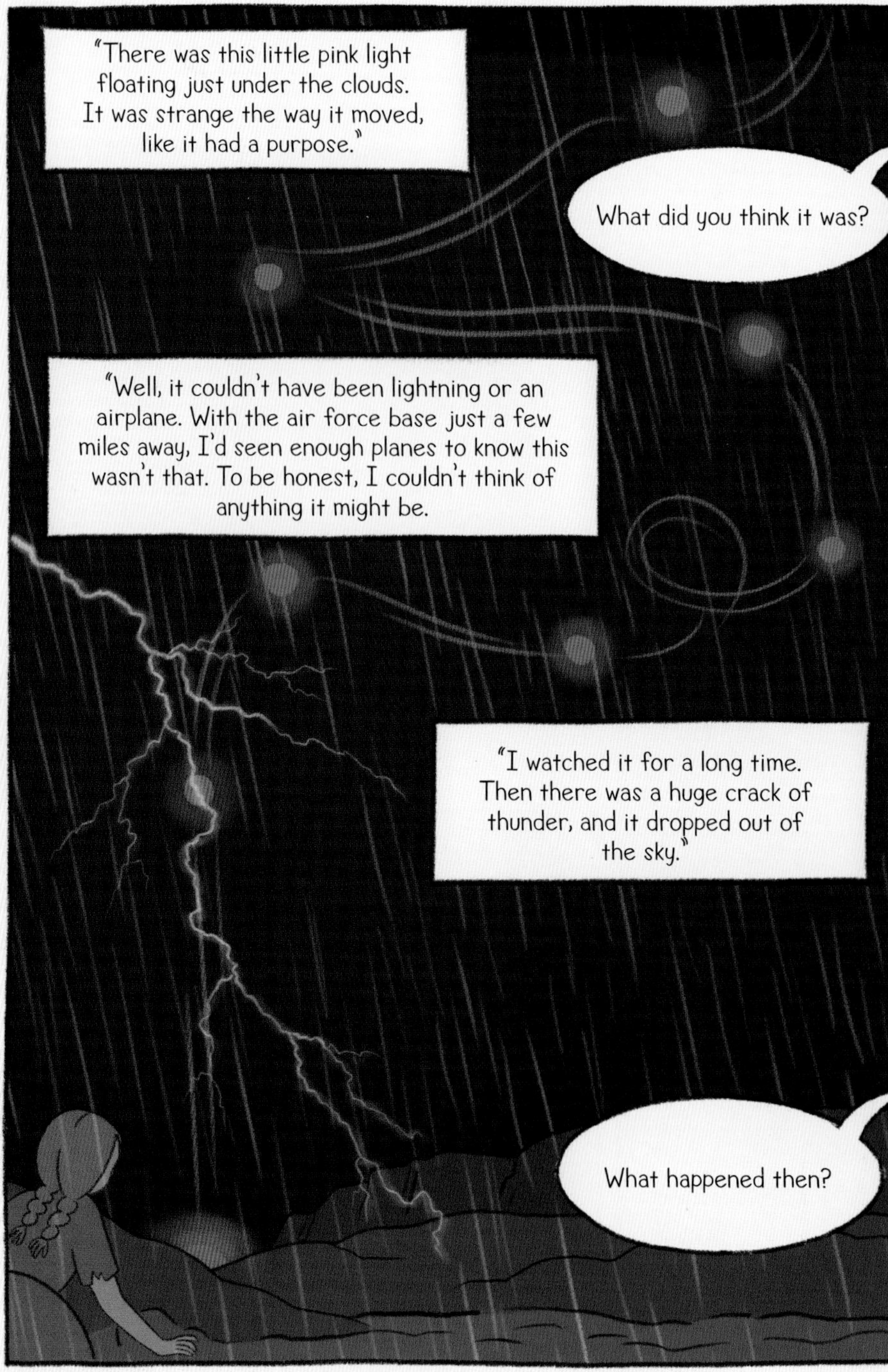

"There was this little pink light floating just under the clouds. It was strange the way it moved, like it had a purpose."
What did you think it was?
"Well, it couldn't have been lightning or an airplane. With the air force base just a few miles away, I'd seen enough planes to know this wasn't that. To be honest, I couldn't think of anything it might be.
"I watched it for a long time. Then there was a huge crack of thunder, and it dropped out of the sky."
What happened then?

"I could see a pink glow just over the horizon, and I began to walk toward it.

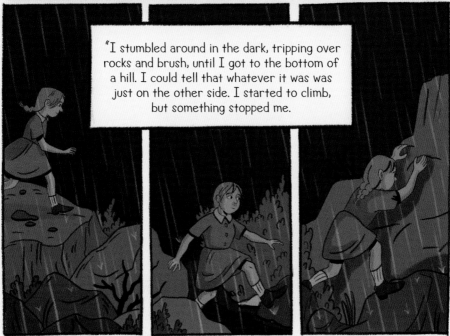

"I stumbled around in the dark, tripping over rocks and brush, until I got to the bottom of a hill. I could tell that whatever it was was just on the other side. I started to climb, but something stopped me.

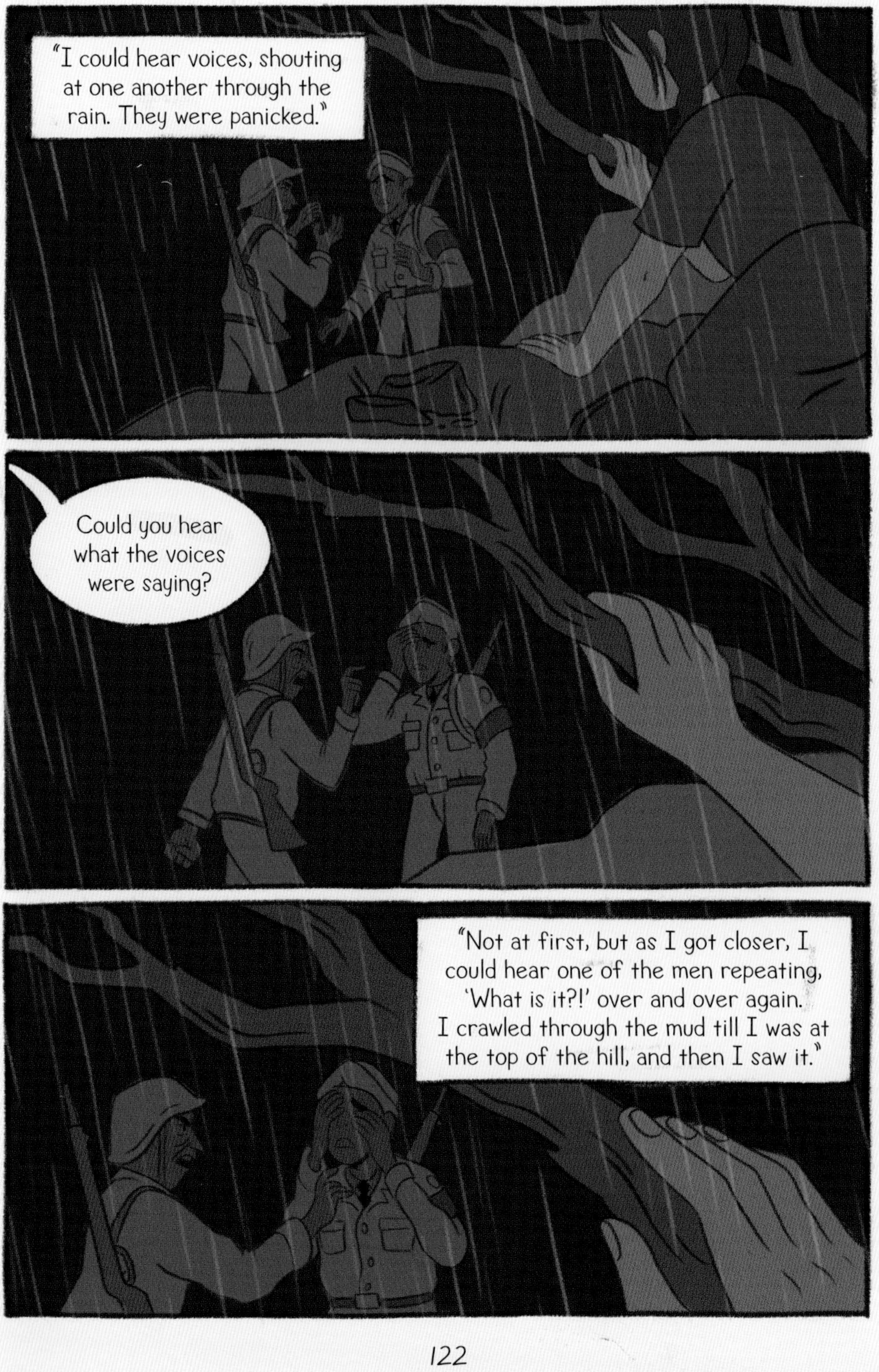
"I could hear voices, shouting at one another through the rain. They were panicked."
Could you hear what the voices were saying?
"Not at first, but as I got closer, I could hear one of the men repeating, 'What is it?!' over and over again. I crawled through the mud till I was at the top of the hill, and then I saw it."

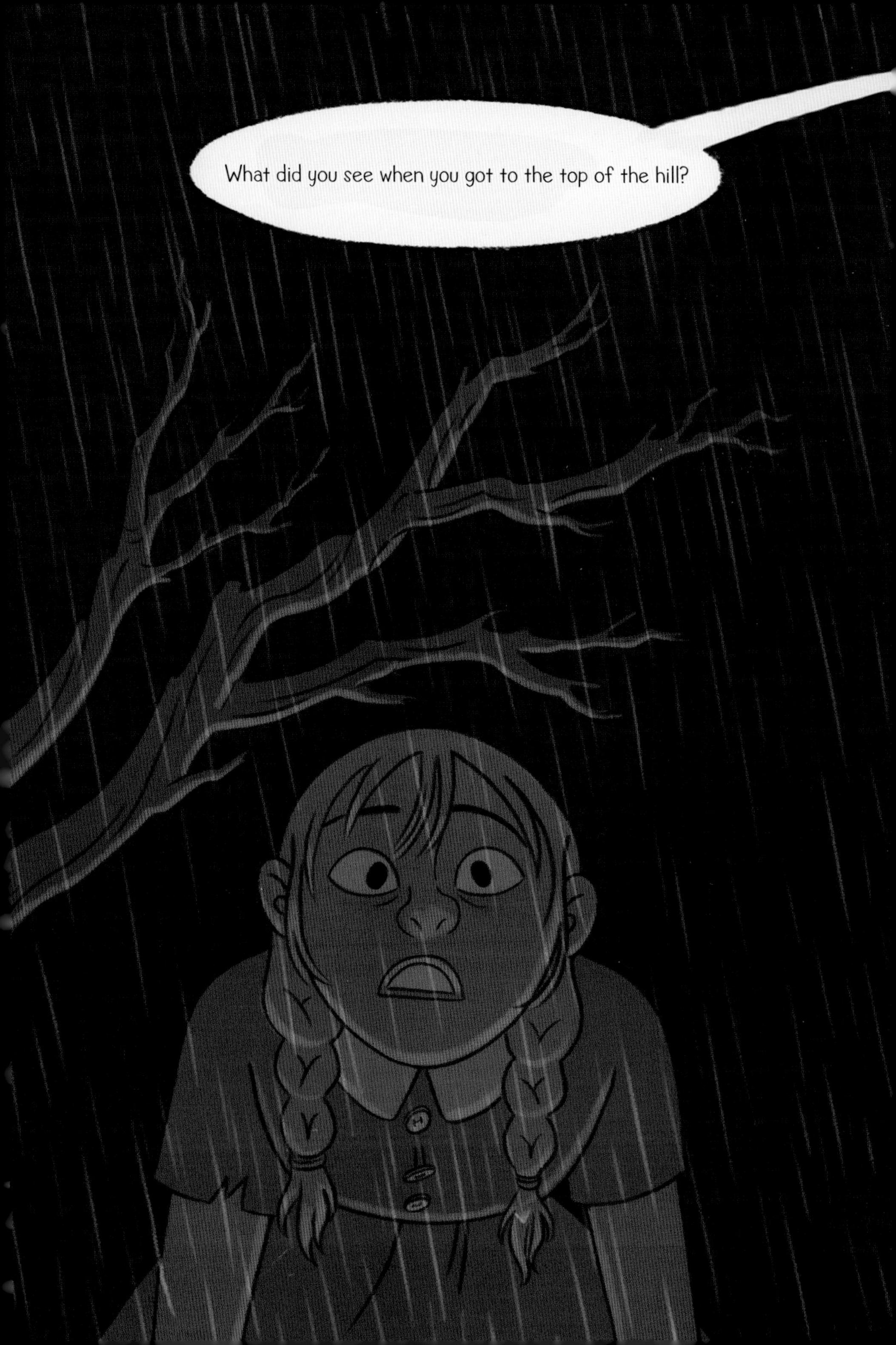
What did you see when you got to the top of the hill?

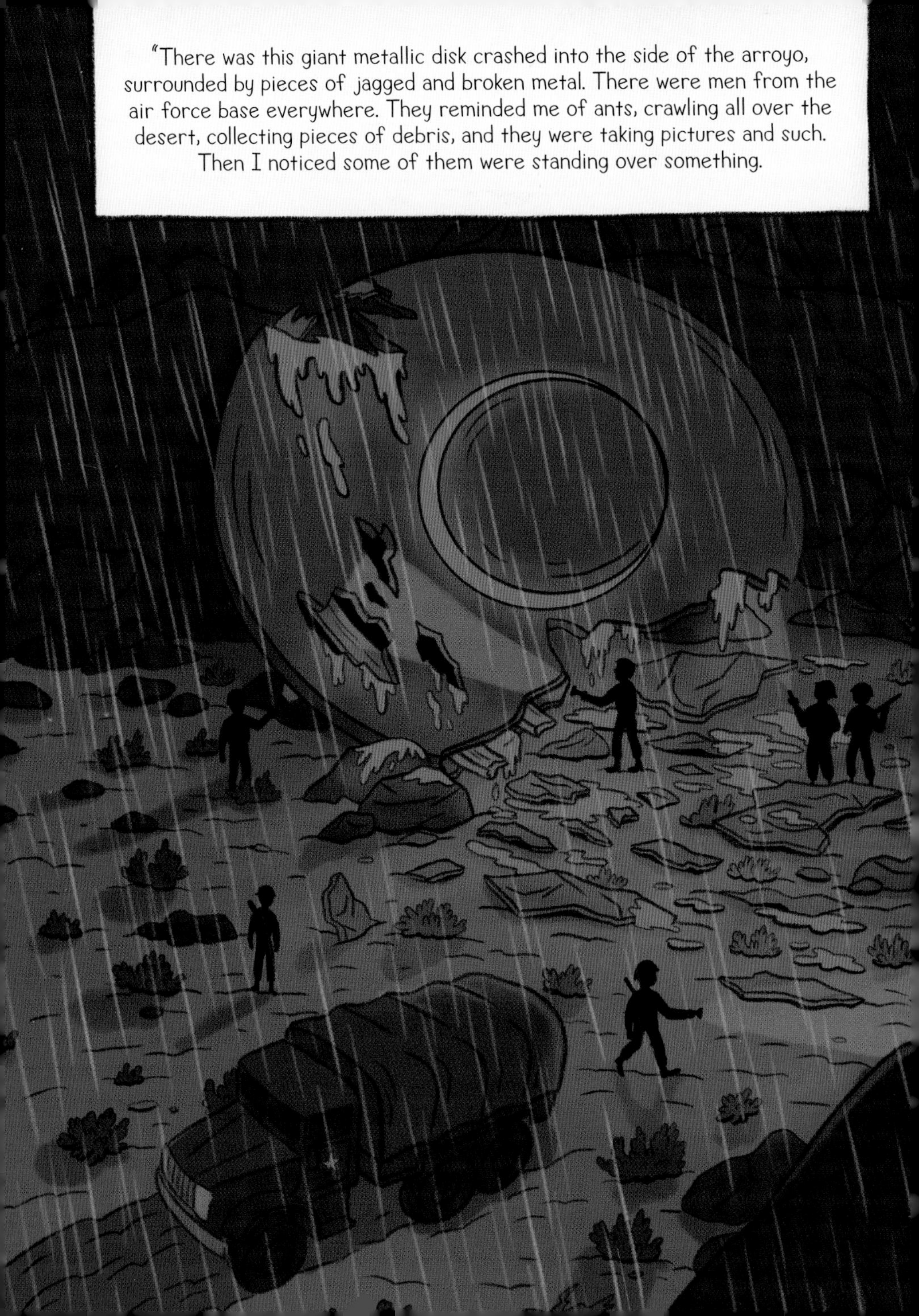
"There was this giant metallic disk crashed into the side of the arroyo, surrounded by pieces of jagged and broken metal. There were men from the air force base everywhere. They reminded me of ants, crawling all over the desert, collecting pieces of debris, and they were taking pictures and such. Then I noticed some of them were standing over something.

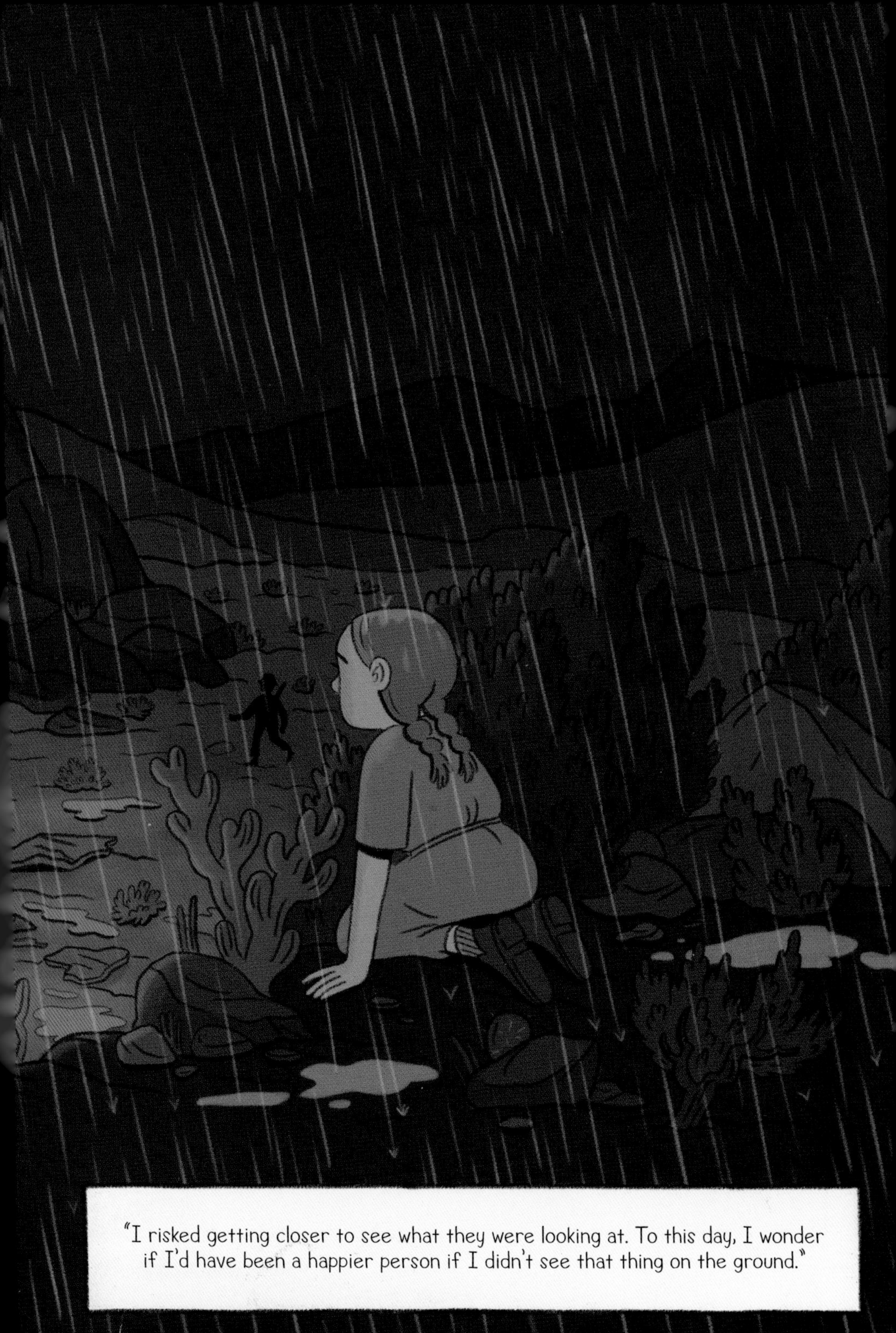
"I risked getting closer to see what they were looking at. To this day, I wonder if I'd have been a happier person if I didn't see that thing on the ground."

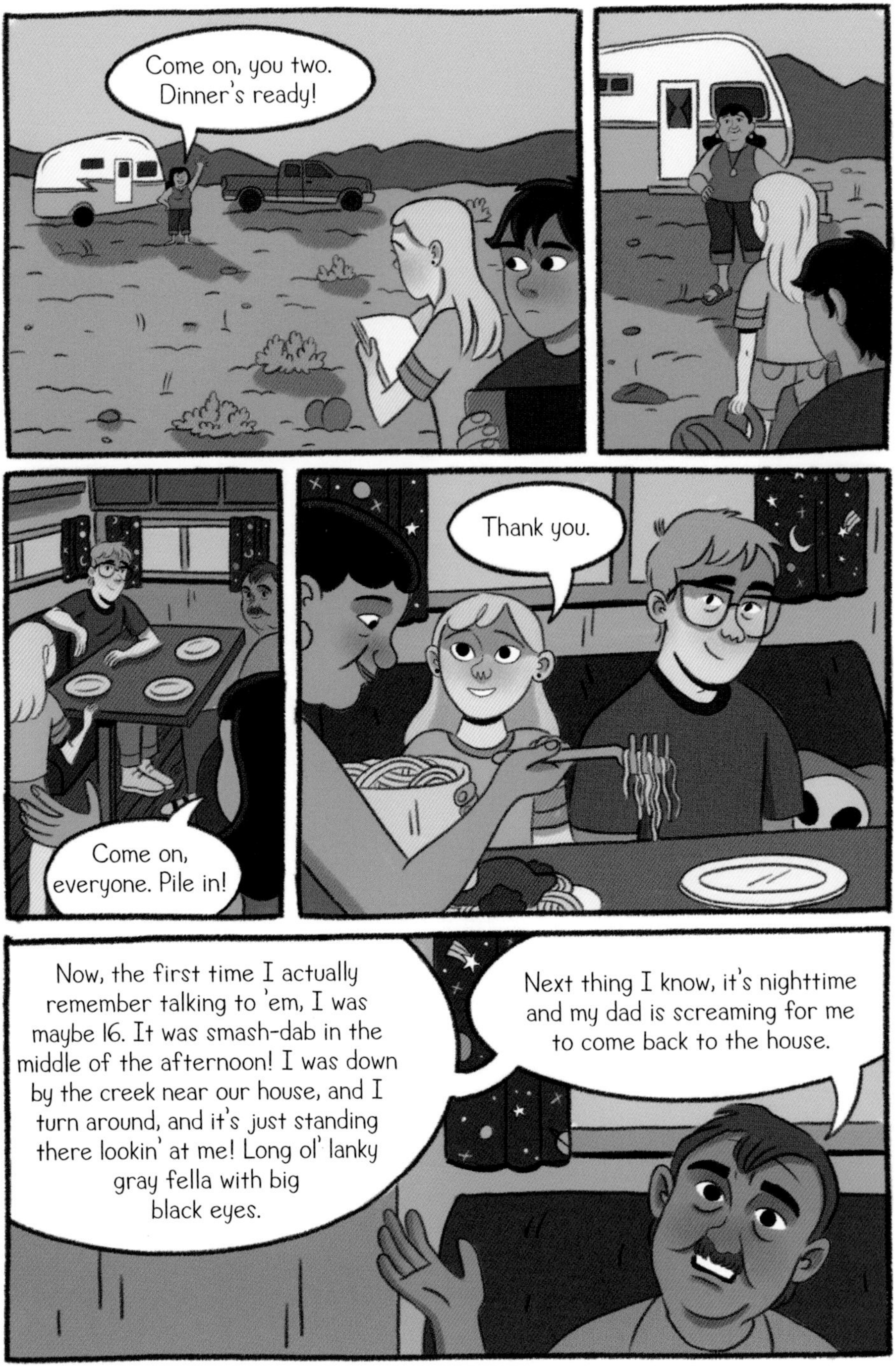

Come on, you two. Dinner's ready!
Thank you.
Come on, everyone. Pile in!
Now, the first time I actually remember talking to 'em, I was maybe 16. It was smash-dab in the middle of the afternoon! I was down by the creek near our house, and I turn around, and it's just standing there lookin' at me! Long ol' lanky gray fella with big black eyes.
Next thing I know, it's nighttime and my dad is screaming for me to come back to the house.

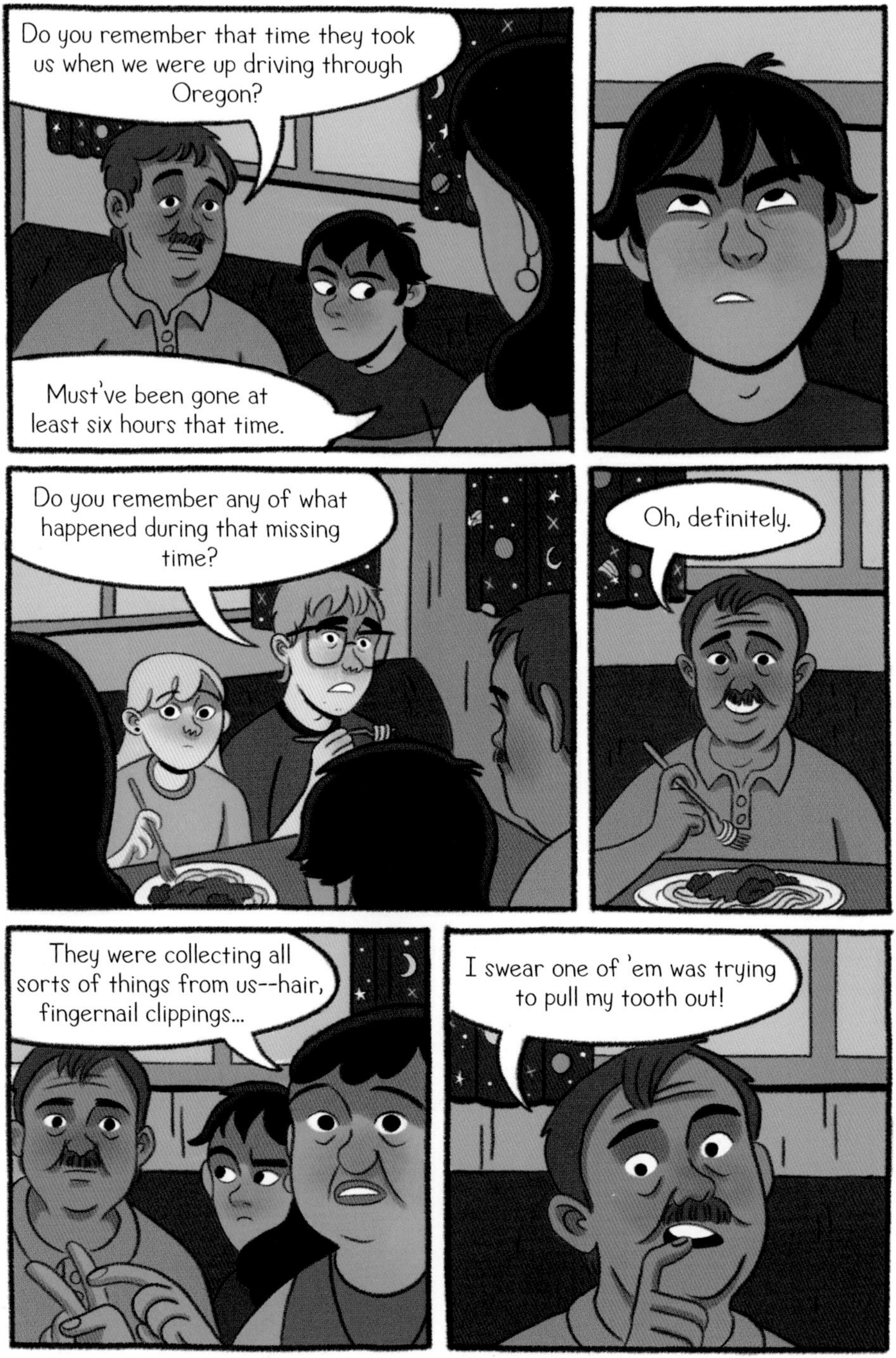
Do you remember that time they took us when we were up driving through Oregon?
Must've been gone at least six hours that time.
Do you remember any of what happened during that missing time?
Oh, definitely.
They were collecting all sorts of things from us--hair, fingernail clippings...
I swear one of 'em was trying to pull my tooth out!

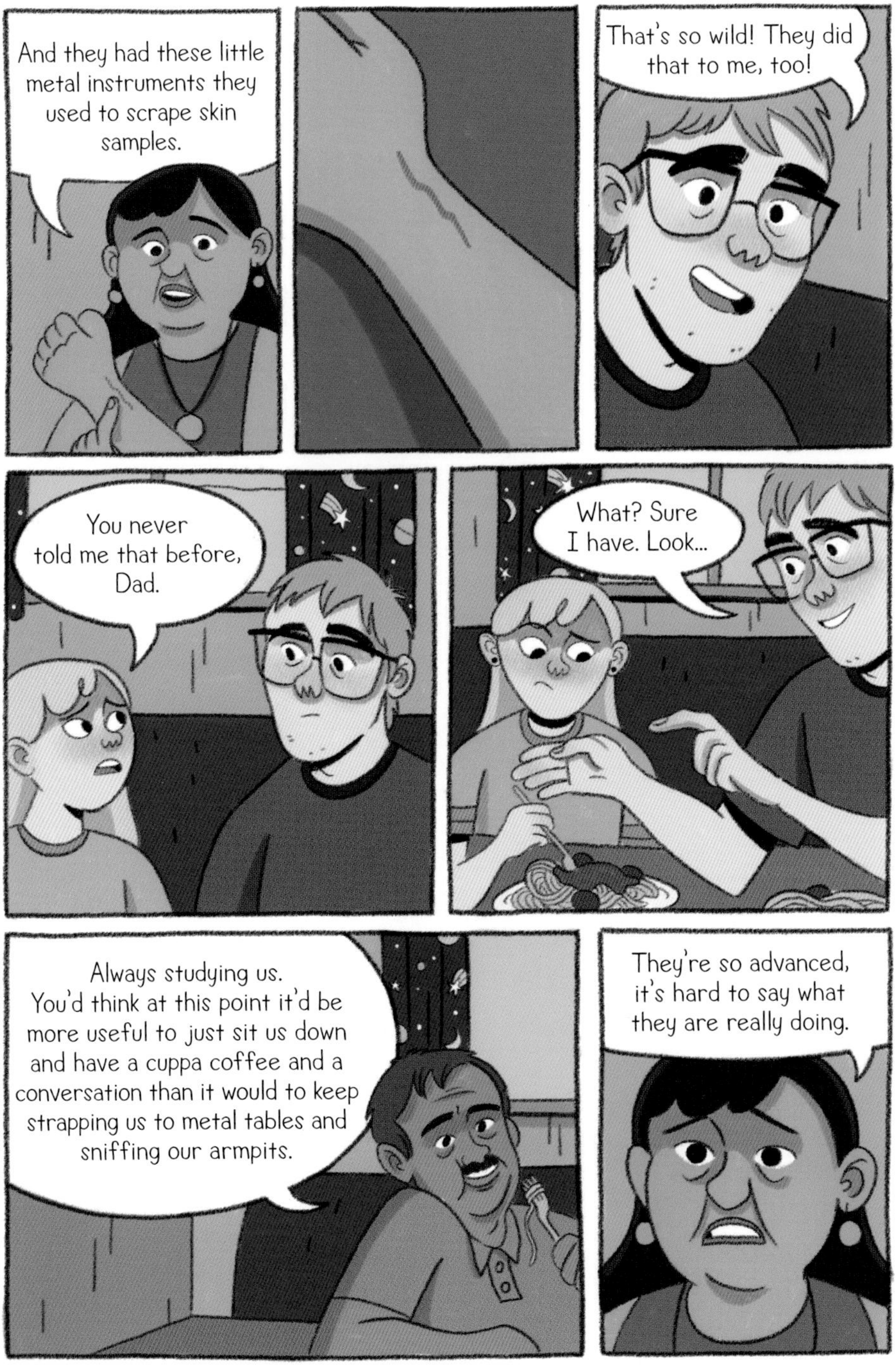
And they had these little metal instruments they used to scrape skin samples.
That's so wild! They did that to me, too!
You never told me that before, Dad.
What? Sure I have. Look...
Always studying us. You'd think at this point it'd be more useful to just sit us down and have a cuppa coffee and a conversation than it would to keep strapping us to metal tables and sniffing our armpits.
They're so advanced, it's hard to say what they are really doing.

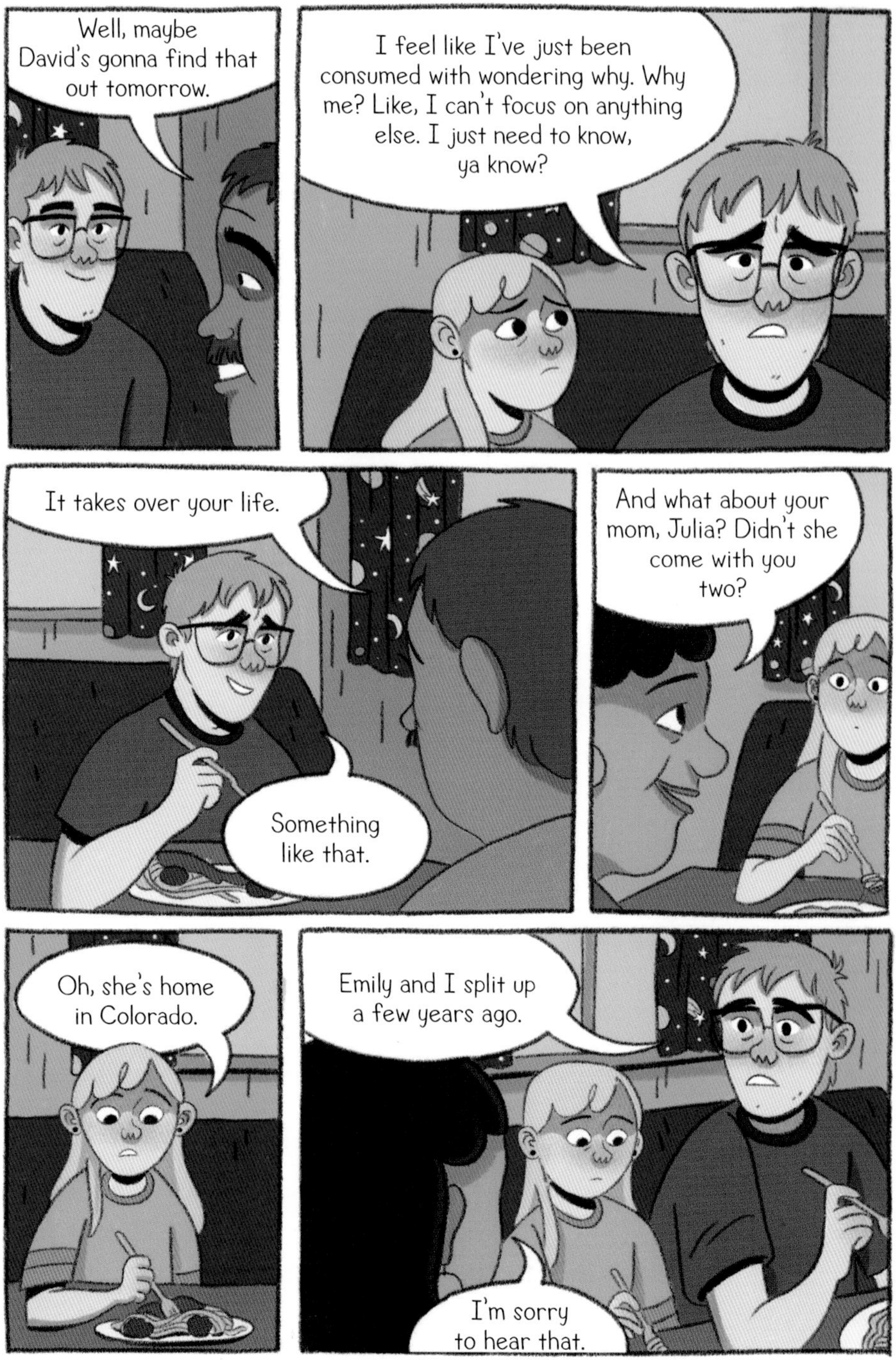
Well, maybe David's gonna find that out tomorrow.
I feel like I've just been consumed with wondering why. Why me? Like, I can't focus on anything else. I just need to know, ya know?
It takes over your life.
Something like that.
And what about your mom, Julia? Didn't she come with you two?
Oh, she's home in Colorado.
Emily and I split up a few years ago.
I'm sorry to hear that.

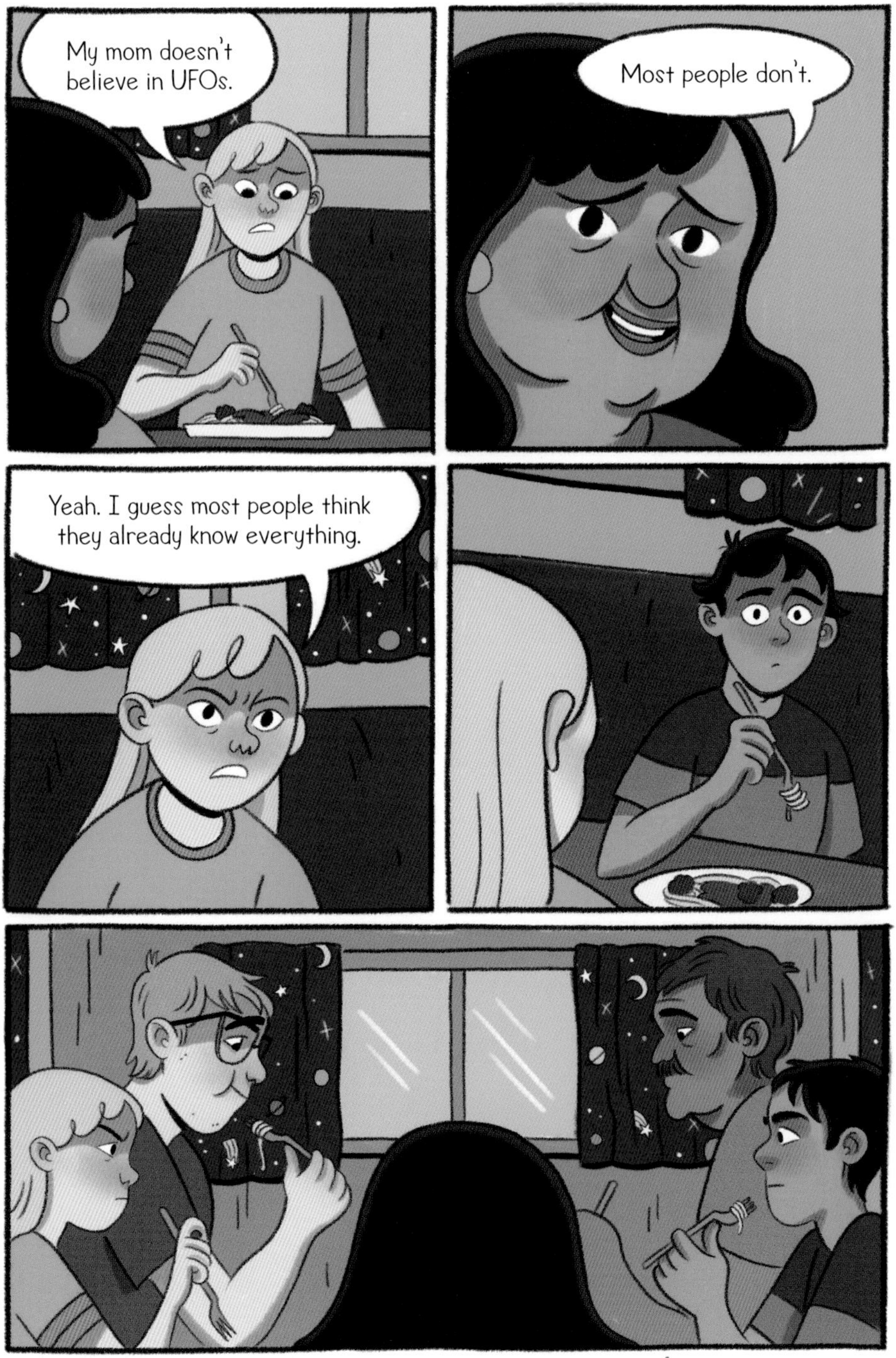
My mom doesn't believe in UFOs.
Most people don't.
Yeah. I guess most people think they already know everything.

Bye!

Thanks for dinner!

They sure are nice, don't you think?

Yeah.

That Josh kid was kinda cute...

Dad! Gross!

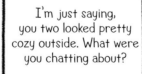

I'm just saying, you two looked pretty cozy outside. What were you chatting about?

He was a jerk.

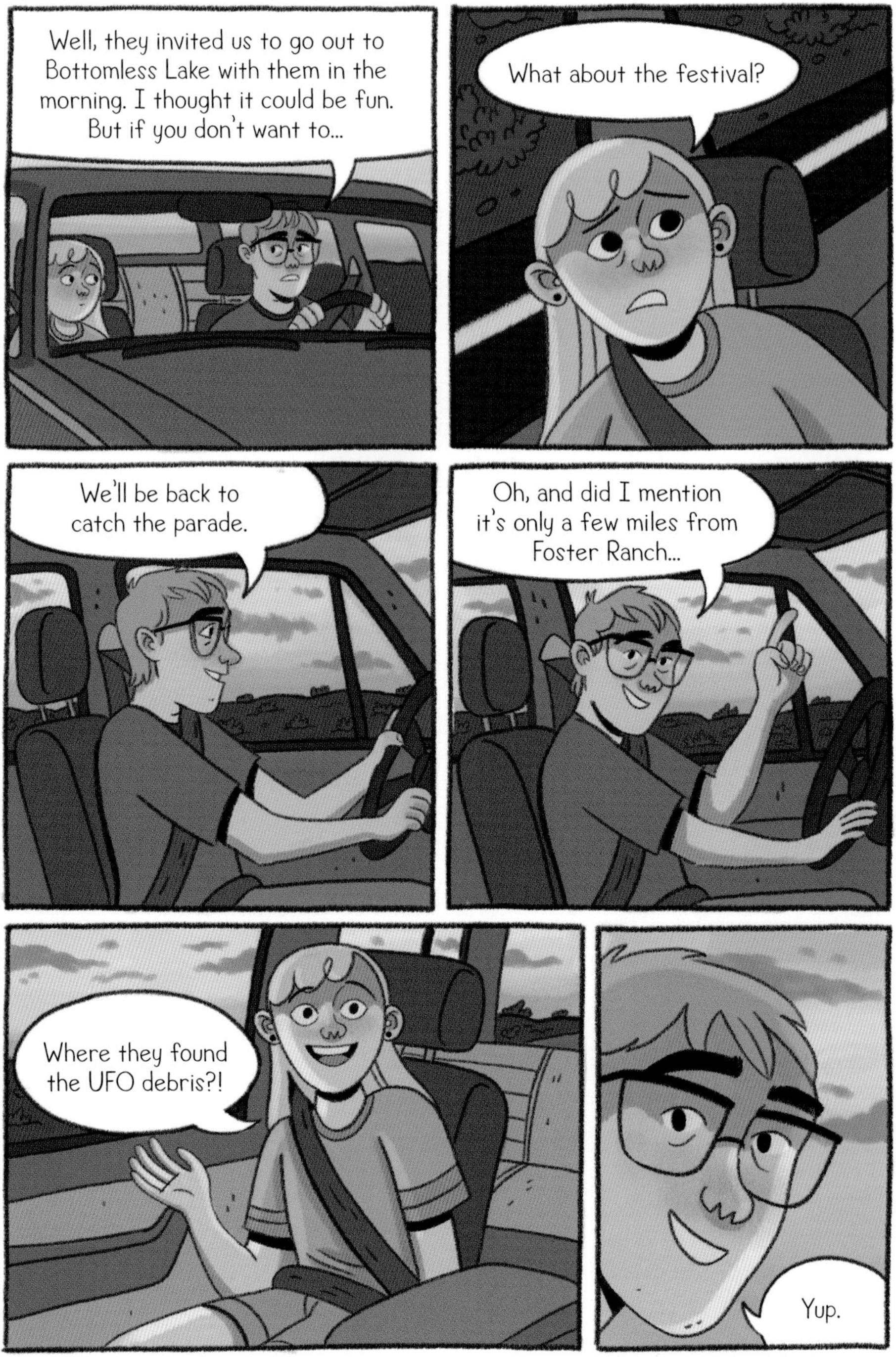

Well, they invited us to go out to Bottomless Lake with them in the morning. I thought it could be fun. But if you don't want to...
What about the festival?
We'll be back to catch the parade.
Oh, and did I mention it's only a few miles from Foster Ranch...
Where they found the UFO debris?!
Yup.

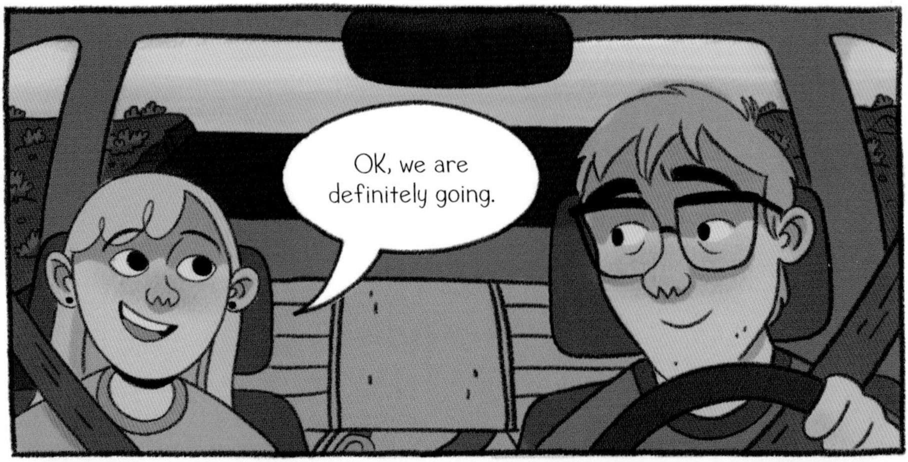
OK, we are definitely going.

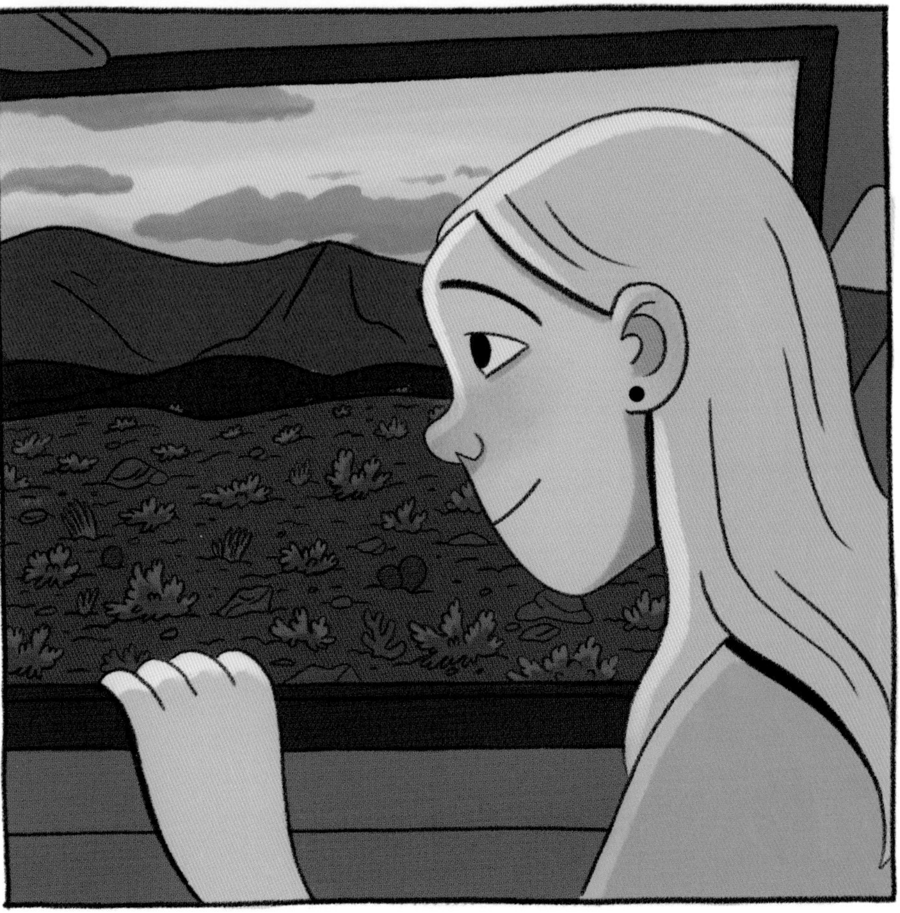

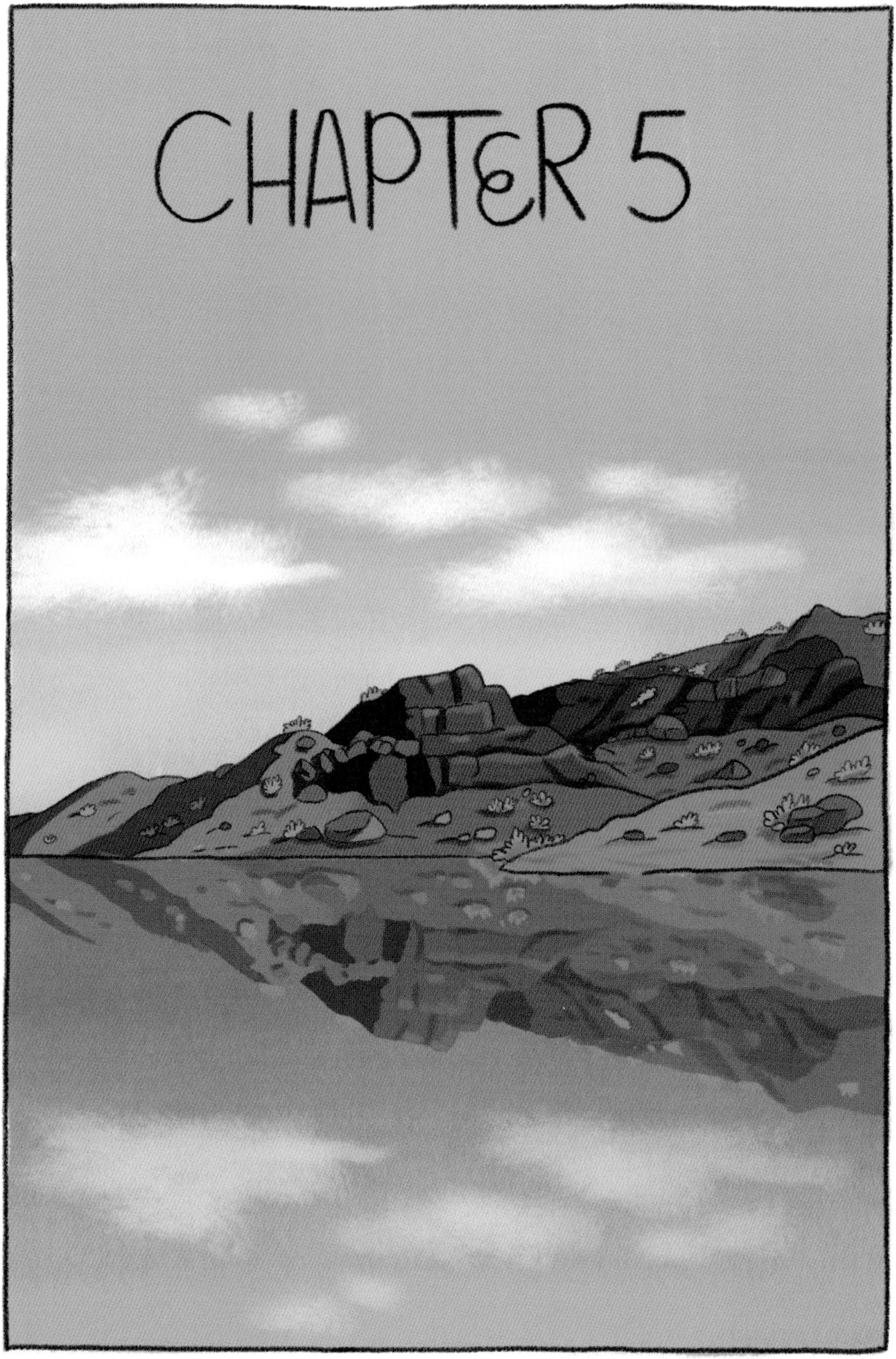
CHAPTER 5

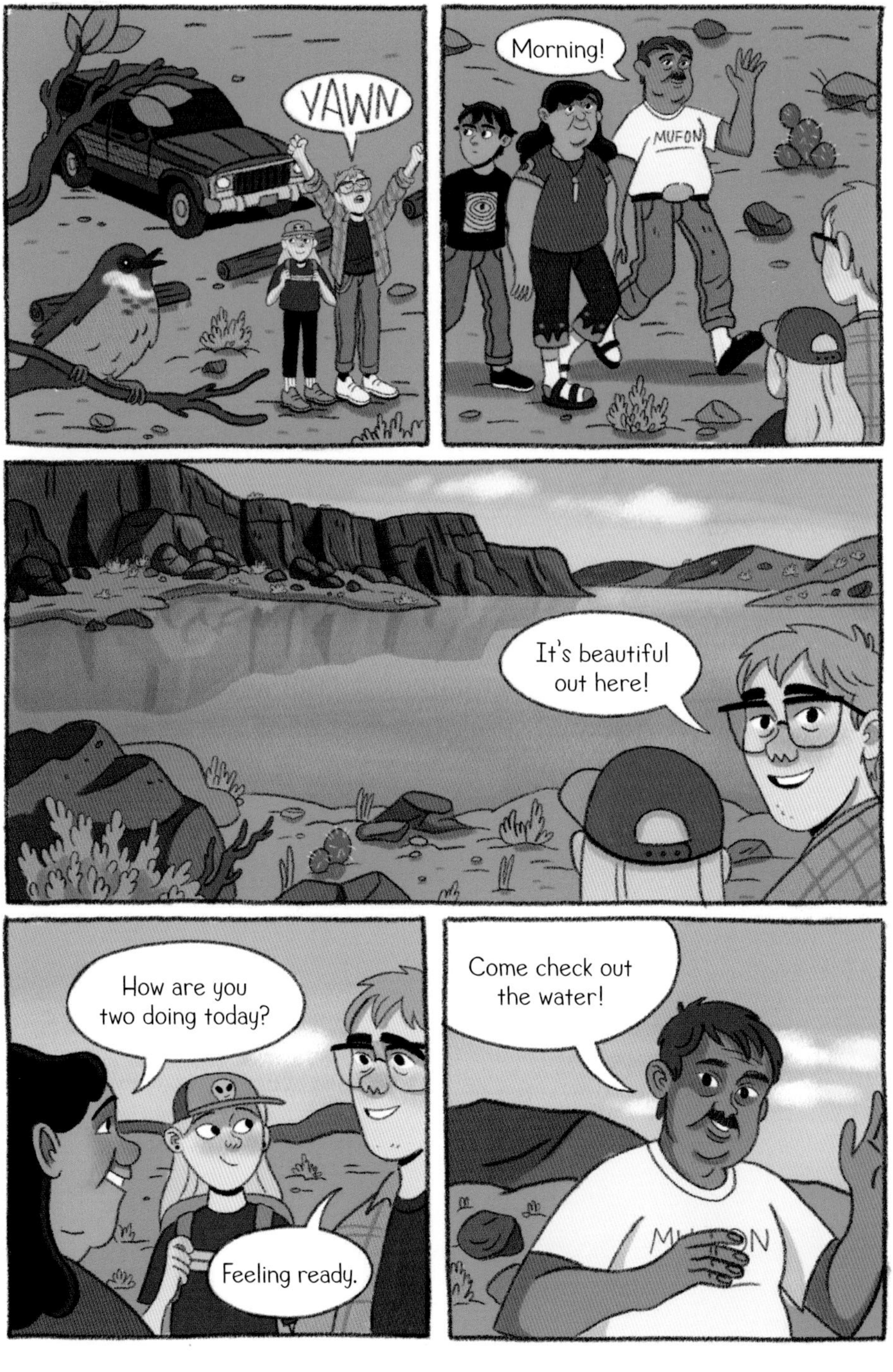
YAWN
Morning!
MUFON
It's beautiful out here!
How are you two doing today?
Feeling ready.
Come check out the water!

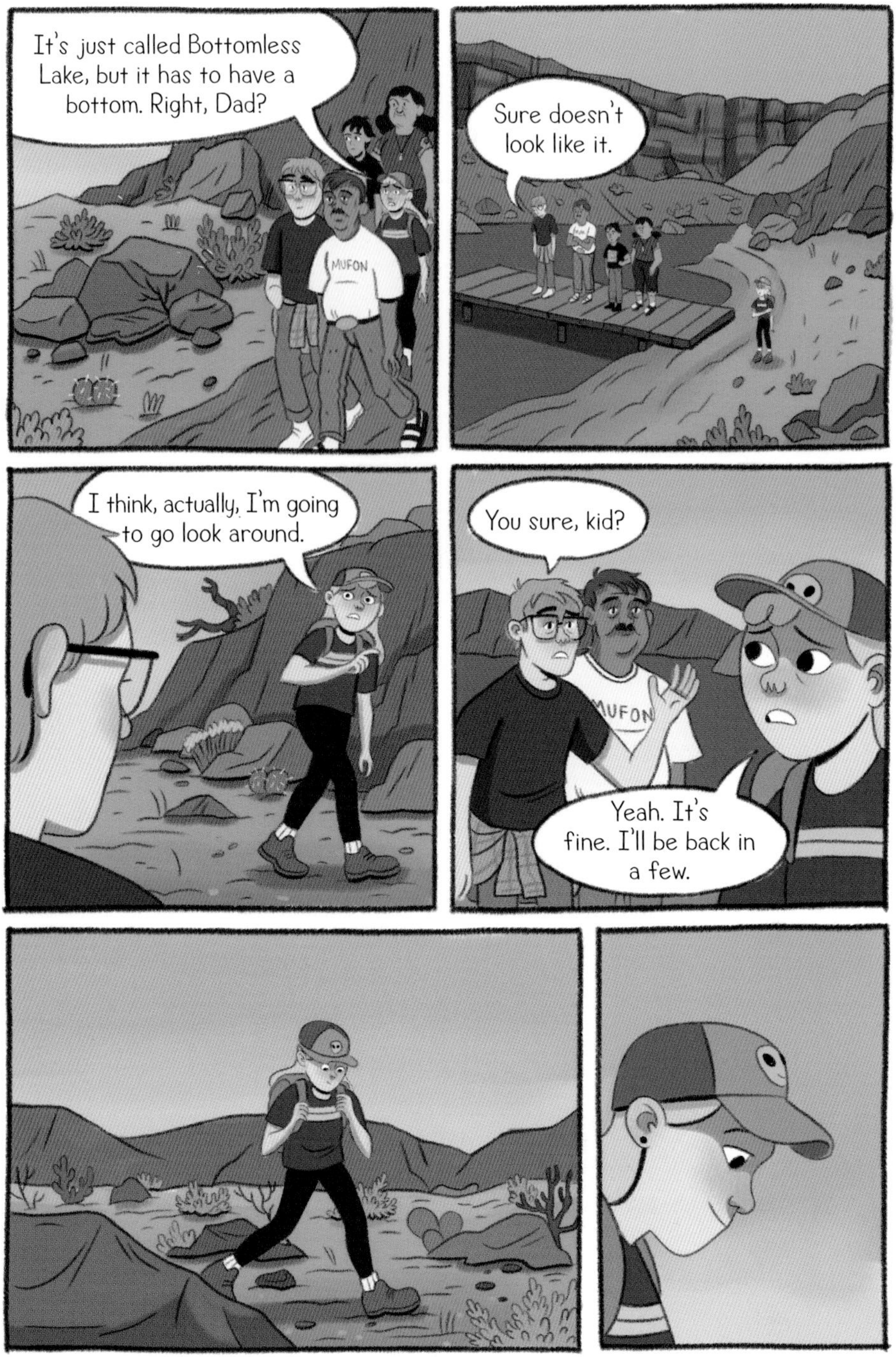
It's just called Bottomless Lake, but it has to have a bottom. Right, Dad?
MUFON
Sure doesn't look like it.
I think, actually, I'm going to go look around.
You sure, kid?
MUFON
Yeah. It's fine. I'll be back in a few.

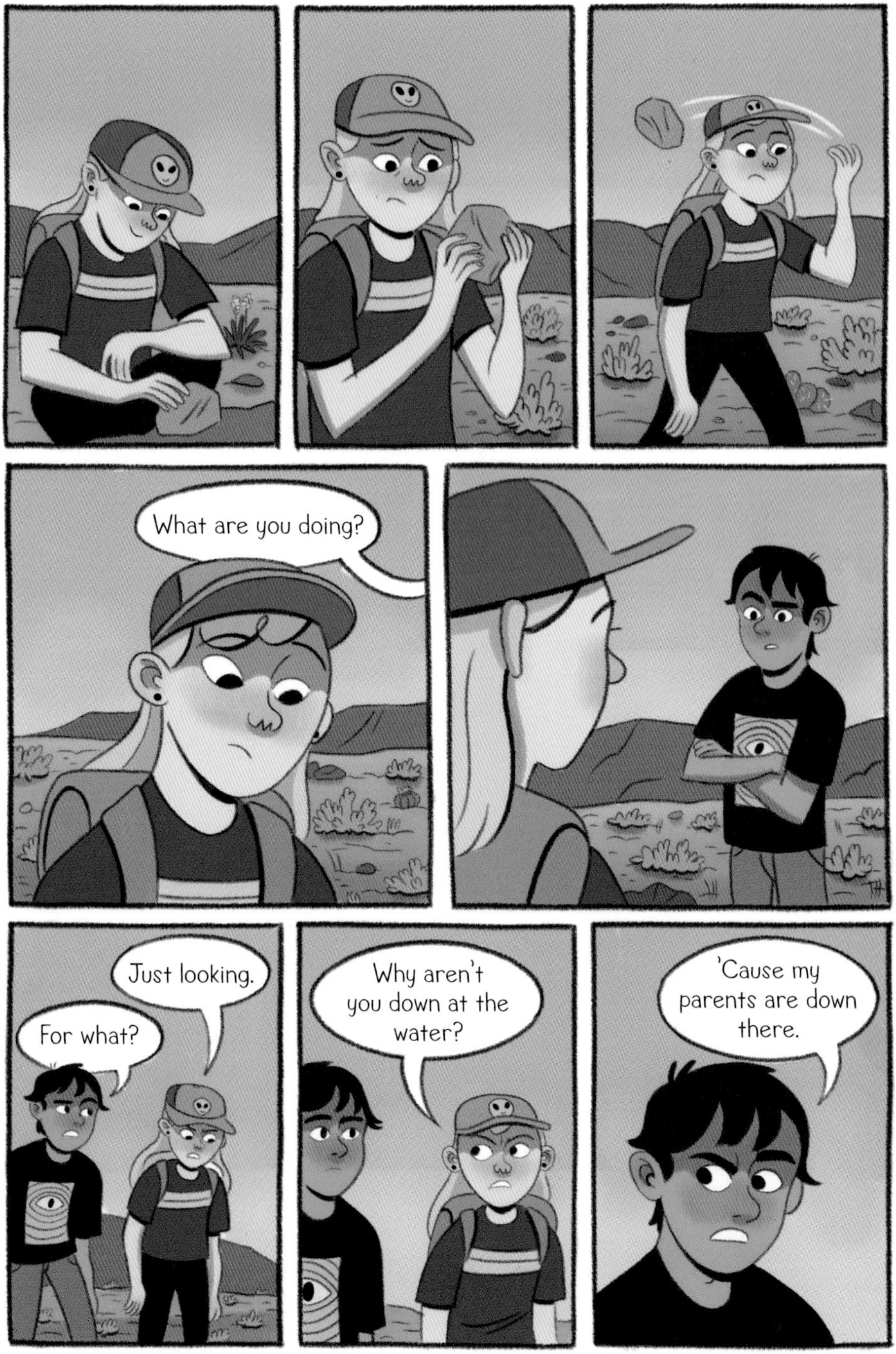
What are you doing?
Just looking.
For what?
Why aren't you down at the water?
'Cause my parents are down there.

Your parents seem really nice.

I guess.

BZZZT

BZZZT

Sara Calling

Who was that?

Just my friend Sara.

So why didn't you answer?

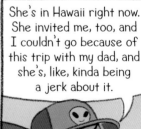

She's in Hawaii right now. She invited me, too, and I couldn't go because of this trip with my dad, and she's, like, kinda being a jerk about it.

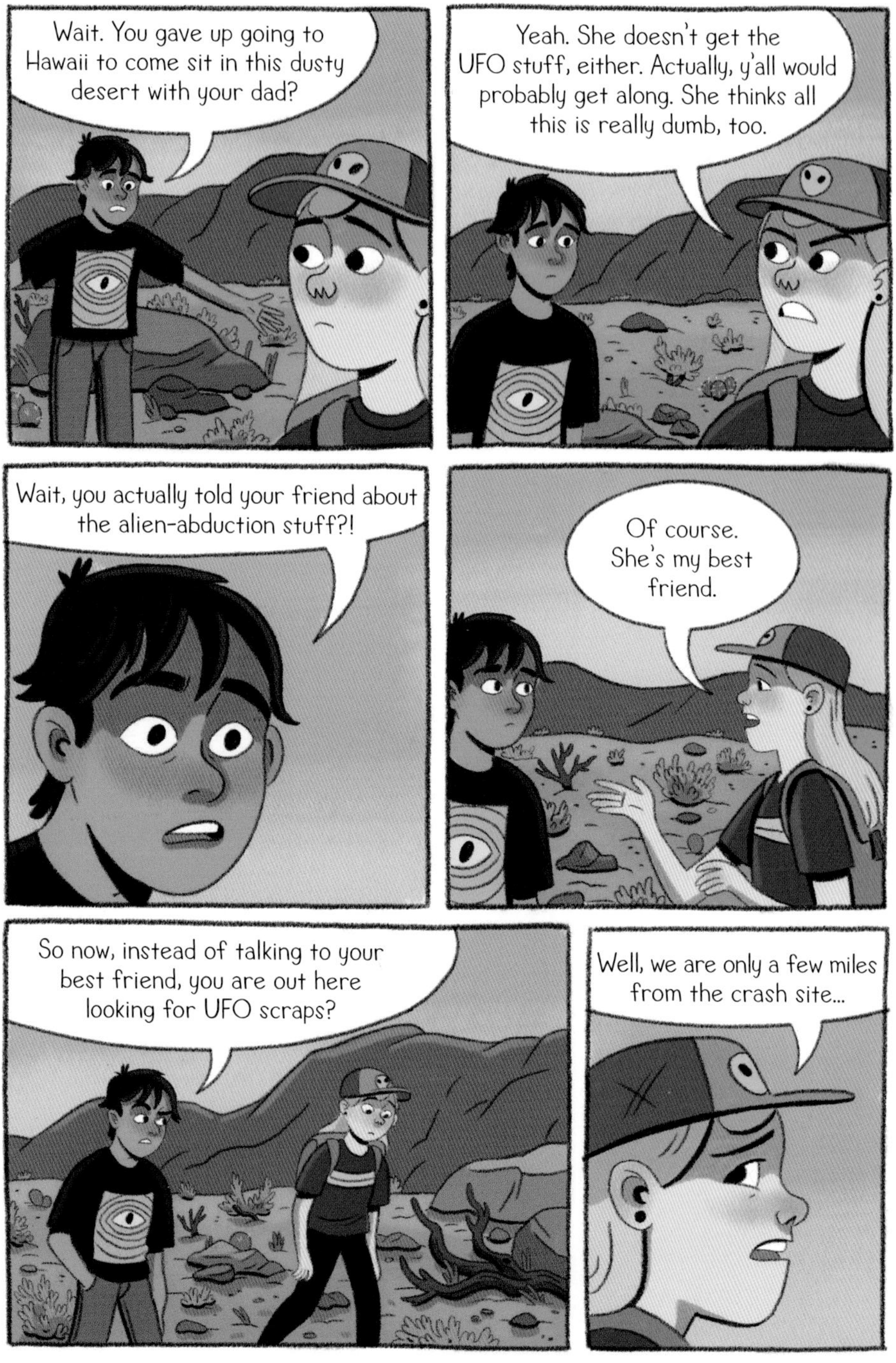

Wait. You gave up going to Hawaii to come sit in this dusty desert with your dad?
Yeah. She doesn't get the UFO stuff, either. Actually, y'all would probably get along. She thinks all this is really dumb, too.
Wait, you actually told your friend about the alien-abduction stuff?!
Of course. She's my best friend.
So now, instead of talking to your best friend, you are out here looking for UFO scraps?
Well, we are only a few miles from the crash site...

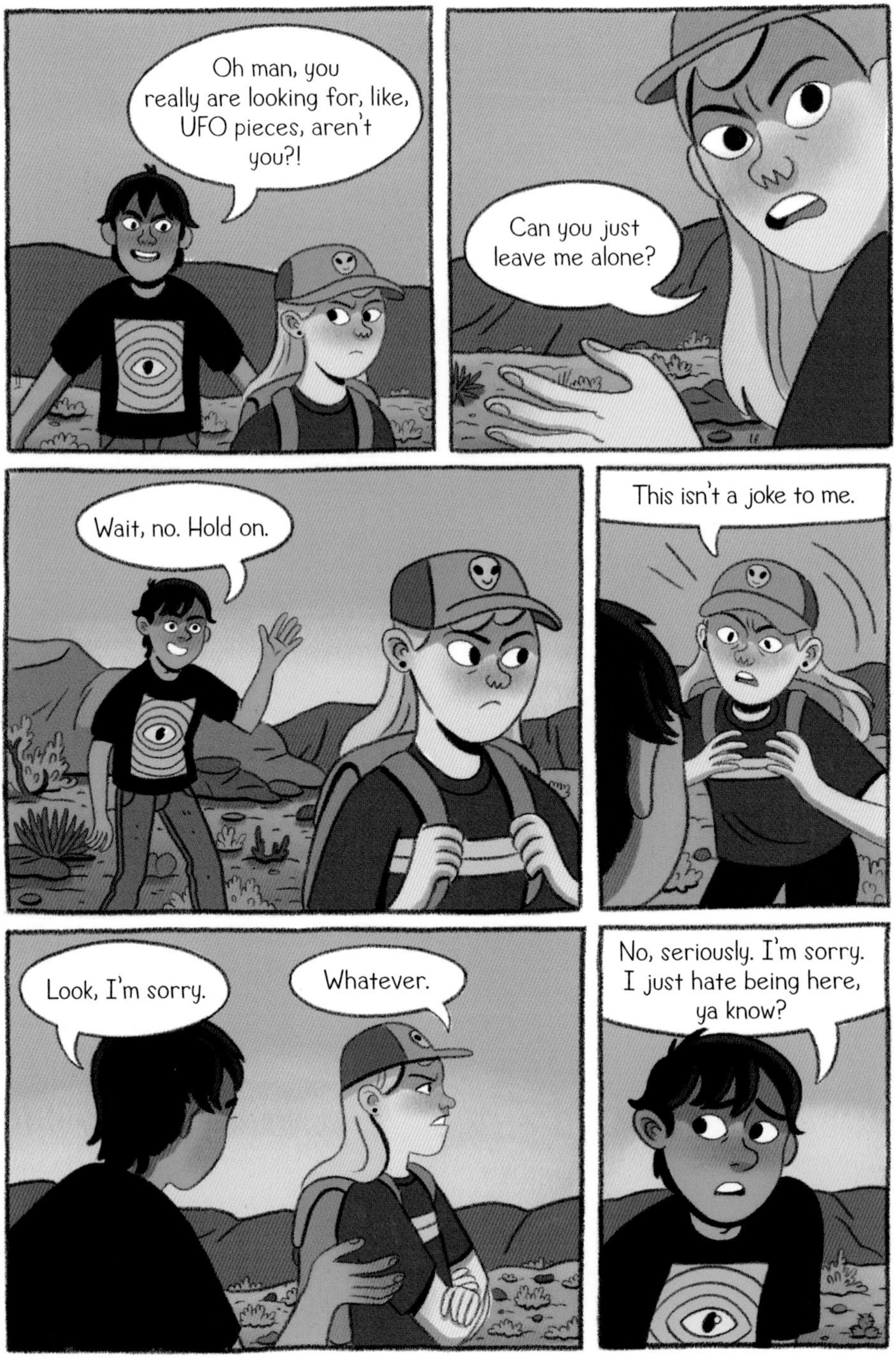
Oh man, you really are looking for, like, UFO pieces, aren't you?!
Can you just leave me alone?
Wait, no. Hold on.
This isn't a joke to me.
Look, I'm sorry.
Whatever.
No, seriously. I'm sorry. I just hate being here, ya know?

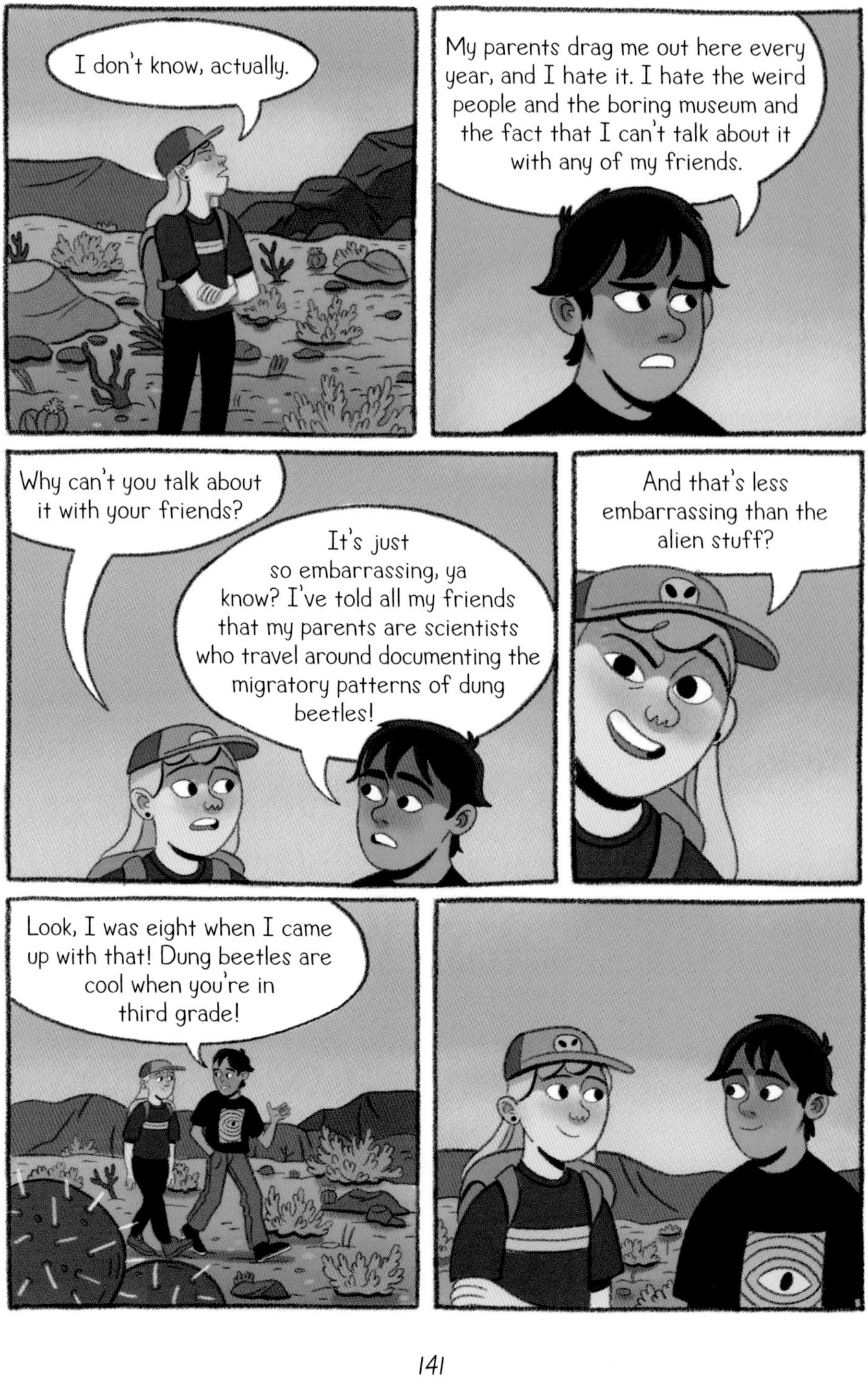
I don't know, actually.
My parents drag me out here every year, and I hate it. I hate the weird people and the boring museum and the fact that I can't talk about it with any of my friends.
Why can't you talk about it with your friends?
It's just so embarrassing, ya know? I've told all my friends that my parents are scientists who travel around documenting the migratory patterns of dung beetles!
And that's less embarrassing than the alien stuff?
Look, I was eight when I came up with that! Dung beetles are cool when you're in third grade!

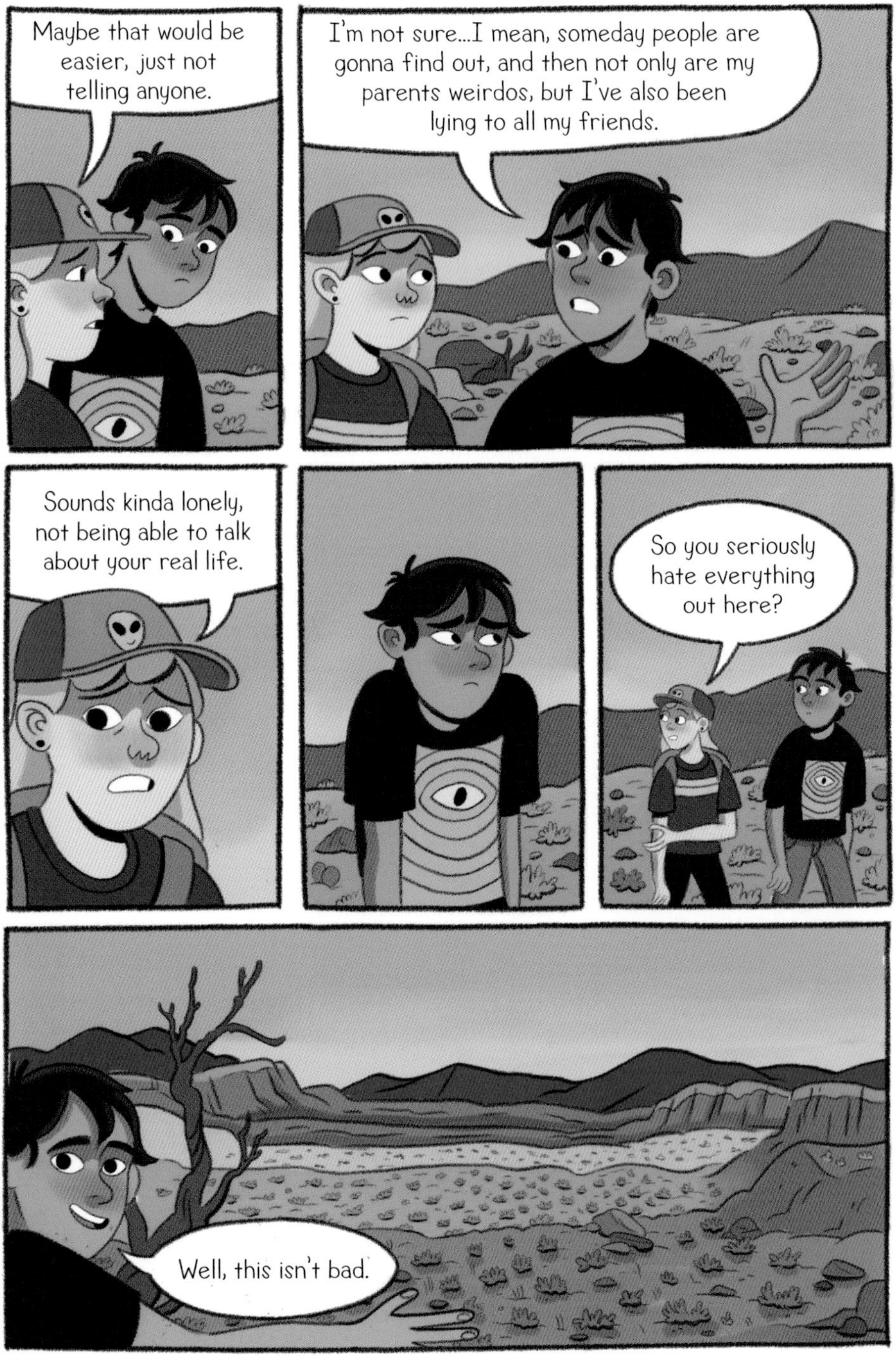
Maybe that would be easier, just not telling anyone.
I'm not sure...I mean, someday people are gonna find out, and then not only are my parents weirdos, but I've also been lying to all my friends.
Sounds kinda lonely, not being able to talk about your real life.
So you seriously hate everything out here?
Well, this isn't bad.

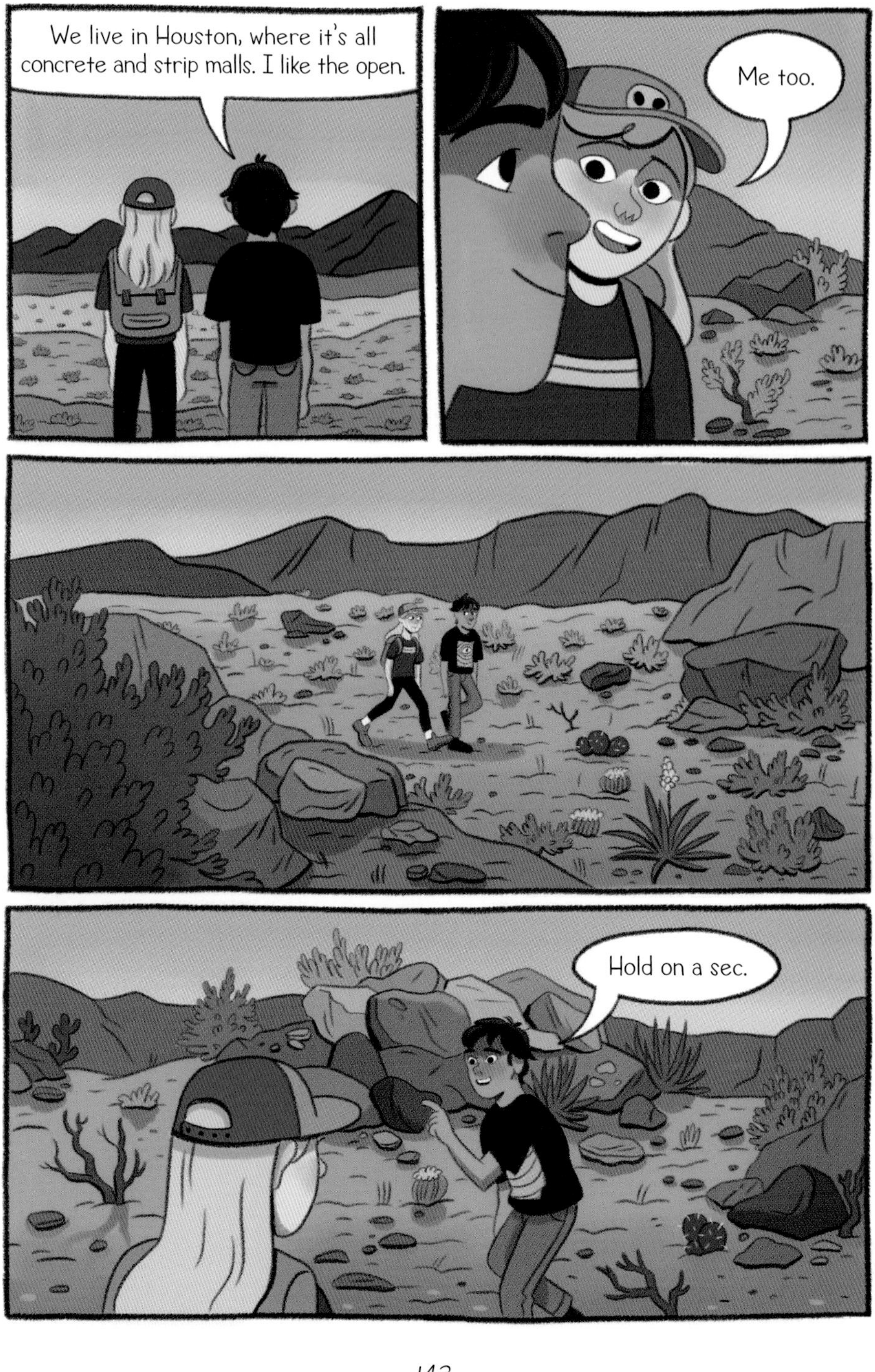
We live in Houston, where it's all concrete and strip malls. I like the open.
Me too.
Hold on a sec.

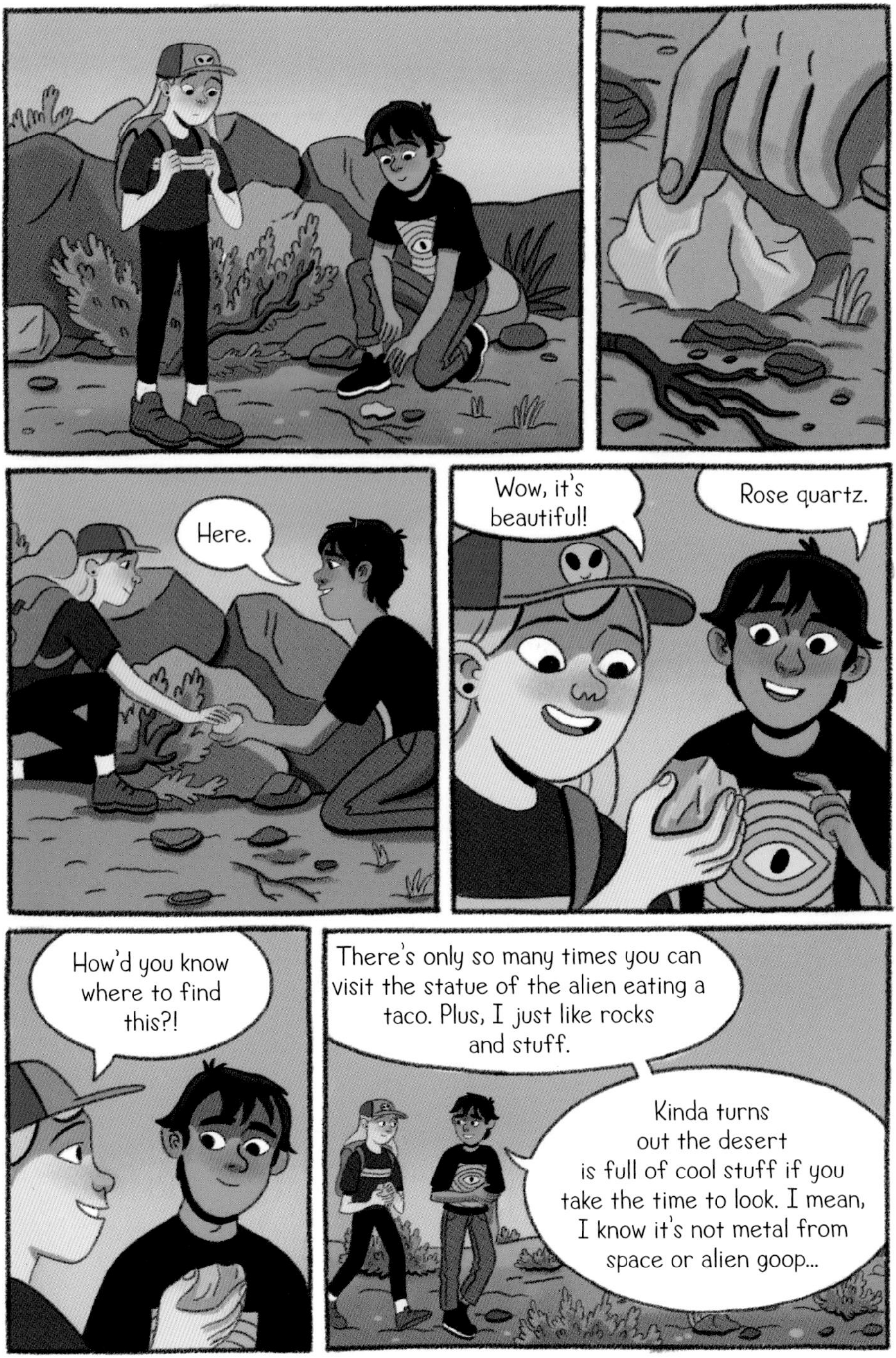
Here.
Wow, it's beautiful!
Rose quartz.
How'd you know where to find this?!
There's only so many times you can visit the statue of the alien eating a taco. Plus, I just like rocks and stuff.
Kinda turns out the desert is full of cool stuff if you take the time to look. I mean, I know it's not metal from space or alien goop...

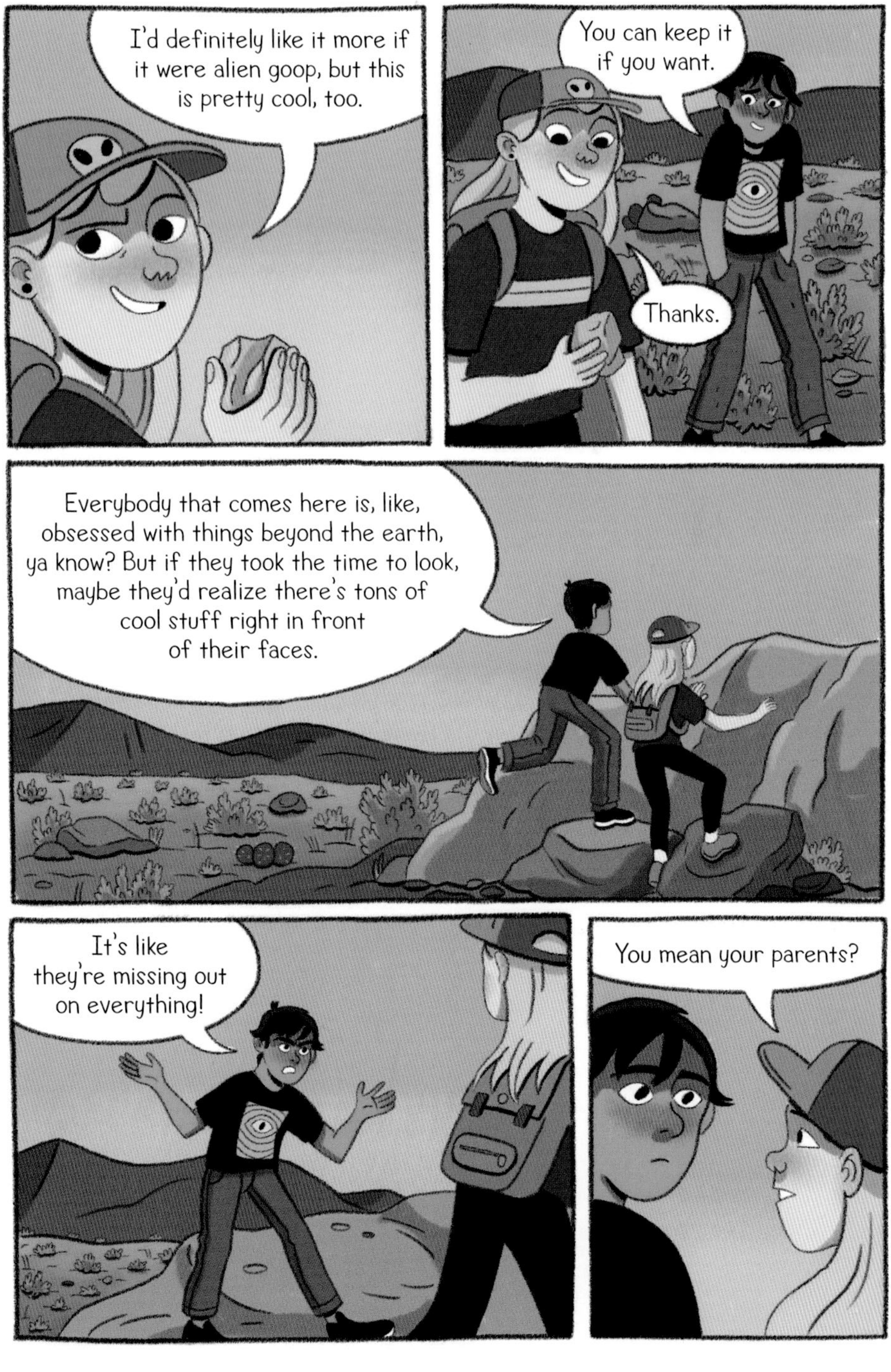
I'd definitely like it more if it were alien goop, but this is pretty cool, too.
You can keep it if you want.
Thanks.
Everybody that comes here is, like, obsessed with things beyond the earth, ya know? But if they took the time to look, maybe they'd realize there's tons of cool stuff right in front of their faces.
It's like they're missing out on everything!
You mean your parents?

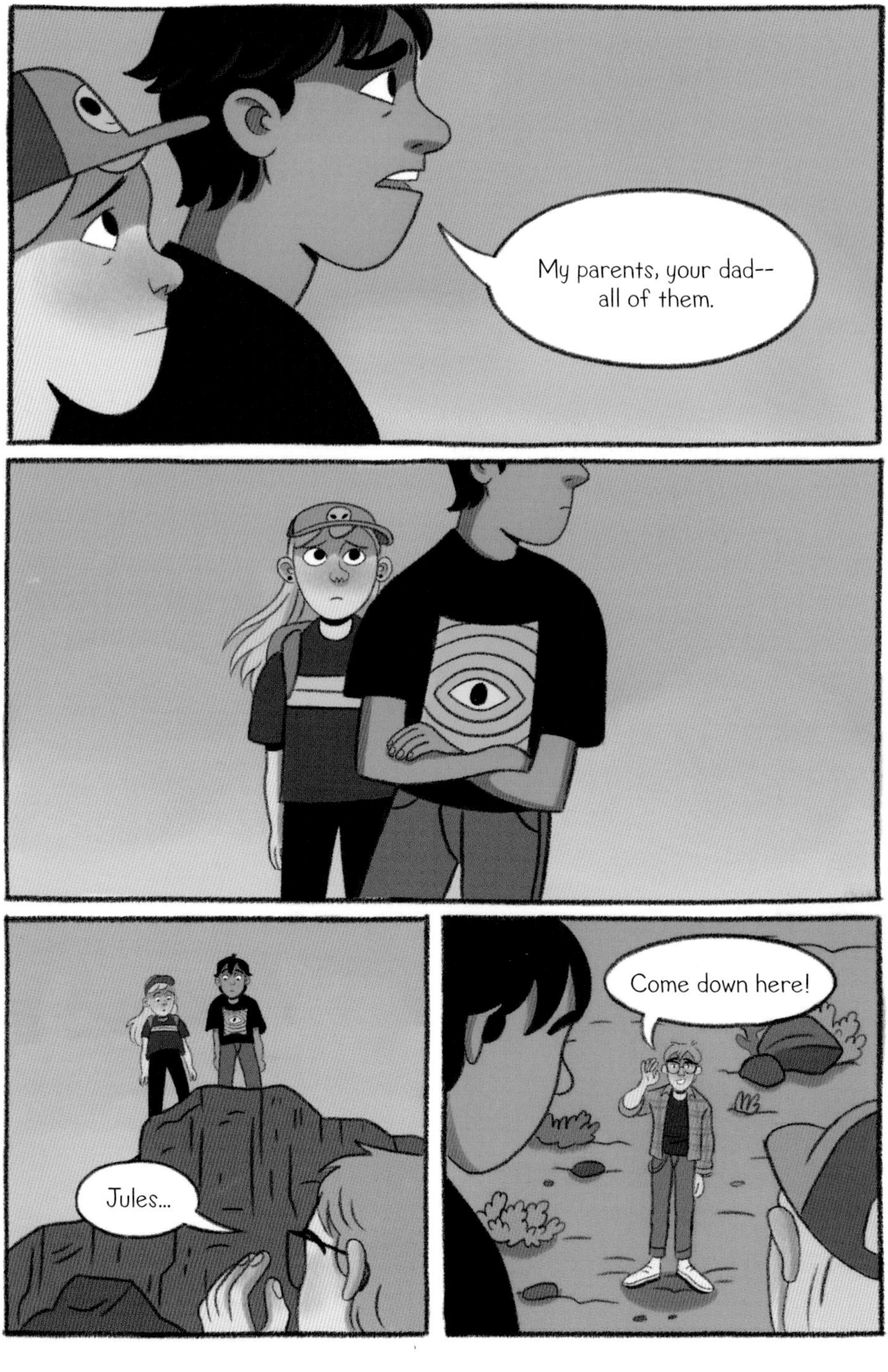
My parents, your dad--
all of them.
Jules...
Come down here!

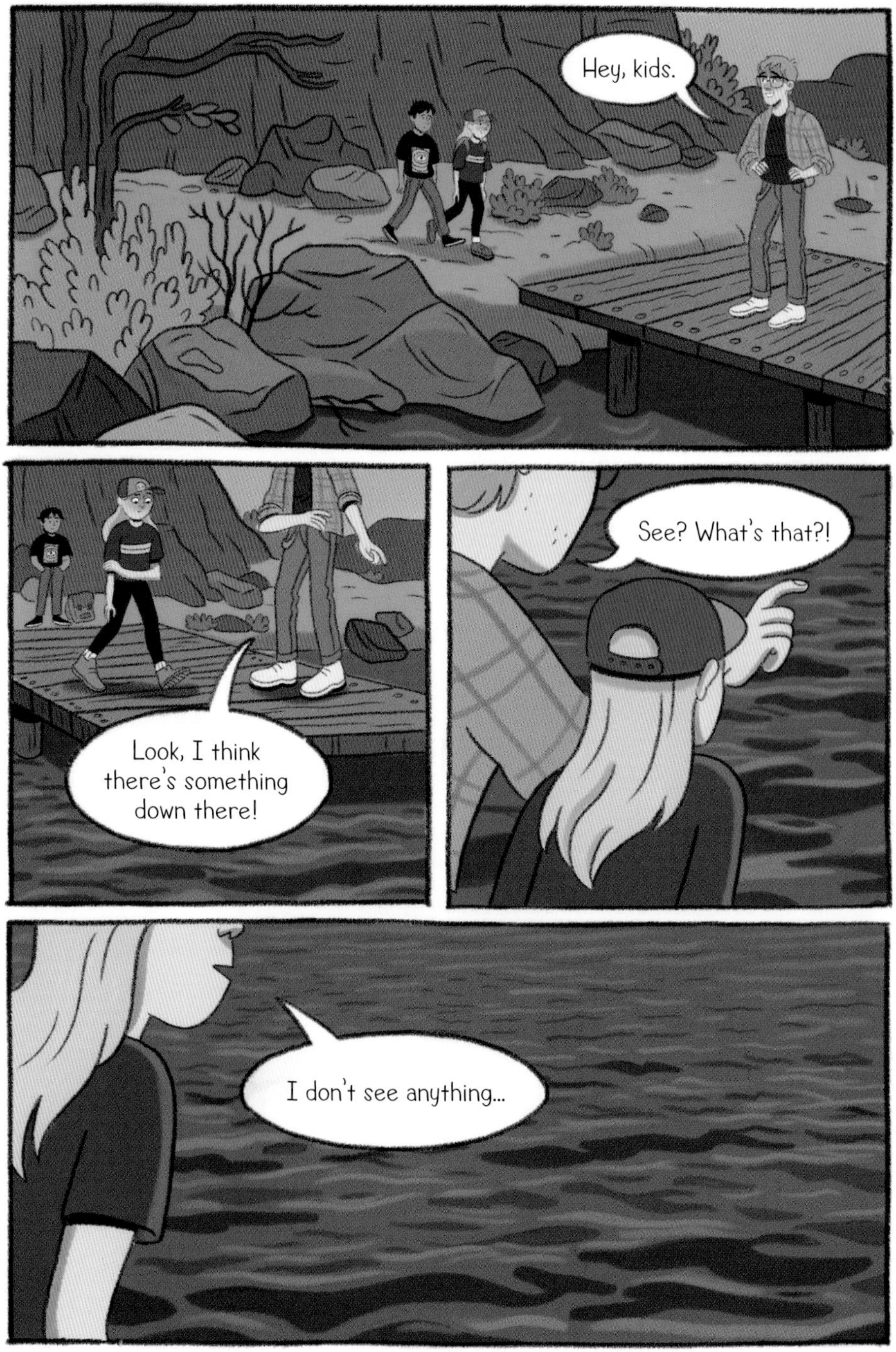
Hey, kids.
Look, I think there's something down there!
See? What's that?!
I don't see anything...

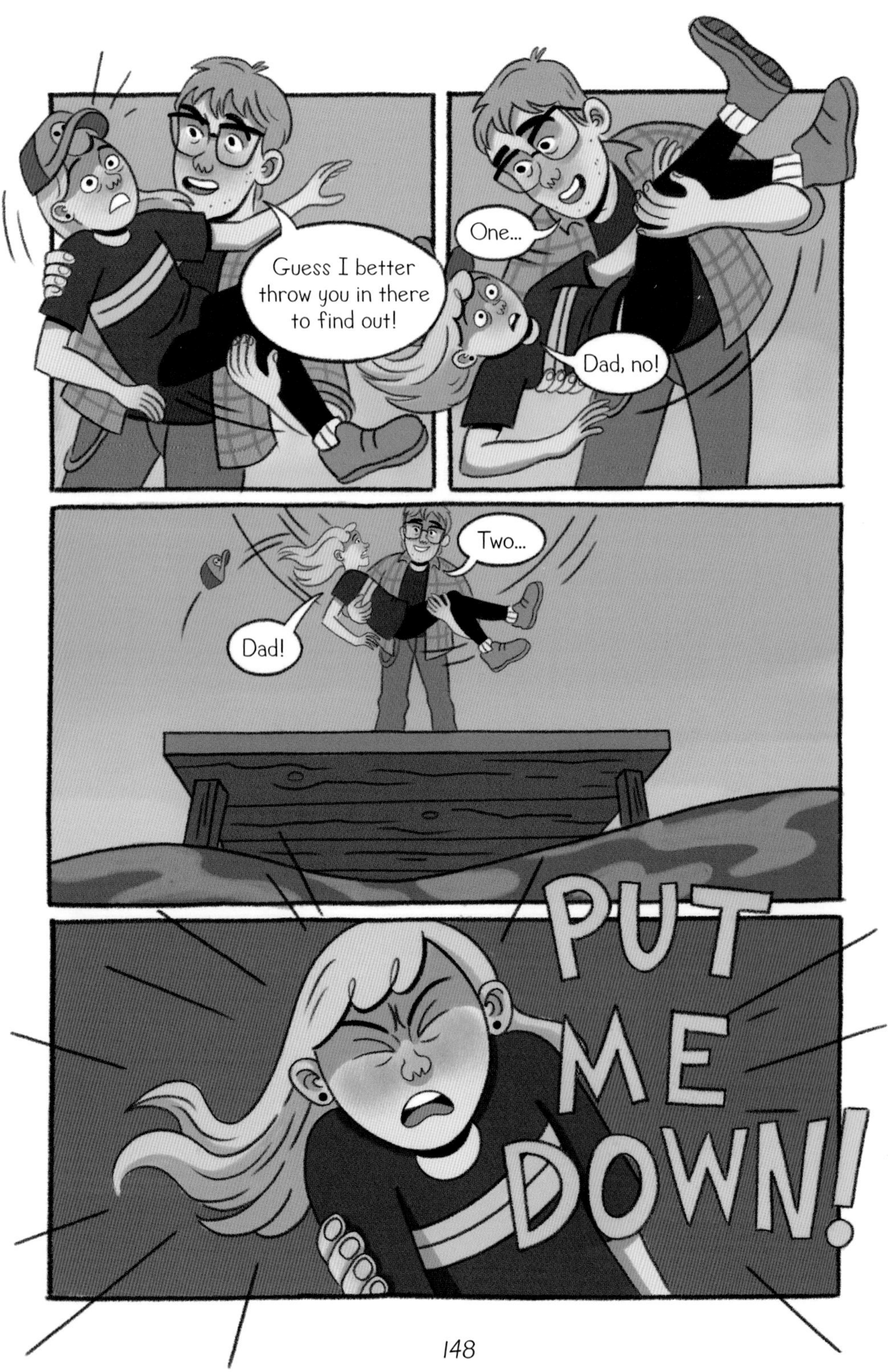
Guess I better throw you in there to find out!
One...
Dad, no!
Two...
Dad!
PUT ME DOWN!

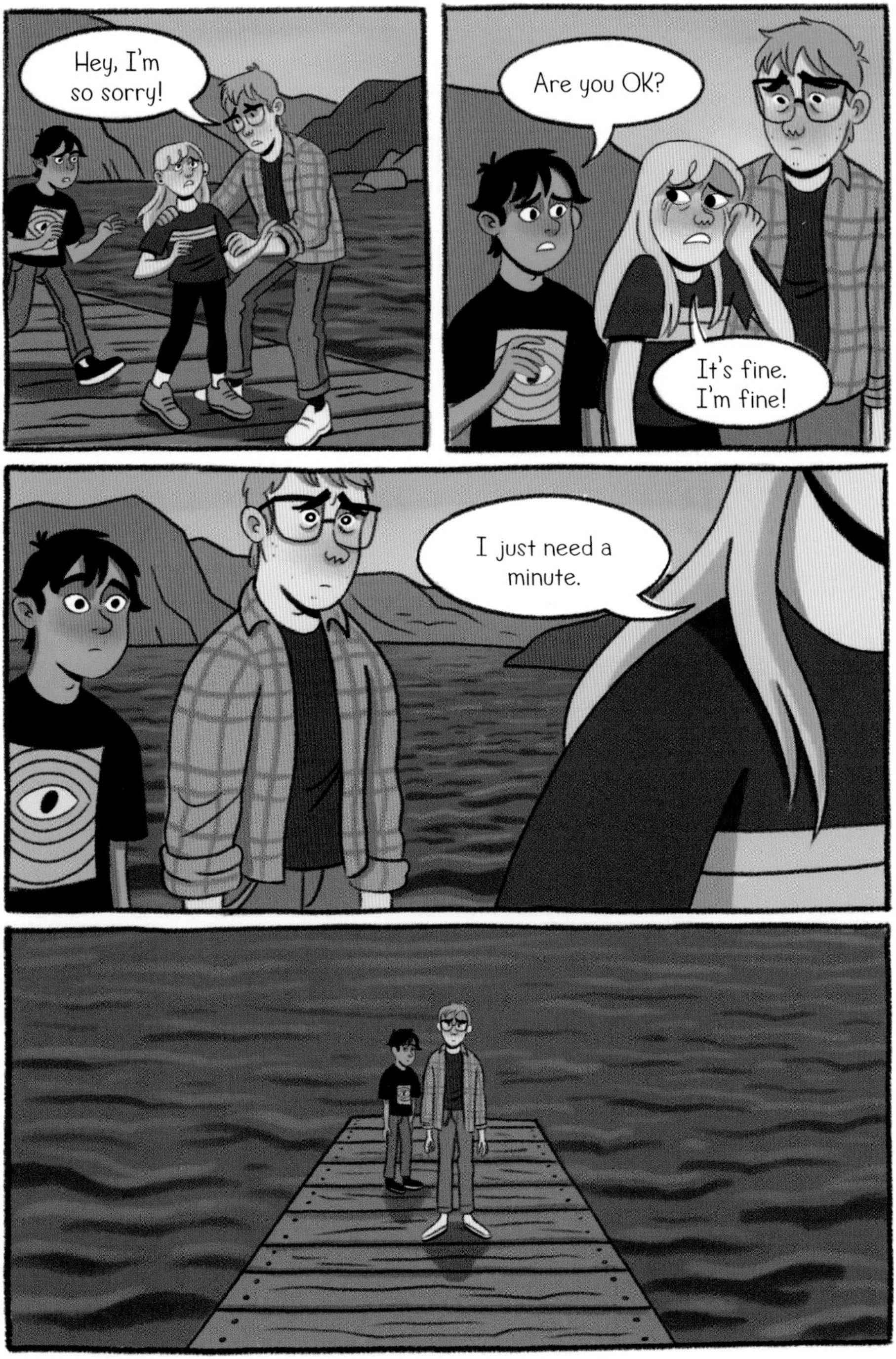
Hey, I'm so sorry!
Are you OK?
It's fine. I'm fine!
I just need a minute.

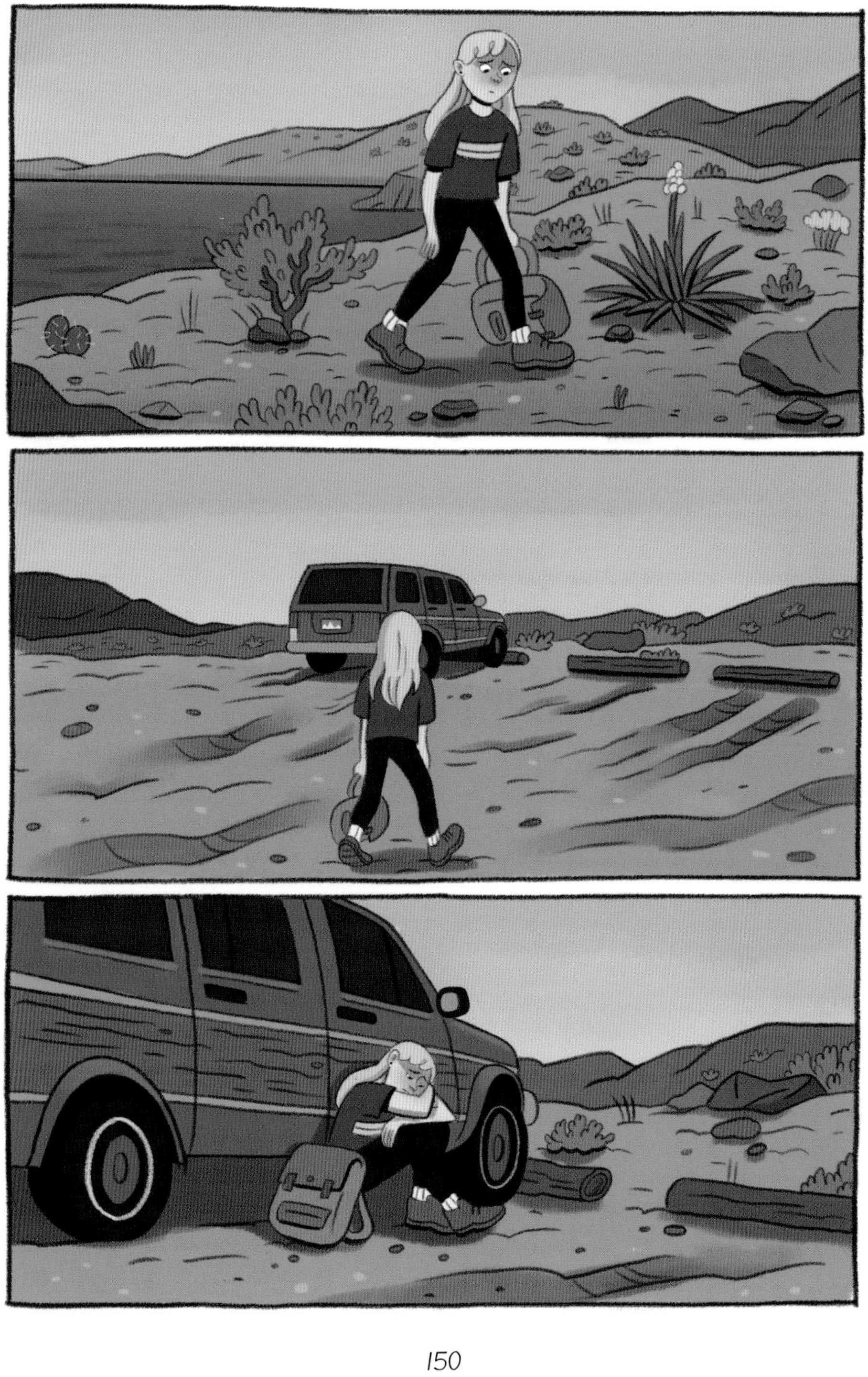

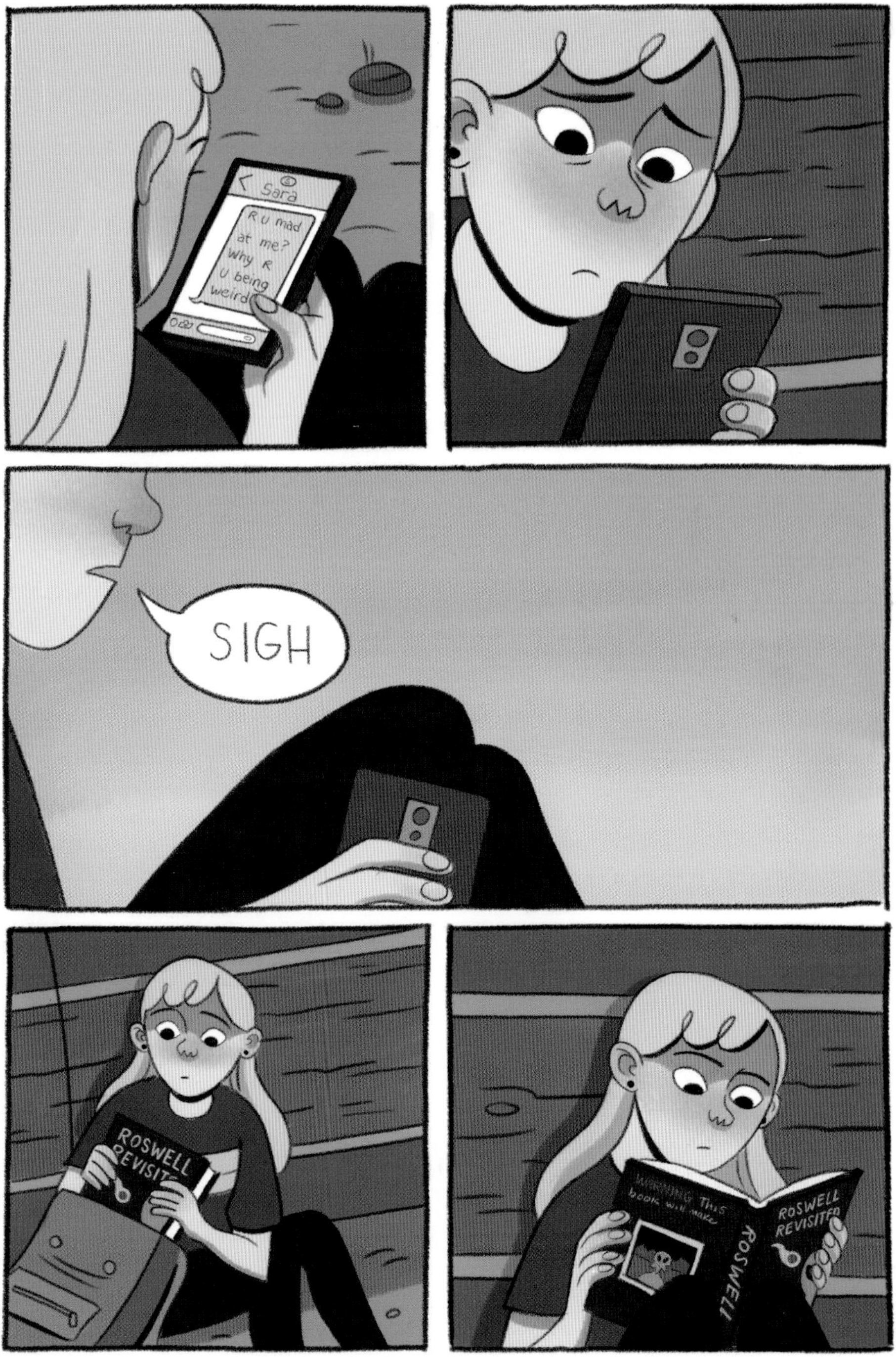
Sara
R U mad at me? Why R U being weird
SIGH
ROSWELL REVISITED
ROSWELL

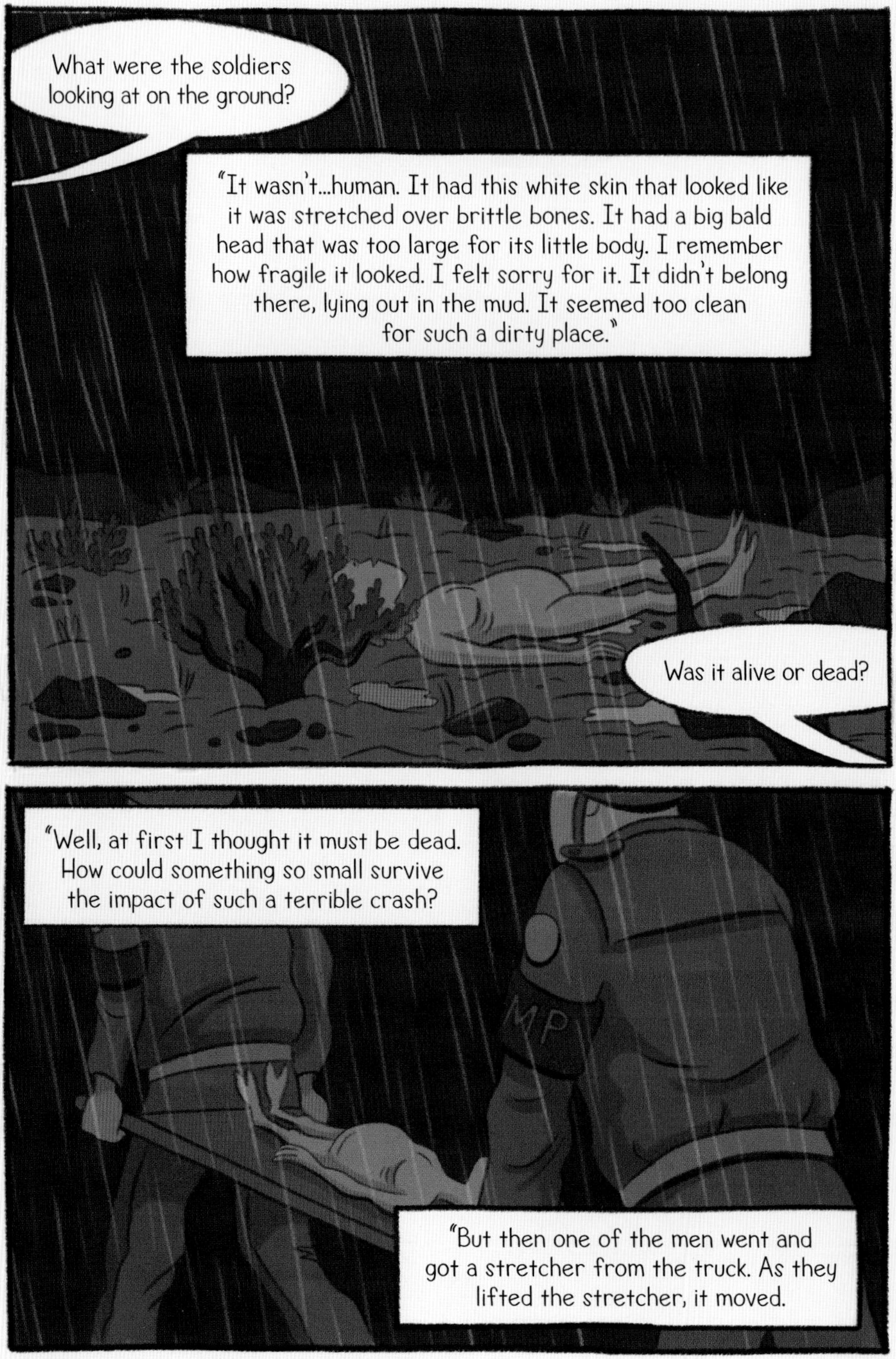
What were the soldiers looking at on the ground?
"It wasn't...human. It had this white skin that looked like it was stretched over brittle bones. It had a big bald head that was too large for its little body. I remember how fragile it looked. I felt sorry for it. It didn't belong there, lying out in the mud. It seemed too clean for such a dirty place."
Was it alive or dead?
"Well, at first I thought it must be dead. How could something so small survive the impact of such a terrible crash?
MP
"But then one of the men went and got a stretcher from the truck. As they lifted the stretcher, it moved.

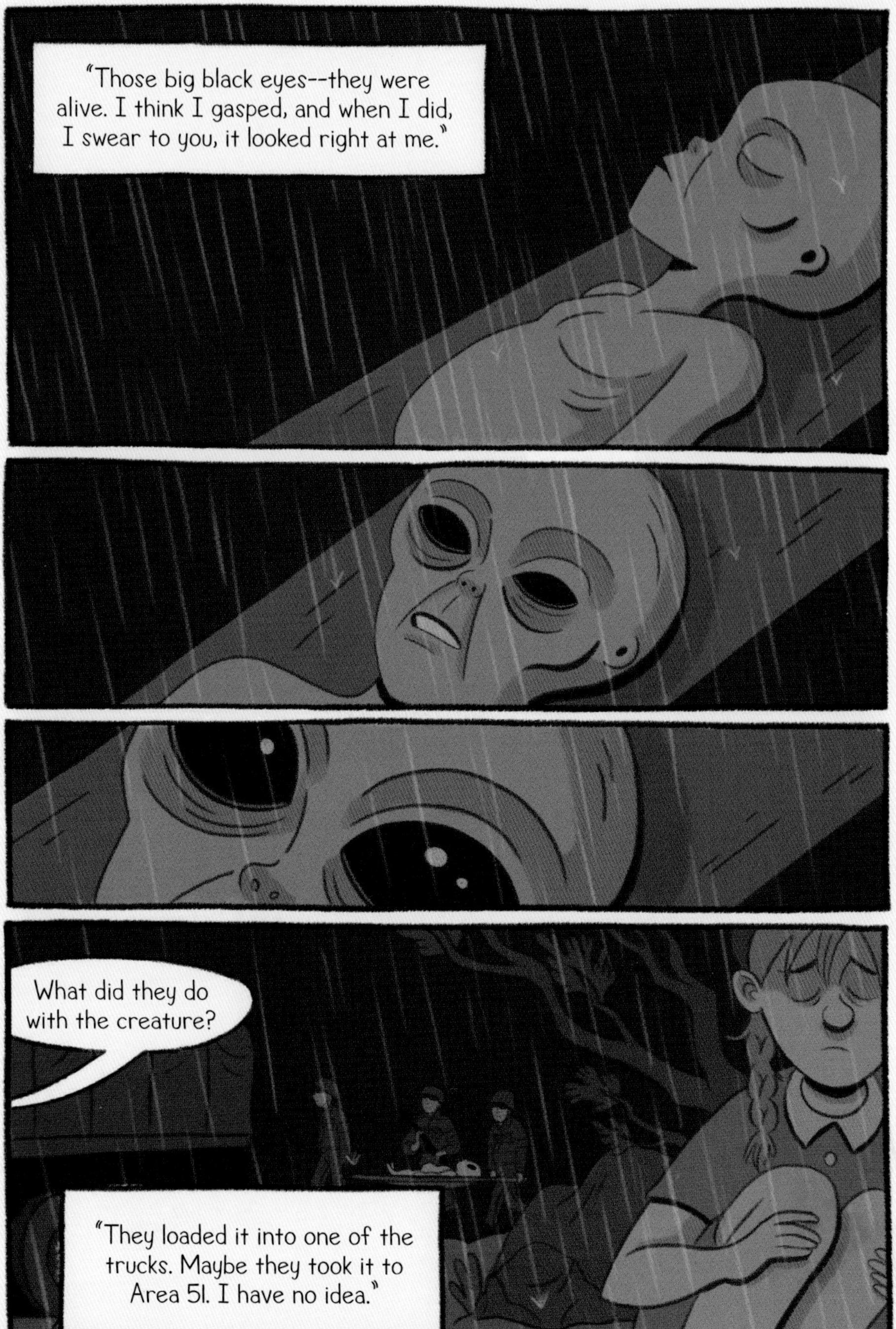
"Those big black eyes--they were alive. I think I gasped, and when I did, I swear to you, it looked right at me."
What did they do with the creature?
"They loaded it into one of the trucks. Maybe they took it to Area 51. I have no idea."

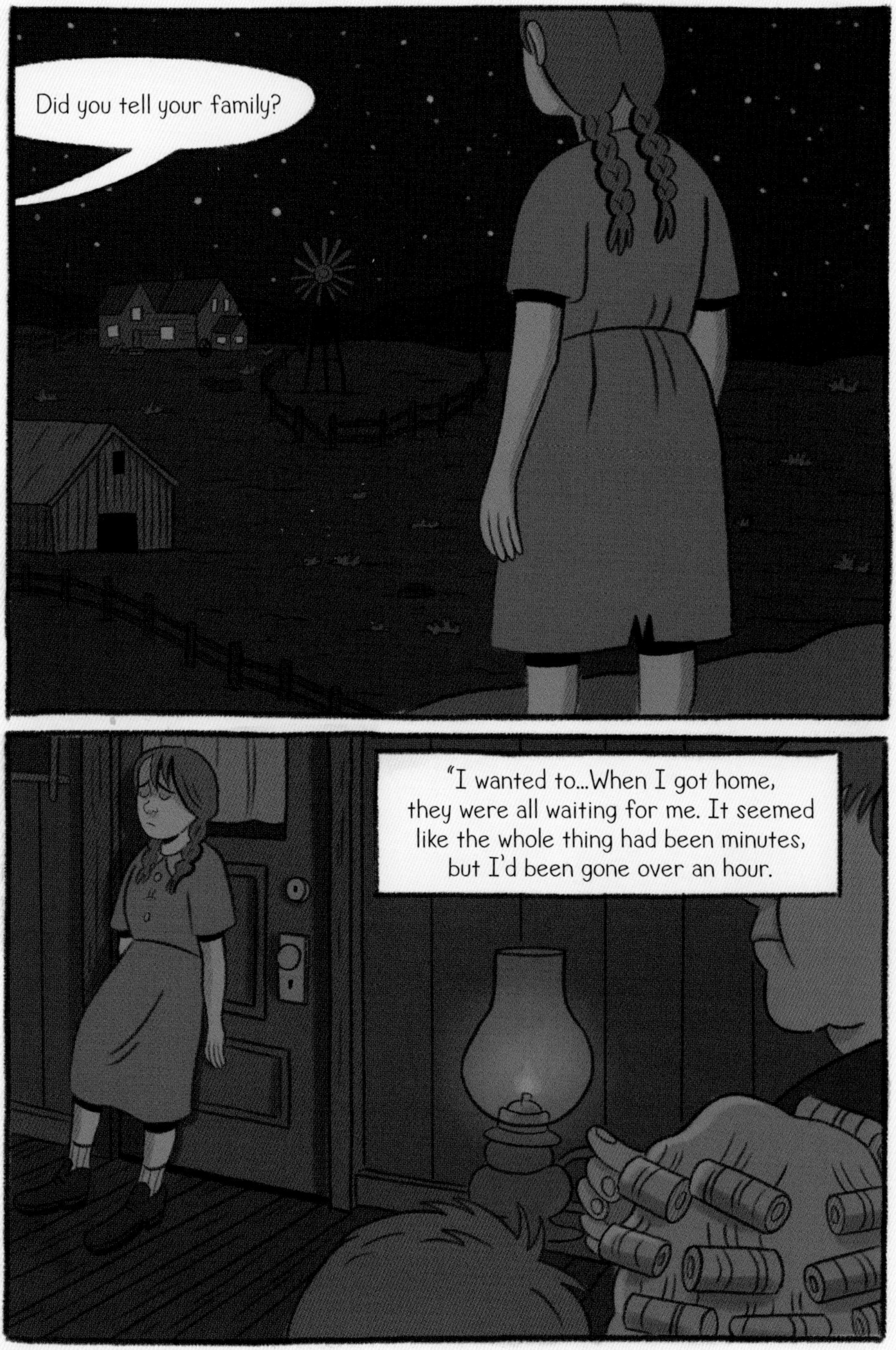
Did you tell your family?
"I wanted to...When I got home, they were all waiting for me. It seemed like the whole thing had been minutes, but I'd been gone over an hour.

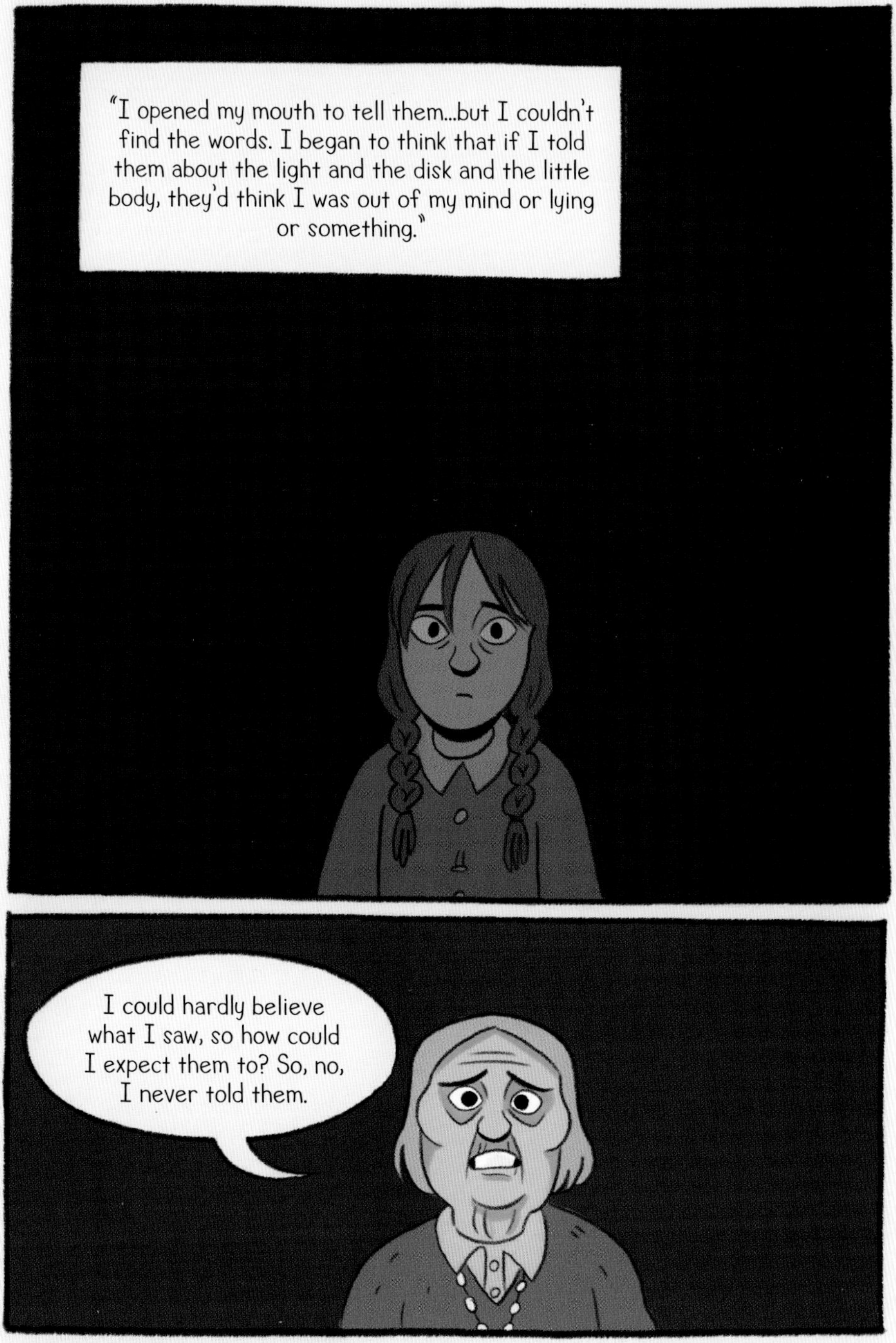
"I opened my mouth to tell them...but I couldn't find the words. I began to think that if I told them about the light and the disk and the little body, they'd think I was out of my mind or lying or something."
I could hardly believe what I saw, so how could I expect them to? So, no, I never told them.

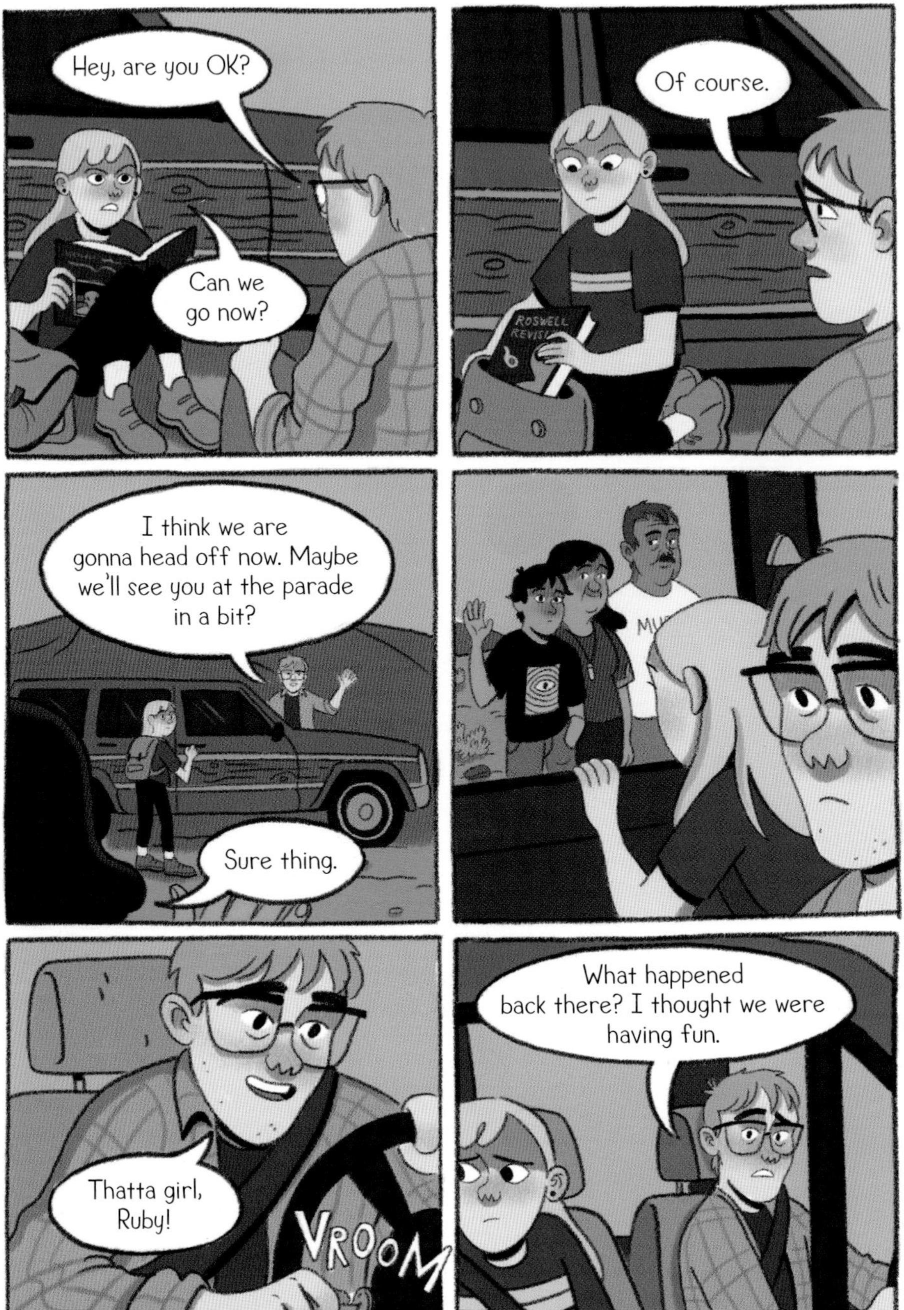
Hey, are you OK?
Can we go now?
Of course.
I think we are gonna head off now. Maybe we'll see you at the parade in a bit?
Sure thing.
Thatta girl, Ruby!
VROOM
What happened back there? I thought we were having fun.

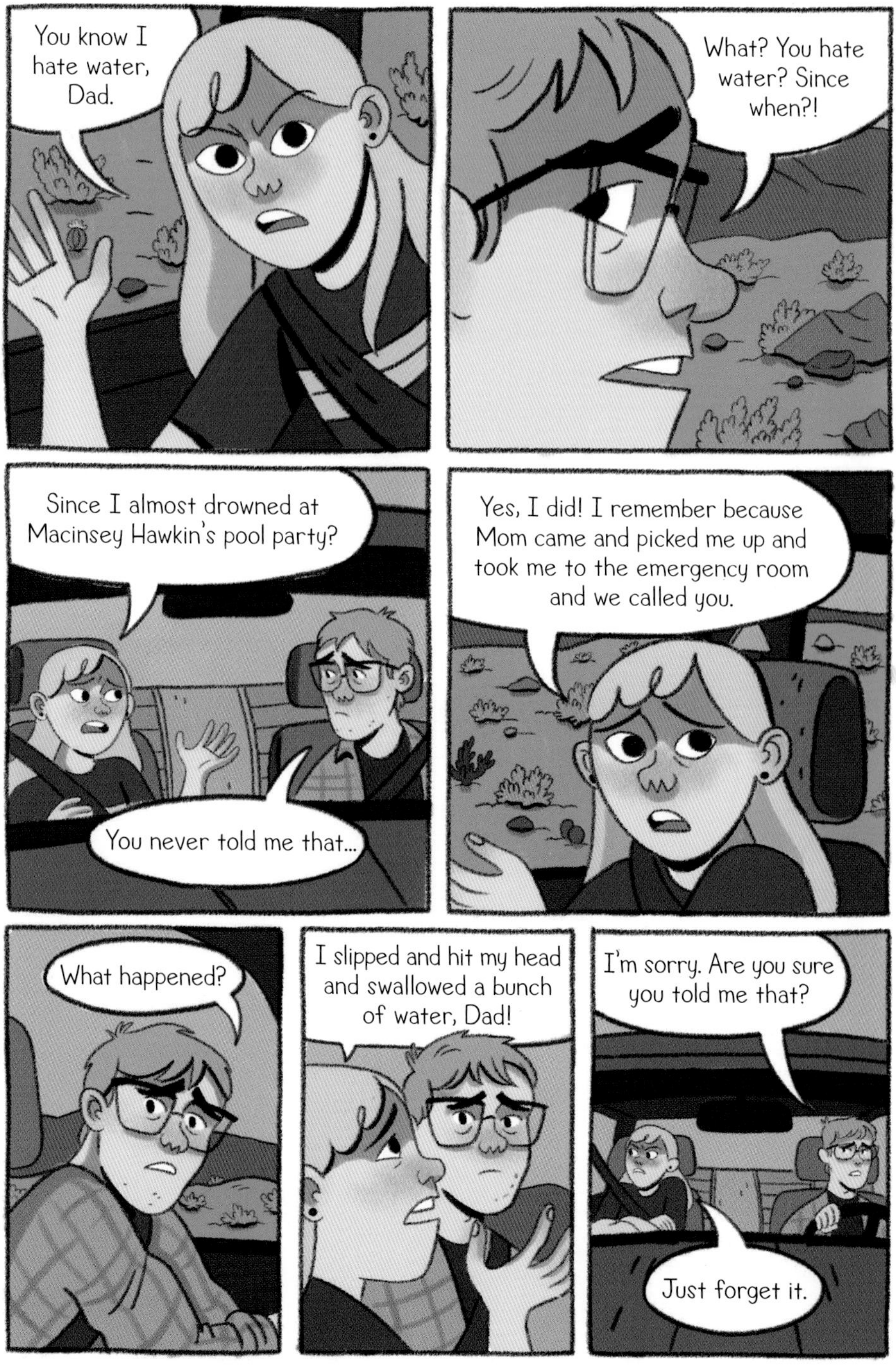

You know I hate water, Dad.
What? You hate water? Since when?!
Since I almost drowned at Macinsey Hawkin's pool party?
You never told me that...
Yes, I did! I remember because Mom came and picked me up and took me to the emergency room and we called you.
What happened?
I slipped and hit my head and swallowed a bunch of water, Dad!
I'm sorry. Are you sure you told me that?
Just forget it.

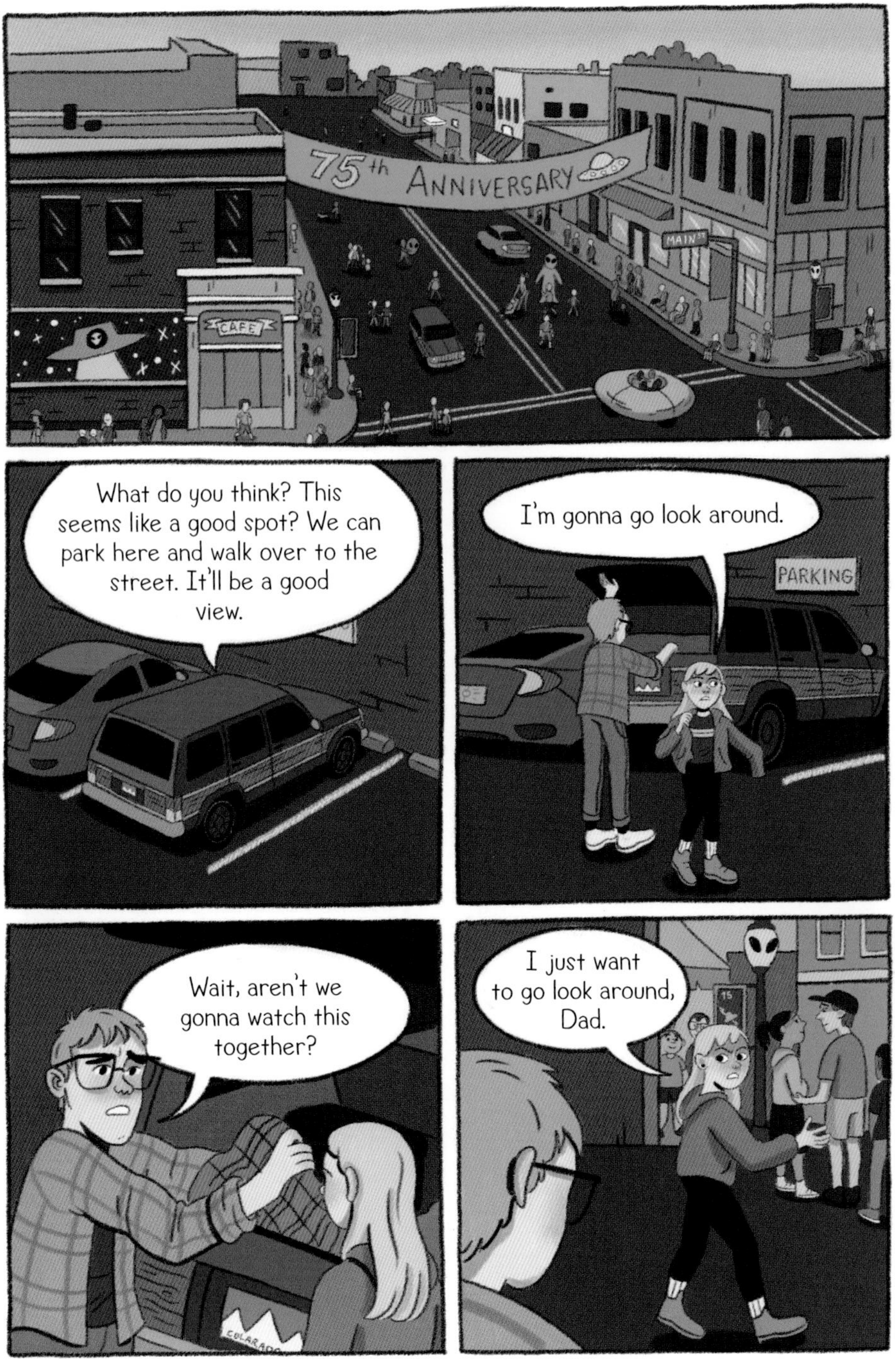
75th ANNIVERSARY
CAFE
MAIN ST
What do you think? This seems like a good spot? We can park here and walk over to the street. It'll be a good view.
I'm gonna go look around.
PARKING
Wait, aren't we gonna watch this together?
I just want to go look around, Dad.

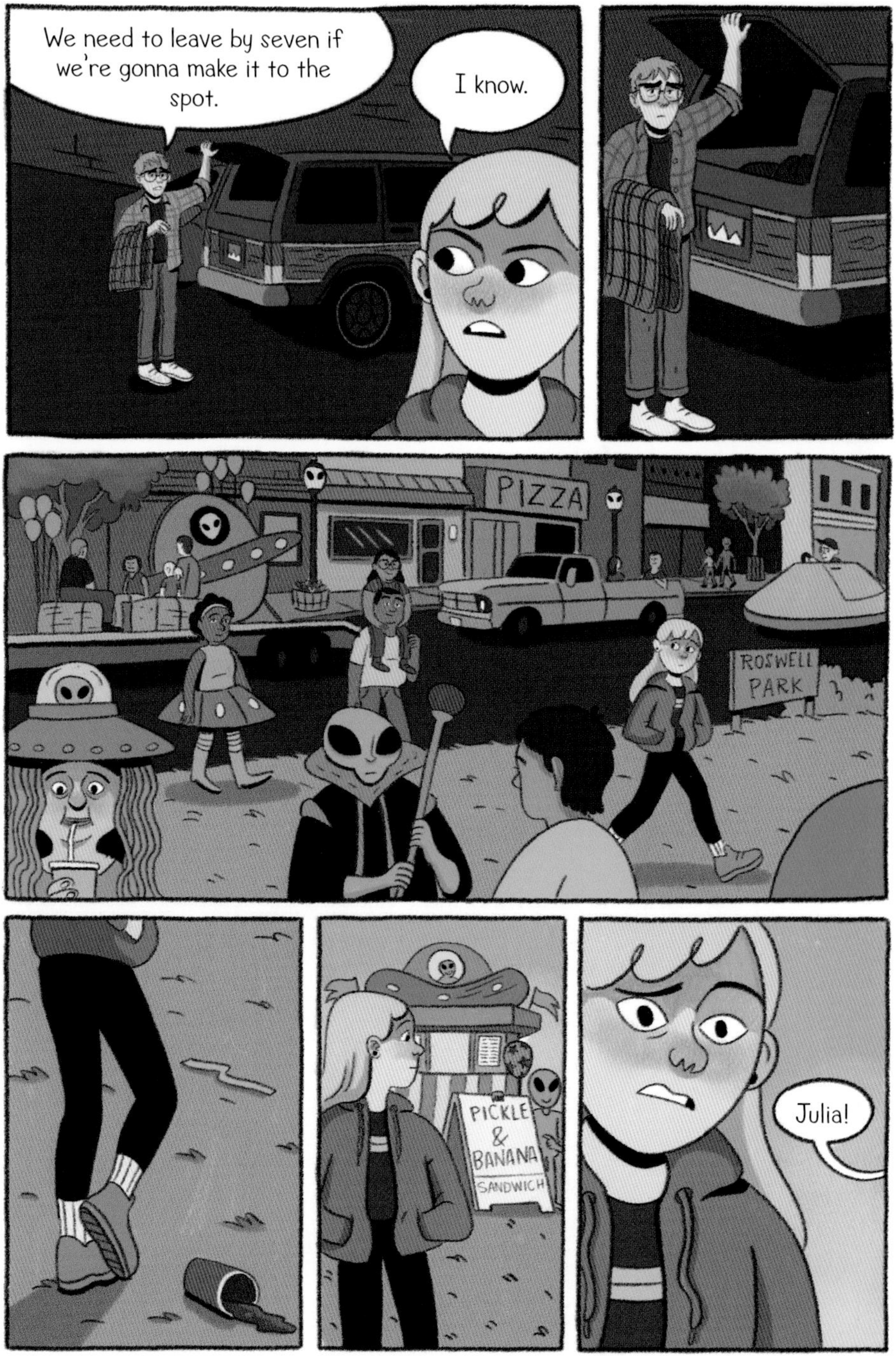
We need to leave by seven if we're gonna make it to the spot.
I know.
PIZZA
ROSWELL PARK
PICKLE & BANANA SANDWICH
Julia!

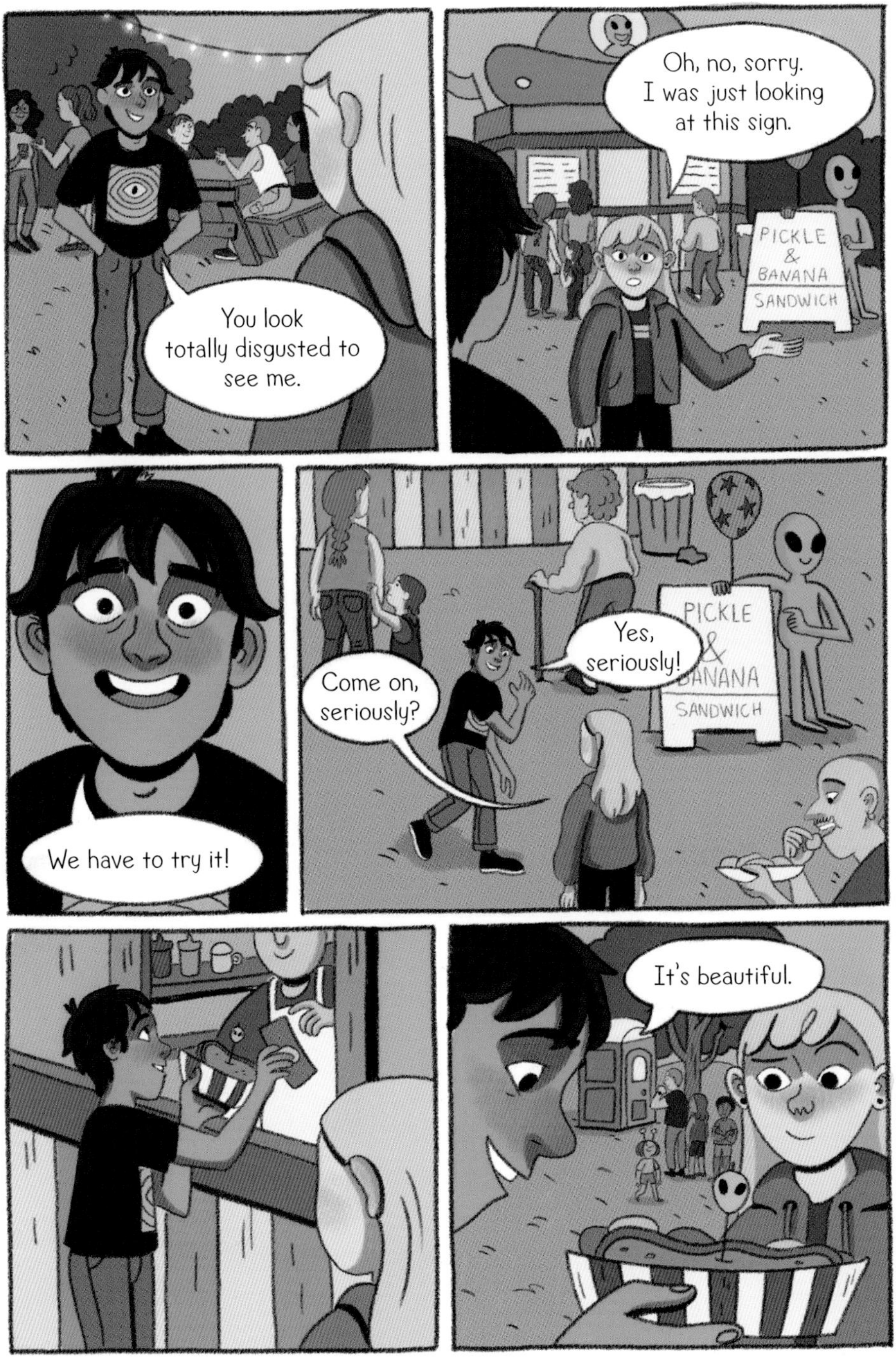
You look totally disgusted to see me.
Oh, no, sorry. I was just looking at this sign.
PICKLE & BANANA SANDWICH
We have to try it!
Come on, seriously?
Yes, seriously!
PICKLE & BANANA SANDWICH
It's beautiful.

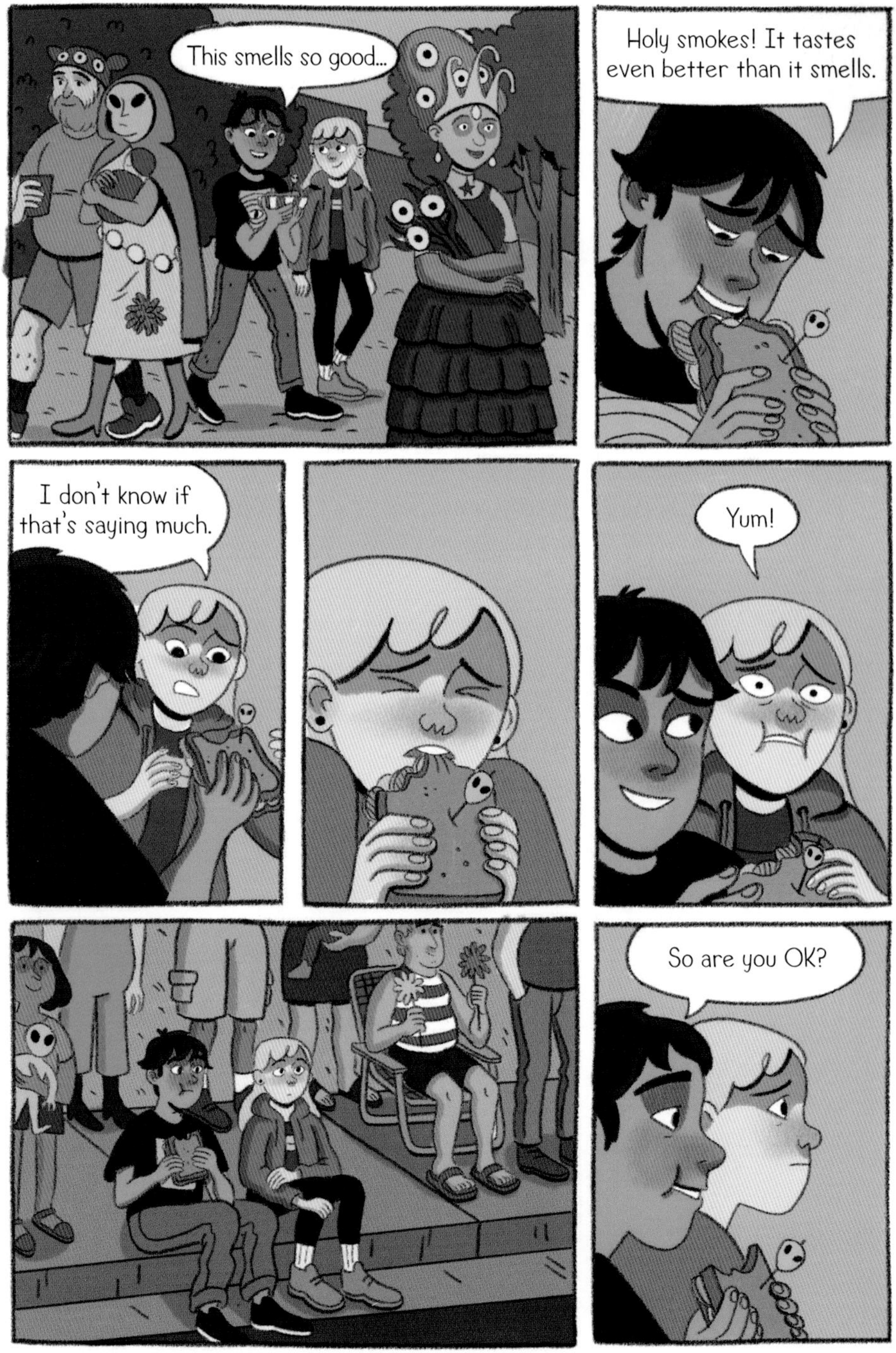
This smells so good...
Holy smokes! It tastes even better than it smells.
I don't know if that's saying much.
Yum!
So are you OK?

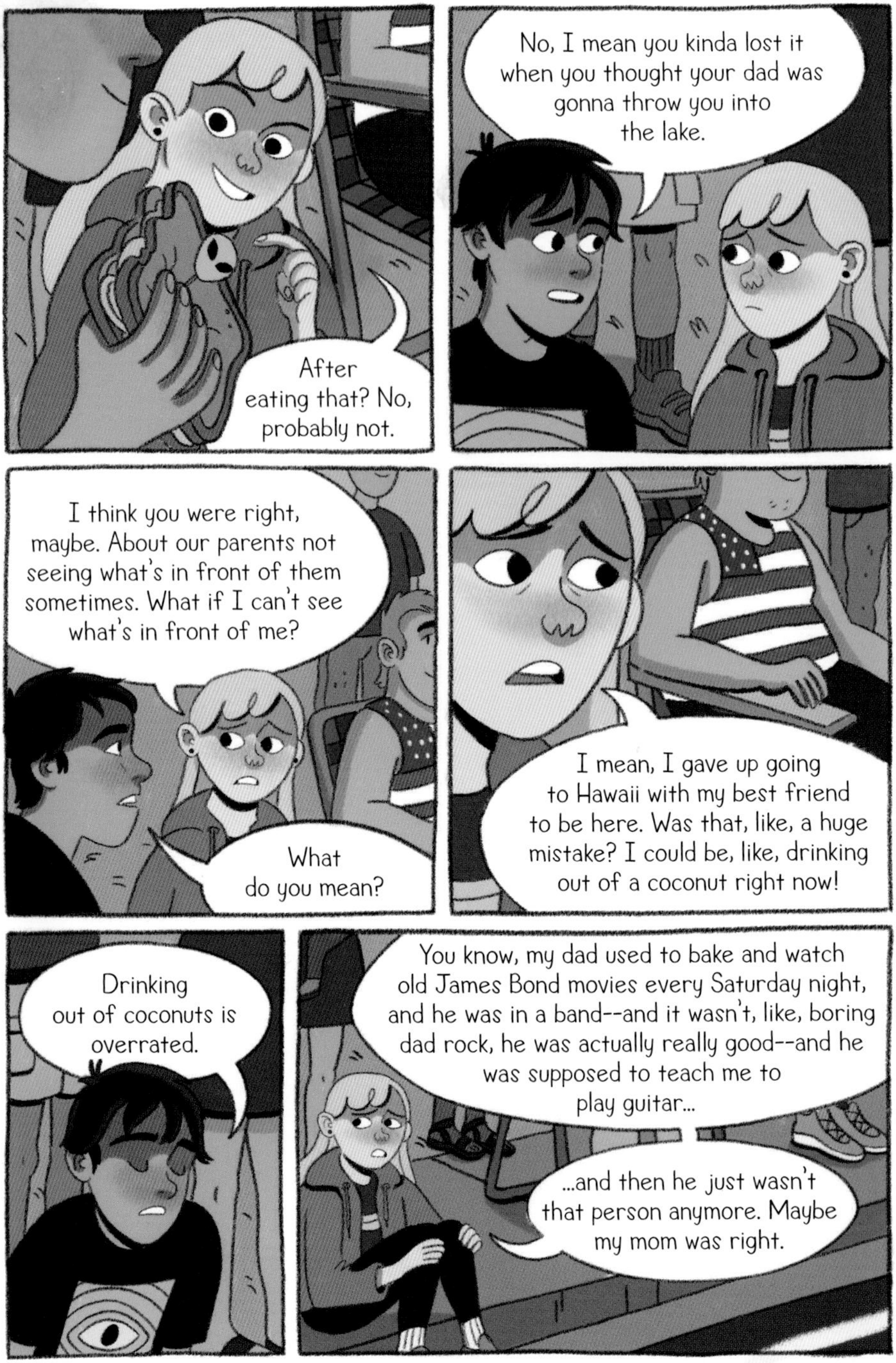
After eating that? No, probably not.
No, I mean you kinda lost it when you thought your dad was gonna throw you into the lake.
I think you were right, maybe. About our parents not seeing what's in front of them sometimes. What if I can't see what's in front of me?
What do you mean?
I mean, I gave up going to Hawaii with my best friend to be here. Was that, like, a huge mistake? I could be, like, drinking out of a coconut right now!
Drinking out of coconuts is overrated.
You know, my dad used to bake and watch old James Bond movies every Saturday night, and he was in a band--and it wasn't, like, boring dad rock, he was actually really good--and he was supposed to teach me to play guitar...
...and then he just wasn't that person anymore. Maybe my mom was right.

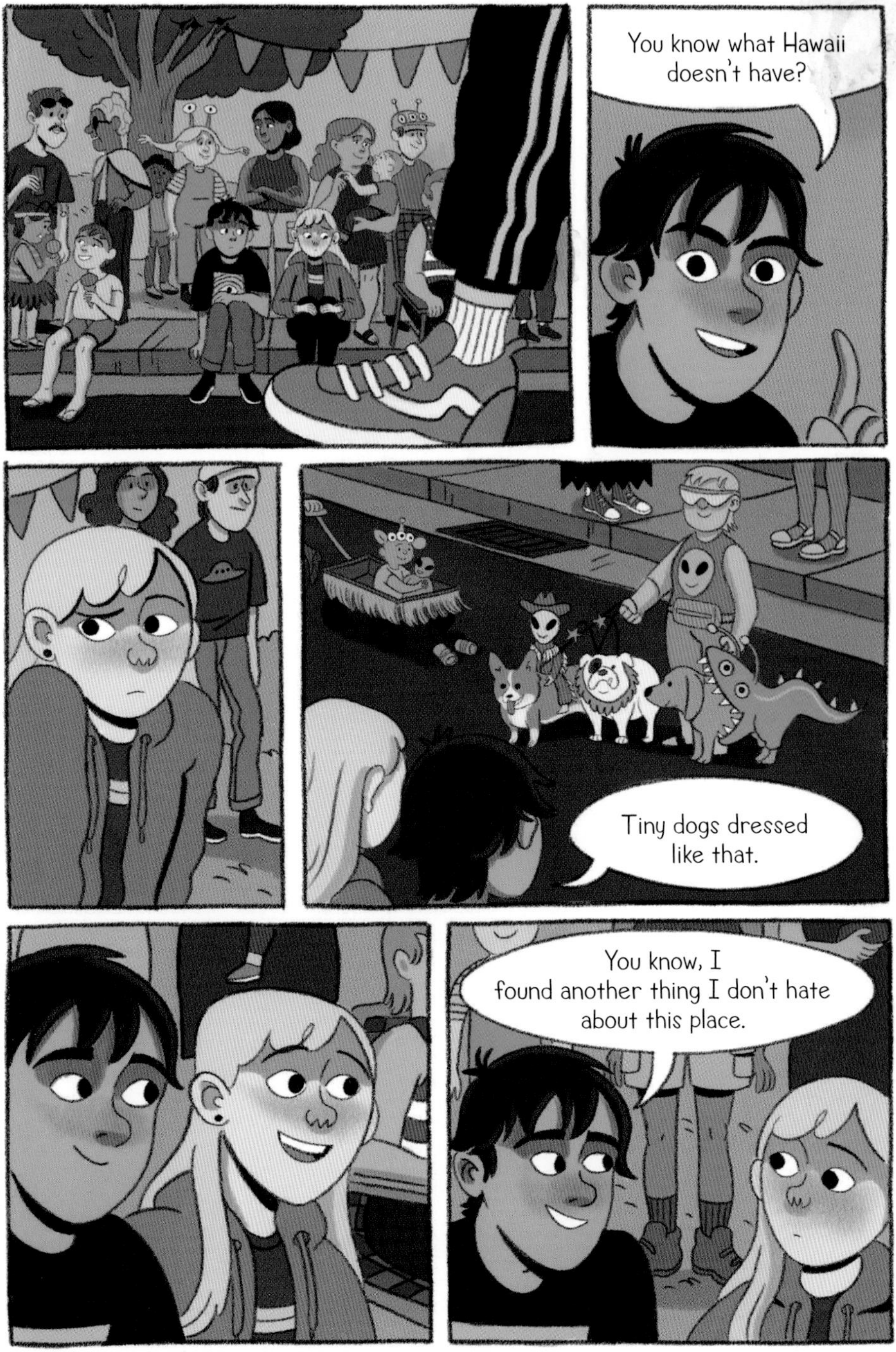
You know what Hawaii doesn't have?
Tiny dogs dressed like that.
You know, I found another thing I don't hate about this place.

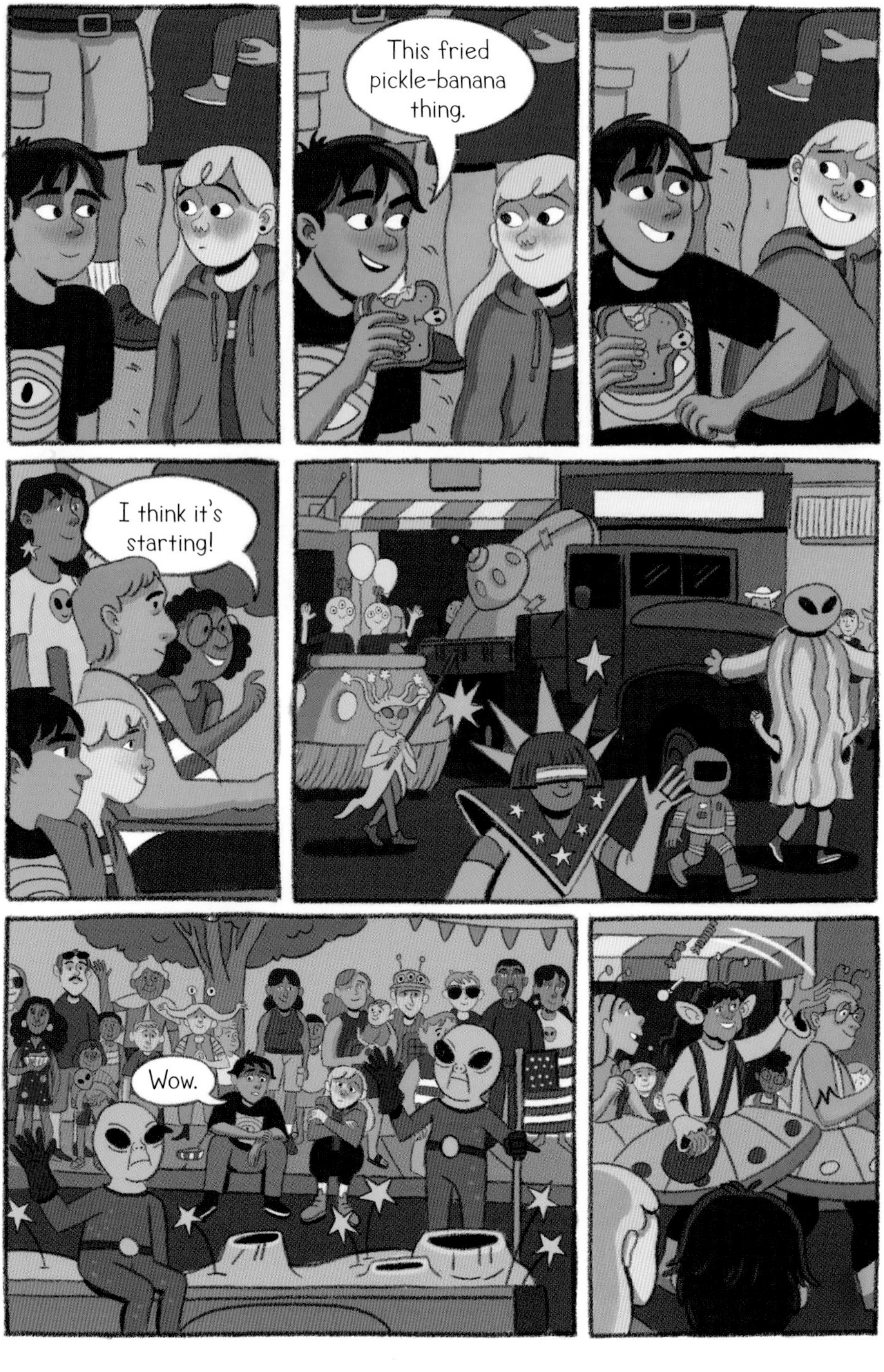
This fried pickle-banana thing.
I think it's starting!
Wow.

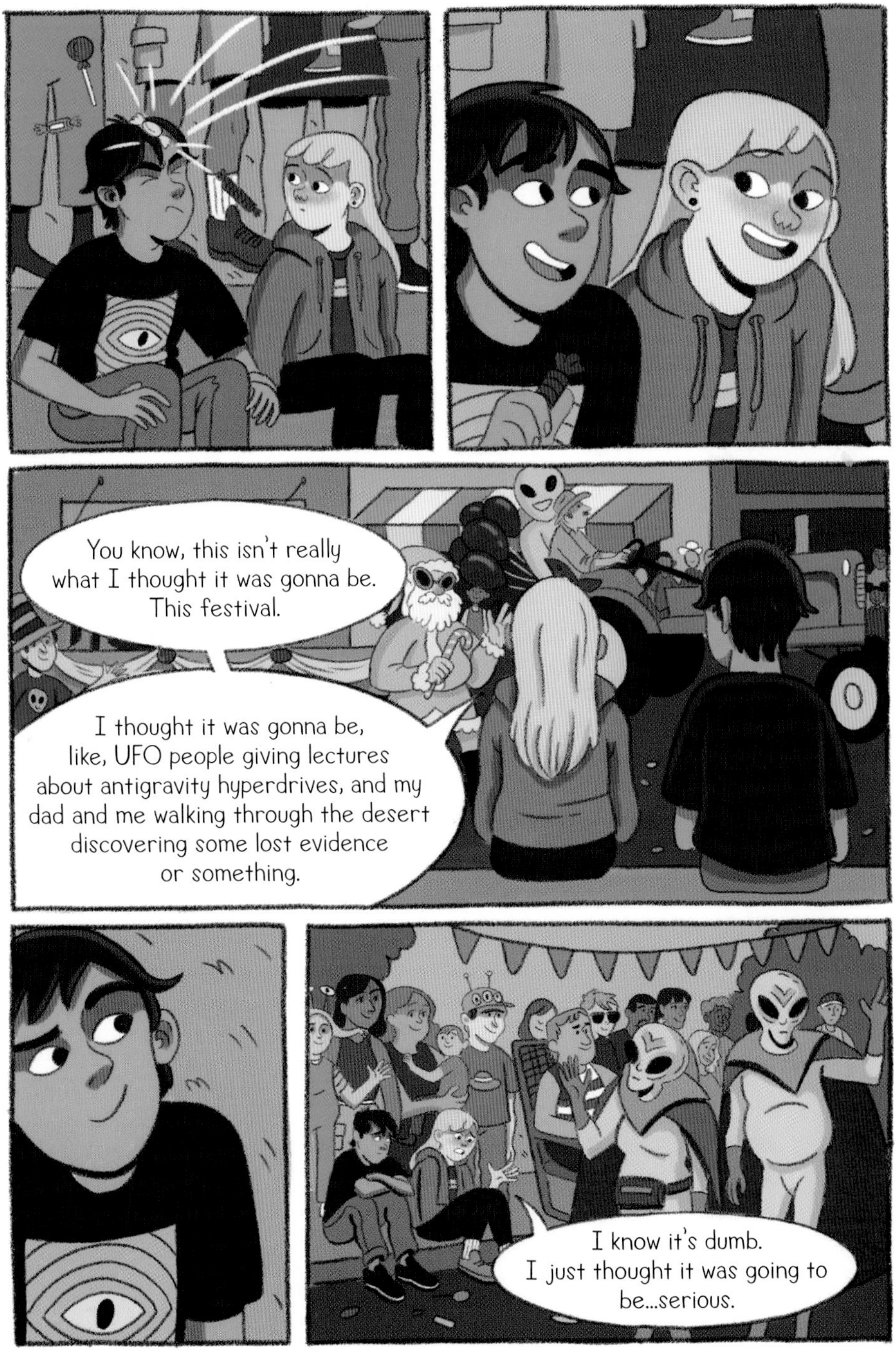
You know, this isn't really what I thought it was gonna be. This festival.
I thought it was gonna be, like, UFO people giving lectures about antigravity hyperdrives, and my dad and me walking through the desert discovering some lost evidence or something.
I know it's dumb. I just thought it was going to be...serious.

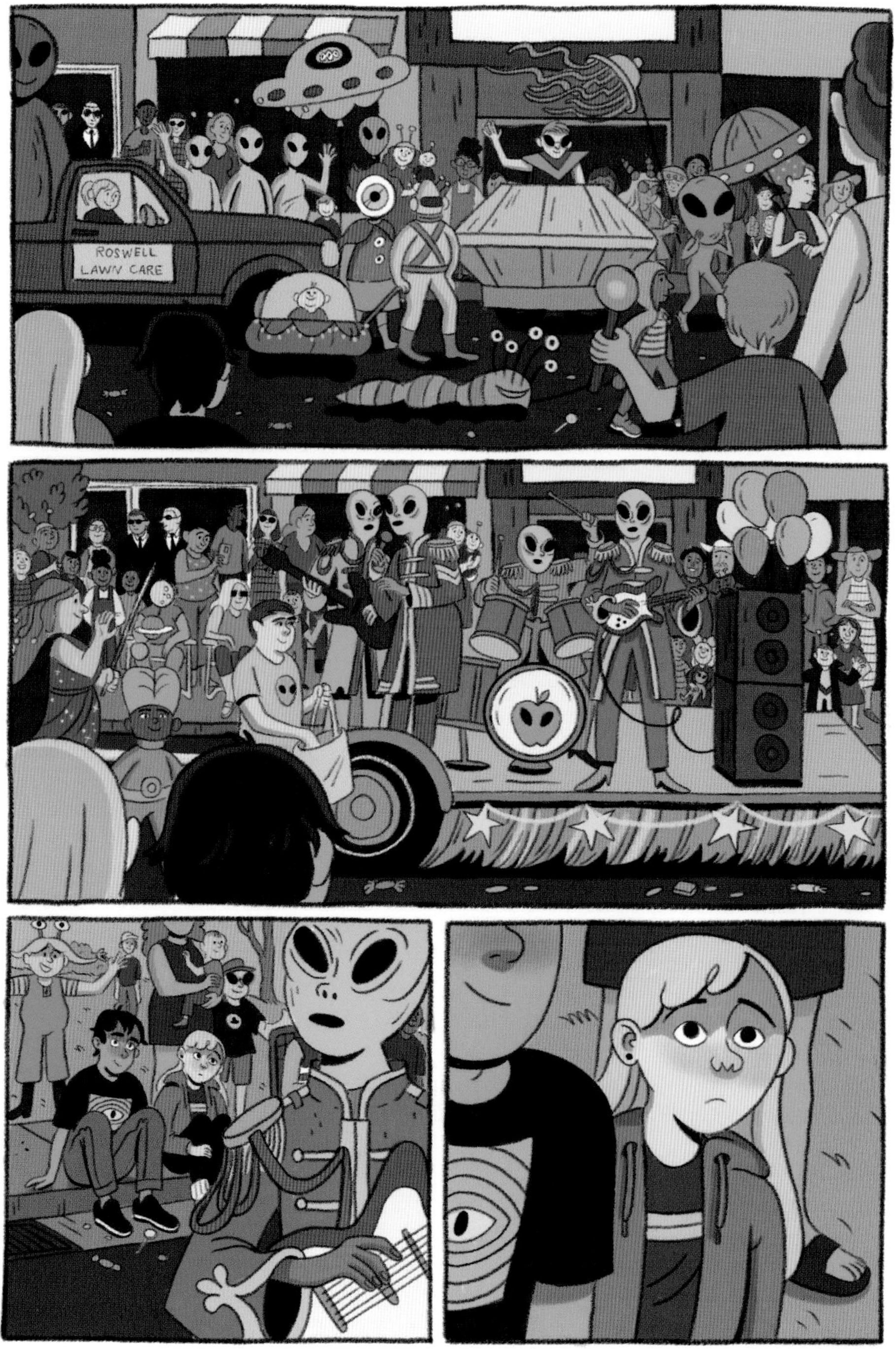
ROSWELL
LAWN CARE

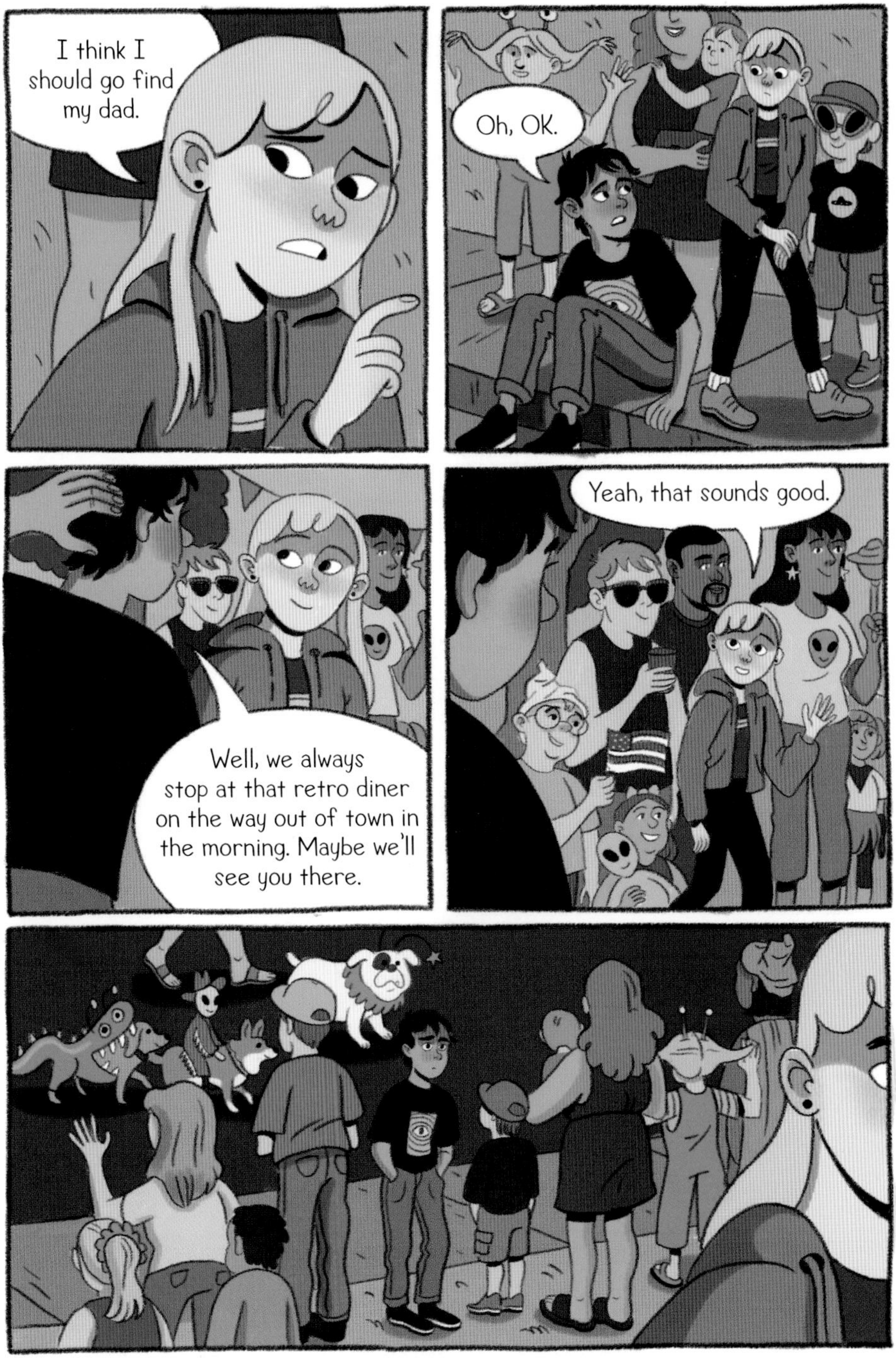
I think I should go find my dad.
Oh, OK.
Well, we always stop at that retro diner on the way out of town in the morning. Maybe we'll see you there.
Yeah, that sounds good.

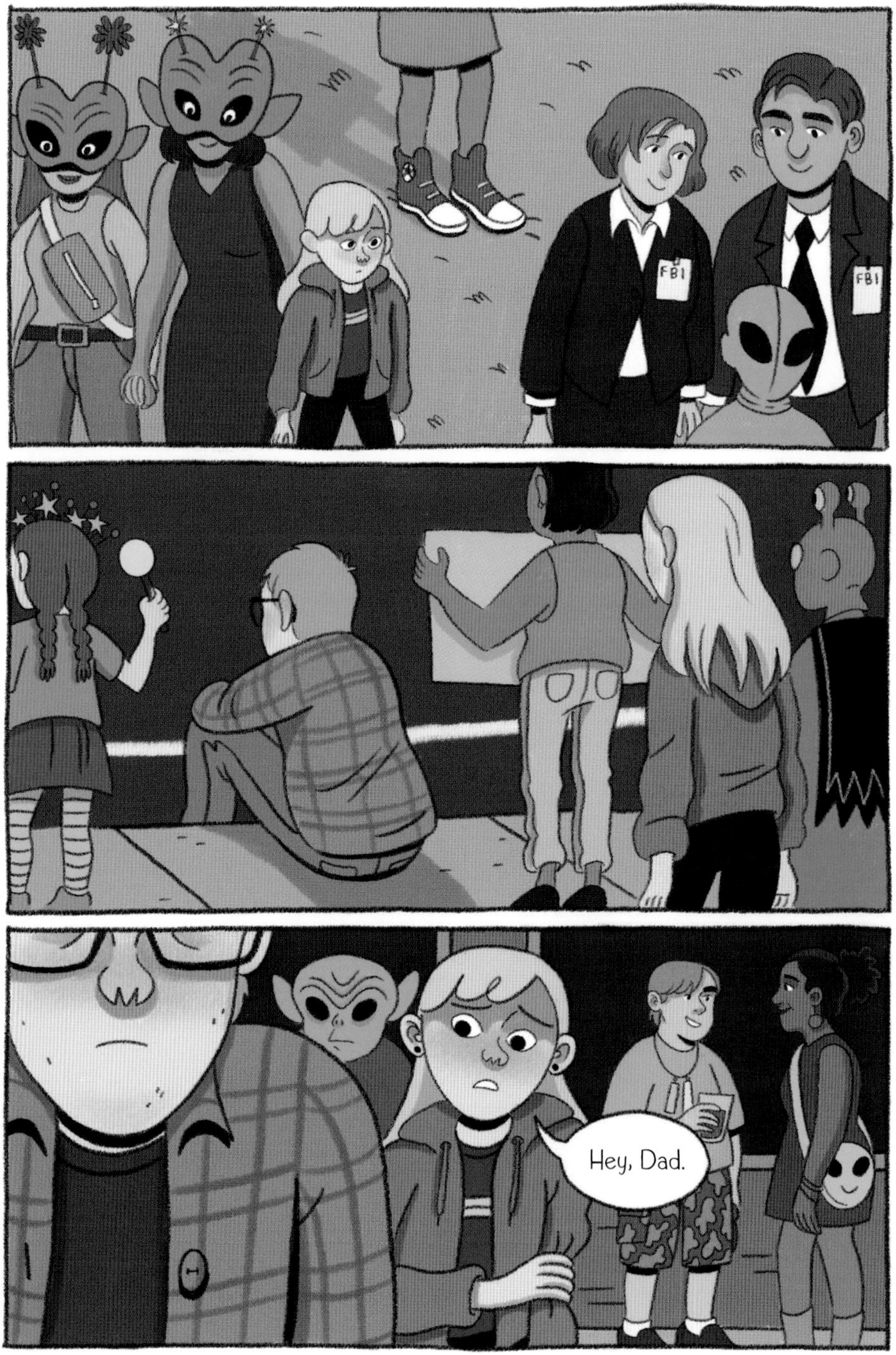
FBI
FBI
Hey, Dad.

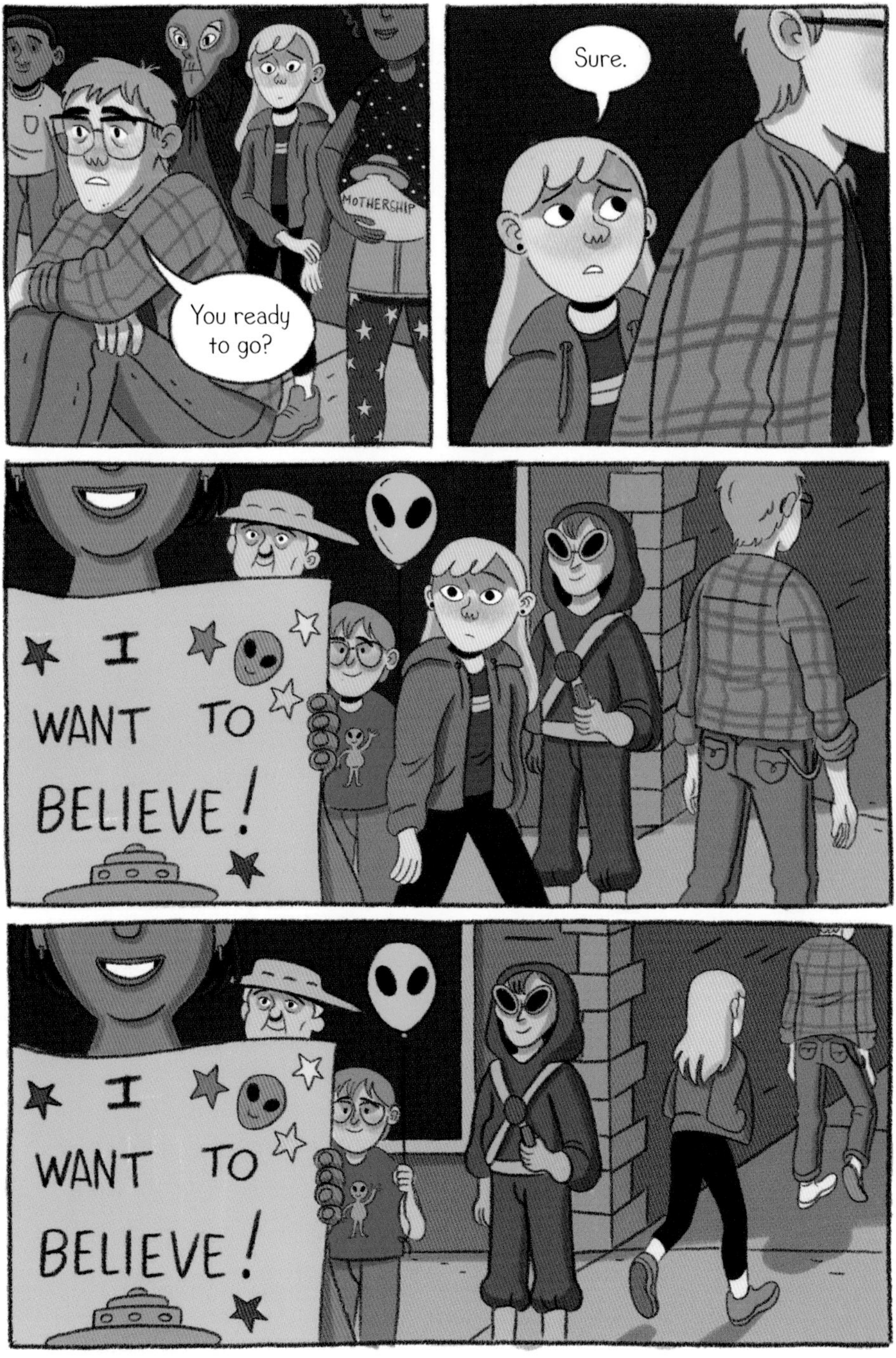
MOTHERSHIP
You ready to go?
Sure.
I WANT TO BELIEVE!
I WANT TO BELIEVE!

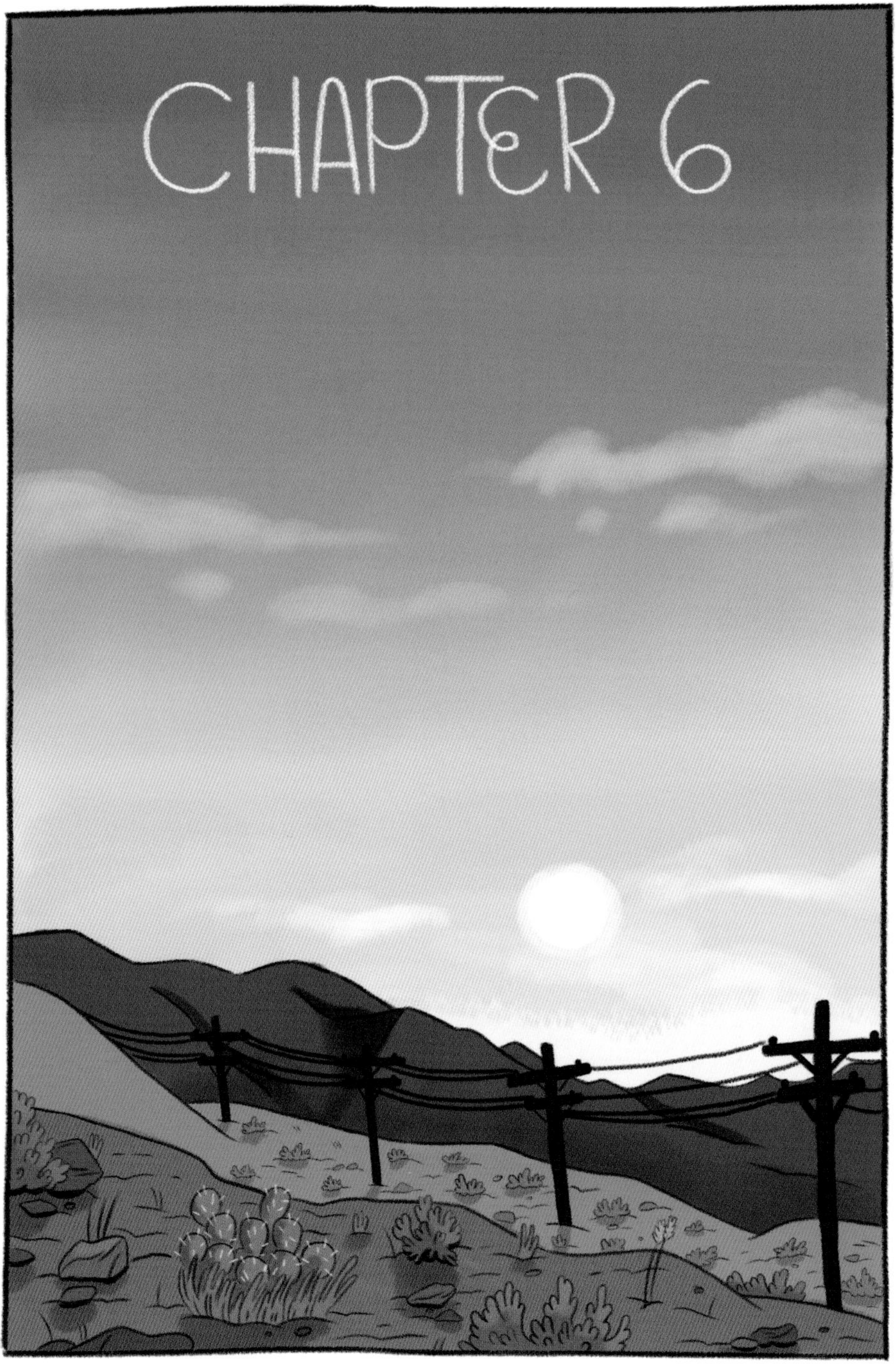
CHAPTER 6

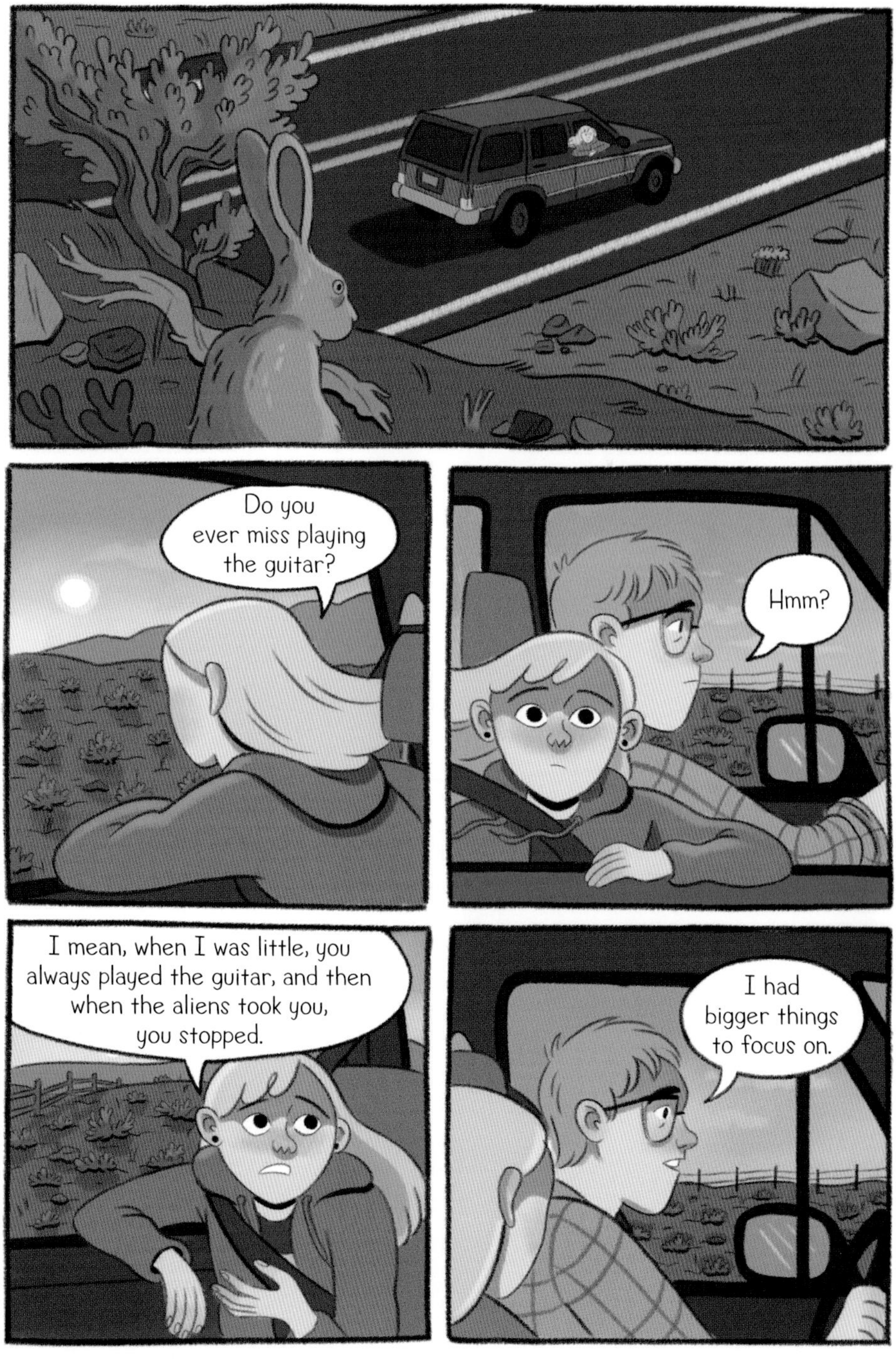
Do you ever miss playing the guitar?
Hmm?
I mean, when I was little, you always played the guitar, and then when the aliens took you, you stopped.
I had bigger things to focus on.

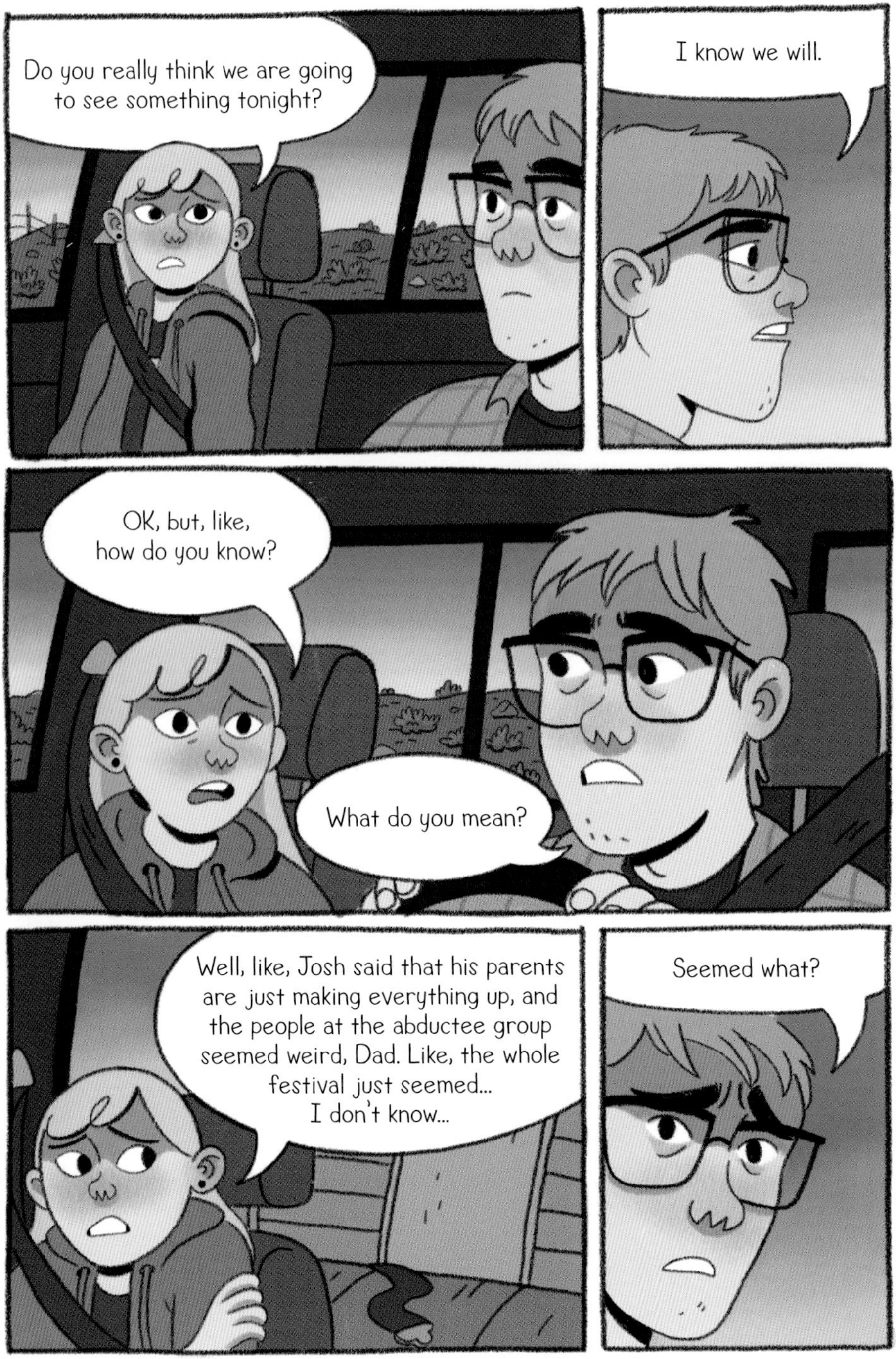
Do you really think we are going to see something tonight?
I know we will.
OK, but, like, how do you know?
What do you mean?
Well, like, Josh said that his parents are just making everything up, and the people at the abductee group seemed weird, Dad. Like, the whole festival just seemed... I don't know...
Seemed what?

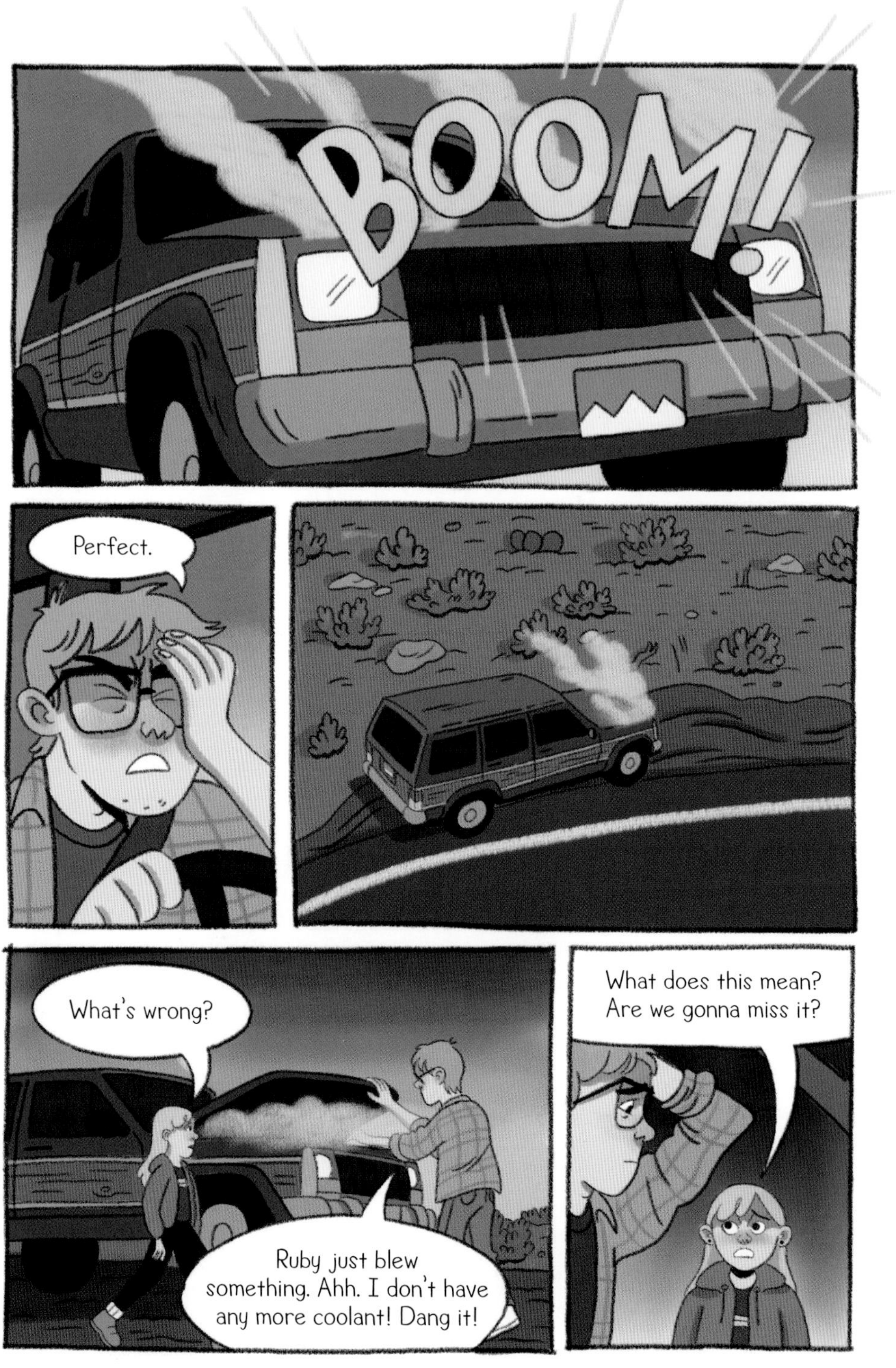
BOOM!
Perfect.
What's wrong?
Ruby just blew something. Ahh. I don't have any more coolant! Dang it!
What does this mean? Are we gonna miss it?

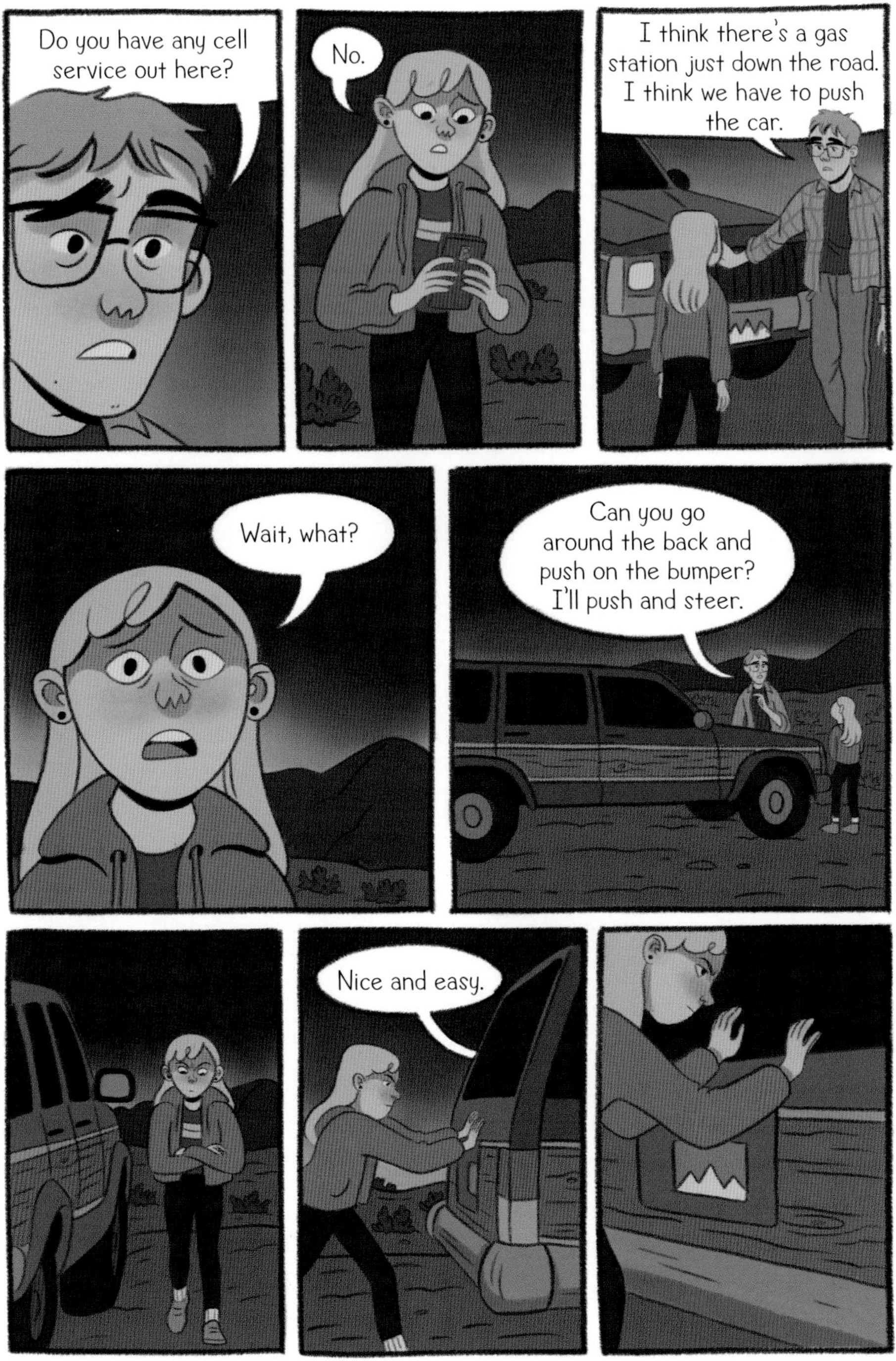
Do you have any cell service out here?
No.
I think there's a gas station just down the road. I think we have to push the car.
Wait, what?
Can you go around the back and push on the bumper? I'll push and steer.
Nice and easy.

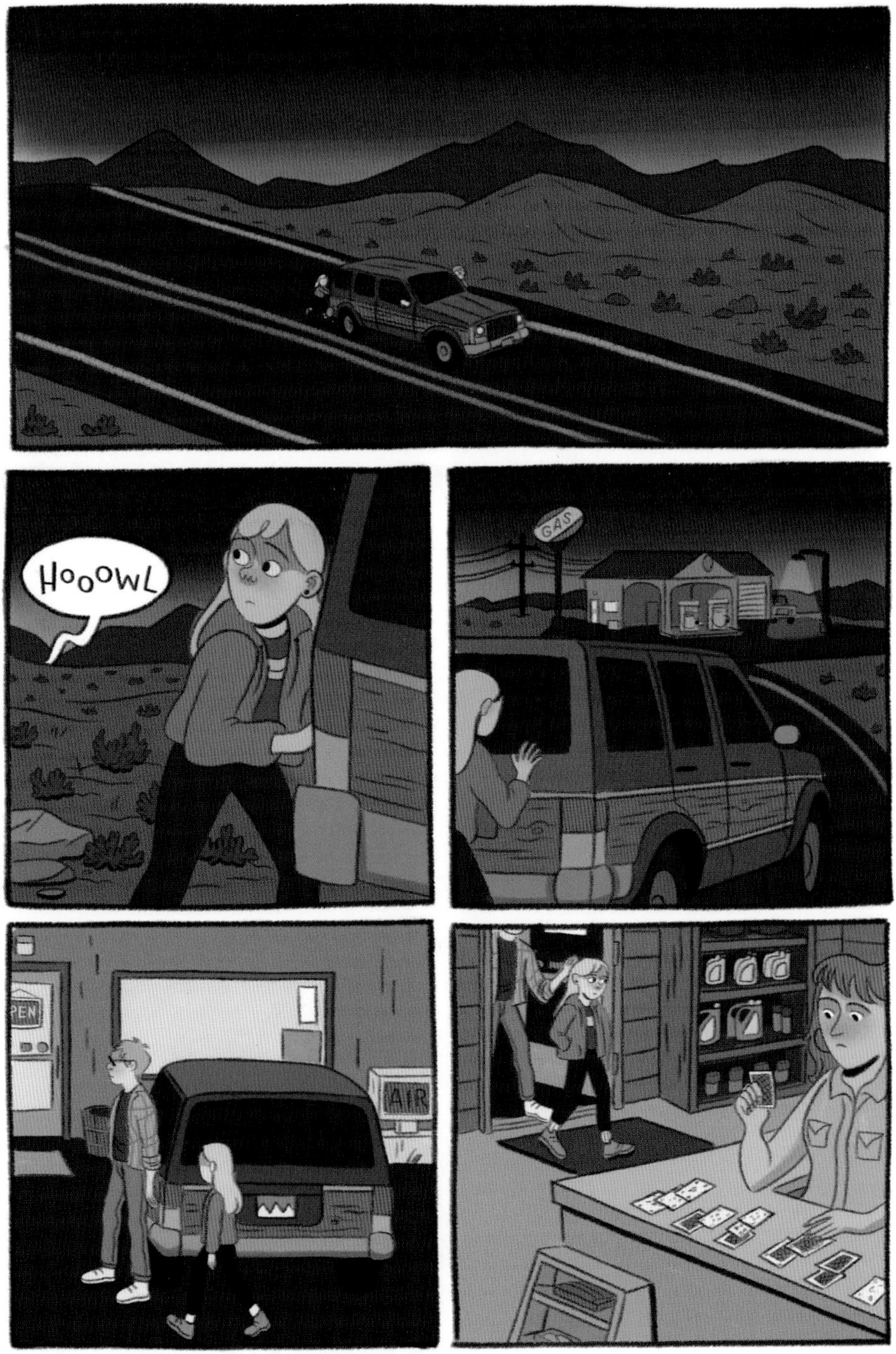
HOOOWL
GAS
OPEN
AIR

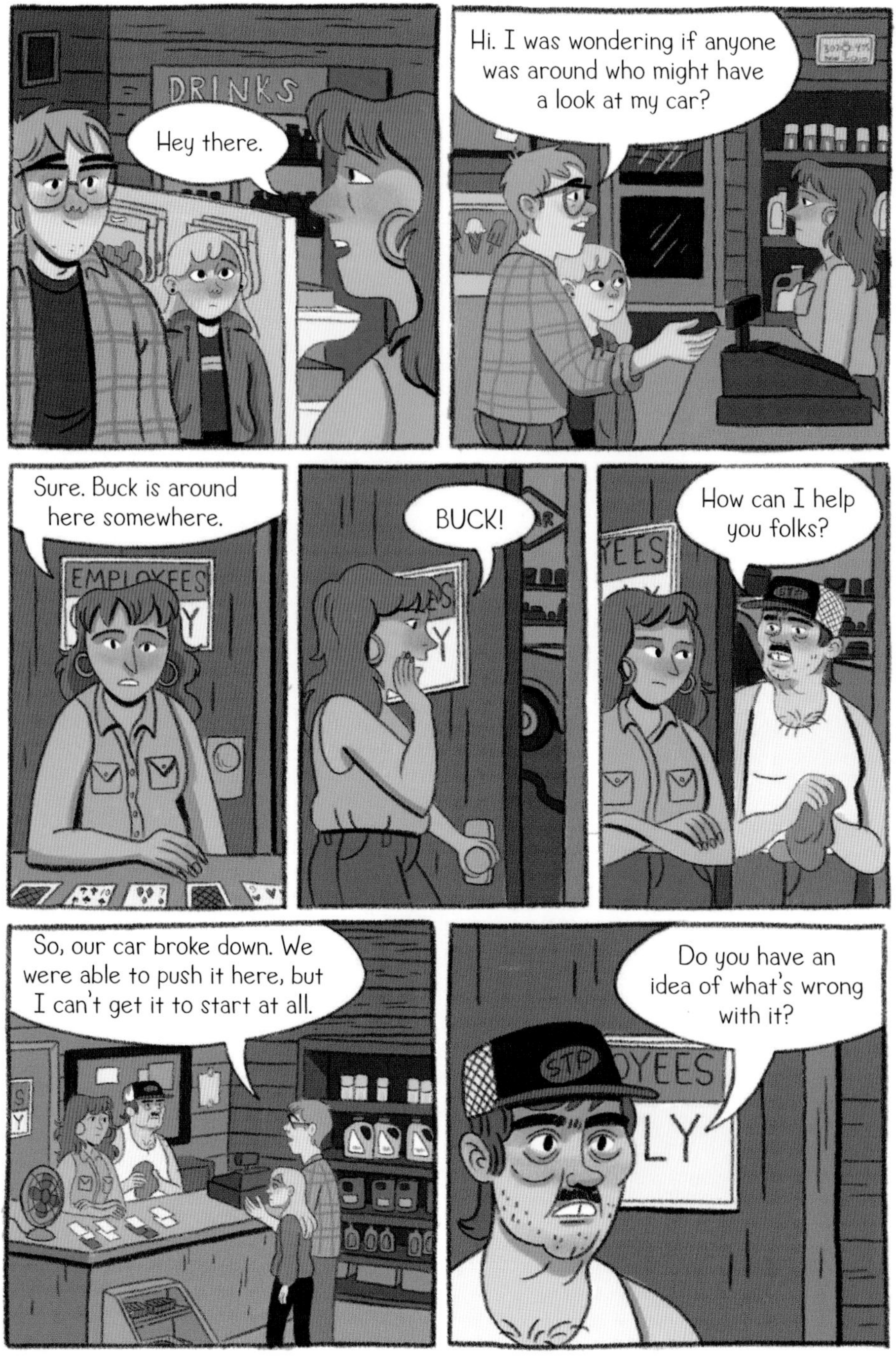
DRINKS
Hey there.
Hi. I was wondering if anyone was around who might have a look at my car?
Sure. Buck is around here somewhere.
EMPLOYEES
BUCK!
How can I help you folks?
So, our car broke down. We were able to push it here, but I can't get it to start at all.
STP
Do you have an idea of what's wrong with it?

No, we were just driving down the road, and it seized up and died.

It keeps overheating, so we can't run the air-conditioning.

Yeah, I have to top it off with coolant sometimes.

Well, let's go have a look.

You and your dad been at the festival?

Jimmy: Yeah.

I went a few years back. Just to see what all the hubbub was about, ya know?

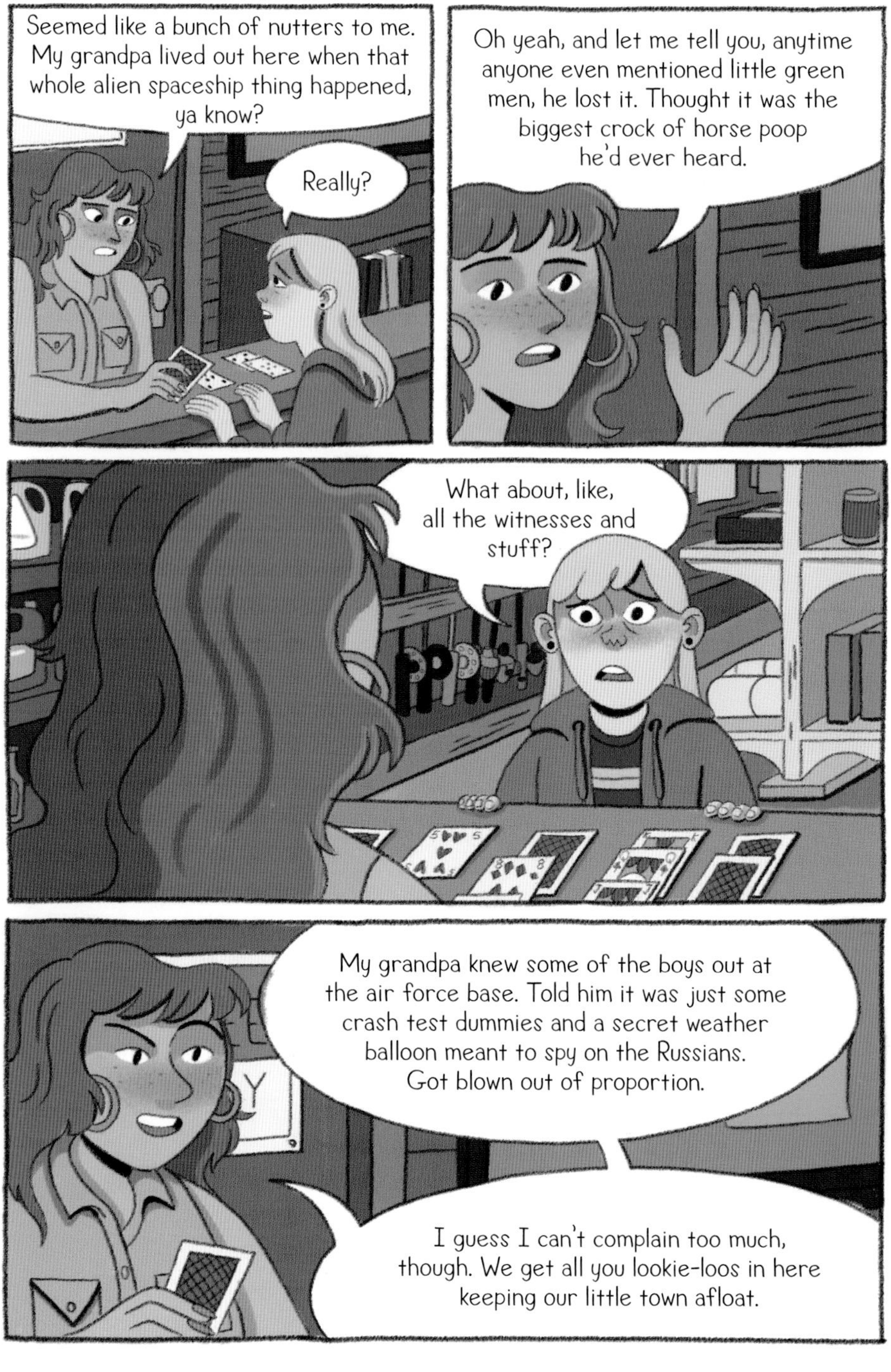
Seemed like a bunch of nutters to me. My grandpa lived out here when that whole alien spaceship thing happened, ya know?
Really?
Oh yeah, and let me tell you, anytime anyone even mentioned little green men, he lost it. Thought it was the biggest crock of horse poop he'd ever heard.
What about, like, all the witnesses and stuff?
My grandpa knew some of the boys out at the air force base. Told him it was just some crash test dummies and a secret weather balloon meant to spy on the Russians. Got blown out of proportion.
I guess I can't complain too much, though. We get all you lookie-loos in here keeping our little town afloat.

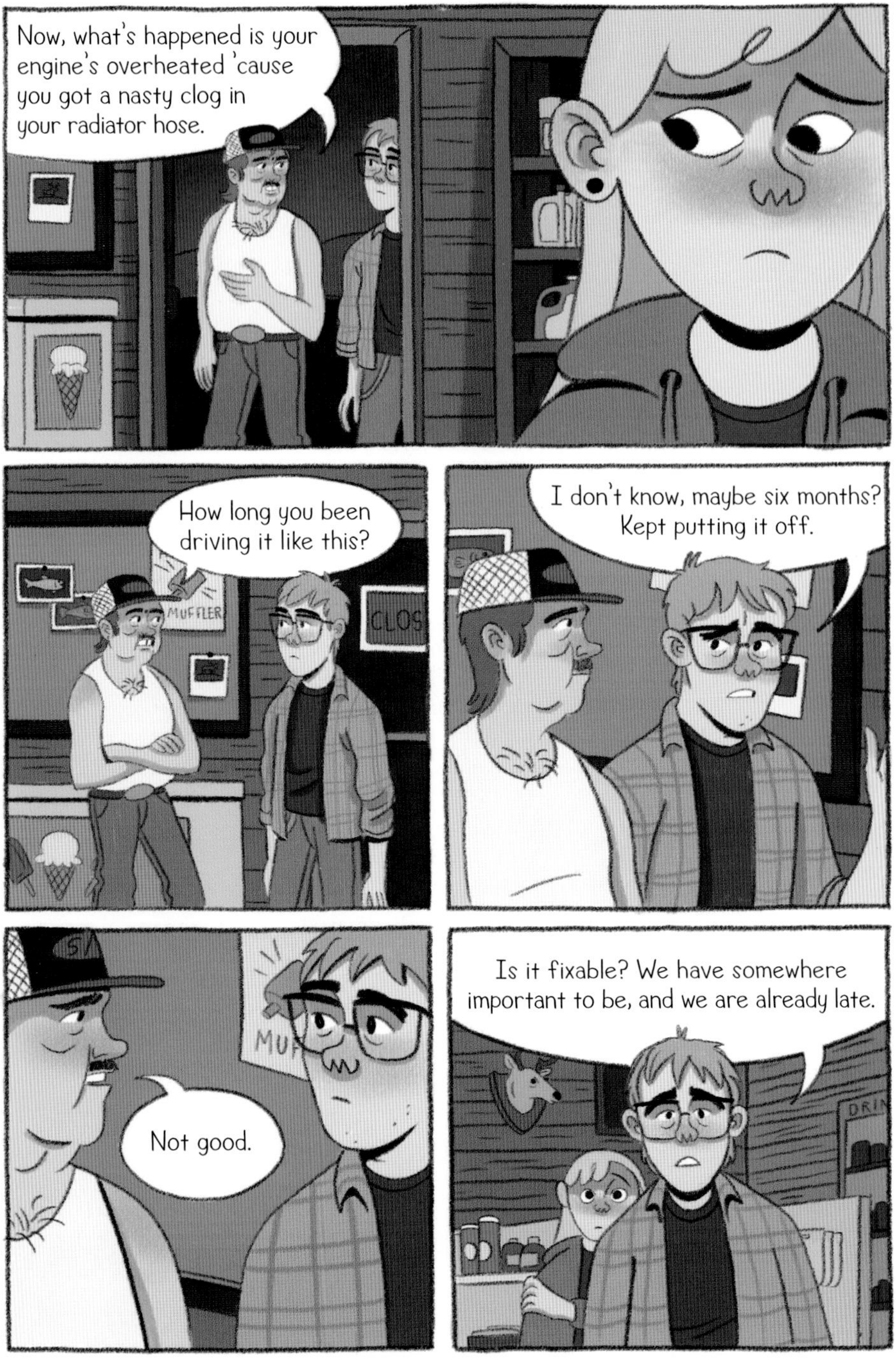
Now, what's happened is your engine's overheated 'cause you got a nasty clog in your radiator hose.
How long you been driving it like this?
MUFFLER
I don't know, maybe six months? Kept putting it off.
Not good.
Is it fixable? We have somewhere important to be, and we are already late.

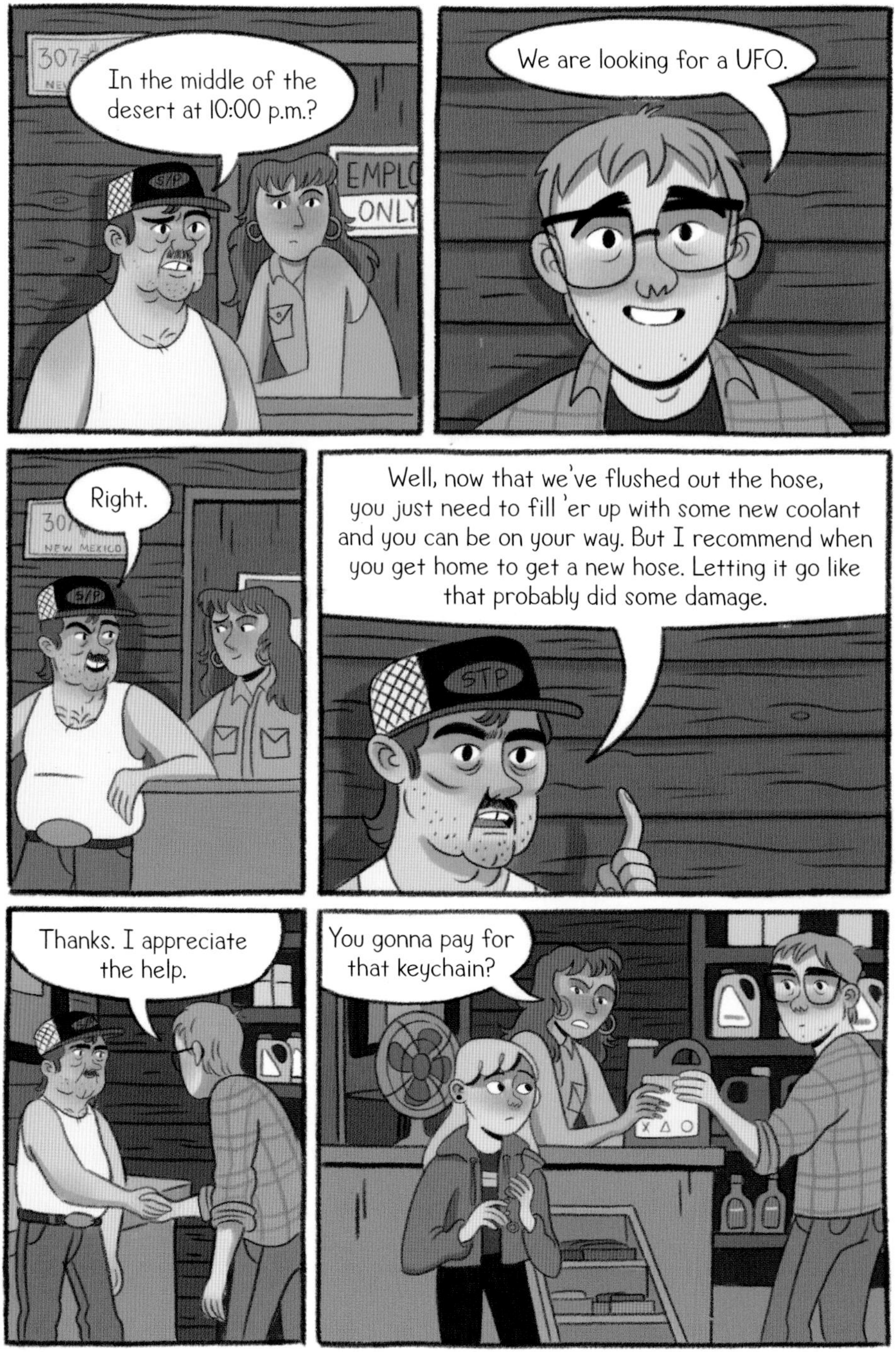
307
NEW
In the middle of the desert at 10:00 p.m.?
EMPLO
ONLY
We are looking for a UFO.
Right.
307
NEW MEXICO
STP
Well, now that we've flushed out the hose, you just need to fill 'er up with some new coolant and you can be on your way. But I recommend when you get home to get a new hose. Letting it go like that probably did some damage.
STP
Thanks. I appreciate the help.
You gonna pay for that keychain?

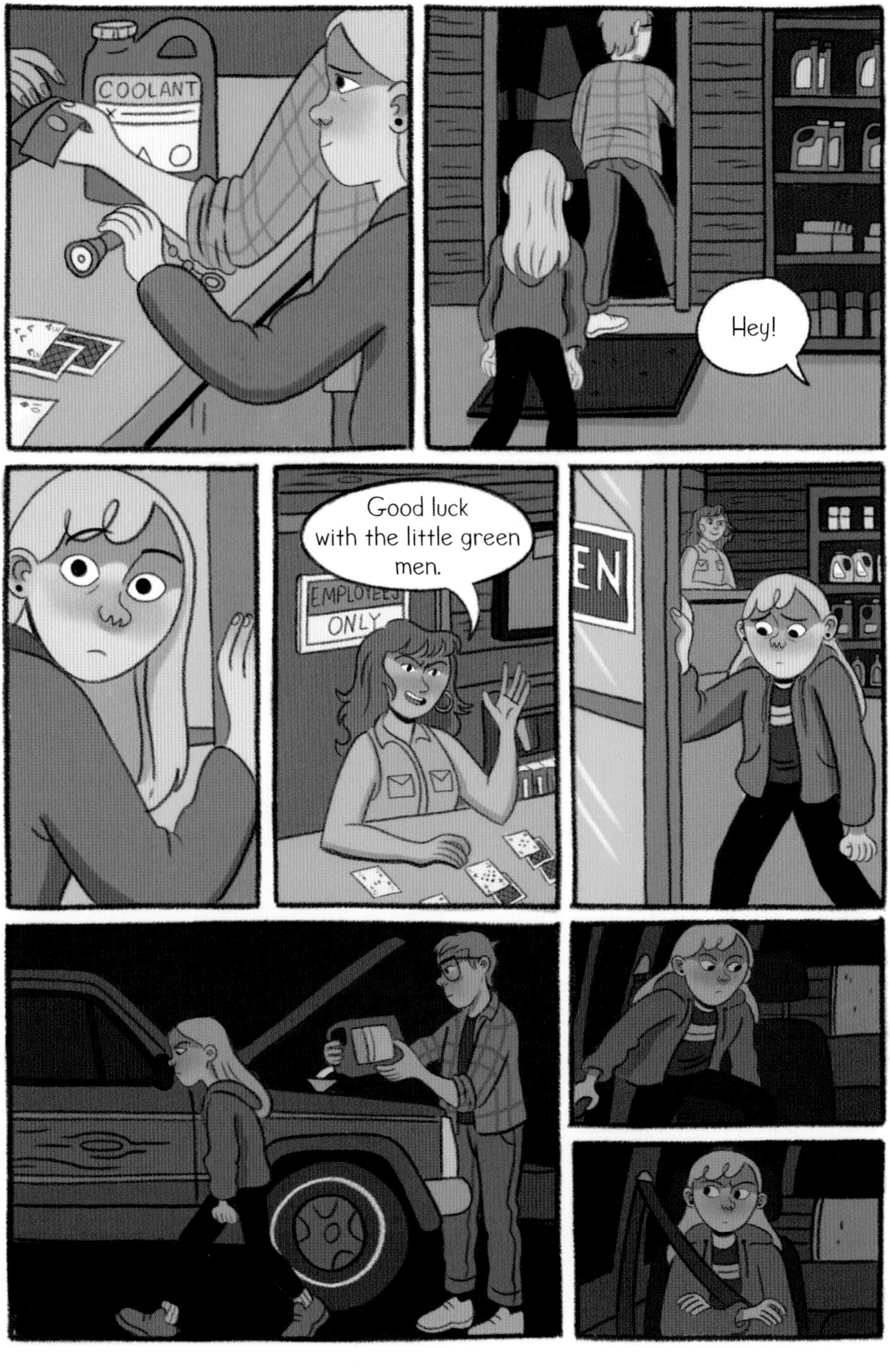
COOLANT
Hey!
Good luck with the little green men.
EMPLOYEES ONLY
EN

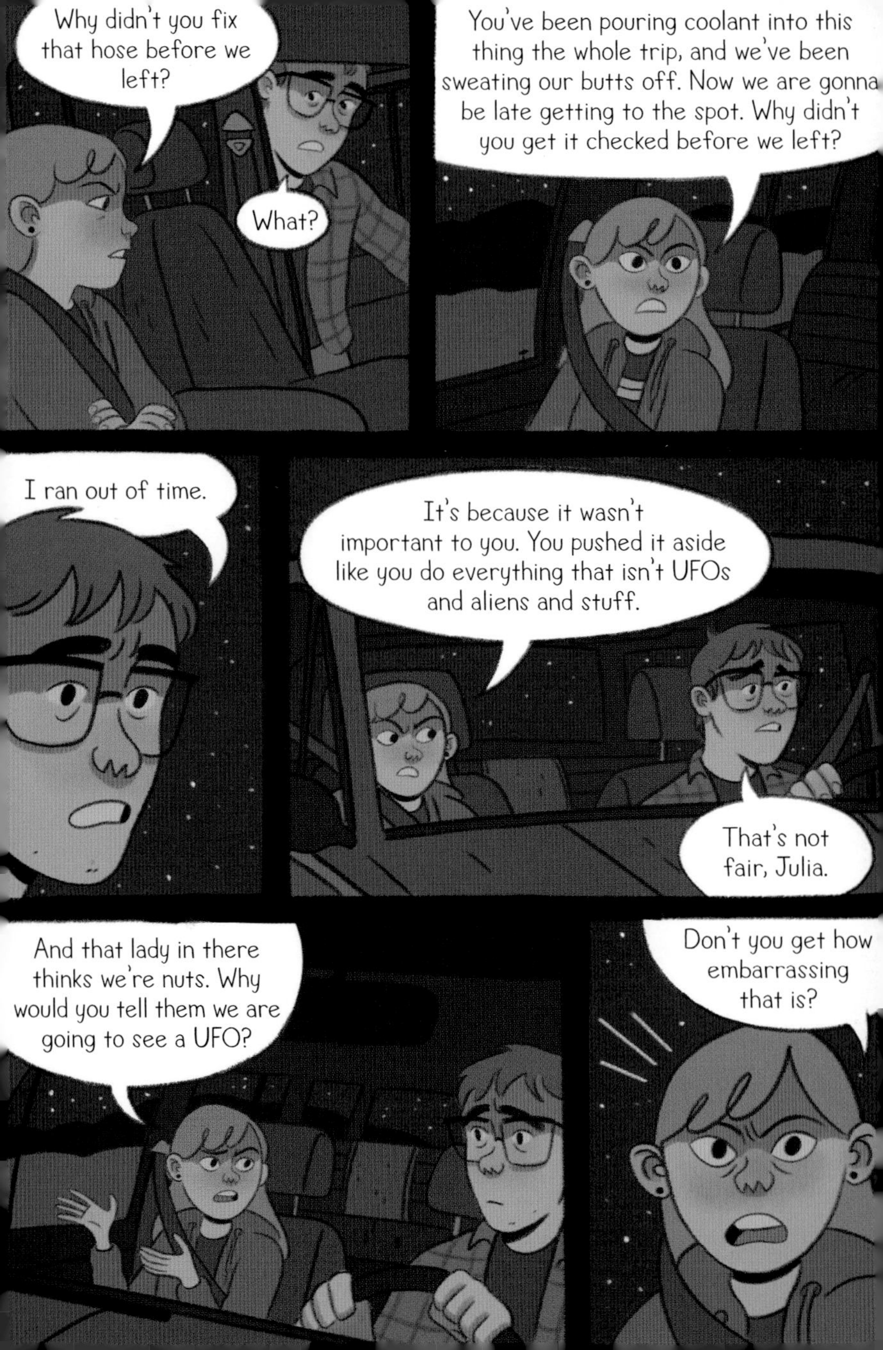
Why didn't you fix that hose before we left?
What?
You've been pouring coolant into this thing the whole trip, and we've been sweating our butts off. Now we are gonna be late getting to the spot. Why didn't you get it checked before we left?
I ran out of time.
It's because it wasn't important to you. You pushed it aside like you do everything that isn't UFOs and aliens and stuff.
That's not fair, Julia.
And that lady in there thinks we're nuts. Why would you tell them we are going to see a UFO?
Don't you get how embarrassing that is?

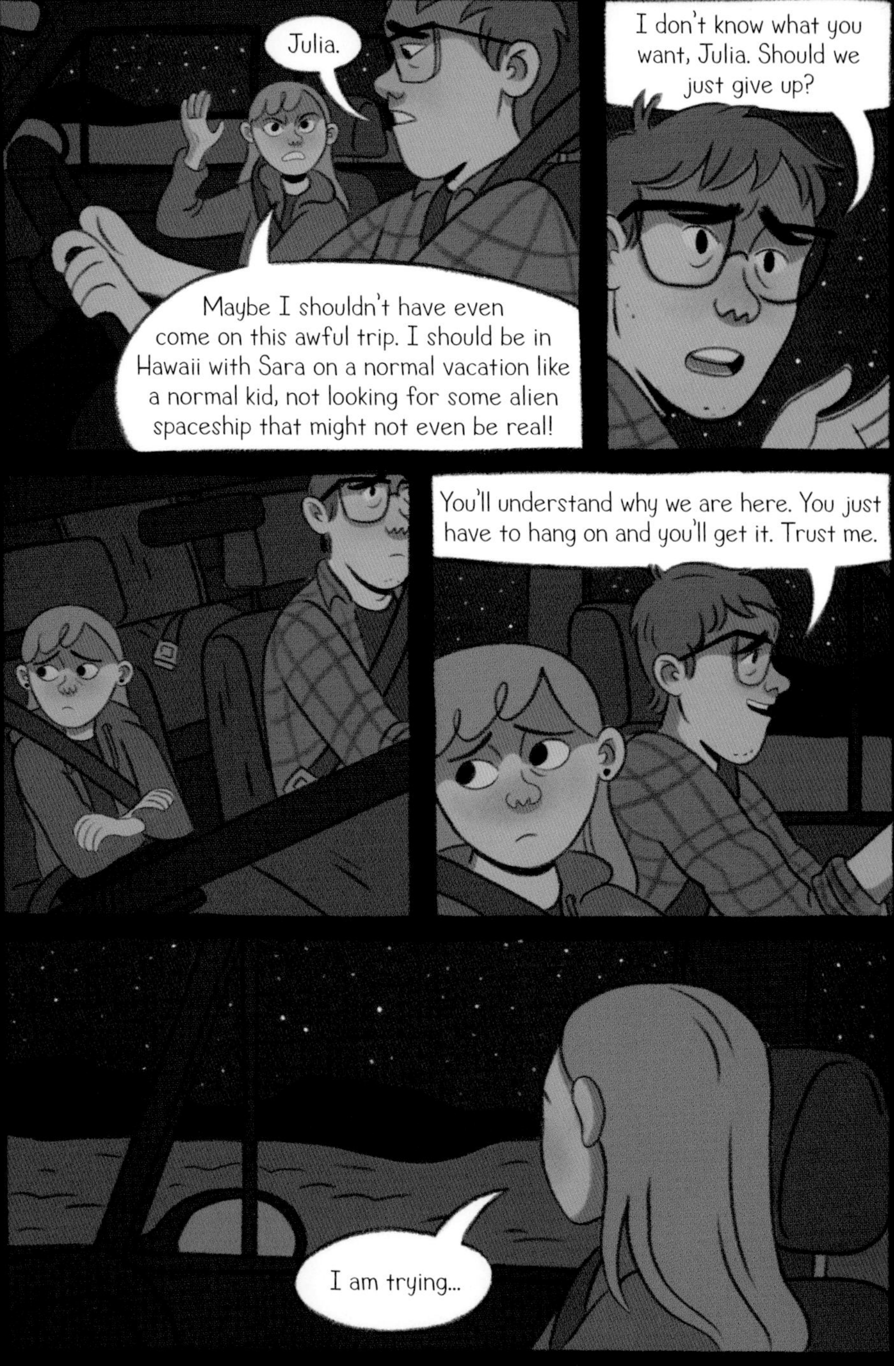
Julia.
Maybe I shouldn't have even come on this awful trip. I should be in Hawaii with Sara on a normal vacation like a normal kid, not looking for some alien spaceship that might not even be real!
I don't know what you want, Julia. Should we just give up?
You'll understand why we are here. You just have to hang on and you'll get it. Trust me.
I am trying...

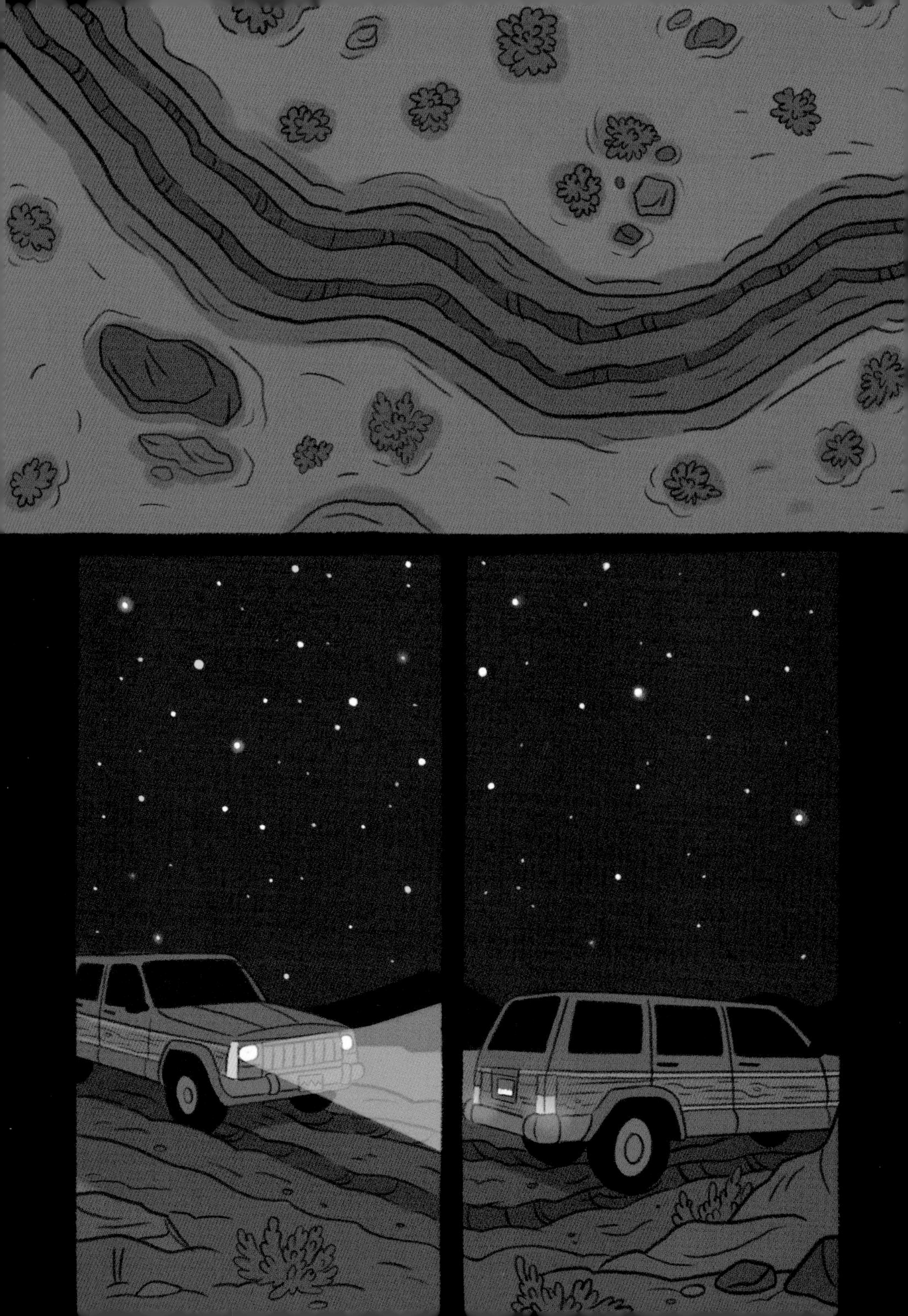

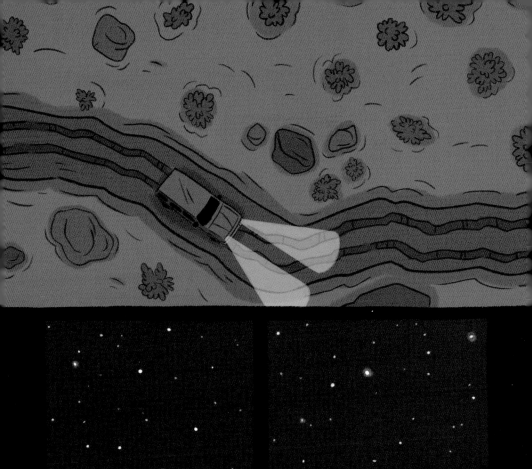

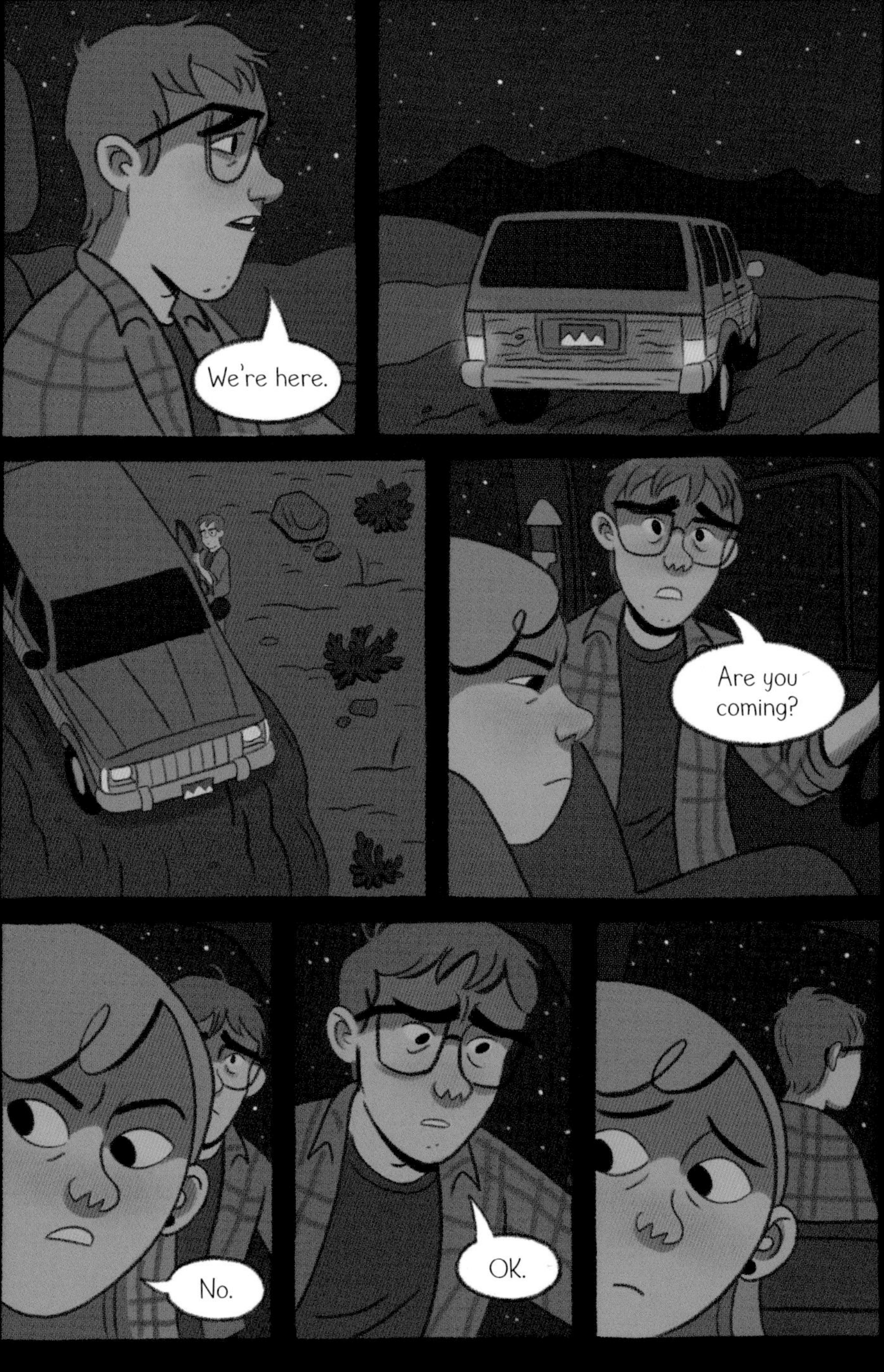
We're here.
Are you coming?
No.
OK.

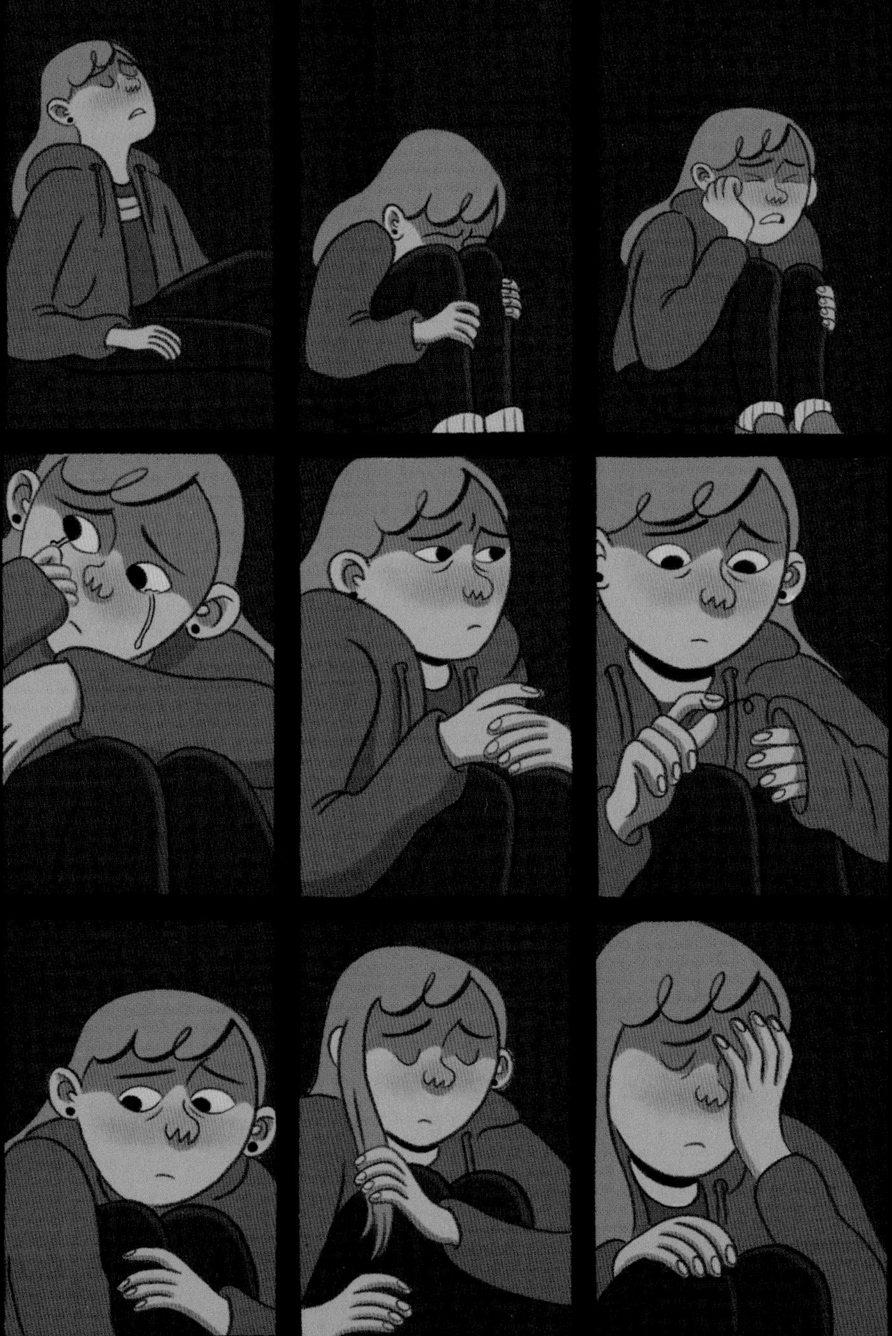

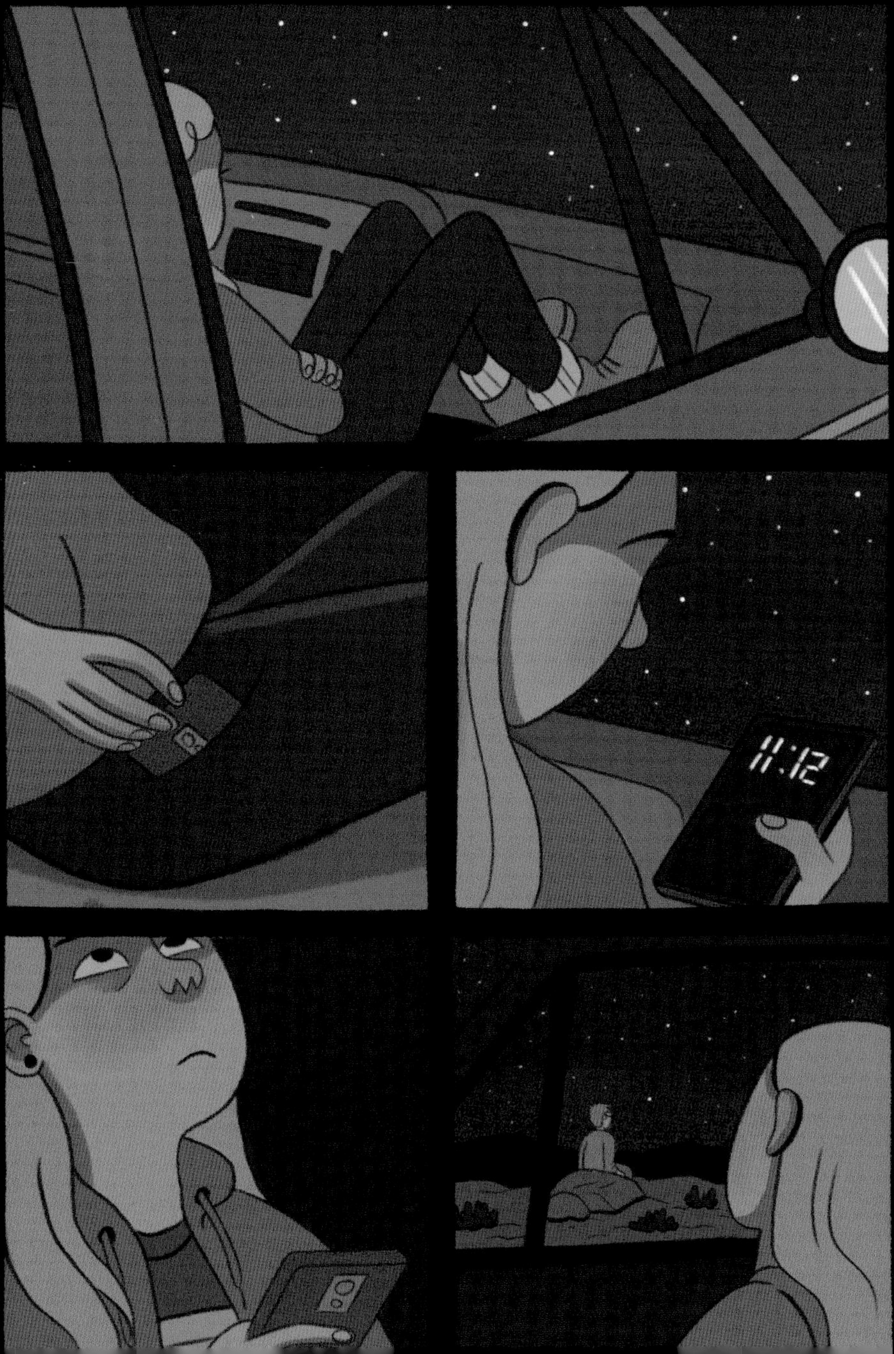
11:12

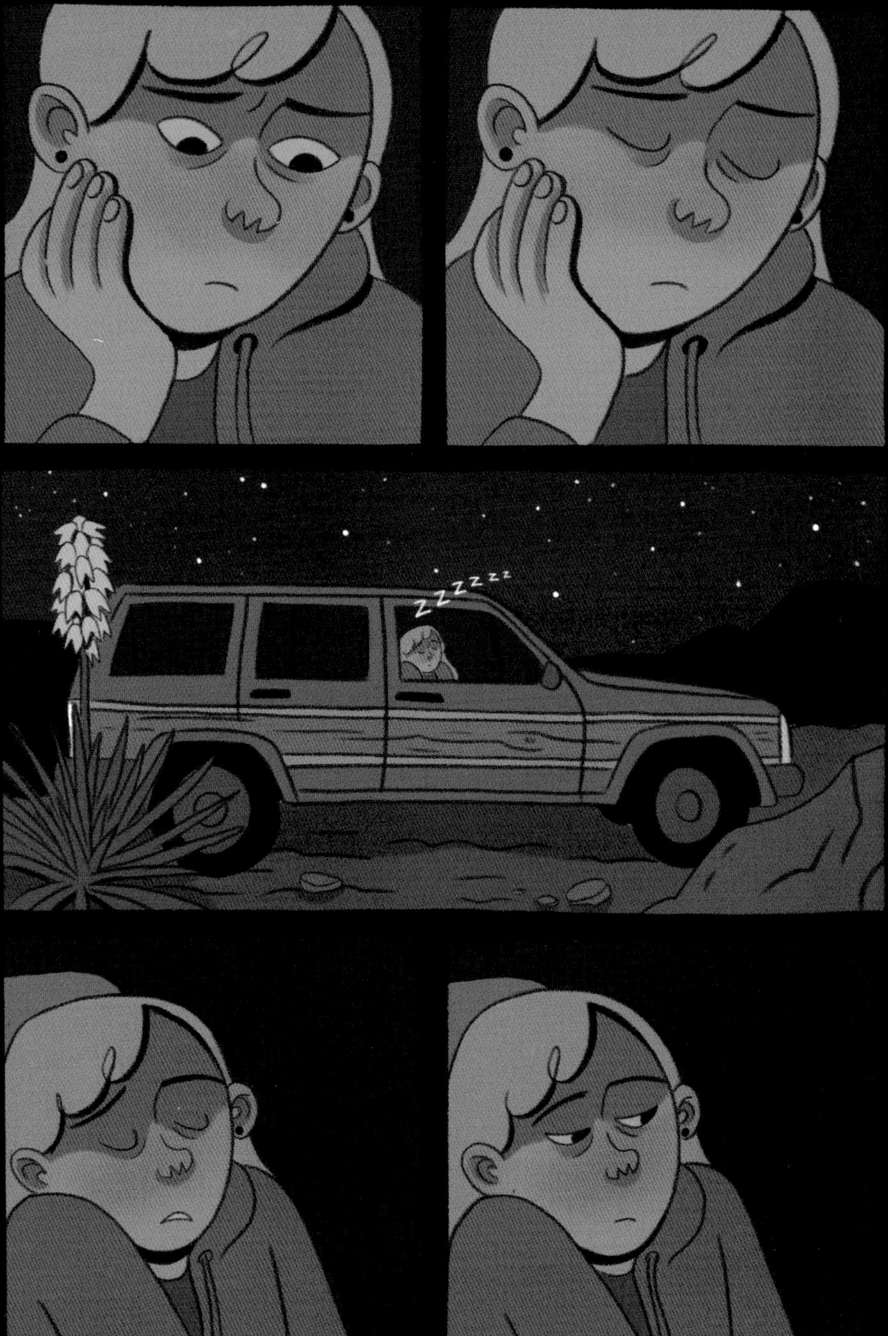
ZZZZZZZ

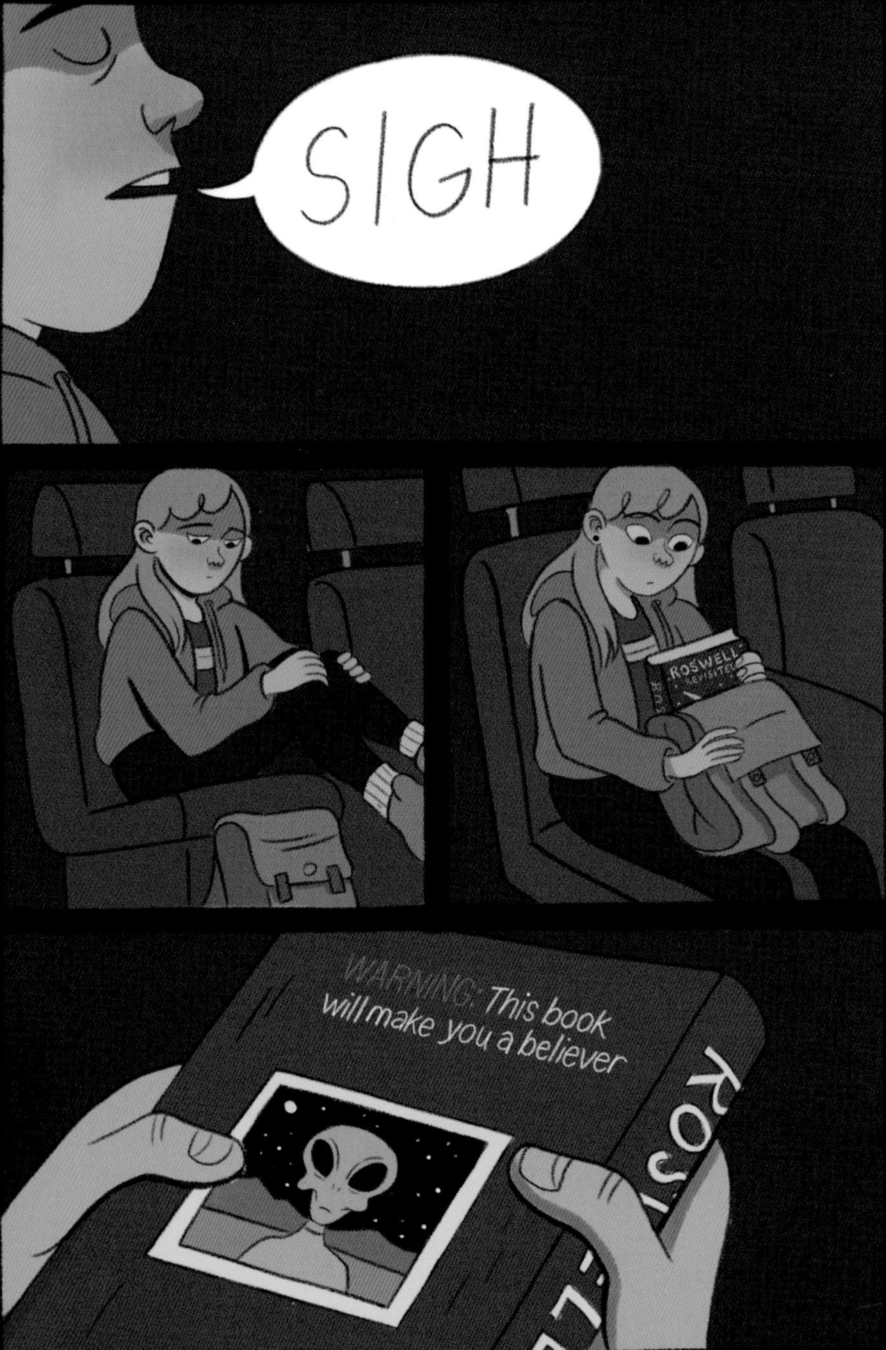
SIGH
ROSWELL REVISITED
WARNING: This book will make you a believer

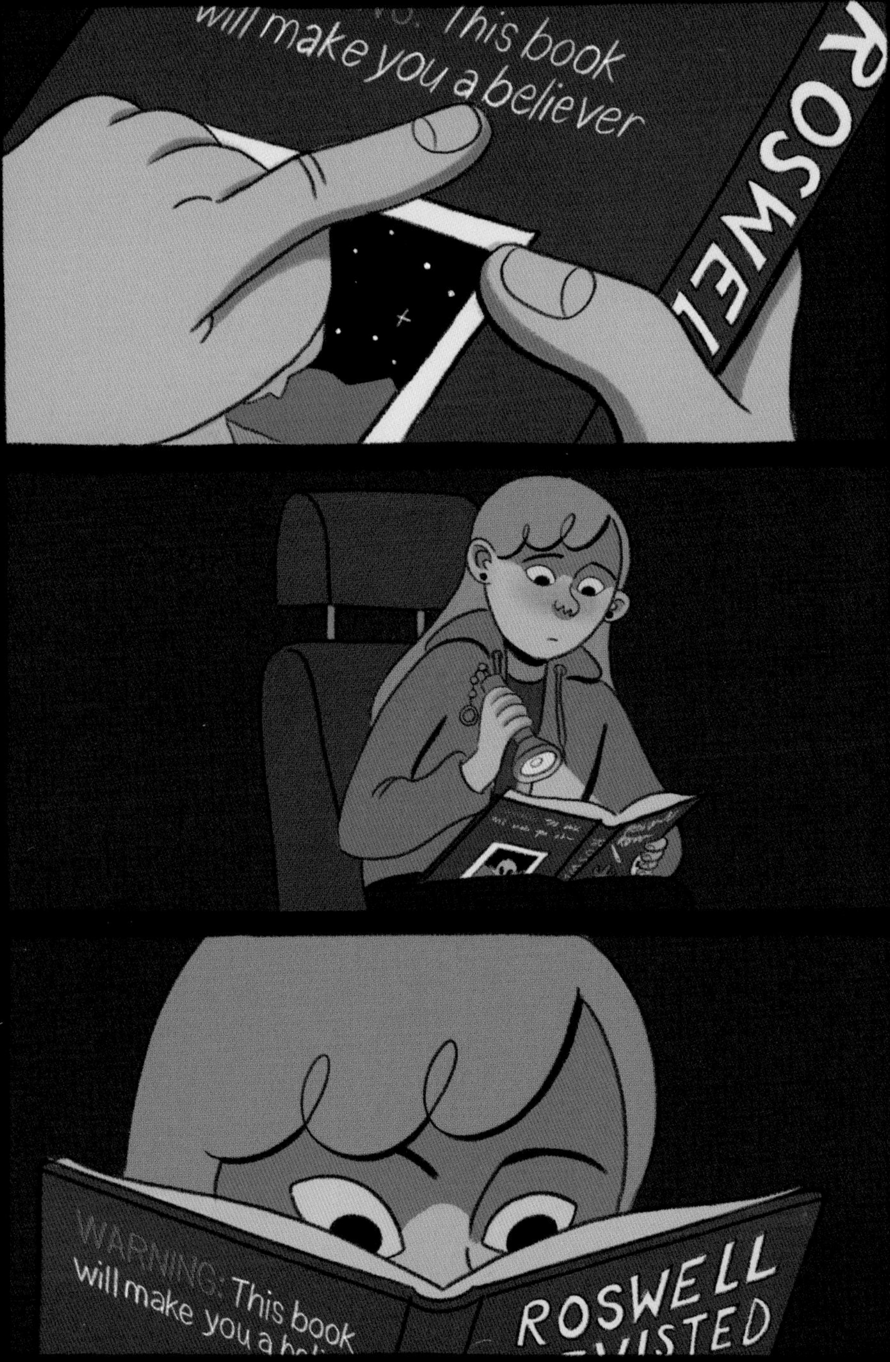
This book
will make you a believer
ROSWEL
WARNING: This book
will make you a
ROSWELL

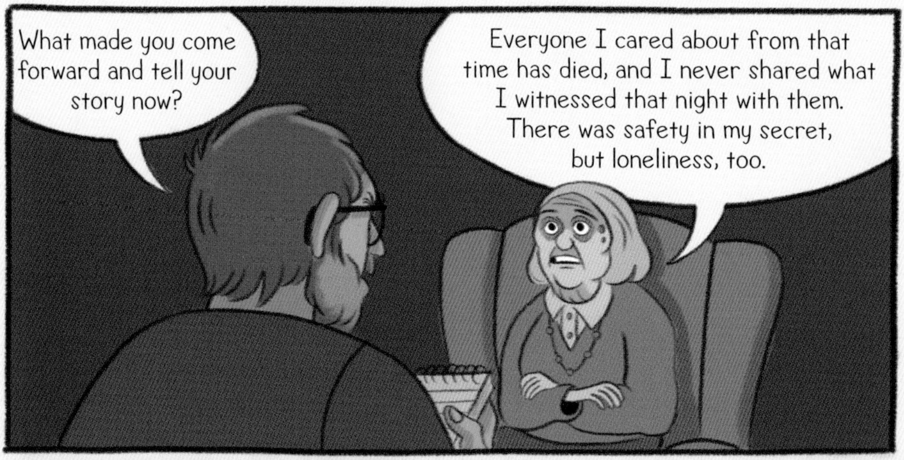
What made you come forward and tell your story now?
Everyone I cared about from that time has died, and I never shared what I witnessed that night with them. There was safety in my secret, but loneliness, too.

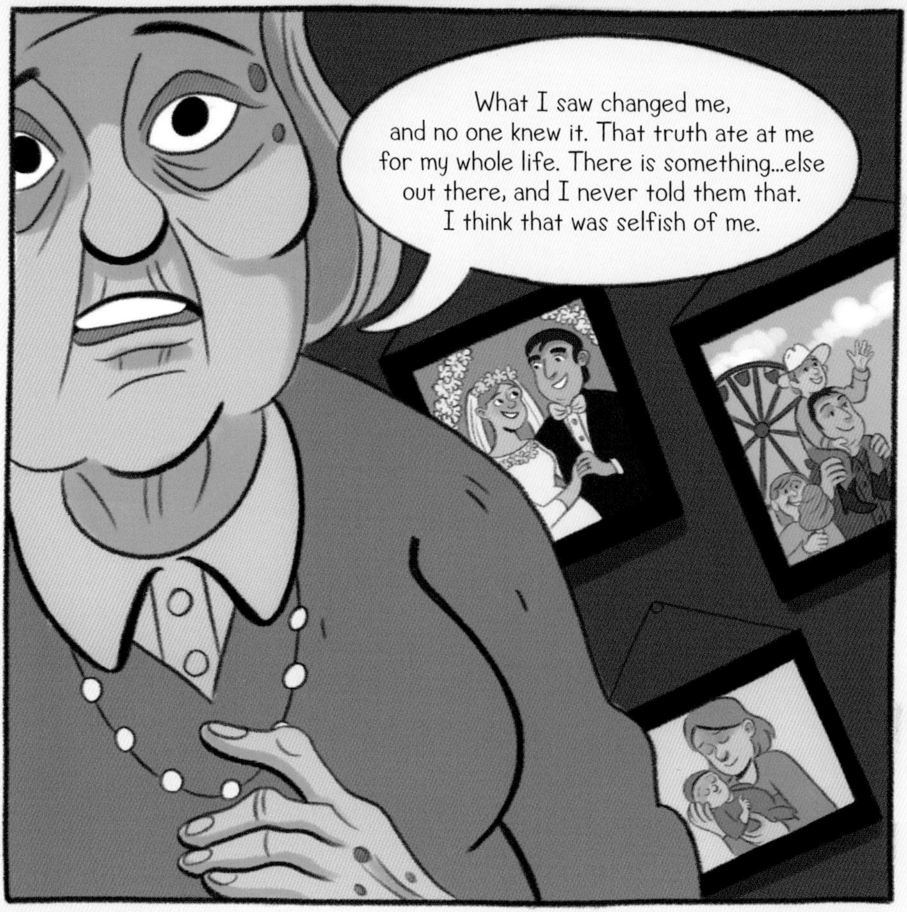
What I saw changed me, and no one knew it. That truth ate at me for my whole life. There is something...else out there, and I never told them that. I think that was selfish of me.

Selfish? In what way?

I know for a fact that the universe isn't dead and empty.

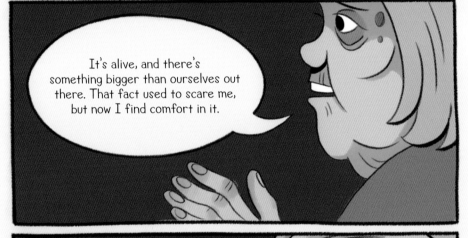

It's alive, and there's something bigger than ourselves out there. That fact used to scare me, but now I find comfort in it.

I denied the people I love the most that comfort. I never even gave them the chance to believe me. I wish I could tell them that I'm sorry I didn't trust them. Sorry that I wasn't brave.

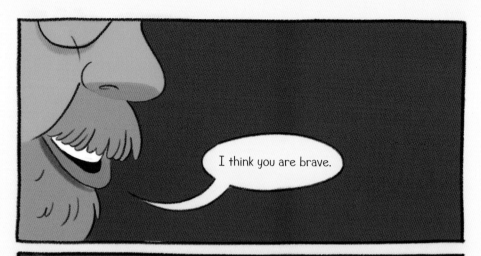

I think you are brave.

Thank you, Mr. Bell.
I think I've reached the point where it doesn't matter anymore what people say about me. I need to tell my story for my own peace of mind.

I can't give anyone proof of what I saw that night. I can't make anyone believe me, but maybe someone out there will, and they will feel a little less alone.

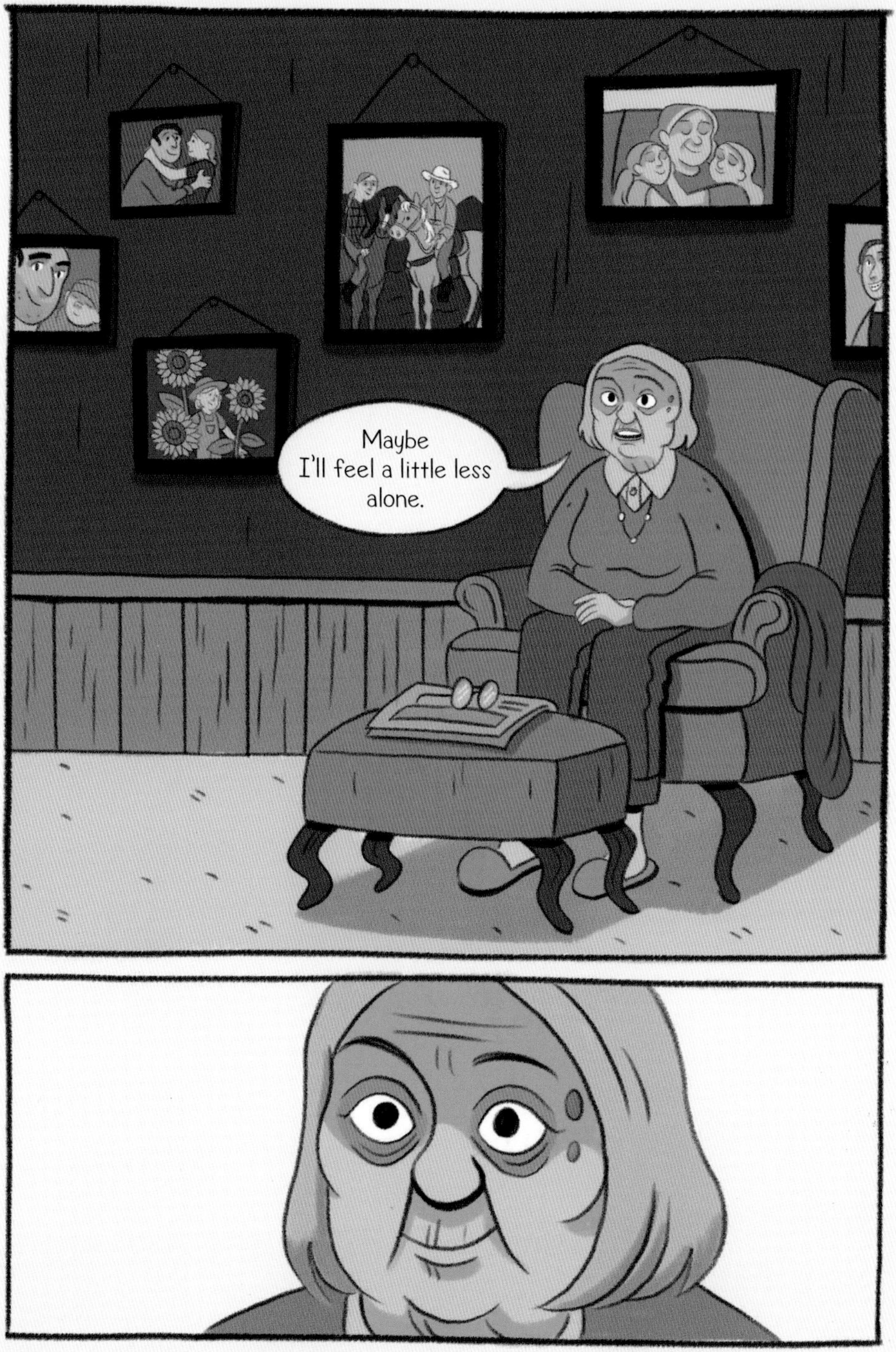
Maybe
I'll feel a little less
alone.

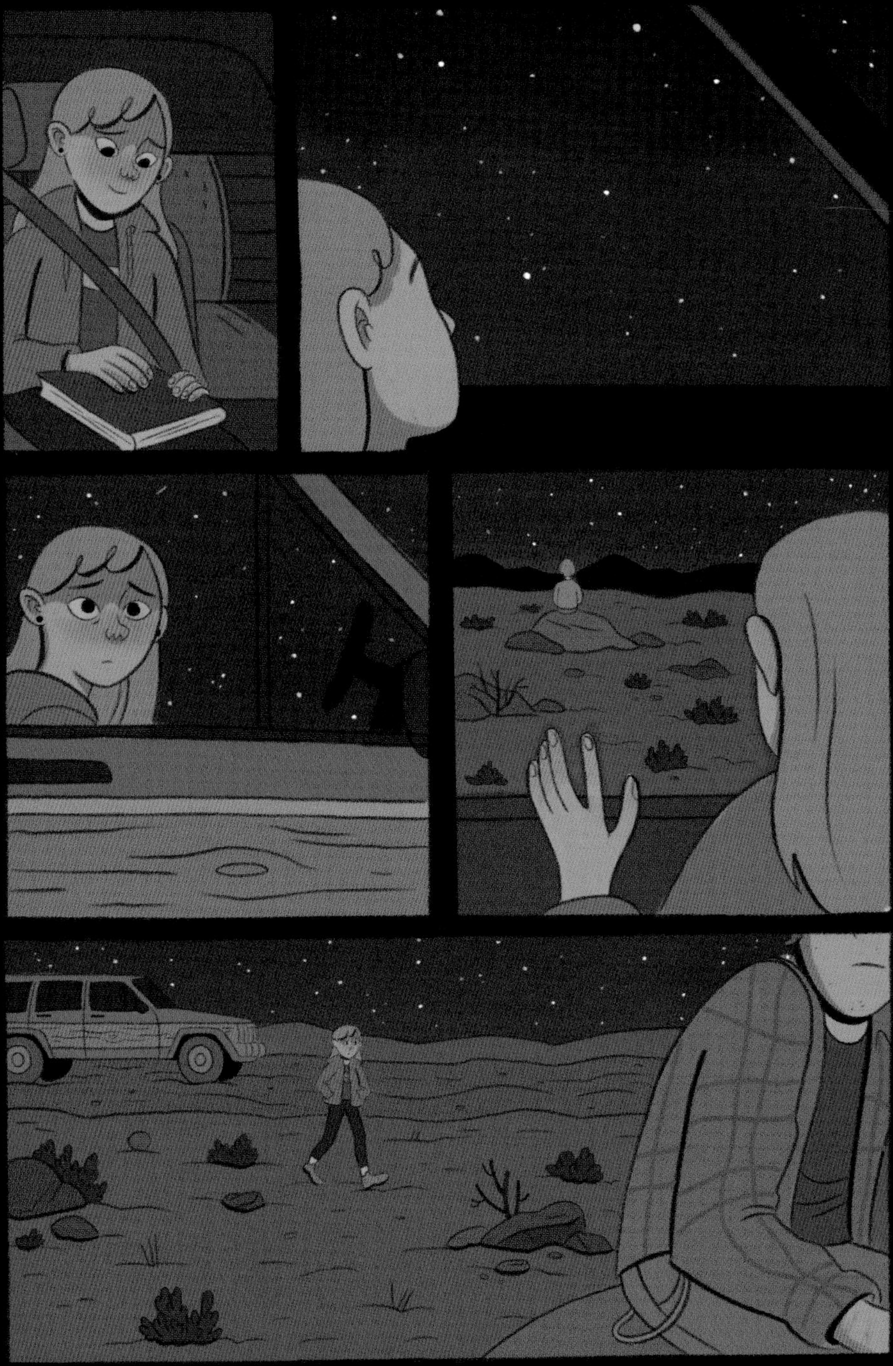

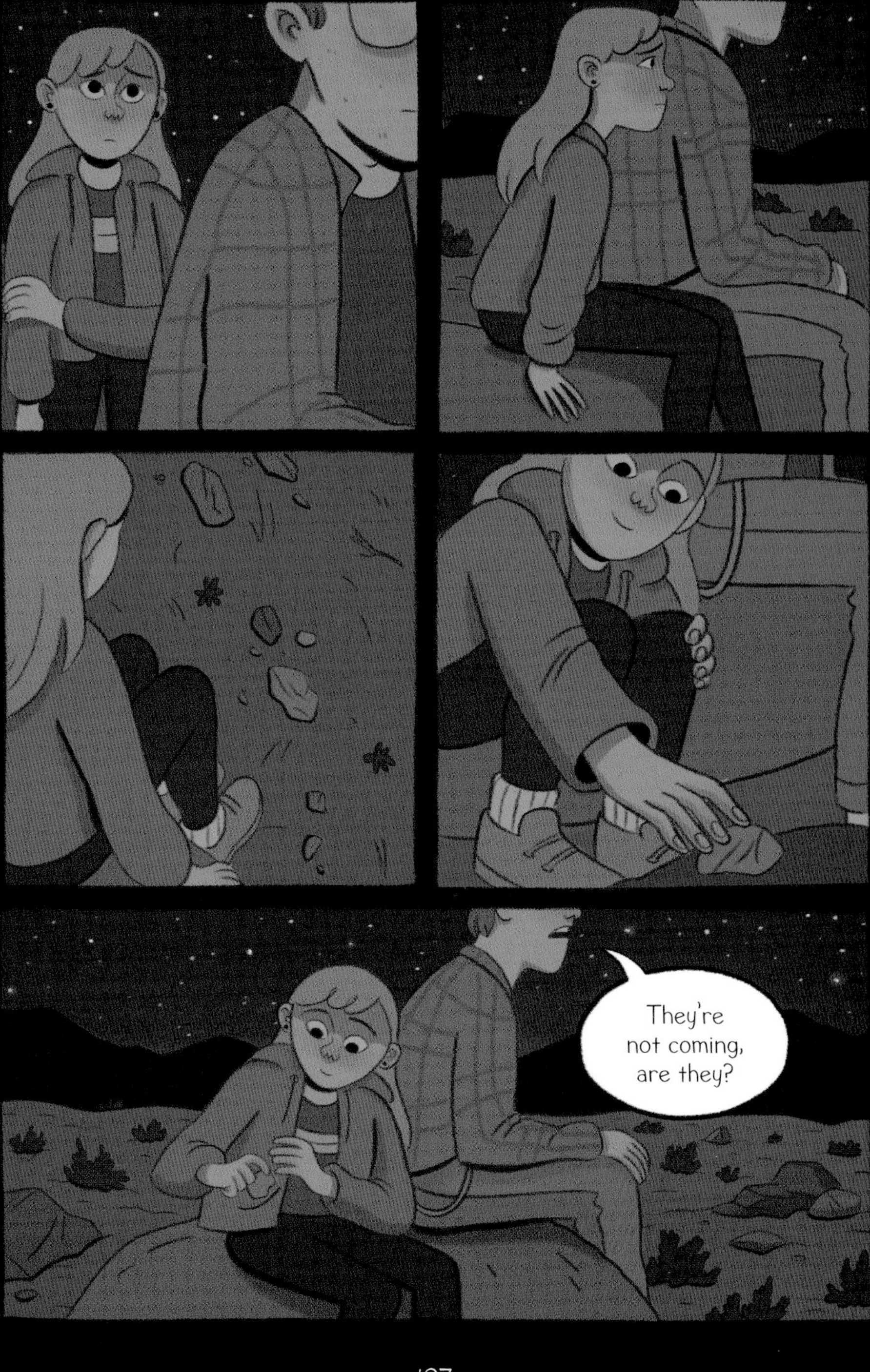
They're not coming, are they?

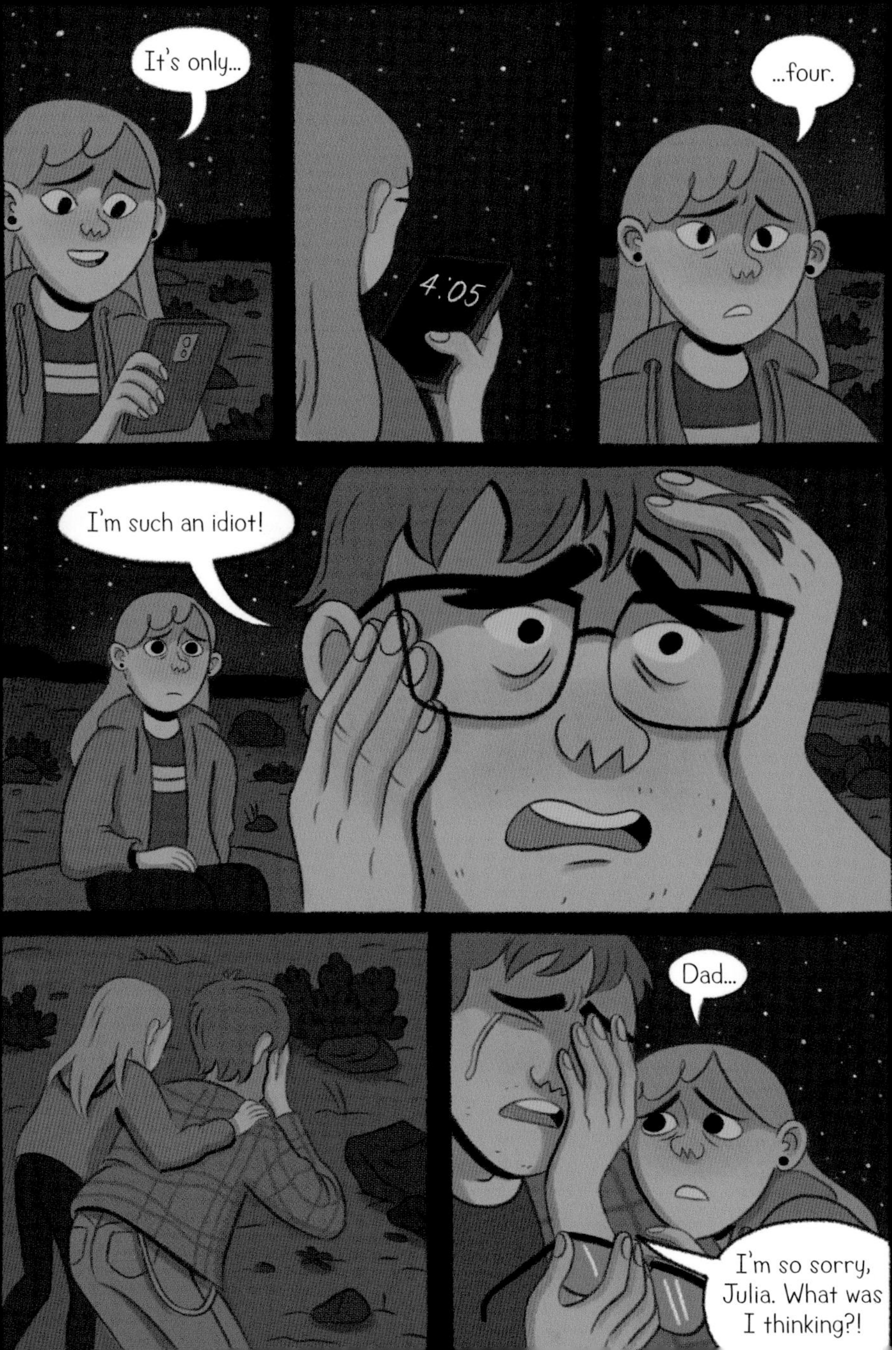
It's only...
4:05
...four.
I'm such an idiot!
Dad...
I'm so sorry, Julia. What was I thinking?!

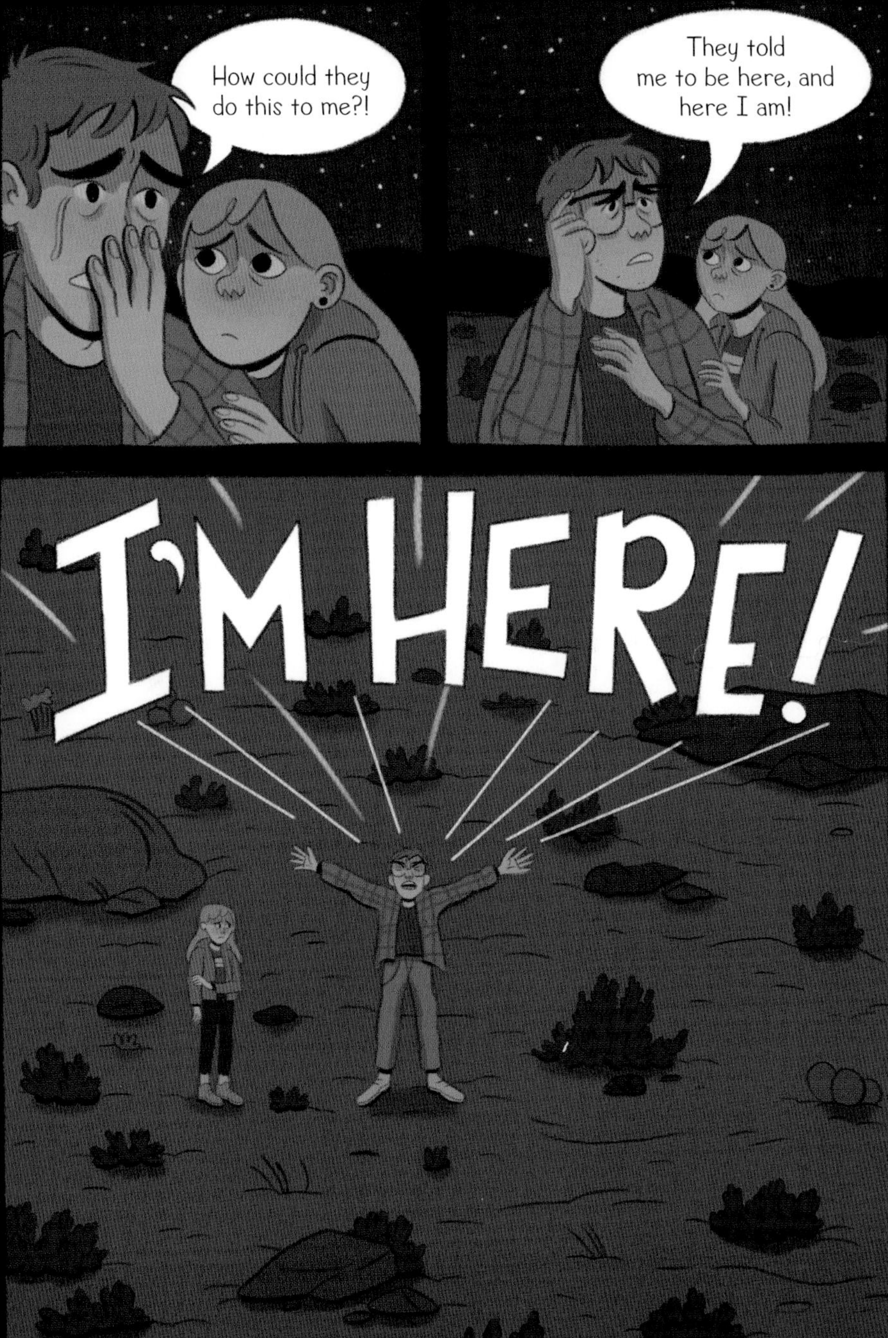
How could they do this to me?!
They told me to be here, and here I am!
I'M HERE!

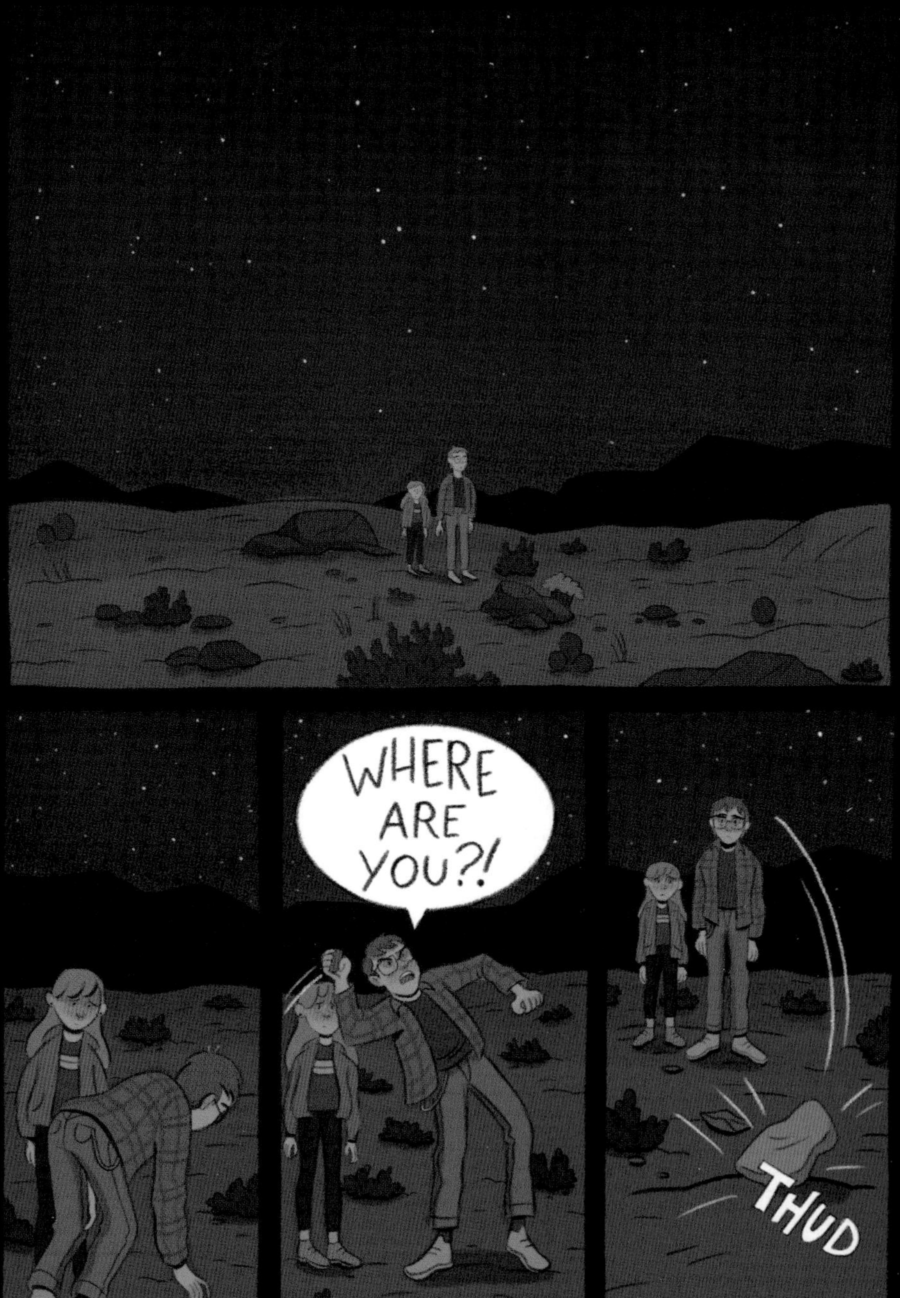
WHERE ARE YOU?!
THUD

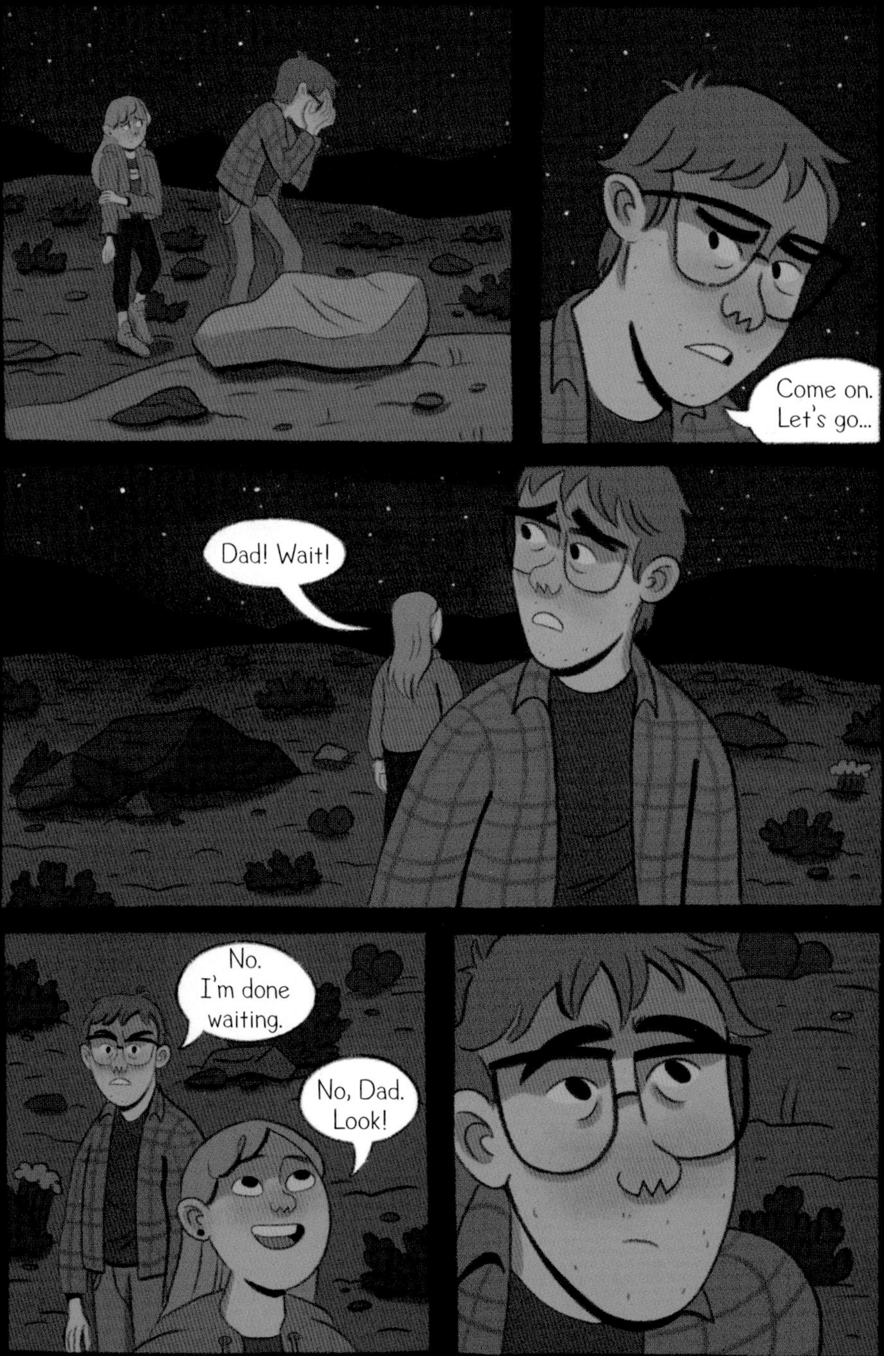
Come on. Let's go...
Dad! Wait!
No. I'm done waiting.
No, Dad. Look!

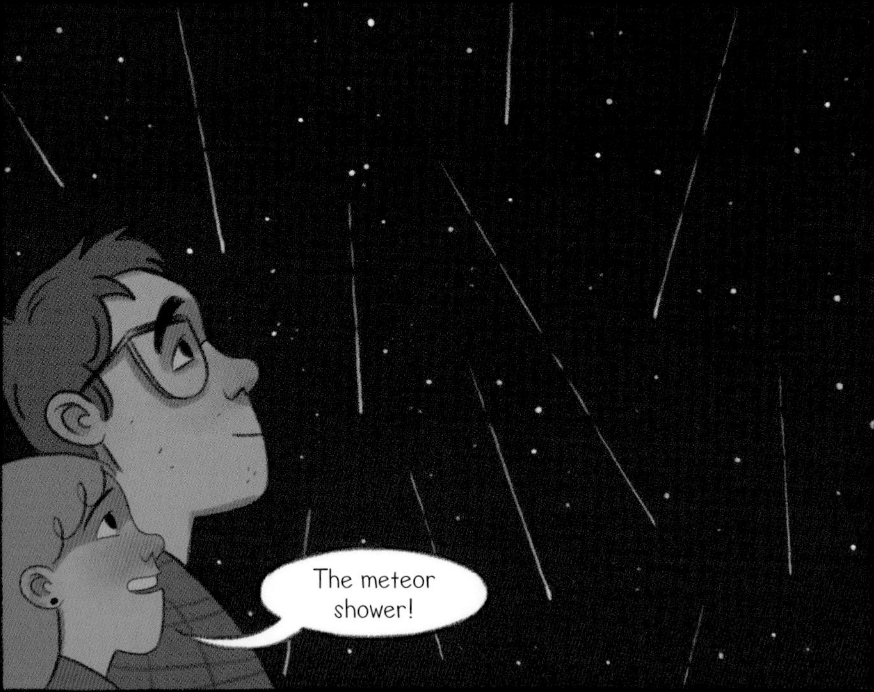
The meteor shower!

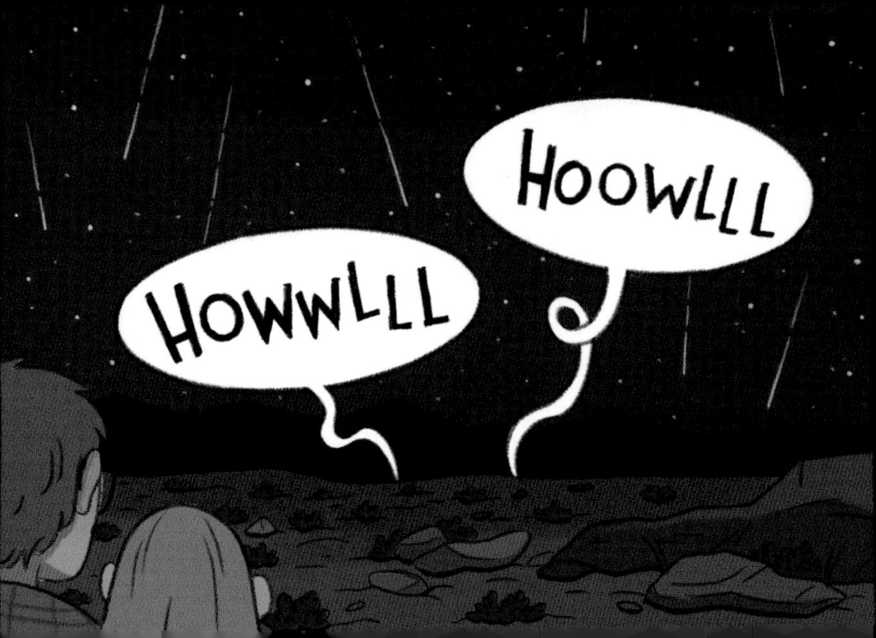
HOOWLLL
HOWWLLL

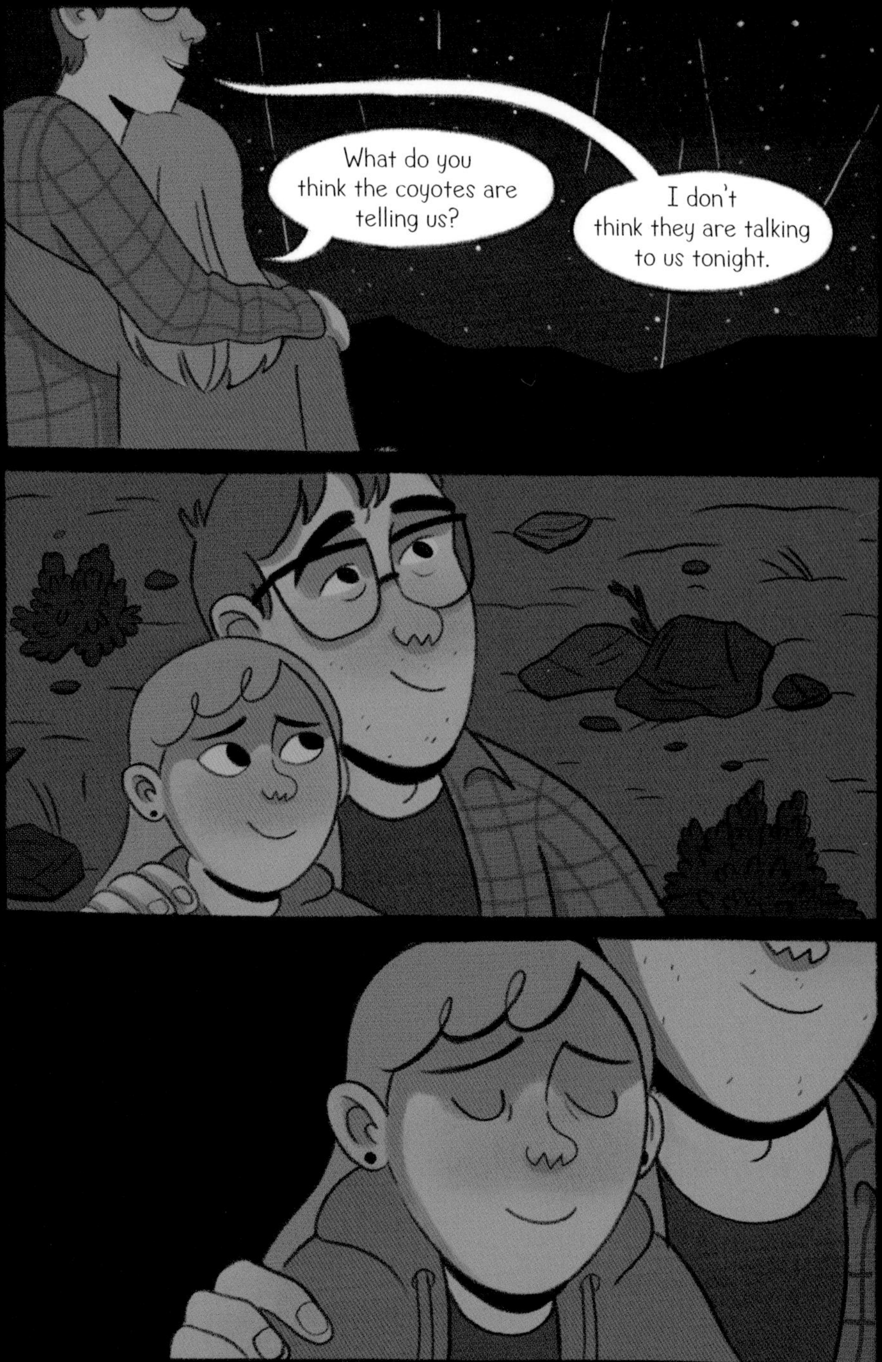
What do you think the coyotes are telling us?
I don't think they are talking to us tonight.

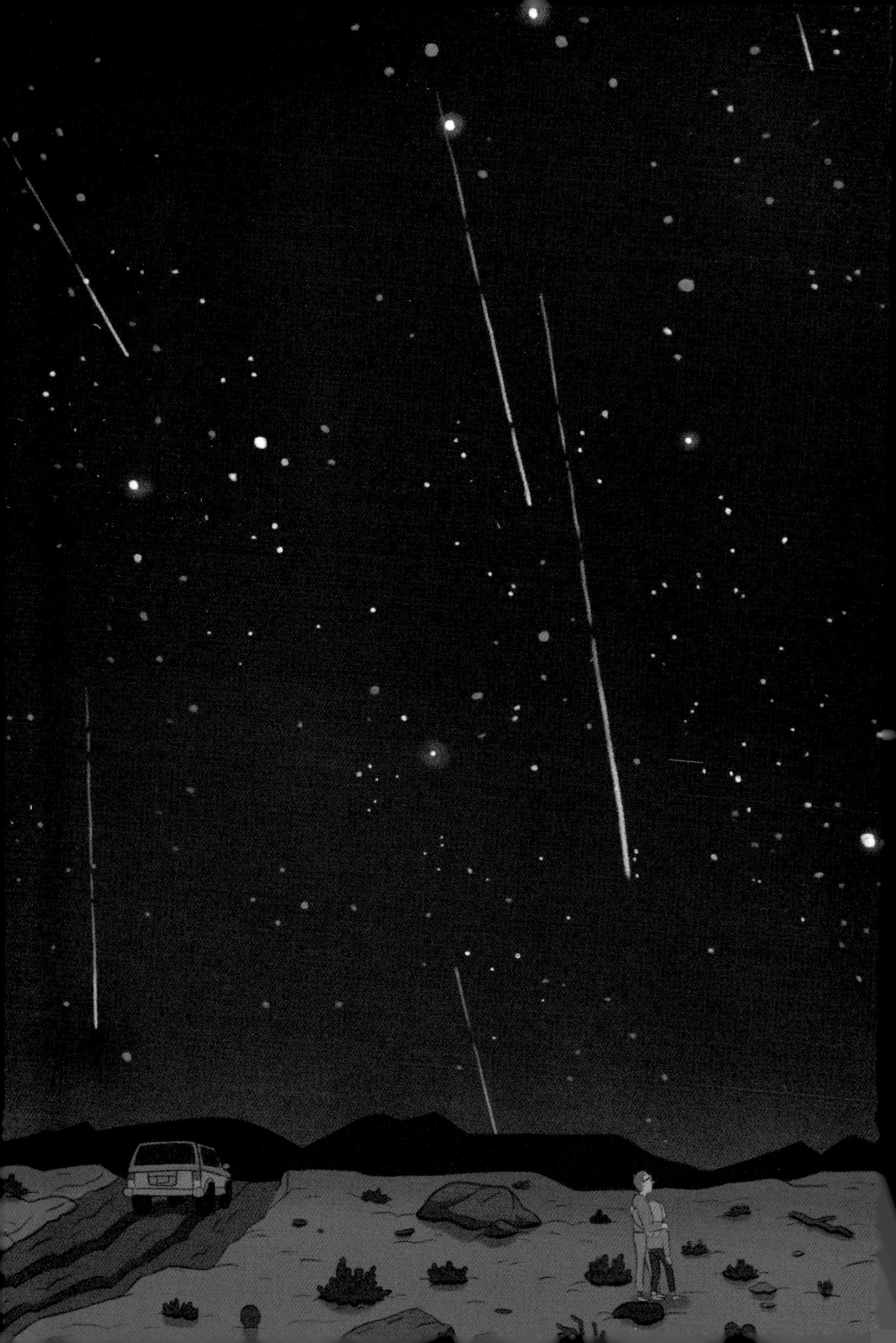

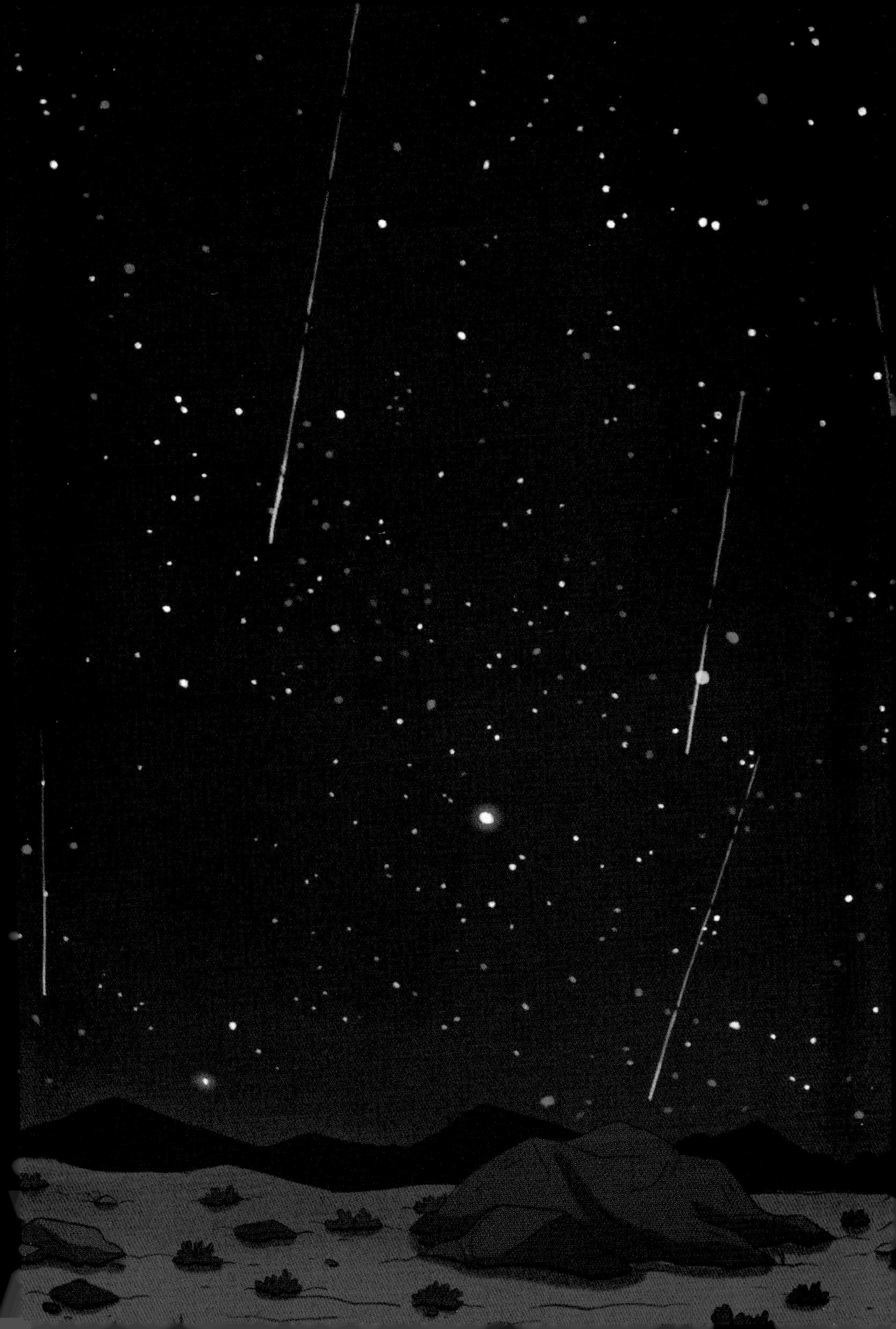

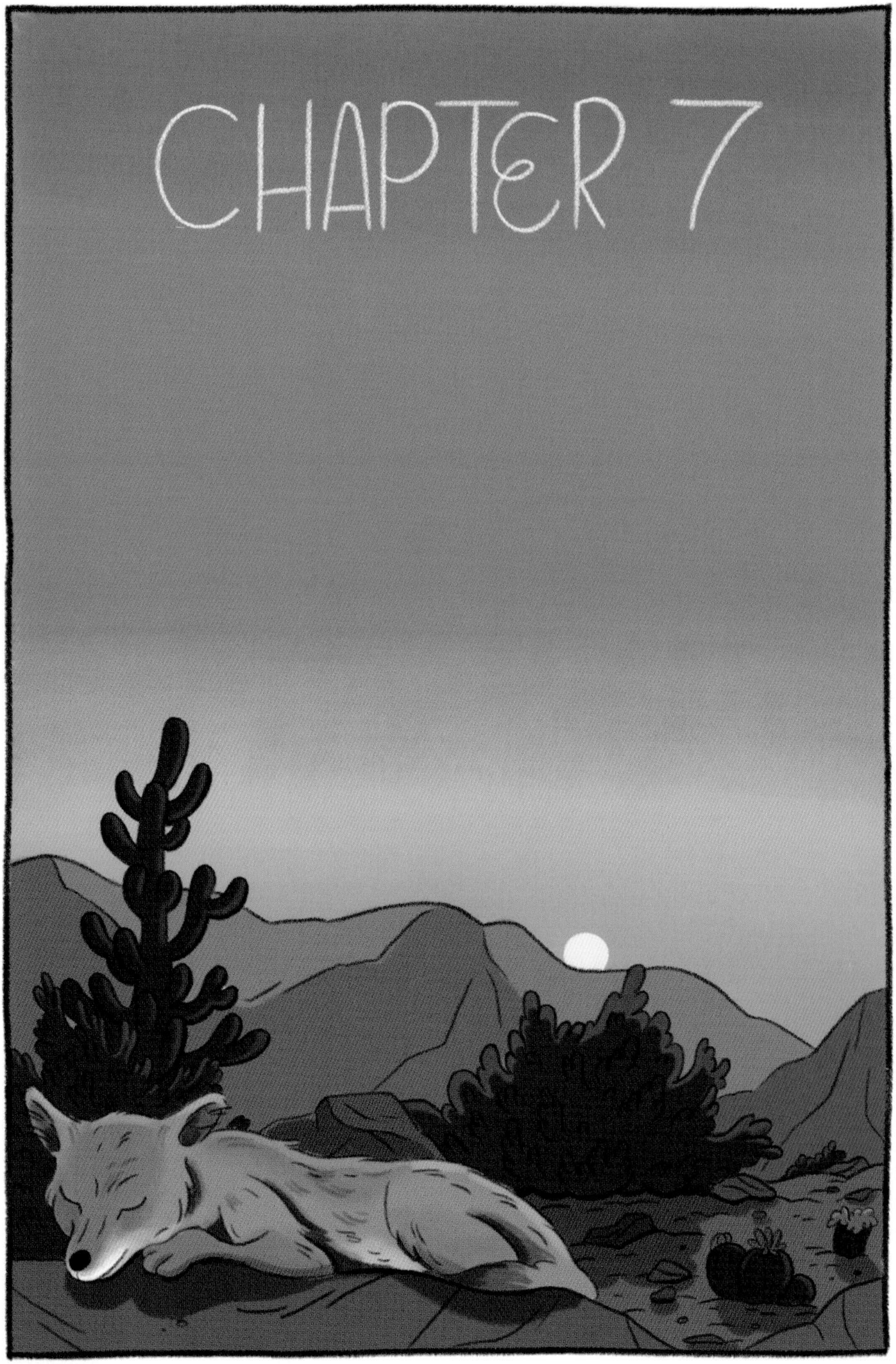
CHAPTER 7

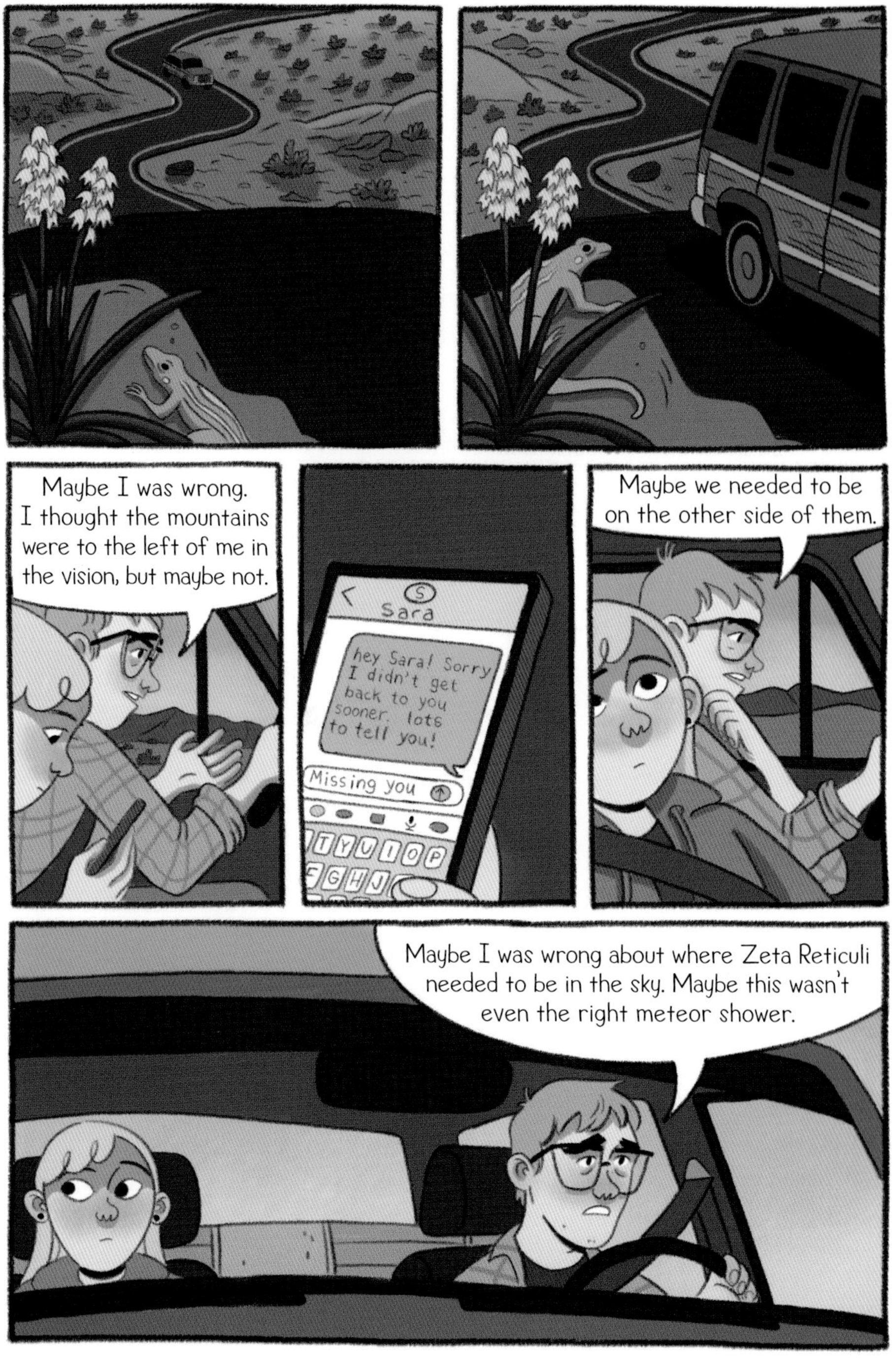
Maybe I was wrong. I thought the mountains were to the left of me in the vision, but maybe not.
Sara
hey Sara! Sorry I didn't get back to you sooner. lots to tell you!
Missing you
Maybe we needed to be on the other side of them.
Maybe I was wrong about where Zeta Reticuli needed to be in the sky. Maybe this wasn't even the right meteor shower.

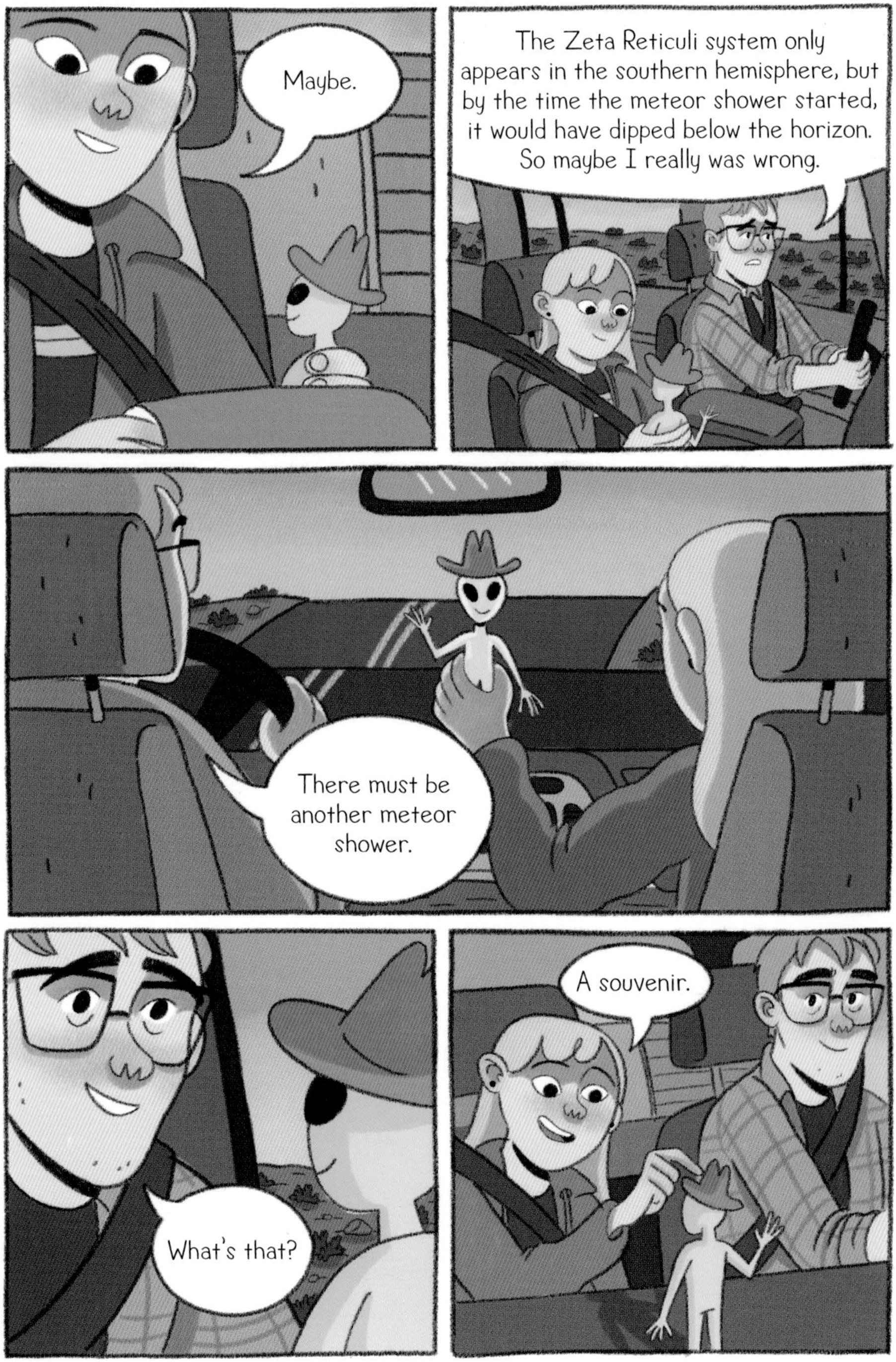
Maybe.
The Zeta Reticuli system only appears in the southern hemisphere, but by the time the meteor shower started, it would have dipped below the horizon. So maybe I really was wrong.
There must be another meteor shower.
What's that?
A souvenir.

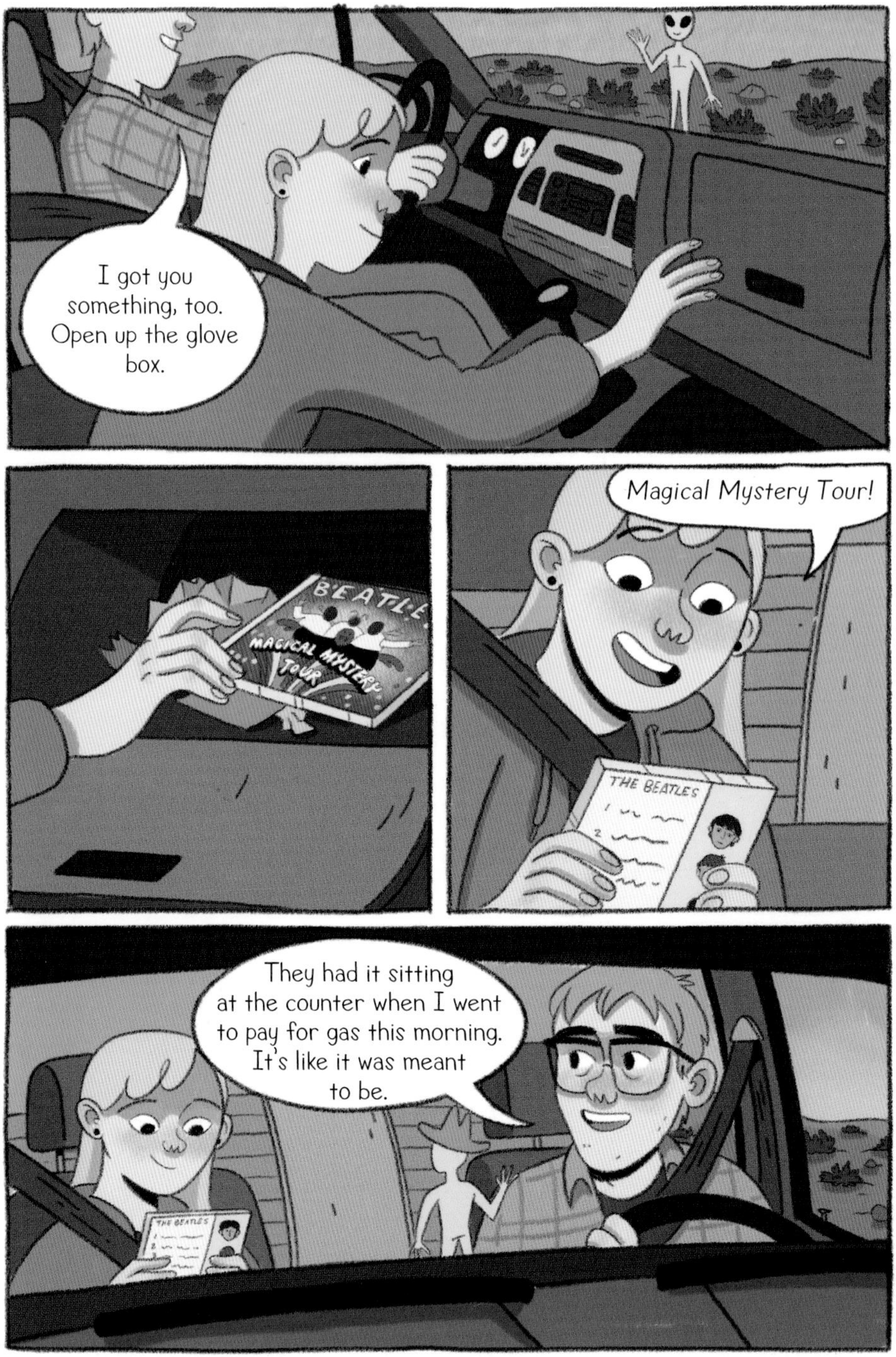
I got you something, too. Open up the glove box.
BEATLE
MAGICAL MYSTERY TOUR
Magical Mystery Tour!
THE BEATLES
They had it sitting at the counter when I went to pay for gas this morning. It's like it was meant to be.

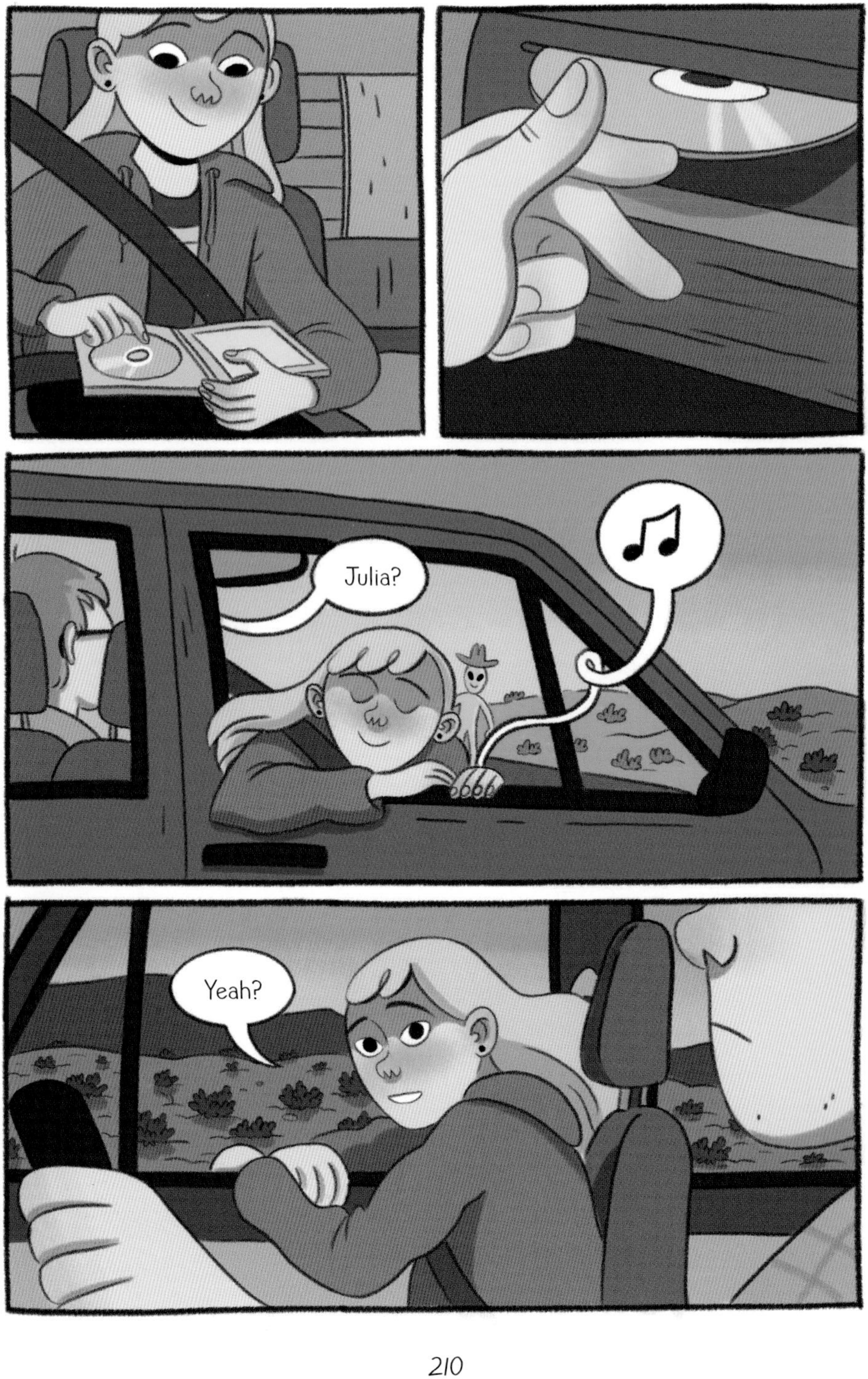
Julia?
Yeah?

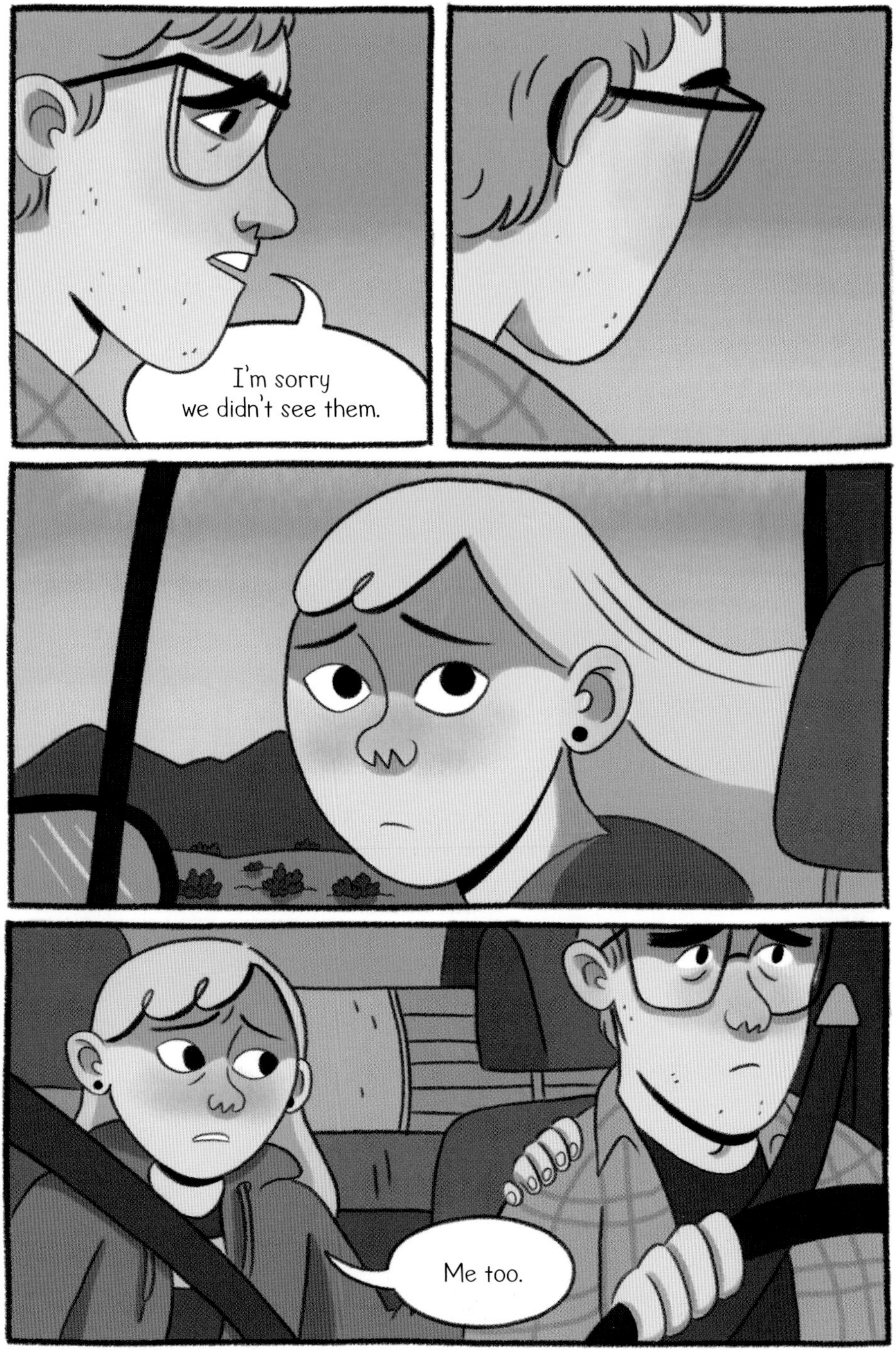
I'm sorry
we didn't see them.
Me too.

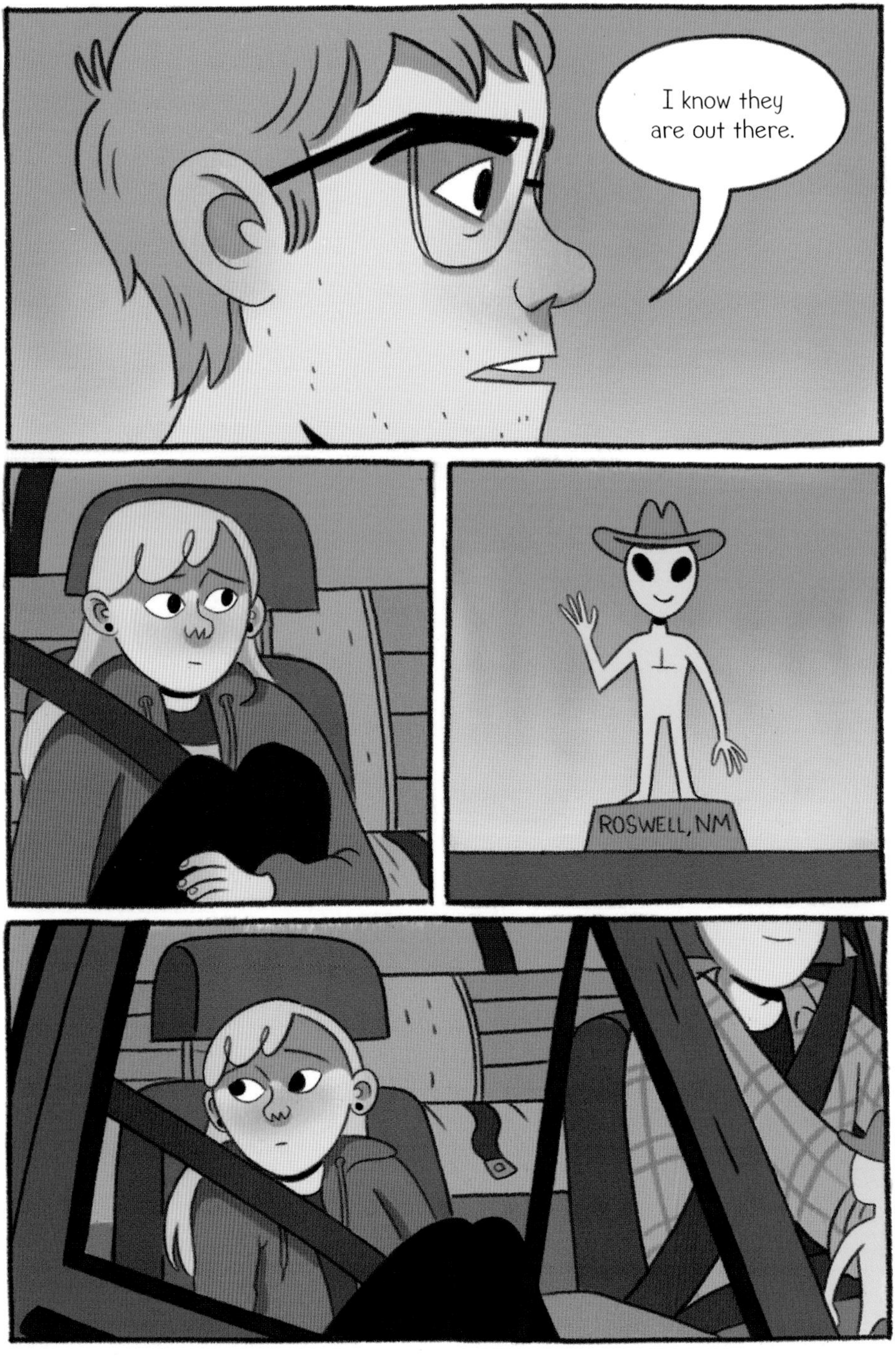
I know they are out there.
ROSWELL, NM

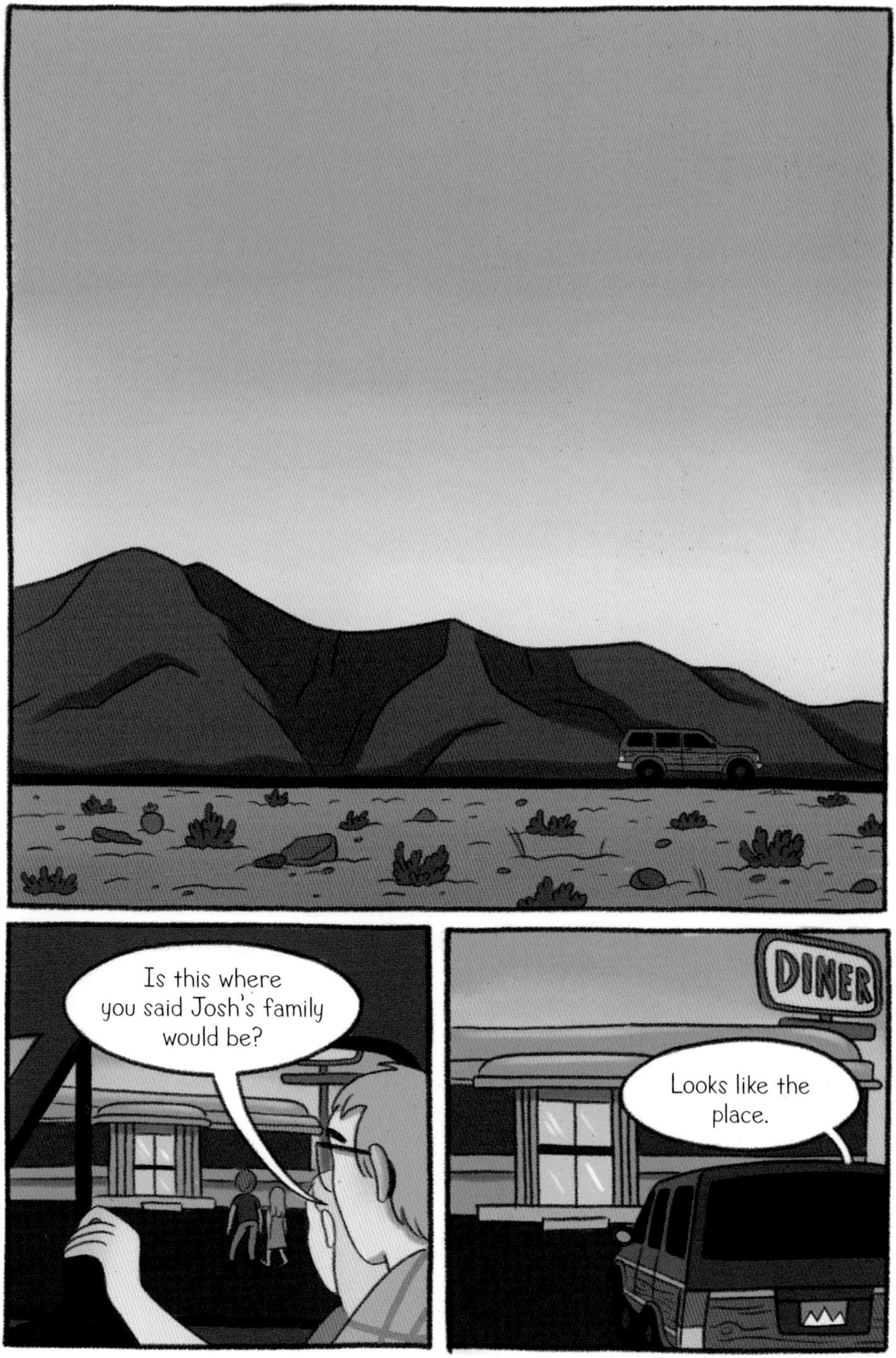
Is this where you said Josh's family would be?
DINER
Looks like the place.

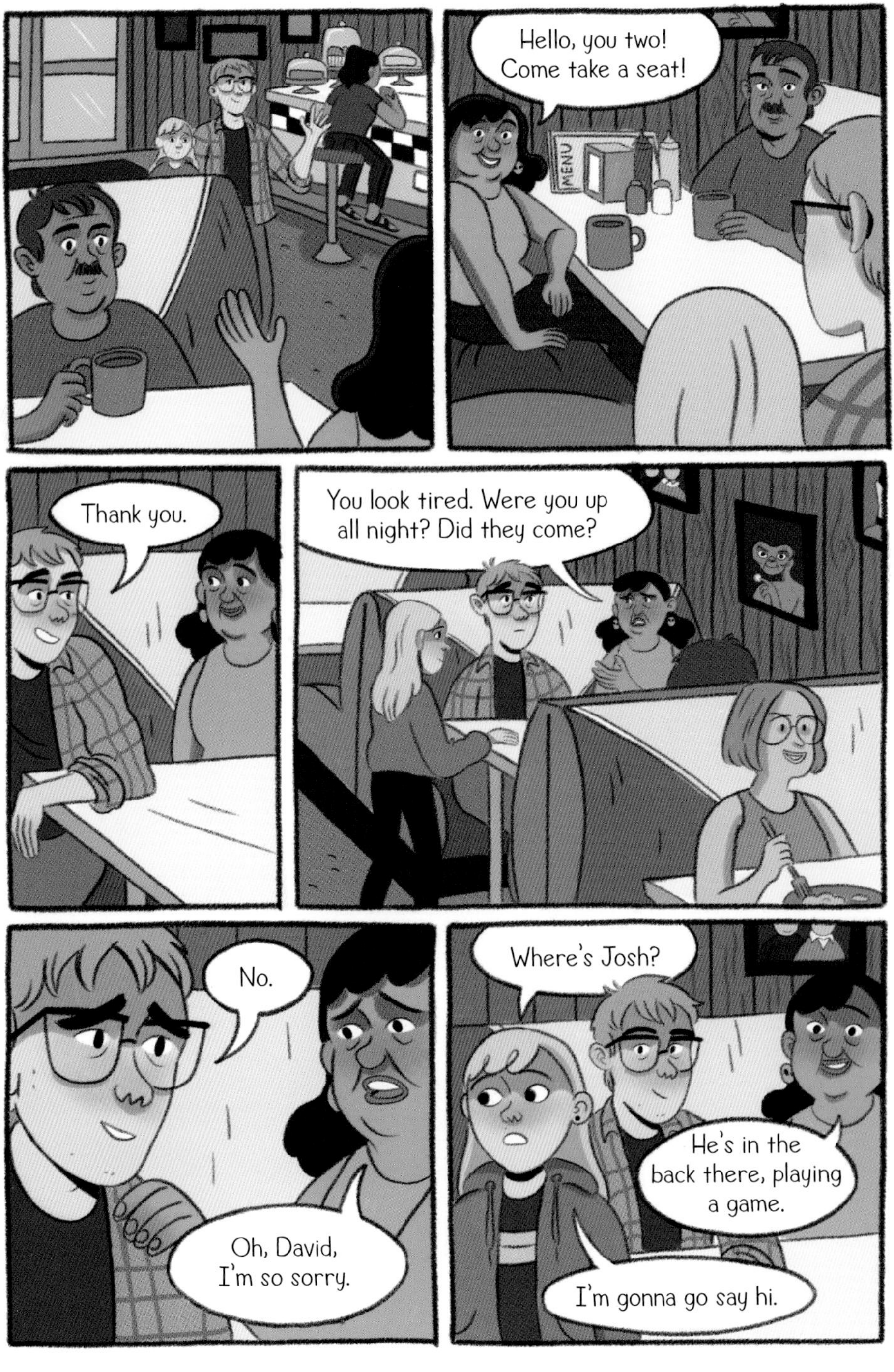
Hello, you two! Come take a seat!
Thank you.
You look tired. Were you up all night? Did they come?
No.
Oh, David, I'm so sorry.
Where's Josh?
He's in the back there, playing a game.
I'm gonna go say hi.

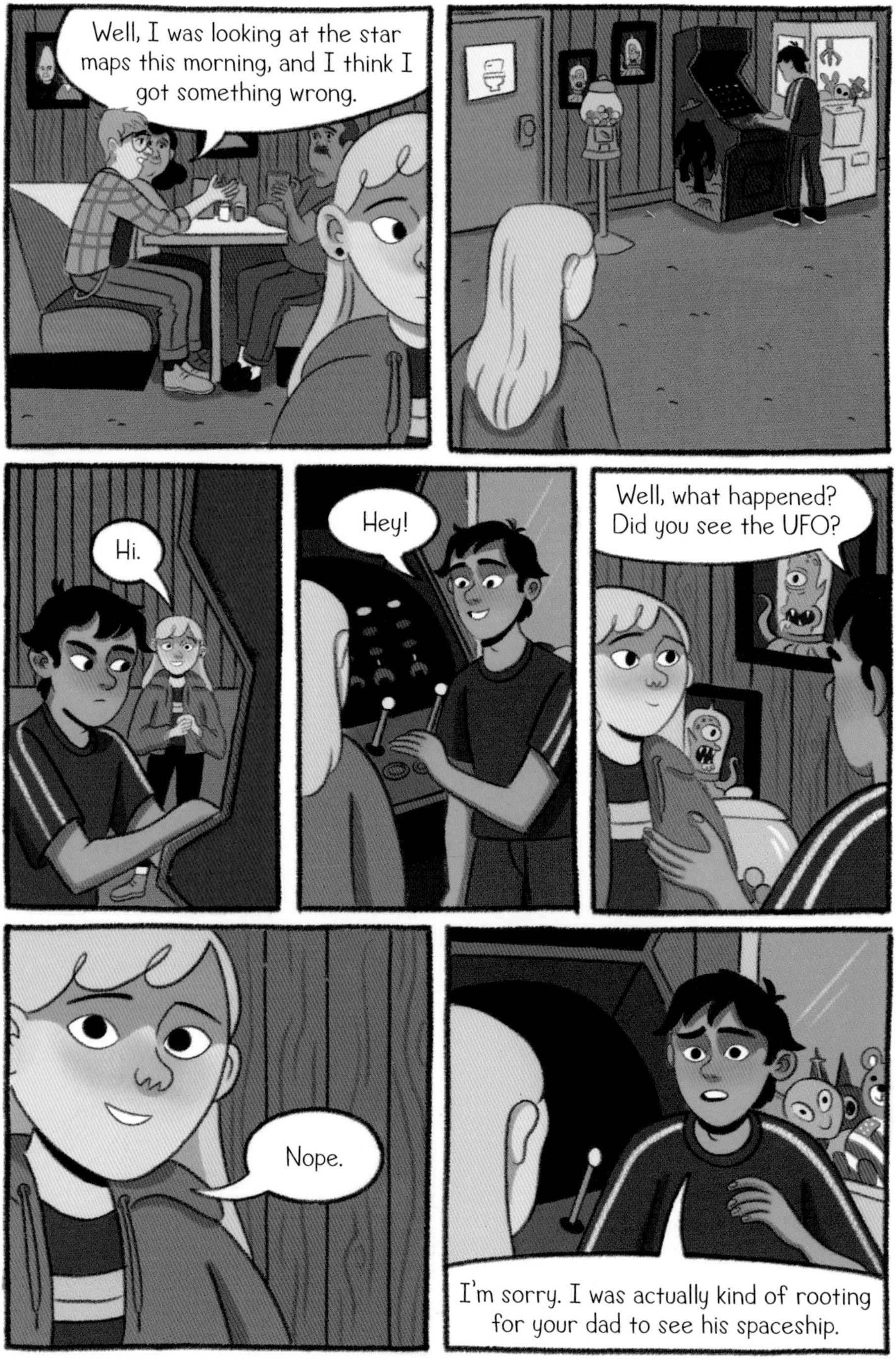

Well, I was looking at the star maps this morning, and I think I got something wrong.
Hi.
Hey!
Well, what happened? Did you see the UFO?
Nope.
I'm sorry. I was actually kind of rooting for your dad to see his spaceship.

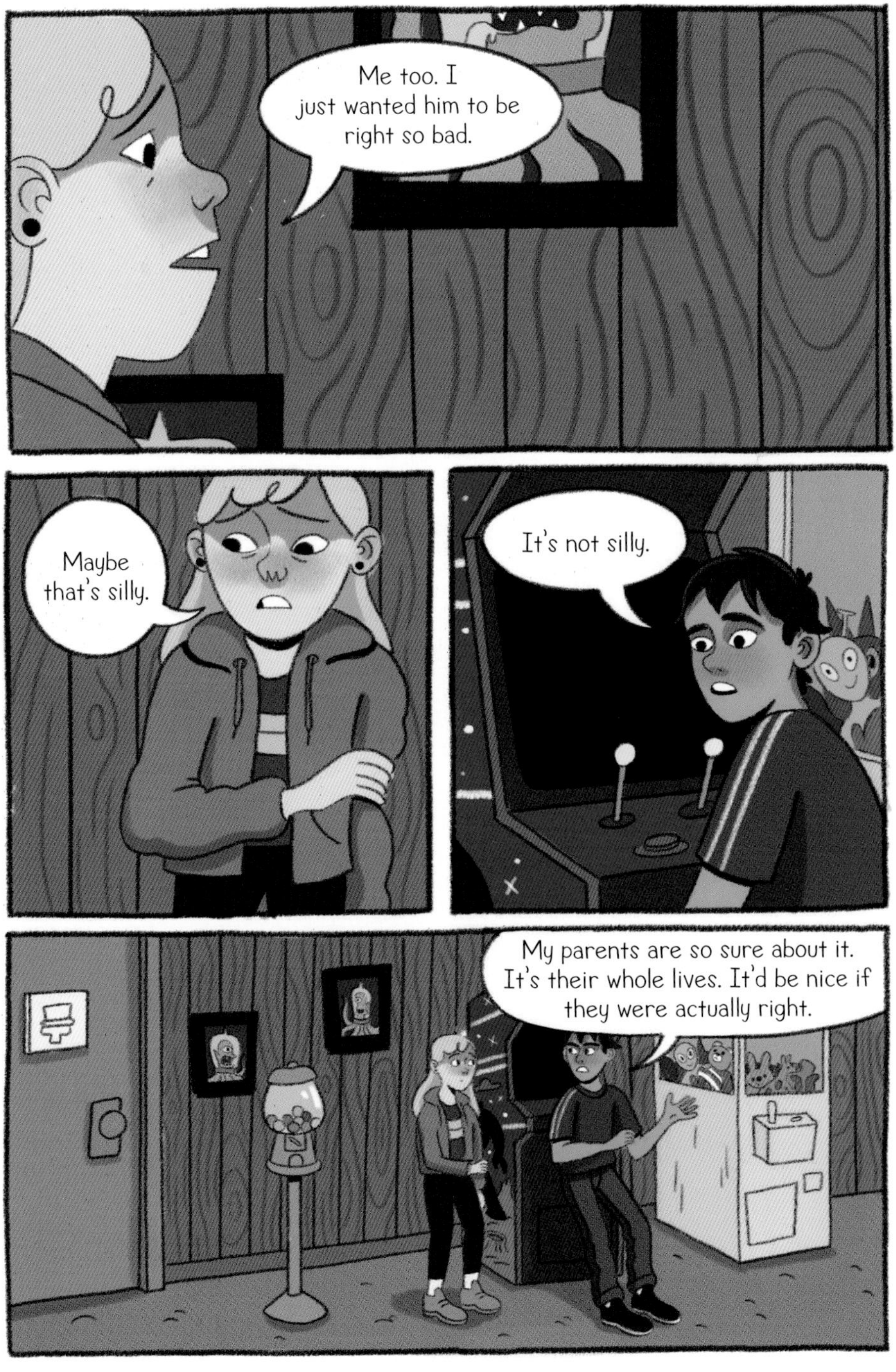
Me too. I just wanted him to be right so bad.
Maybe that's silly.
It's not silly.
My parents are so sure about it. It's their whole lives. It'd be nice if they were actually right.

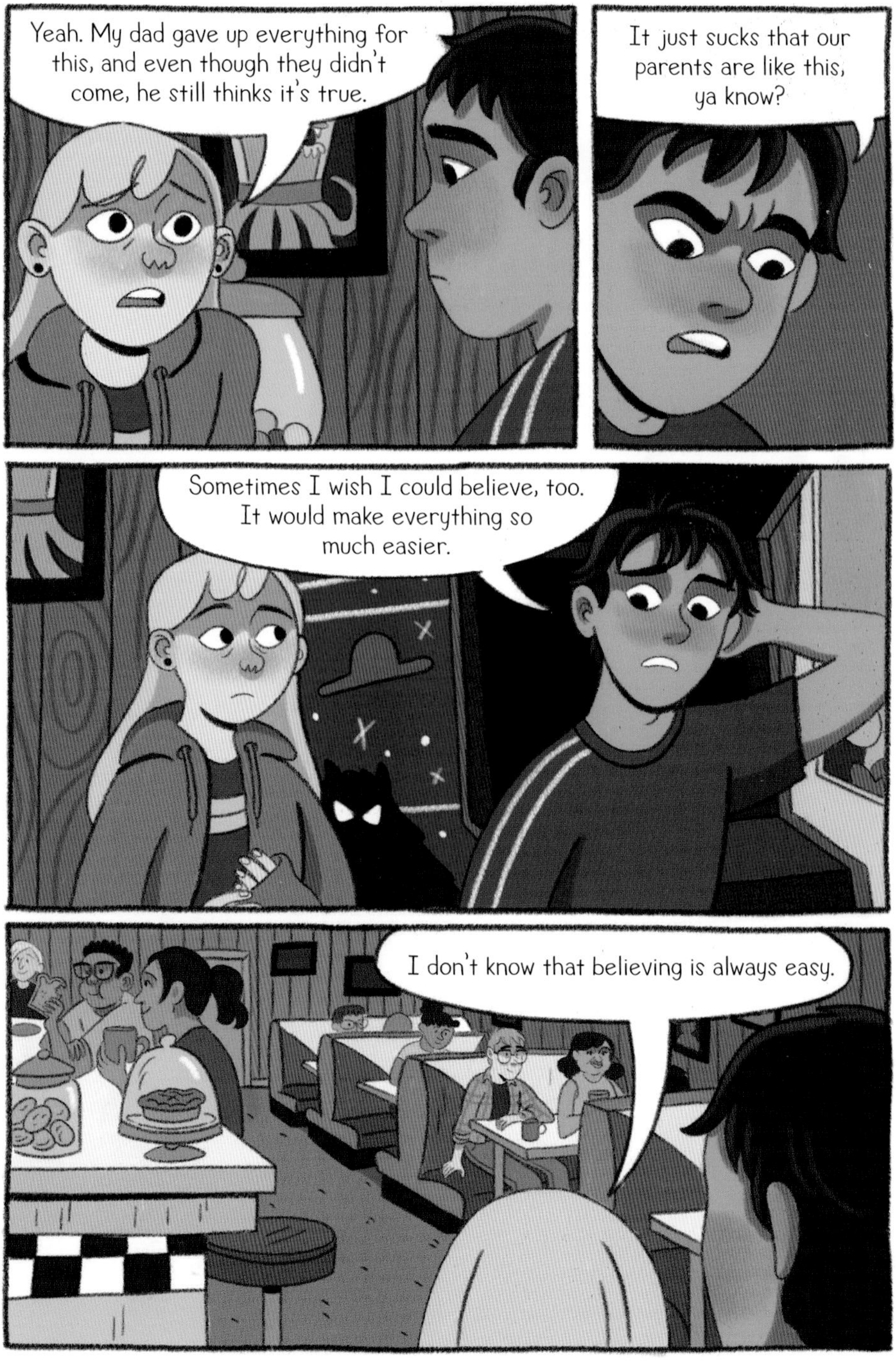
Yeah. My dad gave up everything for this, and even though they didn't come, he still thinks it's true.
It just sucks that our parents are like this, ya know?
Sometimes I wish I could believe, too. It would make everything so much easier.
I don't know that believing is always easy.

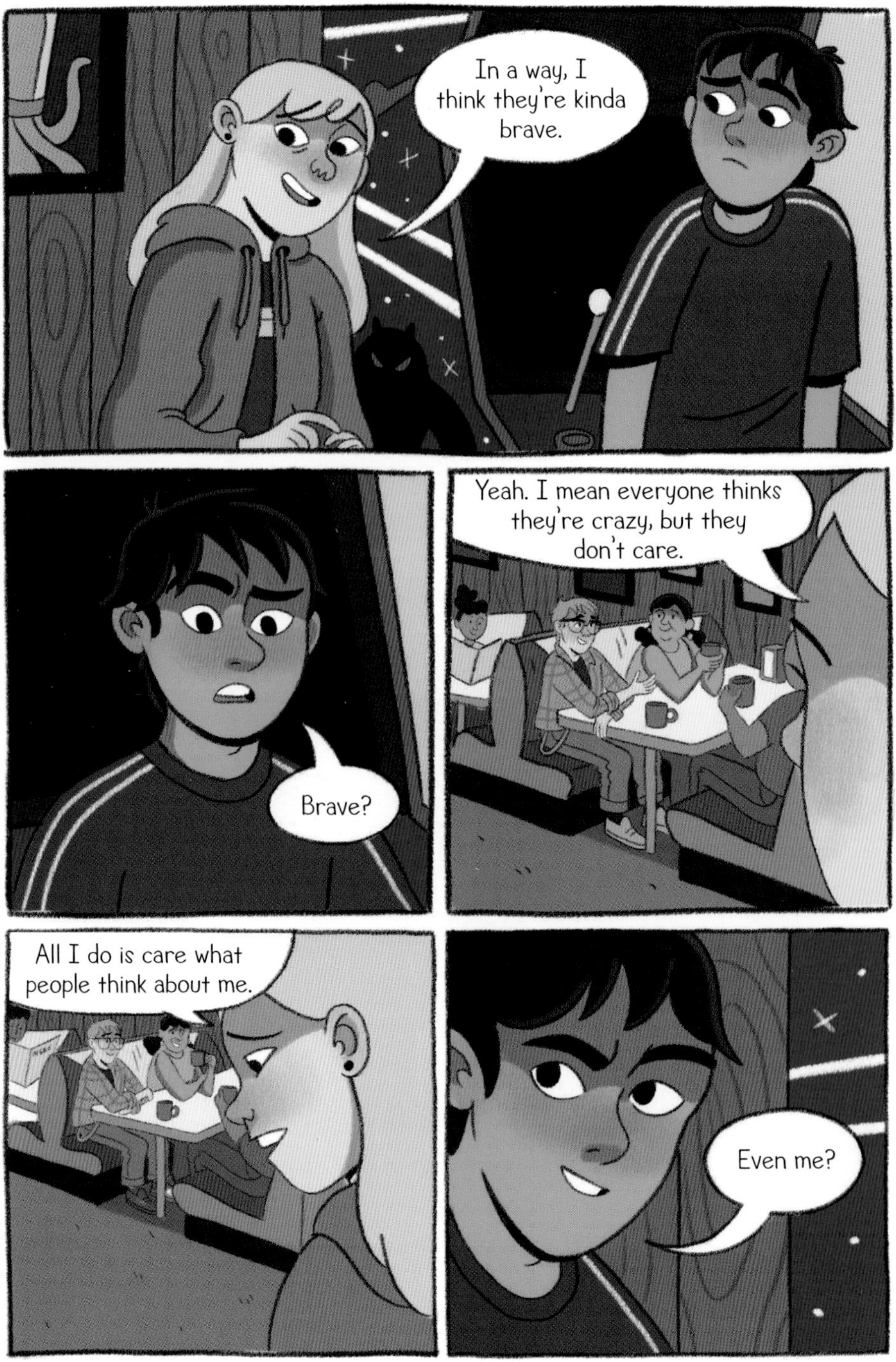
In a way, I think they're kinda brave.
Brave?
Yeah. I mean everyone thinks they're crazy, but they don't care.
All I do is care what people think about me.
Even me?

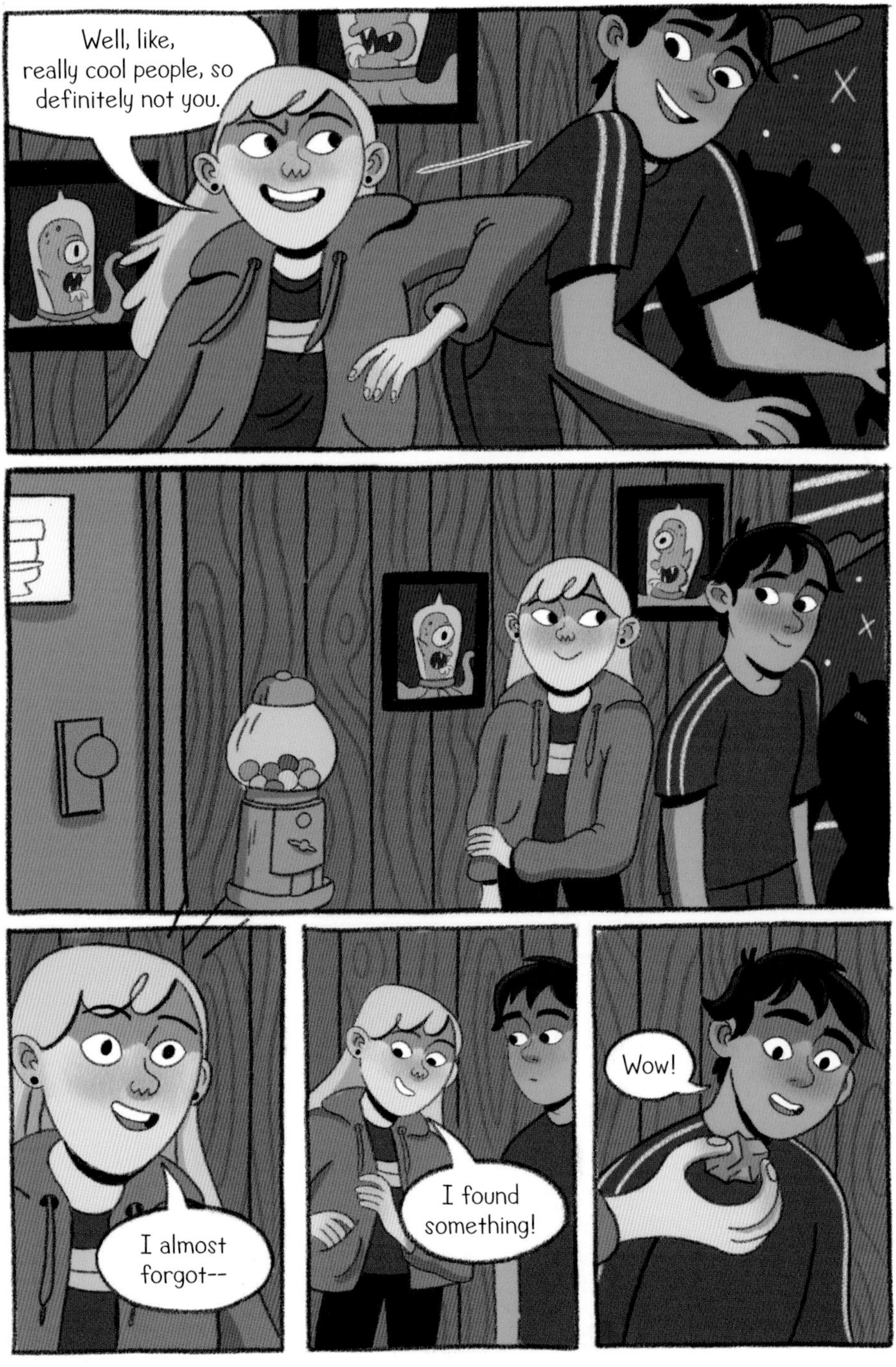
Well, like, really cool people, so definitely not you.
I almost forgot--
I found something!
Wow!

This is chalcedony! It's, like, super rare!

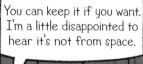

You can keep it if you want. I'm a little disappointed to hear it's not from space.

BZZT

Sara

Is that your friend? The one in Hawaii?

Yeah.

Looks kinda boring.

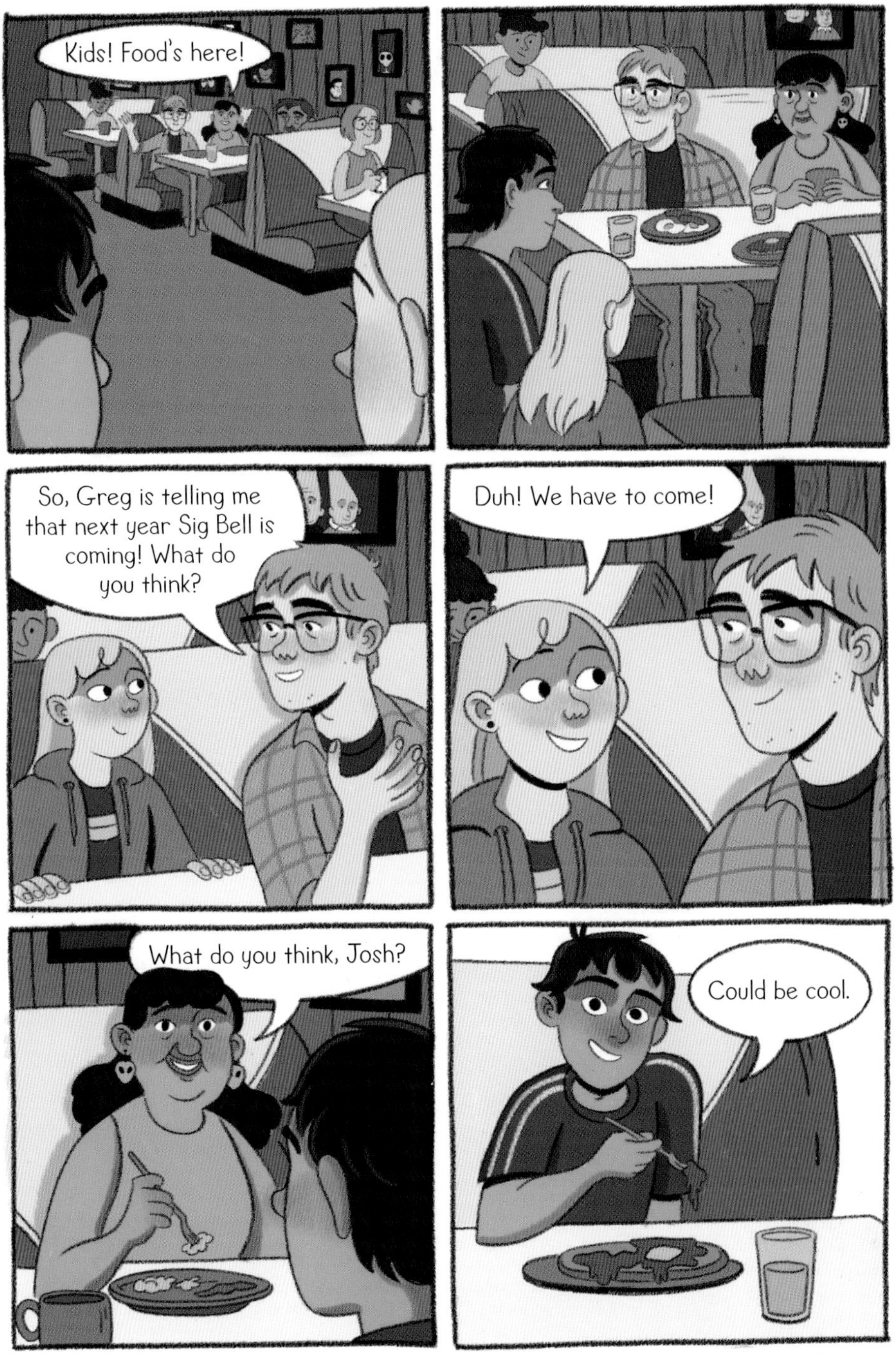

Kids! Food's here!
So, Greg is telling me that next year Sig Bell is coming! What do you think?
Duh! We have to come!
What do you think, Josh?
Could be cool.

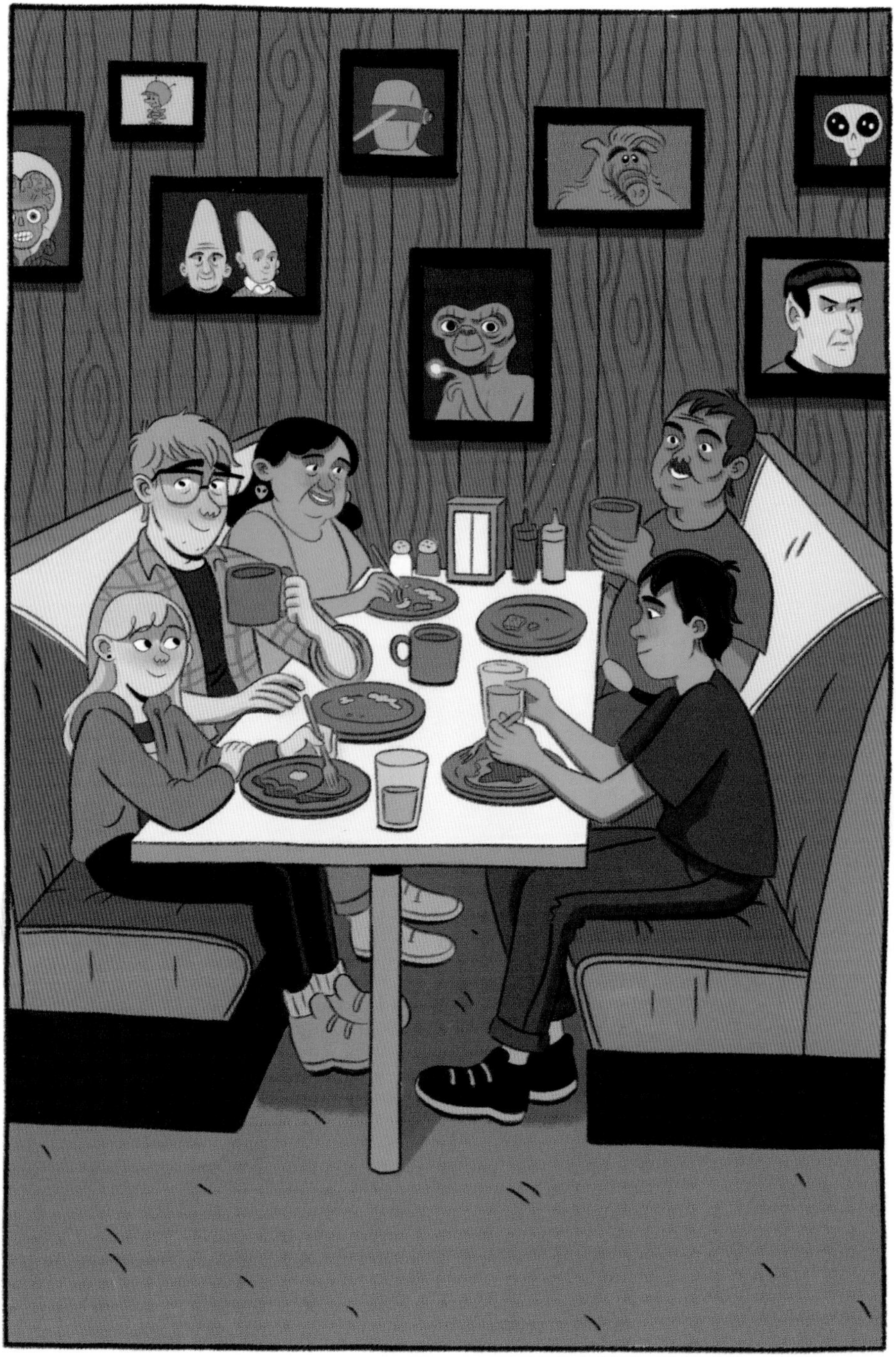

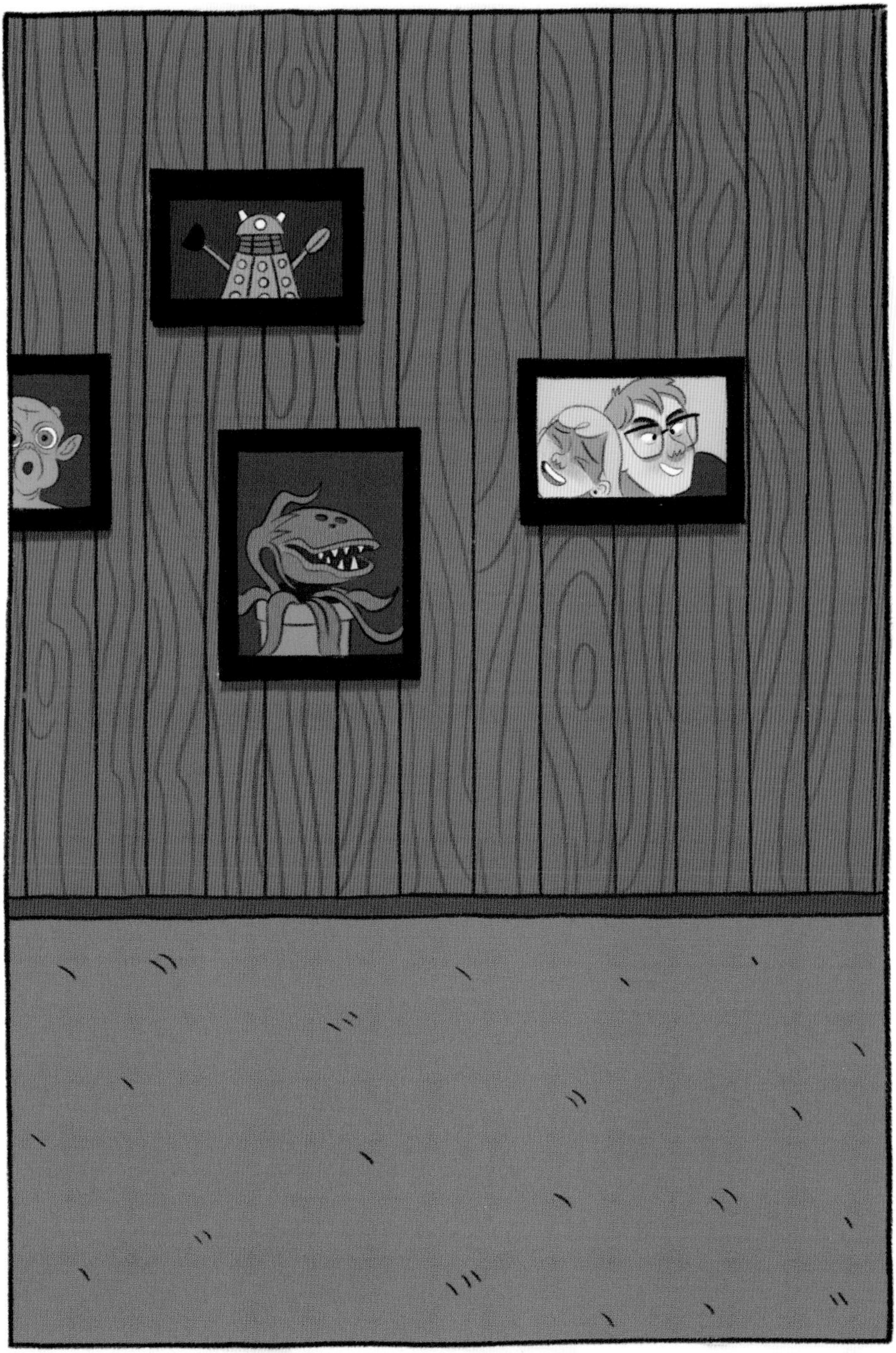

Acknowledgments

First, I'd like to thank my weird, wonderful, eccentric, amazing family—my mom, Melanie; my dad, Jason; and my brother, Jack. I definitely wouldn't have the career I have without all the love and support you've given me over my entire life. Thank you, Mom, for reading every draft of this book and assuring me it was good and that no one was going to fire me for all the misspelled words. You are an amazing writer and storyteller, and your advice always makes everything I do better. Plus, you put up with my sass, and for that, you are a saint.

I'd like to thank my sweet, funny friends Clive and Jonathan, who helped me make this book by giving me really helpful edits, like "This part is bad" and "Why did you do this part so bad?" Okay, that's just what I hear in my head when you tell me it isn't perfect. In reality, you guys always make my work better with incredibly smart and insightful comments. You guys are the best.

My generous, wonderful friends Michele and Glenn have put up with my baloney for many years and somehow still like having me around. You both inspire me to step out of my comfort zone and have new experiences that shape my storytelling for the better. You even put up with all my worries, like "What if I fall off a cliff?" or "What if that cute dog falls off a cliff?"

My loving grandparents, Linda, Carl, and Janet, who always hung up my weird childhood drawings like they were masterpieces, even that one where the mermaid had some really big seashells, if you know what I mean.

My dear friend and mentor Rilla, who helped me get my start. Your joy and enthusiasm for storytelling and characters have been so inspiring to me. I'm still always trying to get an A from you on every project I do.

My agent, Alex, who is always there, ready to write the emails I really don't want to write. You are so kind and amazing. Thank you so much for believing in this book and helping it find its way to Little, Brown Books for Young Readers.

The wonderful people at Little, Brown, but especially my editor, Andrea. Working with you has been a dream. You really helped me make this book exactly what I wanted it to be, and you didn't even call me out for the millions of grammatical mistakes.

I'd also like to thank Lonnie, Carissa, Kelsey, Maria, Lara, Brandy, Jamie, Dayna, Evony, Nate, Colton, and Honeydew for being such an amazing support system.

Lastly, thank you to the History channel for playing marathons of questionable UFO TV shows while I was growing up. I never would have written this book without you.

Seaerra Miller

Seaerra Miller grew up in a small town in Wyoming, where she spent her days picking dandelions and watching old Westerns from her grandma's small movie collection. In 2015, she moved to Portland, Oregon, to study art at the Pacific Northwest College of Art. Since graduating in the spring of 2017, she has worked for several publications and organizations, such as Cricket Media, Apartment Therapy, Oni Press, and Snapchat. She is now working with Flying Eye Books to create her own comics series and illustrate companion novels for the *Hilda* series on Netflix. Her work is often narrative, whimsical, and aimed toward kids, with bold color palettes and unique characters.